EB

Also by Danielle Steel

DANIELLE STEEL

WINGS

Delacorte Press

Published by
Delacorte Press
Bantam Doubleday Dell Publishing Group, Inc.
1540 Broadway
New York, New York 10036

Library of Congress Cataloging in Publication Data

Steel, Danielle.
Wings / by Danielle Steel.
p.   cm.
ISBN 0-385-30605-9
ISBN 0-385-31295-4 (large-print ed.)
ISBN 0-385-31381-0 (limited ed.)
I. Title.
PS3569.T33828W5   1994
813'.54—dc20   93-51253
CIP

Manufactured in the United States of America
Published simultaneously in Canada

December 1994

10 9 8 7 6 5 4 3 2 1

BVG

To the Ace of my heart,
the pilot of my dreams . . .
the joy of my life,
the quiet place I go to
in the dark of night
the bright morning sun
of my soul
at dawn. . . .
the bright shining star
in my sky,
to my love,
to my heart,
to my all,
beloved Popeye,
*   with all my heart and love,*
*   always,*
*   Olive.*

CHAPTER
1

The road to O'Malley's Airport was a long, dusty thin trail that seemed to drift first left, then right, and loop lazily around the cornfields. The airport was a small dry patch of land near Good Hope in McDonough County, a hundred and ninety miles southwest of Chicago. When Pat O'Malley first saw it in the fall of 1918, those seventy-nine barren acres were the prettiest sight he had ever seen. No farmer in his right mind would have wanted them, and none had. The land was dirt cheap, and Pat O'Malley paid for it with most of his savings. The rest went to purchase a beat-up little Curtiss Jenny, it was war surplus, a two-seater plane with dual controls, and he used it to teach flying to the rare visitor who could afford a lesson or two, to fly a passenger to Chicago now and then, or take small cargo loads to anywhere they had to be flown to.

The Curtiss Jenny all but bankrupted him, but Oona, his pretty little redheaded wife of ten years, was the only person he knew who didn't think he was completely crazy. She knew how desperately he had always wanted to fly, ever since he'd seen his first plane on exhibition at a little airstrip in New Jersey. He'd worked two jobs to make enough money to pay for lessons, and he'd dragged her all the way to San Francisco to see the Panama-Pacific Exhibition in 1915, just so he could meet Lincoln Beachey. Beachey had taken Pat up in his plane with him, which had made it all the more painful for Pat when Beachey was killed two months later. Beachey had just made three breathtaking loops in his experimental plane when it happened.

Pat had also met famed aviator Art Smith at the exhibition, and a battalion of other flying fanatics like himself. They were a brotherhood of daredevils, most of whom preferred to fly than to do anything else. They only seemed to come to life when they were flying. They lived it, talked it, breathed it, dreamed it. They knew everything there was to know about all the intricacies of every flying machine ever built, and how best to fly it. They told tales and traded advice, and the most minute bits of information about new planes, and old ones, and seemingly impossible mechanics. Not surprisingly, few of them were interested in anything but flying, nor managed to stay in jobs that had little or nothing to do with flying. And Pat was always in the thick of them, describing some incredible feat he'd seen, or some remarkable airplane that somehow managed to surpass the accomplishments of the last one. He always vowed that he'd have his own plane one day, maybe even a fleet of them. His friends laughed at him, his relatives said he was daft. Only sweet, loving Oona believed him. She followed everything he said and did with total loyalty and adoration. And when their little daughters were born, Pat tried not to let her know how disappointed he was that none of them were sons, so as not to hurt her feelings.

But no matter how much he loved his wife, Pat O'Malley was not a man to waste his time with his daughters. He was a man's man, a man of precision and great skill. And the money he had spent on flying lessons had paid off quickly. He was one of those pilots who knew instinctively how to fly almost every machine, and no one was surprised when he was one of the first Americans to volunteer, even before the United States had entered the Great War. He fought with the Lafayette Escadrille, and transferred into the 94th Aero Squadron when it was formed, flying with Eddie Rickenbacker as his commander.

Those had been the exciting years. At thirty, he had been older than most of the other men, when he volunteered in 1916. Rickenbacker was older than many of the men too. He and Pat had that and their love for flying in common. And also like Rickenbacker, Pat O'Malley always knew what he was doing. He was tough and smart and sure, he took endless risks, and the men said he had more guts than anyone in the squadron. They loved flying with him, and Rickenbacker had said himself that Pat was one of the world's great pilots. He tried to encourage Pat to stick with it after the war, there were frontiers to be explored, challenges to be met, new worlds to discover.

But Pat knew that, for him, that kind of flying was over. No matter how good a pilot he was, for him, the great years had come and gone. He had to take care of Oona and the girls now. He was thirty-two, at the war's end in 1918, and it was time to start thinking about his future. His father had died by then, and left him a tiny bit of money from his savings. Oona had managed to put a little money aside for them too. And it was that money he took with him when he went to scout around the farmlands west of Chicago. One of the men he had flown with had told him about land going dirt cheap out there, especially if it was unsuitable for farming. And that's when it had all started.

He had bought seventy-nine acres of miserable farmland, at a good price, and hand-painted the sign which still stood there eighteen years later. It said simply "O'Malley's Airport," and in the past eighteen years, one of the l's and the y had all but faded.

He'd bought the Curtiss Jenny with the last money he had left in 1918, and managed to bring Oona and the girls out by Christmas. There was a small shack on the far edge, near a stream, shaded by some old trees. And that was where they lived, while he flew anyone who had the price of a charter, and did frequent mail runs in the old Jenny. She was a reliable little plane, and he saved every penny he could. By spring he was able to buy a de Havilland D.H.4.A, which he used to carry mail and cargo.

The government contracts he got to do mail runs were profitable, but they took him away from home a lot. Sometimes Oona had to manage the airport alone for him, as well as take care of the children. She'd learned how to fuel the planes, and take calls concerning their contracts or charters. And more often than not, it was Oona flagging in someone's plane for them on the narrow runway, while Pat was away on a flight, carrying mail, passengers, or cargo.

They were usually startled to see that the person flagging them in was a pretty young woman with red hair, particularly that first spring, when she was very obviously pregnant. She had gotten especially big that time, and at first she'd thought it might be twins, but Pat knew for certain that it wasn't twins. It was his life's dream . . . a son to fly planes with him, and help him run the airport. This was the boy he had waited ten years for.

Pat delivered the baby himself, in the little shack he had slowly begun to add on to. They had their own bedroom by then, and the three girls were sharing the other room. There was a warm, cozy kitchen and a big spacious parlor. There was nothing fancy about the house where they lived, and they had brought few things with them. All of their efforts, and everything they had, had been sunk into the airport.

Their fourth child had come easily on a warm spring night, in scarcely more than an hour, after a long, peaceful walk, beside their neighbor's cornfield. He'd been talking to her about buying another airplane, and she'd been telling him about how excited the girls were about the new baby. The girls were five, six, and eight by then, and to them it seemed more like a doll they were waiting for than a real brother or sister. Oona felt a little bit that way too, it had been five years since she'd held a baby in her arms, and she was longing for this one to arrive. And it did, with a long, lusty wail, shortly before midnight. Oona gave a sharp cry when she looked down at it and saw it for the first time, and then she burst into tears, knowing how disappointed Pat would be. It was not Pat's long-awaited son, it was another girl. A big, fat, beautiful nine-pound girl with big blue eyes, creamy skin, and hair as bright as copper. But no matter how pretty she was, Oona knew only too well how badly he had wanted a son, and how devastated he was now not to have one.

"Never mind, little one," he said, watching her turn away from him, as he swaddled his new daughter. She was a pretty one, probably the prettiest of all, but she wasn't the boy he had planned on. He touched his wife's cheek, and then pulled her chin around and forced her to look at him. "It's no matter, Oona. She's a healthy little girl. She'll be a joy to you one day."

"And what about you?" she asked miserably. "You can't run this place alone forever." He laughed at her concern, as the tears coursed down her cheeks. She was a good woman, and he loved her, and if they weren't destined to have sons, so be it. But there was still a little ache in his heart where the dream of a boy had been. And he didn't dare think that there would be another. They had four children now, and even this mouth to feed would be hard for them. He wasn't getting rich running his airport.

"You'll just have to keep helping me fuel the planes, Oonie. That's the way it'll have to be," he teased, as he kissed her and left the room for a shot of whiskey. He had earned it. And as he stood looking up at the moon, after she and the baby had gone to sleep, he wondered at the quirk of fate that had sent him four daughters and no sons. It didn't seem fair to him, but he wasn't a man to waste time worrying about what wasn't. He had an airport to run, and a family to feed. And in the next six weeks, he was so busy, he scarcely had time to even see his family, let alone mourn the son who had turned out to be a beautiful, healthy daughter.

It seemed as though the next time he noticed her again, she had doubled in size, and Oona had already regained her girlish figure. He marveled at the resiliency of women. Six weeks before she had been lumbering and vulnerable, so full of promise, and so enormous. Now she looked young and beautiful again, and the baby was already a fiery-tempered, little redheaded hellion. If her mother and sisters didn't tend to her needs immediately, the entire state of Illinois and most of Iowa could hear it.

"I'd say she's the loudest one of all, wouldn't you, m'dear?" Pat said one night, exhausted from a long round-trip flight to Indiana. "She's got great lungs." He grinned at his wife over a shot of Irish whiskey.

"It's been hot today, and she has a rash." Oona always had an explanation as to why the children were out of sorts. Pat marveled at her seemingly endless patience. But she was equally patient with him. She was one of those quiet people, who spoke little, saw much, and rarely said anything unkind to or about anyone. Their disagreements had been rare in nearly eleven years of marriage. He had married her at seventeen, and she had been the ideal helpmate for him. She had put up with all his oddities and peculiar plans, and his endless passion for flying.

Later that week, it was one of those airless hot days in June, when the baby had fussed all night, and Pat had had to get up at the crack of dawn for a quick trip to Chicago. That afternoon when he got home, he found that he'd have to leave again in two hours on an unscheduled mail run. It was hard times and he couldn't afford to turn any work down. It was a day when he'd wished more than ever that there had been someone there to help him, but there were few men he'd have trusted with his precious planes, none he'd seen recently, and certainly none of the men who'd applied for work there since he'd opened the airport.

"Got any planes to charter, mister?" a voice growled at him, as

Pat pored over his log, and went through the papers on his desk. He was about to explain, as he always did, that they could rent him, but not his planes. And then he looked across the desk and grinned in amazement.

"You sonofabitch." Pat smiled delightedly at a fresh-faced kid with a broad smile, and a thatch of dark hair hanging into his blue eyes. It was a face he knew well, and had come to love in their turbulent time together in the 94th Aero Squadron. "What's a matter, kid, can't afford a haircut?" Nick Galvin had thick straight black hair, and the striking good looks of the blue-eyed, black-haired Irish. Nick had been almost like a son to Pat, when he'd flown for him. He had enlisted at seventeen, and was only a year older than that now, but he had become one of the squadron's outstanding pilots, and one of Pat's most trusted men. He'd been shot down twice by the Germans, and both times managed to come in, with a crippled engine, making a dead stick landing and somehow saving both himself and the plane. The men in the squadron had called him "Stick" after that, but Pat called him "son" most of the time. He couldn't help wondering if, now that his latest child had turned out to be yet another girl, this was the son he so desperately wanted.

"What are you doing here?" Pat asked, leaning back in his chair, and grinning at the boy who had defied death almost as often as he had.

"Checking up on old friends. I wanted to see if you'd gotten fat and lazy. Is that your de Havilland out there?"

"It is. Bought that instead of shoes for my kids last year."

"Your wife must have loved that," Nick grinned, and Pat was reminded of all the girls in France who had pined for him. Nick Galvin was a good-looking lad, with a very persuasive manner with the ladies. He had done well for himself in Europe. He told most of them he was twenty-five or twenty-six, and they always seemed to believe him.

Oona had met him once, in New York, after the war, and she had thought him charming. She'd said, blushing, that she thought he was exceptionally handsome. His looks certainly outshone Pat's, but there was something appealing and solid about the older man that made up for a lack of Hollywood movie-star looks. Pat was a fine-looking man, with light brown hair, warm brown eyes, and an Irish smile that had won Oona's heart. But Nick had the kind of looks that made young girls' hearts melt.

"Has Oona gotten smart and left you yet? I figured she would pretty quick after you brought her out here," Nick said casually, and let himself into the chair across from Pat's desk, as he lit a cigarette, and his old friend laughed and shook his head in answer.

"I kind of thought she might too, to tell you the truth. But she hasn't, don't ask me why. When I brought her out here, we lived in a shack my grandfather wouldn't have put his cows in, and I wouldn't have been able to buy her a newspaper if she'd wanted one, which she didn't. Thank God. She's one hell of an amazing woman." He'd always said that about her during the war, and Nick had thought as much too when he'd met her. His own parents were dead, and he had no family at all. He had just been floating around since the war ended, getting short-term jobs here and there at various small airports. At eighteen, he had no place to go, nowhere to be, and no one to go home to. Pat had always felt a little sorry for Nick when the men talked about their families. Nick had no sisters or brothers, and his parents had died when he was fourteen. He'd been in a state orphanage until he'd enlisted. The war had changed everything for him, and he had loved it. But now there was nowhere for him to go home to.

"How are the kids?" Nick had been sweet with them when he met them. He loved kids, and he'd seen plenty in the orphanage. He had always been the one to take care of the younger children, read them stories at night, tell them wild tales, and hold them in the middle of the night, when they woke up, crying for their mothers.

"They're fine." Pat hesitated, but only for a moment. "We had another one last month. Another girl. Big one this time. Thought it might be a boy, but it wasn't." He tried not to sound disappointed but Nick could hear it in his voice, and he understood it.

"Looks like you'll just have to teach your girls to fly eventually, huh, Ace?" he teased, and Pat rolled his eyes in obvious revulsion. Pat had never been impressed by even the most extraordinary female fliers.

"Not likely, son. What about you? What are you flying these days?"

"Egg crates. War junk. Anything I can lay my hands on. There's a lot of war surplus hanging around, and a lot of guys wanting jobs flying them. I've kind of been hanging around the airports. You got anyone working with you here?" he asked anxiously, hoping that he didn't.

Pat shook his head, watching him, wondering if this was a sign, or merely a coincidence, or just a brief visit. Nick was still very young. And he had raised a lot of hell during wartime. He loved taking chances, coming in by the skin of his teeth. He was hard on planes. And harder on himself. Nick Galvin had nothing to lose and no one to live for. Pat had everything he owned in those planes, and he couldn't afford to lose them, no matter how much he liked the boy or wanted to help him.

"You still like taking chances like you used to?" Pat had almost killed him once after watching him come in too close to the ground under a cloud bank in a storm. He'd wanted to shake him till his teeth rattled, but he was so damn relieved Nick had survived that he ended up shouting right in his face. It was inhuman to take the chances he did. But it was what had made him great. In wartime. But in peacetime who could afford his bravado? Planes were too expensive to play with.

"I only take chances when I have to, Ace." Nick loved Pat. He admired him more than any man he had ever known or flown with.

"And when you don't have to, Stick? You still like to play?" The two men's eyes met and held. Nick knew what he was asking. He didn't want to lie to him, he still liked raising hell, still loved

9

the danger of it, playing and taking chances, but he had a lot of respect for Pat, and he wouldn't have done anything to hurt him. He had grown up that much. And he was more careful now that he was flying other people's planes. He still loved the thrills, but not enough to want to jeopardize Pat's future. Nick had come here, all the way from New York, on the last dollar he had to see if there was a chance that Pat could use him.

"I can behave myself if I have to," he said quietly, his ice blue eyes never leaving Pat's kindly brown ones. There was something boyish and endearing about Nick, and yet at the same time he was a man. And once they had almost been brothers. Neither one of them could forget that time. It was a bond that would never change, and they both knew that.

"If you don't behave, I'll drop you out of the Jenny at ten thousand feet without thinking twice. You know that, don't you?" Pat said sternly. "I'm not going to have anyone destroying what I'm trying to do here." He sighed then. "But I have to be honest, there's almost too much work for one man. And there's going to be entirely too much for one, and maybe even two, if these mail contracts keep coming in the way they have. I never seem to stop flying anymore. I can't catch up with myself. I could use a man to do some of these runs, but they're rough, and long. Lots of bad weather sometimes, especially in the winter. And no one gives a damn. No one wants to hear how hard it is. The mail's got to get there. And then there's all the rest of it, the cargo, the passengers, the short runs here and there, the thrill seekers who just want to go up and look down, the occasional lesson."

"Sounds like you've got your hands full." Nick grinned at him. He loved every word of what he was hearing. This was what he had come for. That and his memories of the Ace. Nick needed a job desperately. And Pat was happy to have him.

"This isn't a game here. It's a serious business I'm trying to run, and one day I want to put O'Malley's Airport on the map. But," Pat explained, "it'll never happen if you knock out all my planes, Nick, or even one. I've got everything riding on those two out there, and this patch of dry land with the sign you saw when you drove in here." Nick nodded, fully understanding everything he said, and loving him more than ever. There was something about flying men, they had a bond like no one else. It was something only they understood, a bond of honor like no other.

"Do you want me to fly some of the long hauls for you? You could spend more time here with Oona and the kids. And I could do the night stuff maybe. I could start with those and see what you think," Nick asked him nervously. He was desperate for a job with him, and scared he might not get it. But there was no way Pat O'Malley wasn't going to hire him. He just wanted to be sure Nick understood the ground rules. He would have done anything for him. Given him a home, a job, adopted him if he had to.

"The night runs might be a start. Even though"—he looked ruefully at his young friend. There were fourteen years separating them, but the war had long since dissolved the differences between them—"some nights that's the most restful place to be. If that new baby of ours doesn't start sleeping nights pretty soon, I'm going to start dosing her with whiskey. Oona says it's a heat rash, but I swear it's the red hair and the disposition that goes with it. Oona's the only redhead I've ever known with those quiet, gentle ways. This one is a real little hellion." But despite his complaints, Pat seemed taken with her, and for the most part, he'd gotten over his disappointment about not having a son. Particularly now that Nick was here. His arrival was just the godsend he had prayed for.

"What's her name?" Nick looked amused. From the moment he'd laid eyes on them, he'd loved their family, and everything about them.

"Cassandra Maureen. We call her Cassie." He glanced at his watch then. "I'll take you over to the house, and you can have dinner with Oona and the girls. I've got to be back out here at five-thirty." He looked apologetic then. "And you'll have to find a place to stay in town. There are some rooms to rent at old Mrs.

11

Wilson's, but I don't have a place for you to stay here, except a cot in the hangar where I keep the Jenny."

"That would do for now. Hell, it's warm enough. I don't care if I sleep on the runway."

"There's an old shower out back, and a bathroom here, but this is a little primitive," Pat said hesitantly, and Nick grinned as he shrugged his shoulders.

"So's my budget, until you start paying me."

"You can sleep on our couch, if Oona doesn't mind. She's got a soft spot for you anyway, always telling me how handsome you are, and how lucky the girls are with a lad like you. I'm sure she won't mind having you on the couch, till you're ready to rent a room at Mrs. Wilson's."

But he never had done either. He had moved into the hangar immediately, and a month later he'd built himself a little shack of his own. It was barely more than a lean-to, but it was big enough for him. It was tidy and clean, and he spent every spare moment he had in the air, flying for Pat, and helping him to build his business.

By the following spring they were able to buy another plane, a Handley Page. It had a longer range than either the de Havilland or the Jenny, and it could carry more passengers and cargo. Nick spent most of his time flying it, while Pat stayed closer to home, did the short runs, and ran the airport. The arrangement worked perfectly for both of them. It was as though everything they touched turned to magic. The business went beautifully. Their reputation spread rapidly through the Midwest. The word that two hotshot flying aces were operating out of Good Hope seemed to reach everyone who mattered. They handled cargo, passengers, lessons, mail, and within a very reasonable time, began turning over a fairly respectable profit.

And then the ultimate bit of luck occurred. Thirteen months after Cassie was born, Christopher Patrick O'Malley appeared, a tiny, wizened, screaming, scrawny little infant. But a lovelier sight his parents had never seen, and his four sisters stared at his unfamiliar anatomy in utter amazement. The second coming could have made no greater stir than the arrival of Christopher Patrick O'Malley at O'Malley's Airport.

A large blue banner was flown, and every pilot who came through for a month was handed a cigar by the beaming father. He'd been worth waiting for. Almost twelve years of marriage, and finally he had his dream, a son to fly his planes and run his airport.

"Guess I might as well pack up and leave," Nick said mock glumly the day after Chris was born. He had just taken an order for a huge shipment of cargo to be delivered to the West Coast by Sunday. It was the biggest job they'd had so far, and a real victory for them.

"What do you mean, *leave?*" Pat asked, with a terrible hangover from celebrating the birth of his son, and a look of panic. "What the hell does that mean?"

"Well, I figured now that Chris is here, my days are numbered." Nick was grinning at him. He was happy for both of them about the baby, and thrilled to be Chris's godfather. But the one who had stolen his heart from the first moment he'd laid eyes on her was Cassie. She was just what Pat had said she was from the very first, a little monster, and everything everyone had ever said about a redhead. And Nick adored her. Sometimes he almost felt as though she were his baby sister. He couldn't have loved her more if she were his own child.

"Yeah, your days are numbered," Pat growled at him, "for about another fifty years. So get off your lazy behind, Nick Galvin, and check out the mail they just dumped out there on our runway."

"Yes, sir . . . Ace, sir . . . your honor . . . your excellence . . ."

"Oh, never mind the blarney!" Pat shouted at his back, as he poured himself a cup of black coffee and Nick ran out to the runway to meet with the pilot before he took off again. Nick had been just what Pat had hoped from the first, a godsend. And there had been no funny stuff in the past year. He'd taken his share of chances flying in bad weather the previous winter, and they both made their share of forced landings and emergency repairs. But there was nothing really outrageous that Pat could complain about, nothing Nick did he wouldn't have done himself, nothing that truly jeopardized one of Pat's precious airplanes. And Nick loved those planes as much as Pat did. And the truth was, having Nick there had really allowed Pat to build up his business.

And that was just what they had continued to do for the next seventeen years. The years had rushed past them faster than their planes taking off from the four meticulously kept runways at O'Malley's Airport. They had built three of them in the form of a triangle, and the fourth, running north/south, bisected it, which meant that they could land in almost any wind, and never had to close the airport due to problems with planes blocking one of their runways. They had a fleet of ten planes now too. Nick had actually bought two of them himself, and the rest were Pat's. Nick only worked for him, but Pat had always been generous with him. The two were fast friends after long years of working together, and building up the airport. He'd asked Nick to become partners with him more than once, but Nick always said he didn't want the headaches that went with it. He liked being a hired hand, as he put it, although everyone knew that he and Pat O'Malley moved as one, and to cross one was to risk death at the hands of the other. Pat O'Malley was a special man, and Nick loved him as a father, brother, friend. He loved his children as he would his own. He loved everything about him.

But other than Pat's, families and relationships were generally not Nick's strong suit. He had married once in 1922, at twenty-one. It had lasted all of six months, and his eighteen-year-old bride had gone running back to her parents in Nebraska. Nick had met her on a mail route late one night, in the town's only restaurant, which was owned by her mother and father.

The only thing she had hated more than Illinois was everything that had anything to do with flying. She got sick every time Nick took her up, she cried every time she saw a plane, and she whined every time he left to go fly one. It was definitely not the match for him, and the only one more relieved than his bride when her parents came to pick her up was Nick himself. He had never been more miserable in his life, and he had vowed never to let it happen again. There had been women since, a number of them, but Nick always kept quiet about what he did. There had been rumors about him and a married woman in another town, but no one was ever quite sure if they were true or not, and Nick never even said anything to Pat. From his striking boyish good looks, he had become a handsome man, but no one ever knew his business. The women in his life were never obvious. There was nothing anyone could talk about, except how hard he worked, or how much time he spent with the O'Malleys. He still spent most of his spare time with them and their kids. He was like an uncle to them. And Oona had long since given up trying to fix him up with any of her friends. She had even tried to start something between him and her youngest sister when she'd come out to visit years before, she was pretty and young and a widow. But it had been obvious for years that Nick Galvin was not interested in marriage. Nick was interested in airplanes, and not much more, except the O'Malleys, and an occasional quiet affair. He lived alone, he worked hard, and he minded his own business.

"He deserves so much better than that," Oona had complained to Pat for years.

"What makes you think that marriage is so much better?" Pat had teased, but no matter how convinced she was of what would be good for him, even Oona no longer broached it with Nick. She had given up. At thirty-five, he was happy as he was, and too busy to give much time and attention to a wife and kids. Most days, he spent fifteen or sixteen hours a day at Pat's airport. And the only other person there as much as Pat and Nick was Cassie.

She was seventeen by then, and for most of her life Cassie had been a fixture at the airport. She could fuel almost any plane, signal a plane in, and prepare them for takeoff. She cared for the runways, cleaned the hangars, hosed down the planes, and spent every spare moment she had hanging out with the pilots. She knew the engines and the workings of every plane they had. And she had an uncanny sense of what ailed them. There was no detail too small, too intricate, too complicated to escape her attention. She noticed everything about every plane, and could probably have described almost everything in the air with her eyes closed. She was remarkable in many ways, and Pat had to fight with her most of the time to make her go home to help her mother. She always insisted that her sisters were there and her mother didn't need her. Pat wanted her out of his hair, and at home where she belonged, but if he succeeded in driving her off one day, like the sun, she'd be back at six o'clock the next morning, to spend an hour or two at the airport before school. Eventually, Pat just threw up his hands and ignored her.

At seventeen she was a tall, striking, beautiful blue-eyed redhead. But the only thing Cassie knew or cared about was planes. And Nick knew, without ever seeing her fly a plane, that she was a born flier. He sensed that Pat had to know it too, but he was adamant about Cassie not learning to fly. And he didn't give a damn about Amelia Earhart, or Jackie Cochran or Nancy Love, Louise Thaden, or any of those female pilots, or the Women's Air Derby. No daughter of his was going to fly, and that was final. He and Nick had occasionally argued over it, but Nick had also come to understand that it was a losing battle. There were plenty of women in aviation these days, many of them quite remarkable, but Pat O'Malley thought that things had gone far enough, and as far as he was concerned, no woman would ever fly like a man. And no woman was ever going to fly his planes. Certainly not Cassie O'Malley.

Nick had taken him on more than once, and pointed out that in his opinion, some of the women flying these days were better than Lindbergh. Pat had become so apoplectic he had almost thrown a punch at Nick for that. Charles Lindbergh was Pat's God, second only to Rickenbacker in the Great War. In fact, Pat had had his picture taken with Lindy when he had landed at O'Malley's in 1927, on his three-month tour of the country. The photograph still hung, nine years later, dusty and much loved, over Pat's desk, in a place of honor.

There was no question whatsoever in Pat's mind that no woman pilot would ever top or even match Charles Lindbergh's skill, or his prowess. Lindbergh's own wife, after all, was only a navigator and radio operator—to Pat, Lindy was a kind of God, and to compare anyone to him was a sacrilege, and one he didn't intend to listen to from Nick Galvin. It made Nick laugh when he saw how excited Pat got about it, and he loved goading him. But it was an argument he knew he would never win. Women just weren't up to it, according to Pat, no matter how much they flew, how many records they broke, or races they won, or how good they looked in their flight suits. Women, according to Patrick O'Malley, were not meant to be pilots.

"And *you*," he looked pointedly at Cassie as she came in from the runway in a pair of old overalls, having just fueled a Ford Tri-Motor before it took off for Roosevelt Field on Long Island, "should be at home helping your mother cook dinner." It was a familiar refrain she always pretended not to hear, and today was no different. She strode across the room, almost as tall as most of the men who worked for him. She had shoulder-length red hair that was as bright as flame, and big lively blue eyes that met Nick's as he grinned at her mischievously from behind her father.

"I'll go home in a while, Dad. I just want to do some stuff here." At seventeen, she was a real beauty. But she was completely unconscious of it, which was part of her charm. And the overalls she wore molded her figure in a way that only irritated her father more. As far as he was concerned, she didn't belong here. It was not an opinion that was going to change, and theirs was an argument that everyone had heard at least a thousand times if they'd ever been to O'Malley's Airport, and today was no different. It was a hot June day, and she was out of school for the summer. Most of her friends had summer jobs in the drugstore, the coffee shop, or stores. But all she wanted to do was help out, for free, at the airport. It was her life and soul, and the only time she worked anywhere else was when she was desperate for a little money. But no job, no friend, no boy, no fun could ever keep her away from the airport for long. She just couldn't help it.

"Why can't you do something useful, instead of getting in the way here?" her father shouted at her from across his office. He never thanked her for the work she did. He didn't want her there in the first place.

"I just want to pick up one of the cargo logs, Dad. I need to make a note in it." She said it quietly, looking for the book and then the page that she needed. She was familiar with all their logs, and all their procedures.

"Get your hands off my logs! You don't know what you're doing!" He was enraged, as usual. He had grown irascible over the years, though at fifty he was still one of their finest pilots. But he was adamant about his philosophies and ideas, although no one paid much attention, not even Cassie. At the airport, his word was law, but his battle against women pilots and his arguments with her were fruitless. She knew enough not to argue with him. Most of the time she didn't even seem to hear him. She just quietly went about her business. And to Cassie, the only business she cared about was her father's airport.

When she'd been a little girl, sometimes she'd sneaked out of the house at night, and come to look at the planes sitting shimmering in the moonlight. They were so beautiful, she just had to see them. He had found her there once, after looking for her for an hour, but she was so reverent about his planes, so in awe of them, and of him, that he hadn't had the heart to spank her, no matter how much she'd scared them by disappearing. He had told her never to do it again, and had taken her back to her mother without saying another word about it.

Oona knew too how much Cassie loved planes, but like Pat, she felt it just wasn't fitting. What would people think? Look what she looked like, and smelled like, when she came home from fueling planes, or loading cargo or mail, or worse yet, working on the engines. But Cassie knew more about the inner workings of planes than most men knew about their cars. She loved everything about them. She could take an engine apart and put it back together again faster and better than most men, and she had borrowed and read more books on flying than even Nick or her parents suspected. Planes were her greatest love and passion.

Only Nick seemed to understand her love for them, but even he had never succeeded in convincing her father that it was a suitable pastime for her, and he shrugged now, as he went back to some work on his desk, and Cassie went back out to the runway. She had learned long since that if she stayed away from Pat, she could hang around for hours at the airport.

"I don't know what's wrong with her . . . it's unnatural . . ." Pat complained. "I think she does it just to annoy her brother." But Nick knew better than anyone that Chris didn't give a damn. He was about as interested in flying as he was in getting to the moon, or becoming an ear of corn. He hung out at the airport occasionally, to please his dad, and now that he was sixteen, he was taking flying lessons, to satisfy him, but the truth was, Chris didn't know anything, and didn't care, about airplanes. He had about as much interest in them as he did in the big yellow bus which took him to school every day. But Pat was convinced, or had convinced himself, that one day Chris would become a great pilot.

Chris had none of Cassie's instinct for it, or her passionate love of the machine, or her genius about an engine. He only hoped that Cassie's interest in planes would get his father off his back, but instead it seemed to make him even more anxious for Chris to become a pilot. He wanted Chris to become who Cassie was, and Chris couldn't. Chris wanted to be an architect. He wanted to build buildings, not fly planes, but as yet, he had never dared to tell his father. Cassie knew. She loved the drawings he did, and the models for school. He had built a whole city once out of tiny little boxes and cans and jars, he had even used the tops of bottles and all sorts of tiny gadgets from their mother's kitchen to complete it. For weeks she had been looking for things, bottle caps had disappeared, small tools, and vital utensils. And then it all reappeared in Chris's remarkable creation. Their father's only comment had been to ask him why he hadn't designed an airport. It had been an intriguing idea, and Chris still said he was going to try it. But the truth was, absolutely nothing about flying enticed him. He was intelligent and precise and thoughtful, and the flying lessons he was taking seemed incredibly boring. Nick had already taken him up dozens of times, and he had logged quite a few hours. But none of it interested him. It was like driving a car. So what? To him, it meant nothing. And to Cassie, it was life itself. It was more than that, it was magic.

She stayed out of her father's office that afternoon, and at six o'clock, Nick saw her far down the runway, signaling a plane in, and then disappearing into one of the hangars with the pilot. He sought her out a little while later, and she had oil on her face, and her hair was tied in a knot on her head. She had a huge smudge of grease on the tip of her nose, and her hands were filthy. He couldn't help laughing as he looked at her. She was quite a picture.

"What's funny?" She looked tired, but happy, as she smiled up at him. He had always been like a brother to her. She was aware of how handsome he was, but it didn't mean anything. They were good friends, and she loved him.

"You're funny. Have you looked in the mirror today? You're wearing more oil than my Bellanca. Your father is going to love that look."

"My father wants me cleaning house in a housedress, and boiling potatoes for him."

"That's useful too."

"Yeah?" She cocked her head to one side, and was an intriguing combination of absurdity and sheer beauty. "Can you cook potatoes, Stick?" She called him that sometimes and it always made him smile as he did now when he answered.

20

"If I have to. I can cook too, you know."

"But you don't *have* to. And when was the last time you cleaned house?"

"I don't know . . ." He looked thoughtful, "Ten years ago maybe . . . about 1926?" He was grinning at her and they were both laughing.

"See what I mean?"

"Yeah. But I see what he means too. I'm not married and I don't have kids. And he doesn't want you to end up like me. Living in a shack off the runway and flying mail runs to Cleveland." His "shack" was very comfortable by then if not luxurious.

"Sounds good to me." She grinned. "The mail runs I mean."

"That's the problem."

"*He's* the problem," she disagreed. "There are plenty of women flying and leading interesting lives. The Ninety-Nines are full of them." It was a professional organization founded by ninety-nine female pilots.

"Don't try and convince me. Tell him."

"It's pointless." She looked discouraged as she looked up at her old friend. "I just hope he lets me be out here all summer." It was all she wanted to do now that she was out of school until the end of August. It would be a long summer, hiding from him, and trying to avoid confrontations.

"Couldn't you get yourself a job somewhere else, so he doesn't drive us both crazy?" But they both knew that she preferred to do without any extra money at all than miss a moment at the airport.

"There isn't anything else I want to do."

"I know. You don't have to tell me." He knew the extent of her passion better than anyone else. He had suffered from the same disease himself. But he'd been lucky. The war, his sex, and Pat O'Malley had made it possible for him to spend the rest of his life flying. Somehow, he didn't think that Cassie O'Malley was going to be as lucky. In a funny way, he would have loved to take her up in a plane one of these days, just to see how well she would fly, but that was one headache he didn't need, and he knew Pat would kill him for it. Without meddling in Pat's family life, Nick had his own work to do, and there was plenty of it at the airport.

As Nick went back to his desk to clear up the last of his paperwork, he saw Chris arrive. He was a good-looking boy, a handsome blond with fine features like his mother's, and his father's powerful build, and warm brown eyes. He was bright and nice and well liked. He had everything in the world going for him, except a love for airplanes. He was working at the newspaper that summer, doing layouts, and he was grateful he didn't have to work at the airport.

"Is my sister here?" he asked Nick hesitantly. He almost looked as though he wished Nick would say no. He looked as though he couldn't wait to leave the airport. As it was, Cassie had expected him an hour before and she'd asked Nick impatiently half a dozen times if he'd seen him.

"She is indeed." Nick smiled at him. He kept his voice low so he wouldn't irritate Pat, in case he overheard him. "She's in the back hangar with some pilot who just flew in."

"I'll find her." Chris waved at Nick, who promised to take him up again in a few days, when he came back from a run to San Diego. "I'll be here. I came out to practice my solos," he said solemnly.

"I'm impressed." Nick raised an eyebrow, amazed at how badly the boy obviously wanted to please his father. It was no secret to Nick that Chris really didn't enjoy his lessons. It wasn't that he was afraid, it was more that they just bored him. To him, flying meant nothing. "See ya."

Chris found Cassie easily, and she left her newfound friend very quickly once she saw her brother. She was quick to berate him. "You're late, now we're going to be late for dinner. Dad'll have a fit."

"Then let's not do it." He shrugged. He hadn't even wanted to leave work as early as he had, but he knew she'd be furious with him if he didn't.

22

"Come on," she blazed at him. "I've been waiting all day!" She flashed an angry look at him, and he groaned. He knew her too well. There was no escaping Cassie when she set her mind to something. "I'm not going home till we do it."

"Okay, okay. But we can't stay up for long."

"Half an hour." She was begging him, pleading with him, turning her huge blue eyes imploringly to his gentle brown ones.

"Okay. Okay. But if you do anything to get us into trouble, Cass, I swear I'm going to kill you. Dad would have my hide for this."

"I promise. I won't do anything." He searched her eyes as she promised him, and he wanted more than anything to believe her, but he didn't.

Together, they walked toward the old Jenny their father had had for several years. It had been built as a trainer for the military, and Pat had told Chris he could use it now any time he wanted to practice. All he had to do was tell Nick, and he just had. Chris had a copy of the key, and he took it out of his pocket. Cassie almost salivated when she saw it. She was standing close to him, and she could feel her heart beat as Chris opened the door to the small open-cockpit airplane.

"Will you stop it?" He looked annoyed at her, "I can feel you breathing on me. I swear . . . you're sick . . ." He felt as though he were helping an addict supply his habit as they walked around the plane, checking the wires and ailerons. Chris put on his flying helmet and goggles and gloves, and then got into the plane in the rear seat, and Cassie climbed in quickly ahead of him intending to look like a passenger, but somehow she didn't. She looked too knowledgeable, too comfortable, even in the front seat, especially once she put on her own helmet and goggles.

They both buckled in, and Cassie knew the plane was well fueled, because part of her deal with her brother was doing all the scutwork for him; and she had done it herself that afternoon. Everything was ready and she inhaled the familiar smell of castor oil that was characteristic of the Jenny. And five minutes later they were headed down the runway, with Cassie watching Chris's style critically. He was always too cautious, too slow, and once she turned around to signal to him to go faster, and pull up. She didn't care if anyone saw her. She knew that no one was watching now, and everything she knew, she knew from listening and watching. She had watched her father and Nick, transient pilots, and barnstormers. She had picked up some real skills, and a few tricks, and she knew flying by instinct and by sheer intuition. It was Chris who had had the lessons, and yet it was Cassie who knew exactly what to do and they both knew she could have flown the plane easily without him, and a lot more smoothly.

Eventually, she shouted at him over the sound of the engine, and he nodded, willing her not to do anything foolish. But they both knew exactly why they had come up here. Chris was taking lessons from Nick, and in turn he was giving Cassie lessons. Or, in fact, the way it had been working out, Chris was taking her up in the plane, and letting her fly it, and she was giving him lessons. Or just enjoying the opportunity to fly. She seemed to know how to do everything, a lot better than Chris did. She was a natural. And she had promised to pay him twenty dollars a month for unlimited opportunities to fly with him in their father's plane. He wanted the money to spend on his girlfriend, so he had agreed to do it for her. It was a perfect arrangement. And she had worked hard all winter, at odd jobs, baby-sitting, and loading groceries, and even shoveling snow to save the money.

Cassie handled the controls with ease. She did some S turns, and lazy eights, and then moved on to some deep turns, which she did carefully, and with perfect precision. Even Chris was impressed with her easy, careful style, and he was suddenly grateful to her for how good she would make him look, if anyone was watching him from the ground. She was a splendid pilot. She moved into a loop then, and then he started to get nervous. They'd been up together several times before, and he hated it when she did anything fancy. She was too good, too fast, and he was afraid she might get out of control completely and do something really scary. For twenty bucks, he wasn't willing to let her terrify him. But she didn't even notice him. She was concentrating on her flying. So he just glared at the back of her helmet, and watched her red hair fly in the breeze around it. And eventually, totally fed up with her, he tapped her hard on the shoulder. It was time to go back, and she knew it. But for a few minutes, she pretended to ignore him.

She wanted to do a spin, but there was no time and she knew Chris would have a fit if she tried it.

But in his calmer moments, he'd have had to admit that his sister was a very smooth pilot. Even if she did scare the pants off him more than half the time. He just didn't trust her. At any moment, she was perfectly capable of doing something really crazy. There was something about airplanes that went to her head and made her forget all reason.

But she lost altitude carefully, and then let Chris take over the controls again, before they landed. As a result, his landing was not as smooth as hers would have been. They touched down too hard, bumping awkwardly down the runway. She was trying to will him to land the plane properly, but Chris had none of her instincts and as a result he'd done a "pancake" as he landed, hitting the ground hard after leveling off too high for a proper landing.

When they got out of the plane, both of them were surprised to see Nick and their father standing near the runway. They'd been watching them, and Pat was grinning broadly at Chris, while Nick seemed to be staring at Cassie.

"Nice work, son," Pat beamed. "You're a natural pilot." Pat looked immensely pleased and overlooked the shabby landing, as Nick watched them. He'd been watching Chris's face, but he was much more intent on Cassie as he had been from the moment she stepped out of the plane. "How was it being up there with your brother, Cass?" her father asked her with a smile.

"Pretty good, Dad. It was really fun." Her eyes danced like

Christmas as Nick watched, and Pat led Chris back to the office, as Nick and Cass followed behind in silence.

"You like flying with him, huh, Cass?" Nick asked carefully as they sauntered toward the office.

"A lot." She beamed at Nick, and for reasons best known to himself he wanted to reach over and shake her. He knew she wasn't telling the truth, and he wondered why Pat was so easily fooled. Maybe he wanted to be. But those kinds of games could be dangerous, even fatal.

"That loop looked pretty good," Nick said quietly.

"Felt good too," she said, without looking at him.

"I'll bet it did," he said, watching her for a moment, and then, shaking his head, he went back to his office.

A few minutes later, Pat drove the kids home with him. When Nick heard their car leave, he sat at his desk, thinking of them, and the flying he had just seen. He shook his head with a rueful grin. He knew one thing for sure. Chris O'Malley had not been flying that plane. And he couldn't help smiling to himself, as he realized that somehow Cassie had found a way to fly. And maybe, just maybe, after all her hard work to get there, maybe she deserved it. Maybe he wouldn't challenge her for a while. Maybe he'd just watch and see how she did. He smiled to himself again, thinking of the loop he'd seen her do. Next she'd be flying in the air show. But why not? What the hell? Everything about her told him she was a natural. She was more than that. He sensed instinctively that woman or not, she *needed* to fly, just like he did.

CHAPTER
2

When Pat, Cassie, and Chris walked into the house that night, all of Cassie's sisters were in the kitchen helping their mother. Glynnis looked like Pat, and at twenty-five, had four little girls of her own, and had been married for six years. Megan was shy like her mom, and looked like her, though her hair was brown. At twenty-three, she had three sons, and had married six months after Glynnis. Their husbands were farmers, and had small properties nearby. They were decent, hardworking men, and the girls were happy with them. Colleen was twenty-two and blond, she had a little boy and a little girl, both were barely more than toddlers, and Colleen had been married for three years to the English teacher at the local school. She wanted to go to college, but she was pregnant again, and with three kids at home there was no way she could go anywhere, except if she took them with her. It wouldn't be fair to leave three kids with her mother every day just so she could go to school, and her father wouldn't have let her anyway. Maybe when the kids were older. For the moment college was only a dream for her. The reality of her life was three babies and very little money. Her father gave them small "gifts" from time to time, but Colleen's husband was proud, and he hated to take them. But with his own wages so small, and a new baby only a few weeks away, they needed all the help they could get, and Colleen's mother had given her some money that afternoon. She knew they needed it to buy things for the baby. Depression wages had hit the schools, and they could hardly eat on what David made, even with regular gifts from her parents, and food given to them by her sisters.

All three of the girls were staying for dinner with them, their husbands had other plans that night and the girls came home to their parents often. Oona loved seeing the kids, although having them all home at once made the dinner hour unusually chaotic and noisy.

Pat went to change and Chris went to his room, while Cassie tried entertaining the kids and everyone else cooked, and two of her nephews thought the dirt on her face was hysterically funny. One of her nieces did too, and she chased all of them around the living room pretending to be a monster. Chris didn't appear again until dinner was called, and he glared at Cassie when he did. He was still annoyed at her about the loop she had done, but on the other hand she had won his father's praise for him, so he didn't dare complain too much or too loudly. They were both getting what they wanted out of the arrangement. She wanted to fly, and he wanted the money. His father's praise was an added bonus.

Half an hour later, they all sat down to an enormous meal, of corn and pork, corn bread and mashed potatoes. Glynnis had brought the pork, and Megan the corn, and Oona had grown the potatoes. They all grew their own food, and when they needed more they bought it at Strong's. It was the only grocery store for miles, and the best one in the region. The Strongs were doing well, even in tough times, and theirs was a solid business. Oona said as much again as they finished the meal, and Cassie heard a familiar sound of wheels outside the house, almost as though on cue. It was easy to guess who it was, he dropped by almost every night after dinner, particularly now that they were both out of school for the summer.

Cassie had known Bobby Strong, the only son of the local grocer, since they were children. He was a good boy, and they had been good friends for years, but for the past two years they'd been more than that, though Cassie insisted she didn't quite know what. But her mother and Megan always reminded her that they had gotten married at seventeen, so she better know what she was doing with Bobby. He was serious and responsible, and her parents liked him too. But Cassie wasn't ready to admit to herself, or to him, that she loved him.

She liked being with him. She liked him, and his friends. She liked his good manners and gentle ways. His thoughtfulness, his patience. He had a kind heart, and she loved the way he was around her nieces and nephews. She enjoyed a lot of things about him, but he still wasn't as exciting as airplanes. She had never met a boy who was. Maybe there was no such thing. Maybe that was something you just had to accept. But she would have loved to know a boy who was as exciting as a "Gee Bee Super Sportster" or a "Beech Staggerwing" or a Wedell-Williams racing plane. Bobby was a nice kid, but he didn't even compare to an airplane.

"Hi, Mrs. O'Malley . . . Glynn . . . Meg . . . Colleen . . . wow! Looks like it'll be pretty soon!" Colleen looked huge as she tried to gather up her kids to leave, and Oona helped her.

"Maybe tonight if I don't stop eating my mother's apple pie," Colleen grinned. She was only five years older than they were, but Cassie felt as though they were light-years apart sometimes. Her sisters were all married and so settled and so different. She knew instinctively that somehow she couldn't be like them. She wondered sometimes if there was a curse on her, if her father had wanted a boy so badly that it had somehow damaged her before birth. Maybe she was a freak. She liked boys. She liked Bobby particularly. But she liked airplanes and her own independence a whole lot better.

Bobby shook hands with her father, and said hi to Chris, and all the little kids climbed all over him. Then a little while later her mother and the oldest sisters went out to the kitchen to clean up, and her mother told her not to bother, and just to go sit with Bobby. At least Cassie had washed her face by then, but you could still see traces of the grease that had been there before dinner.

"How was your day?" he asked with a shy smile. He was awkward, but likable, and he tried to be tolerant of her unusual ideas and her fascination with her father's airplanes. He pretended to be interested, and listened to her rattle on about a new plane that had come through, or her father's cherished Vega. But the truth was, she could have said anything, he just wanted to be near her. He came by faithfully almost every night, and Cassie still acted surprised when he did, much to her parents' amusement.

She was just not ready to face the seriousness of his commitment, or what it might mean if he persisted in visiting her. Only a year from now she would graduate, and if he kept dropping by like this, he might ask her to marry him, and expect to marry her as soon as they finished high school. The very thought of that terrified her and she just couldn't face it. She wanted so much more than that. Time, and space, and college. And the feeling she got when she did a loop, or a spin. Being with Bobby was like driving to Ohio. Safe, and solid and uneventful. He wasn't like flying anywhere. And yet she knew that if he had stopped coming to see her, she would miss him.

"I went up in my dad's Jenny with Chris today." She filled him in, trying to sound casual. Getting too serious with Bobby always scared her. "It was fun. We did some lazy eights, and a loop."

"Sounds like Chris is getting good," Bobby said politely, but like Chris, airplanes didn't do much to excite him. "What else did you do?" He was always interested in her, and secretly he thought her beautiful, not like the other boys who thought she was too tall, or her hair was too red, or liked her because her figure was great, or thought she was weird because she knew a lot about airplanes. Bobby liked her because of who she was, even if at times he recognized the possibility that he might not understand her. But that was endearing about him too. A lot of things were, which was why her feelings about him confused her. Her mother told her that she had felt that way about Pat at first too. Commitment was always hard, Oona said. And that made it even harder for Cassie. She didn't know what to think of what she felt for Bobby.

"Oh, I don't know . . ." Cassie went on to answer his question, trying to remember all she'd done. All of it had to do with airplanes. "I gassed a bunch of planes, tinkered with the engine on the Jenny before Chris took it out. I think I might even have fixed it." She touched her face self-consciously then with a grin. "I got a lot of grease on my face doing it. My dad had a fit when he saw me. I couldn't get it all off. You should have seen me before dinner!"

"I thought maybe you were getting liver spots," he teased and she laughed. He was a good sport, and he knew how much her dreams meant to her, like college. He had no plans to go himself. He was going to stay home and help his father with their business, just as he did every day after school, and all through the summer.

"You know, Fred Astaire's new movie *Follow the Fleet* is coming to the movie theater this Saturday night. Want to go? They say it's a great movie." Bobby looked at her hopefully, she nodded slowly, and smiled up at him.

"I'd like that."

A few minutes later, the last of her sisters and their children left, and Cassie and Bobby were alone on the porch again. Her parents were in the living room. She knew they could see them from where they sat, but her parents were always discreet about Bobby's visits. They liked him, and Pat wouldn't have been unhappy if they'd decided to get married when she finished school next June. As long as they didn't get themselves into trouble first, they could spend all the time they wanted cooing on the front porch. It was fine with him. Better than having her hang around the airport.

Inside the house, Pat was telling Oona about Chris's loop that afternoon. He was so proud of him. "The boy's a natural, Oonie." He grinned and she smiled at him, grateful that he had finally gotten the son he had so desperately wanted.

On the porch, Bobby was telling her about his day at the grocery store, and how the Depression was affecting food prices all over the country, not just in Illinois. He had a dream of opening a series of stores one day, in several towns, maybe as far reaching as Chicago. But they all had dreams. Cassie's were a lot wilder than his, and harder to talk about. His just sounded young and ambitious.

"Do you ever think of doing something totally different, and not what your father does at all?" she asked him, intrigued by the idea, even though all she wanted was to follow in her own father's footsteps. But those footsteps were totally forbidden to her, which made them all the more appealing.

"Not really," Bobby answered quietly. "I like his business actually. People need food, and they need good food. We do something important for people, even if it doesn't seem very exciting. But maybe it could be."

"Maybe it could," she smiled at him, as she heard a sudden droning sound above, and looked up toward the familiar noise of the engines. "That's Nick . . . he's on his way to San Diego with some cargo. Then he's stopping in San Francisco on the way back, to bring back some mail on one of our contracts." She knew he was flying the Handley Page, she could tell just from the sound of the engines.

"He probably gets tired of that too," Bobby said wisely. "It sounds exciting to us, but to him it's probably only a job, just like my father's."

"Maybe." But Cassie knew different. Flying wasn't like that. "Pilots are a different breed. They love what they do. It's almost as though they can't bear the thought of doing anything else. It's in their bones. They live and breathe it. They love it more than anything." Her eyes shone as she said it.

"I guess," Bobby looked baffled by what she was saying, "I can't say I understand it."

"I don't think most people can . . . it's like a mysterious fascination. A wonderful gift. To people who love flying, it means more than anything."

He laughed softly in the warm night air. "I think you just see it as very romantic. I'm not so sure they do. Believe me, to them, it's probably just a job."

"Maybe," she said, not wanting to argue with him, but knowing far more than she let on to. Flying was like a secret brotherhood, one she desperately wanted to join, and so far no one would let her. But for those few moments in the air today, when Chris had let her fly the plane, that was all that mattered.

She sat thinking of it for a long time, staring into the darkness off the porch, forgetting that Bobby was even there, and then suddenly, when she heard him stir, she remembered.

"I guess I should go. You're probably tired from gassing all those planes," he teased her. But actually, she wanted to be alone, to think of what it had been like to fly the plane. It had been so exquisite for those few minutes. "I'll see you tomorrow, Cass."

"Good night." He held her hand briefly and then brushed her cheek with his lips before he walked back to his father's old Model A truck with "Strong's Groceries" written across the side. In the daytime, they used it for deliveries. At night, they let Bobby drive it. "I'll see you tomorrow."

She smiled and waved at him as he drove away, and then she walked slowly back into the house, thinking of how lucky Nick was to be flying through the night, on his way to San Diego.

33

CHAPTER

3

Nick returned to Good Hope from the West Coast late Sunday night, after dropping off cargo and mail in Detroit and Chicago. He was back at his desk at six o'clock Monday morning, looking rested and energetic. It was a busy day, some new contracts had come in, and there was always more mail and cargo to be moved around. They had plenty of pilots working for them, and enough planes, but Nick still volunteered for the longer-range trips himself, and the more difficult flying. It gave him enormous satisfaction to get in a plane, and fly off into the night, especially in rotten weather. And Pat was the perfect balance for him. He was a genius at running the administrative side of their business. He still loved to fly too, but he had less time for it now, and in some ways less patience. It annoyed the hell out of him when something went wrong with a plane, or they were delayed, or their schedules got loused up. He had no patience at all for pilots' quirks and little tricks, and he made them toe the line and be 100 percent reliable, or they never flew again for O'Malley.

"Ya better watch out, Ace," Nick teased him now and again, "you're beginning to sound like Rickenbacker," their old commander.

"I could do a lot worse, Stick. And so could you," Pat would growl back at him, using Nick's old wartime nickname. His wartime history was every bit as colorful as Pat's. Nick had once fought the famed German flying ace Ernst Udet to a standoff, and brought his plane back safely even though he'd been wounded. But that was all behind them now. The only time Nick thought of the war was when he was fighting weather, or bringing in a limping plane. He had had a few close calls in the seventeen years he'd flown for Pat, but none as dramatic as his wartime adventures.

Nick was reminded of one of them late that afternoon, as they watched a storm brewing in the east, and mentioned it to Pat. There had been a terrible storm he'd gotten caught in during the war, and flew so low to the ground to get under the clouds, he had almost scraped the plane's belly. Pat laughed, remembering it; he'd given Nick hell for flying that low, but he'd managed to save himself and the plane. Two other men had gotten lost in the same storm and never made it.

"Scared the hell out of me," Nick admitted, two decades later.

"You looked a little green when you got in, as I recall." Pat needled him a little bit, and they watched the ominous black clouds gather in the distance. Nick was still tired from the long flight from the West Coast the day before, but he wanted to finish his paperwork before he went home to sleep. And when he walked back into the office with Pat, after checking the condition of some planes, he noticed Chris in the distance, chatting with Cassie. They seemed intent in conversation and neither of them noticed him. He couldn't imagine what they were saying. Nor did it worry him. He knew that the weather was looking too ominous for Chris to want to go up with him or practice solo.

Cassie and Chris were still talking after Nick disappeared back into the office, and Cassie was shouting at him over the roar of some nearby engines.

"Don't be stupid! We only have to go up and down for a few minutes. The storm is still hours away. I listened to all the weather reports this morning. Don't be such a damn chicken, Chris."

"I don't want to go up when the weather looks like this, Cass. We can go tomorrow."

"I want to go now." The dark clouds rushing past them overhead only seemed to excite her further. "It would be fun."

"No, it wouldn't. And if I risk the Jenny, Dad'll really be mad at me." He knew his father well and so did Cassie.

"Don't be dumb. We're not risking anything. The clouds are still way up there. If we go now, we can be back in half an hour, and be perfectly safe. Trust me." He watched her eyes unhappily, hating her for being so persuasive. She had always done this to him. After all, she was his big sister. He had always listened to her, and more often than not it had resulted in disaster, mostly when she urged him to trust her. She was the daredevil in the family, and he was always the hesitant, cautious one. But Cassie never listened to reason. Sometimes it was easier just to give in to her than to go on arguing forever. Her blue eyes were pleading with him, and it was obvious she wasn't going to take no for an answer.

"Fifteen minutes and that's it," he finally conceded unhappily. "And I decide when we come back in. I don't give a damn what you think, if it's too soon, or you haven't had enough. Fifteen minutes and we're back. And that's it, Cass. Or forget it. Deal?"

"Deal. I just want to get the feel of the weather." She looked like a girl with a new romance as she beamed at him, her eyes dancing.

"I think you're nuts," he said grumpily. But it seemed easier to get it over with than to stand there yelling at each other till the storm broke.

They went out to where the Jenny was kept, rolled it out, and did the necessary checks on the plane itself, and then they hopped into their respective seats. Cassie sat in front again, and Chris took the instructor's seat behind her. In theory, just as before, she was only a passenger, and since they both had controls, no one could see who handled them, if it was Chris or Cassie.

A few minutes later, Nick heard the hum of the plane overhead, but he didn't pay much attention to it. He figured it was some fool, trying to get home ahead of the weather front right before the storm broke. For once, it wasn't his problem. All his pilots were on the ground, where he had told them to stay, after listening to a news bulletin half an hour before. But as he listened to the sound now, he could have sworn he could hear the Jenny. It seemed impossible, but he wandered over to the window anyway, and then he saw them. He saw Cassie's distinct red hair in the front seat, and Chris right behind her. He was flying the plane, or so Nick thought, and the wind buffeted them terribly and seemed to almost toss them away right after takeoff. They were moving with surprising speed, and then Nick saw them rise dramatically, probably caught in a sudden updraft. He watched them, amazed, unable to believe that Chris had been both brave and foolish enough to take off in a windstorm like this one. And almost as soon as they disappeared into the cloud hanging over him, Nick saw the rain splash down on the ground as though someone in the sky had turned on a faucet.

"Shit!" He muttered to himself as he hurried outside, watching for where the Jenny had been, but he couldn't see anything, and the storm front was moving fast now, with terrifying winds and a flash of lightning. Within minutes he was drenched, and there was no sign of Chris or Cassie.

Chris was fighting with the controls as they gained altitude, and Cassie had turned around and was shouting something to him, but between the storm and the engine's noise, he couldn't hear her.

"Let me take it!" she was shouting, and at last he understood, as she signaled him with gestures. He shook his head, but she kept nodding at him, and it was obvious that he was being overpowered rapidly by the forces of nature. The force of the wind and the storm were too much for him, and the plane was being tossed around like a child's toy, in his unskilled hands. And then, without saying a word to him, she turned her attention to the controls, and by sheer force, she overpowered him and took them from him. She began flying the plane with her stronger hands on the controls, and within moments, despite the ferocious winds, the plane had almost steadied. Chris stopped fighting her then, and near tears, he let his hands go slack on his set of the controls, and let her fly it. She knew less than he did perhaps, but she seemed to have a relationship with the plane that he couldn't come close to. And he knew that in his hands they would almost surely be destroyed. Maybe in Cassie's there was some hope. For an instant, he closed his eyes and prayed, wishing he had never let her talk him into taking off in the storm.

They were both drenched in the open cockpit, and the plane was rising and falling on terrifying downdrafts. They would drop a hundred feet or so, and then rise again, although more slowly. It was like being dropped off a building when they fell, and then crawling up the side again, only to be dropped again, like a paper puppet.

The clouds were almost black as Cassie fought with the stick, but she seemed to sense their altitude almost by instinct. She had an uncanny sense about what the plane would cooperate with, and seemed to work with it to get where she wanted. But they had no idea where they were anymore, how far they had gone, or exactly how high they were. The altimeter was going crazy. Cassie had some idea, but they had totally lost sight of the ground, and a rapidly moving line of clouds had disoriented them completely.

"We're okay," she shouted encouragingly back at Chris, but he couldn't hear her. "We're going to be fine," she kept saying to herself, and then she began talking to the Jenny itself, as though the little plane could follow her directions. She had heard about some of her father's and Nick's tricks, and she knew that there was one that would get them out of this mess, if it didn't kill them. She had to trust her own instincts for this, and she had to be very, very sure . . . she was talking to herself, into the wind, as the plane began to drop dramatically. She was looking for the lowest edge of the clouds, and counting on finding it before they hit the ground, but if it was too low, and she dropped too fast, or if she lost control for a single instant . . . it was called scud running, and if you lost . . . you died. It was as simple as that. And they both knew it, as the little Jenny dropped toward the ground as quickly as Cassie would let it.

Their speed was terrifying by then, the howling of the wind deafening, as they flew through the inky wet blackness. It seemed like a bottomless place they were falling into, filled with horrifying sounds, and terrifying feelings, and then suddenly, almost before she knew, she sensed before she saw, both the treeline, and the ground, and then the airport. She pulled sharply on the stick, and pulled herself up just before they'd have hit the trees. They got lost in the clouds again for a moment or two, but she knew then where she was, and how to approach the airport. She closed her eyes just for a second, feeling where she was, and how fast she could drop, and again she saw the trees, but this time she was in full control. She came in just over them, as the wind tipped her wings, and almost knocked them over. She pulled up and circled the airport again, wondering if they could land at all, or if in the end it would be impossible because of the force of the unpredictable winds. She wasn't afraid, she was just thinking very quietly, and then she saw him. It was Nick waving frantically. He had seen what she'd done, seen her running just under the clouds, and almost hit the ground. She was less than fifty feet above it. He ran to where she should be, and tried to wave her in, on the farthest runway. The angle of the wind was just enough gentler there to allow her to make a breathtaking landing. The little Jenny screeched all the way down the runway, with the wind hard on their faces, and Cassie gritted her teeth so hard her face ached. Her hair was plastered to her head from the rain, and her hands were numb from clutching the stick, and Chris was sitting behind her with his eyes closed. They bounced hard when they hit the ground, and he opened them. He couldn't believe she'd brought them in, he had been sure they were as good as dead; he was still in shock when Nick came rushing up to them, and physically dragged him out of the plane, while Cassie just sat there shaking.

"What the hell are you two lunatics trying to do? Commit suicide, or bomb the airport?" They had come pretty close to the roof on the way down, but Cassie had decided that was the least of their problems. She was still amazed that she'd brought them in at all, and she had to fight to repress a grin of relief. She'd been so damn scared, and yet a part of her had stayed so cool. All she could do was think about how to get out of it, and talk to the little airplane. "Are you crazy?" Nick was shaking him, and glaring at her, as Pat came running out from the airport.

"What the hell is going on here?" he shouted at all of them, as the wind buffeted them, and Cassie began worrying about the plane. She didn't want her turned over and damaged as they sat in the wind on the runway.

"These two fools of yours went out for a joyride in this. I think they're trying to get killed, or destroy your airplanes, I'm not sure which, but they ought to have their butts kicked." Nick was so furious he could hardly speak, and Pat couldn't believe what he was seeing.

He stared at Chris in utter astonishment. "You went out in *this?*" He was referring to the weather not the plane, as his son knew.

"I . . . uh . . . I just thought we'd go up and come right down . . . and . . ." . . . he wanted to whine as he had as a child, "But, Daddy, Cassie made me . . ." But he said not a word

41

as his father tried to hide his pride in him. The kid had guts, and he was a hell of a pilot.

"And you landed her in this? Don't you know how dangerous this kind of weather is? You could have been killed." Pat couldn't hide the pride in his voice, it was beyond him.

"I know, Dad. I'm sorry." Chris was fighting not to cry, and Cassie was watching her father's face. She knew only too well what she saw there. It was raw pride in the accomplishments of his son, or so he thought. It was meant for her, but it went to Chris, because he was a boy, and that was just the way things were. The way they always had been. Whatever she did in life, she knew she had to do it for herself, not for him, because he would never understand it or give her credit for it. She was "only a girl" to him. That was all she ever would be.

Pat turned to look at Cassie then, almost as though he could hear her thinking. And then he looked at his son again with an angry scowl. "You should never have taken her up in this. It's too dangerous for passengers to be out in bad conditions. You shouldn't have gone up yourself. But never take a passenger into weather like this, son." She was someone to be protected, but never admired. It was her destiny, and she knew it.

"Yes, sir." There were tears standing out in Chris's eyes as his father glanced at the plane, and his son, in fresh amazement.

"Put her away then." And with that he walked away, and Nick watched Chris and Cassie put the plane away. Chris looked so shaken he could hardly walk, but Cassie was calm, as she wiped the rain off the plane, and checked the engine. Her brother only looked at her angrily and stalked away, determined never to forgive her for almost killing him. He would never forget how close they had come, and all because of one of her whims. She was completely crazy. She had proved it.

She put the last of her tools away, and she was surprised when she turned to find Nick standing just behind her. He looked very much like the storm she had just flown through. Her brother was gone, and her father was waiting for them inside the airport.

"Don't *ever* do that again. You're a damn fool, and you could have been killed. That little trick only works once in a while for the greats, and usually not for them. It won't work for you again, Cass. Don't try it." But it had worked for him more than once. And years before, watching him, it had made Pat as angry as Nick was now. His eyes were like steel as he looked at her. He was furious, but there was something else there too. And her heart gave a little leap as she saw it. It was what she had wanted from Pat, and knew she would never get from him. It was admiration, and respect. It was all she wanted.

"I don't know what you mean." She looked away from him. Now that she was back on the ground, she felt drained. The exhilaration was almost gone, and what she felt now was the backlash of the terror, and the exhaustion.

"You know damn well what I mean!" he shouted at her and grabbed her arm, his black hair matted around his face. He had stood staring up at her plane, willing her in, willing her to find the hole in the clouds, to make it. He couldn't have stood losing both of them, seeing them die, and all for a joyride. In the war, they'd had no choice. But this was different. It was so senseless.

"Let go of me." She was angry at him. She was angry at all of them. Her brother who got all the glory and didn't know how to fly worth a damn, her father who was so obsessed with him he couldn't see anything, and Nick who thought he knew it all. It was their secret club, they had all the toys, and they would never let her play. She was good enough to fuel their machines and work on their engines, and get their oil and grease in her hair, but never to fly their planes. "Leave me alone!" she shouted at him, and he only grabbed her other arm. He had never seen her like this, and he didn't know whether to spank her or hold her.

"Cassie, I saw what you did up there!" He was still shouting at her. "I'm not blind. I know Chris can't fly like that! I know you were flying the plane . . . but you're crazy. You could have gotten yourself killed . . . you can't do that . . ." She looked at him with such misery that his heart went out to her. He had wanted to beat her senseless for almost killing herself, and now instead, he felt sorry for her. He understood now as he never had before what she wanted, and how badly she wanted it, and just how much she was willing to do to get it.

"Cassie, please . . ." He kept a grip on her arms and pulled her closer to him. "Please . . . don't ever do anything like that again. I'll teach you myself. I promise. Leave Chris alone. Don't do that to him. I'll teach you. If you want it so badly, I'll do it." He held her close to him, cradling her like a little girl, grateful that she hadn't been killed by her foolish but daring stunt. He knew he couldn't have stood it. He looked at her unhappily as he held her close to him. They were both badly shaken by what had happened. But she only shook her head at him. She knew how impossible it was. This was the only way she could have it.

"My father will never let you teach me, Nick," she said miserably, no longer denying that she had brought Chris in, instead of the other way around. Nick knew the truth, and she knew that. There was no point lying to him. She had done it.

"I didn't say I'd ask him, Cass. I said I'd do it. Not here." He smiled ruefully at her, and handed her a clean towel to dry her hair with. "You look like a drowned rat."

"At least I don't have grease all over my face for a change," she said shyly. She felt closer to him than she ever had before. And different. She was drying her hair, as she looked at him again. She couldn't believe what she was hearing. "What do you mean 'not here.' Where else would we go?" She felt suddenly grown-up, part of a conspiracy with him. Something had very subtly changed between them.

"There are half a dozen little strips we can go to. It may not be easy. You could catch a bus to Prairie City after school, and I could meet you there. In the meantime, maybe Chris would drop you off there this summer now and then on his way to work. I imagine he'd rather do that than risk his life several times a week flying with you. I know I would." Cassie grinned. Poor Chris. She had scared the pants off him, and she knew it. But it had seemed like such a great idea, and for a few minutes it was fun. And after that, it was the scariest thing she had ever done, and the most exciting.

"Do you mean it?" She looked amazed, but in fact, they both did. He was a little startled himself at what he'd just offered.

"I guess I do. I never thought I'd do something like this. But I think maybe some instruction will keep you out of a lot more trouble. And maybe after you fly respectably for a while," he looked at her pointedly, "we can talk to Pat and see if he'll let you fly from here. He'll come around eventually. He has to."

"I don't think he will," she said gloomily, as they went back out into the rain to meet her father in his office. And then, just before they reached it, soaked again, she stopped and looked at him with a smile that melted his very soul. He didn't want to feel that way with her, and it startled him. But they had been through a lot that evening, and it had brought them closer together.

"Thanks, Nick."

"Don't mention it. And I mean that." Her father would have strangled him for giving her lessons. He tousled her wet hair then, and walked her into her father's office. Chris was looking shaken and gray, and his father had just given him a nip of brandy.

"You okay, Cass?" Pat glanced at her, but saw that she looked none the worse for wear, unlike her brother. But the responsibility had been his after all, and the hard part of landing back at the airport, or at least that was what her father thought, and Chris hadn't told him any different.

"I'm okay, Dad," she assured him.

"You're a brave girl," he said admiringly, but not admiring enough. It was Nick who had understood. Nick who had agreed to give her what she had always dreamed of. Her dream come true, and she was suddenly glad she had gone up in the storm, even if she had taken a hell of a chance. Maybe in the end, it had been worth it.

Pat drove Chris and Cassie home, and their mother was waiting for them. As soon as they sat down to dinner, her father told

Oona the whole story. Or what he thought was the whole story, of how incredible Chris had been, how he had flown by sheer wit and nerve, and after the initial foolishness of going up in the storm, had brought them home safely. Their father was so proud of him, and Chris said nothing at all. He just went to his room, and lay on his bed and cried, with the door closed.

Cassie went in to see him after a while. She knocked for a long time, and he finally let her in, with a look that combined anguish and fury.

"What do *you* want?"

"To tell you I'm sorry I scared you . . . and almost got us killed. I'm sorry, Chris. I shouldn't have done it." She could afford to be magnanimous now, now that Nick had agreed to give her what she had always wanted.

"I'm never going up in a plane with you again," he said ominously, glaring at her like a much younger brother who had been used and betrayed by a wilier older sister.

"You don't have to," she said quietly, sitting on the edge of his bed as he stared at her.

"You're giving up flying?" That he'd never believe.

"Maybe . . . for now . . ." She shrugged, as though it didn't matter to her, but he knew her better.

"I don't believe you."

"I'll see. It doesn't matter now. I just wanted to tell you I was sorry."

"You should be," he fired at her, and then he backed down, and reached out and touched her arm. "Thanks though . . . for saving our asses up there. I really thought we were done for."

"So did I," she grinned excitedly at him. "I really thought for a while there it was over." And then she giggled.

"You lunatic," and then, admiringly, "you're a hell of a pilot, Cass. You gotta learn right one day, and not all this sneaky stuff behind Dad's back. He's got to let you fly. You're ten times the pilot I'll ever be. I'll bet you're as good as he is."

"I doubt that, but you'll be okay. You're a good straightforward pilot, Chris. Just stay out of the tough stuff."

"Yeah, thanks," he grinned at her, no longer wanting to kill her. "I'll remind you of that, next time you offer to take me up and kill me."

"I won't, for a while," she said angelically, but he knew her better.

"What's that all about? You're up to something, Cass."

"No, I'm not. I'm going to behave . . . for a while anyway . . ."

"Lord help us. Just let me know when you decide to go berserk again. I'll be sure to stay away from the airport. Maybe you ought to do that for a while too. I swear, those fumes have made you crazy."

"Maybe so," she said dreamily. But it was more than that, and she knew it. She had those fumes in her blood, her bones, and she knew more than ever that she would never escape them.

Bobby Strong came by after dinner that night, and he was horrified when he heard her father's tale, and furious with Chris a little later when he saw him.

"The next time you take my girl up and almost kill her, you'll have to answer to me," he said, much to Chris's and Cassie's astonishment. "That was a dumb thing to do and you know it." Chris would have liked to tell him Cassie wanted to, he would have liked to tell him a lot of things, but of course he couldn't.

"Yeah, sure," her younger brother mumbled vaguely as he went back to his room. They were all nuts. Bobby, Cass, his father, Nick. None of them knew the truth, none of them knew who was to blame and who wasn't. His father thought he was a criminal, and Cassie had them all bamboozled. But only Cassie knew the truth about that, and Nick, now that he had promised to give her lessons.

Bobby lectured her that night on how dangerous flying was, how useless, and how foolish; he told her that all the men involved in it were immature, and they were just playing like children. He hoped she had learned a lesson that night, and that she would be more reasonable in the future about hanging around the airport. He expected it of her, he explained. How could she expect to have any kind of future at all if she spent her life covered in grease and oil, and was willing to risk her life on a wild adventure with her brother? Besides, she was a girl, and it wasn't proper.

She tried to make herself agree with him, because she knew he meant well. But she was relieved when he left. And all she could think of that night, as she lay in bed listening to the rain, was what Nick had promised her, and how soon they would start flying together. She could hardly wait. She lay awake for hours, thinking about it, and remembering the feeling of the wind on her face, as she dashed beneath the clouds in the Jenny, looking for the edge, waiting to escape, just before they hit the ground, and then soaring free again, shearing the top of the trees, and then coming in safely. It had been an extraordinary day, and she knew that no matter what anyone said to her about how dangerous or improper it was, she would never give it up. Not for any of them. She just couldn't.

CHAPTER
4

Three days after the storm that eventually turned into a tornado, ten miles away in Blandinsville, Cassie got up and did her chores and when she left the house, she told her mother she was going to the library, and then to meet a friend from school who had married that spring, and was expecting a baby. And after that she'd stop by the airport. She had packed an apple and a sandwich in a paper bag, and she had taken a dollar from her savings and hidden it in her pocket. She wasn't sure how much the bus fare would be, but she wanted to be sure she had enough to get to Prairie City. She had promised to meet Nick there at noon, and as she walked toward the bus terminal downtown in the summer sun, she was sorry she hadn't worn a hat. But she knew that if she had, her mother would have suspected something. She never wore one.

As she walked along, she looked like a long, lanky girl, going off to meet friends. She looked her age, but was extraordinarily lovely. She was even prettier than her mother had been, she was taller and thinner, and she had an even more impressive figure. But her looks were something that Cassie never thought about. Looks were something for other girls, who had nothing else in their heads, or girls like her sisters who wanted to get married and have babies. She knew she wanted children one day, or at least she thought she did, but there were so many other things she wanted first, things she would probably never have, like excitement and freedom and flying. She loved reading stories about women pilots, and she read everything she could about Amelia Earhart and Jackie Cochran. She'd read Lindbergh's book *We,* about his Atlantic solo in 1927, and his wife's book *North to the Orient* the year before when it came out, and Earhart's book, *The Fun of It.* All the women involved in aviation were her heroes. She often wondered why they could do what she could only dream of. But maybe now with Nick helping her . . . just maybe . . . if she could just fly . . . if she could just take off as she had the other day with Chris, and soar lazily into the sky forever.

She was so lost in her own thoughts that she almost missed her bus, and she had to run to catch it before it left her. She was relieved to see that no one she knew had gotten on, and the forty-five-minute ride to Prairie City in the dilapidated bus was uneventful. It had only cost fifteen cents, and she spent the entire trip daydreaming about her lessons.

It was a long walk to the airstrip after the bus dropped her off, but Nick had told her exactly how to get there. He had somehow assumed that she would get a ride from someone. It had never dawned on him that she would walk the last two miles to meet him, and when she arrived she looked hot and damp and dusty. He was sitting quietly on a rock, drinking a soda, with the familiar Jenny parked at the end of the deserted airstrip. There was no one else around, just the two of them. It was a runway that was used occasionally for crop dusters, and had been put in originally in barnstorming days. It was only used occasionally, but it was in good repair. Nick had known it would be the perfect place for their lessons.

"You okay?" He looked at her with a fatherly air, as she pushed her bright red hair off her face, and held it off her neck. The sun was blazing. "You look hotter than hell. Here, have something to drink." He handed her his Coke, and watched her admiringly as she took a long swallow. She had a long graceful neck, and the silky whiteness of her throat reminded him of the palest pink marble. She was a striking girl, and there were times lately when he almost wished she weren't Pat's daughter. But it wouldn't have done him any good anyway, he reminded himself. He was thirty-five and she was seventeen, she was hardly fair prey for a man his age. But there were moments when it could have been tempting. "What did you do, you goofball?" he asked, relieving the tension of the moment. It was odd being here, just the two of them, alone on their secret mission. "Did you walk all the way from Good Hope?"

"No," she grinned back at him, quenched by his soda. "Just from Prairie City. It was farther than I thought. And hotter."

"I'm sorry," he said apologetically. He felt bad to have brought her so far, but it had seemed the perfect place for their rendezvous with her father's plane, for their secret lessons.

"Don't be," she grinned, accepting another swig of his soda. "It's worth it." He could see easily in her eyes how much it meant to her. She was crazed over planes, and totally in love with flying. It was exactly how he had been at her age, dragging from airport to airport to airport, happy to do anything, just to be near the planes and get a chance to fly now and then. The war had been like a dream come true for him, flying in the 94th, with men who had almost all become legends. But he was sorry for her, it wouldn't be that easy, particularly if Pat was determined to keep her from flying. Nick was hoping that one of these days he might sway him. And in the meantime, at least he could teach her the important things, so she didn't kill herself doing crazy tricks, or scud running with her brother. He still shuddered when he thought of her flying out of the clouds three days before, just barely above the ground and moving like a bullet. At least now she'd know what she was doing.

"Shall we give it a whirl?" he asked, waving at the Jenny. She was sitting there, waiting for them, an old friend, just as they were.

She was too excited to even speak to him as they walked down the airstrip to the familiar plane. She had gassed her a thousand times, cleaned her engine, lovingly washed her wings, and flown her half a dozen times with Chris pretending that he was taking his sister up for a joyride. But the Jenny had never looked as beautiful to Cassie as she did now. They did a walk around first, checked the landing gear to make sure he hadn't damaged it when he landed. She was a low plane with a broad wingspan and the feel of a larger plane, although she was a modest size, and she wasn't daunting to Cassie. And now Cassie gently stepped into her and buckled her seat belt. She knew that the skies would soon be hers, she had a right to them, just as they all did. And after that, no one could stop her.

"All set?" Nick shouted at her in the first noise of the engine. Cassie nodded with a grin, and he hopped in the seat behind her. At first, he would be flying the plane, and once they were safely in the air, he would turn over the controls to her. This time she wouldn't have to wrest them from him, as she had from Chris. This time it would all be aboveboard, and as they taxied down the runway, Cassie turned to look at him. Nick's was such a familiar face to her, and yet as she saw him now, she felt happier than she had ever been, and she wanted to throw her arms around his neck and kiss him.

"What?" She had said something to him, and at first he couldn't hear her. He didn't think anything was wrong, she looked too happy for there to be a problem. But he leaned forward so he could hear her better. His dark hair was blowing in the wind, his eyes were the same color as the summer sky, and there were lines around his eyes from where he squinted into the sunlight.

"I said . . . thank you! . . ." She shouted back at him, her eyes so filled with joy that it touched his heart. He squeezed her shoulder gently, and she turned forward again, and put her hands on the controls. But there was no question this time as to who was flying the plane. Nick was.

He pushed the throttle forward evenly, and used the rudder pedals. And a moment later, they lifted smoothly off the runway and rose easily into the air, and as they did, Cassie felt her heart soar with the old Jenny. She felt the same thrill she always did when she left the ground. She was *flying*!

He started a gentle turn to move away from the small airstrip, and then rolled the wings to level off, and touched Cassie on the shoulder. She glanced over her shoulder at him, and he pointed at her, indicating to her to take the controls now. She nodded, and as though by instinct, Cassie took over. She knew what she needed to do, and they flew easily through the bright blue sky, as though she had been flying all her life. And in some ways she had. He was amazed at her skill, and her natural instincts. She had picked up a lot of his own and her father's tricks, just by watching them, and she seemed to have a style of her own, which was surprisingly smooth and easy. She seemed totally at ease at the controls of the small plane, and Nick decided to see how much she could do on their first lesson.

He had her do turns and banks in different directions, first moving left and then right; he was going to tell her to keep the nose up, to maintain altitude, but she seemed to know automatically that the plane would fall during turns, and she kept the nose up without his telling her anything. Her natural sense for the plane was uncanny. She kept back pressure on the stick with a steady hand, and the nose stayed up in response to her movements.

He had her do S turns then, using a small dirt road as a guide, and he noticed as she did them, that she controlled her altitude easily. She seldom seemed to look at the instruments yet she knew when she needed to compensate, or rise higher in the sky. She seemed to fly primarily by feel and sight, which was a sure sign of a natural pilot. It was rare to see one like her, and he knew he had seen damn few in his lifetime.

He had her fly circles for a while, around a silo they spotted on a distant farm, and she complained at how boring it was, but he had wanted to check her precision. She was careful and precise, and astonishingly accurate, particularly for someone who had scarcely flown. And then finally, he let her try a loop, and the double loop she had wanted to terrify her brother with. But after that, he taught her how to recover from a stall, which was far more important. But she seemed to know that by instinct too. Her total calm going into the stall impressed him, as the Jenny began to fall nose down with alternate wings dipping. But within seconds, she released the pressure on the stick that had created the stall in the first place and in a totally fearless move, she allowed the dive to increase their airspeed. He had explained how to do it at first, but she seemed to have no trouble at all figuring it out, and no lack of courage in following the procedure. Most young pilots were terrified at the drop and the sudden zero gravity. Cassie was awed by none of it, as the Jenny plummeted briefly, and when the Jenny had gained just enough speed, she pushed the throttle, gave it power, and leveled out like a baby eagle, soaring gently back to where she wanted to be, without a murmur.

Nick had never been so impressed by anything he'd seen. And he made her do it again, to see if she could maintain the same cool hands and cool head, and quick reactions, or if it had just been beginner's luck. But the second stall and recovery were even smoother than the first, and she swooped him right back up again from a stall that even had him worried. She was good. She was very good. She was brilliant.

He had her do a few lazy eights then, an Immelmann, and their last lesson of the day was a spin recovery, which was not unlike the stall, but first she had to give it right rudder pedal to induce a spin to the right, and then left rudder pedal to recover. She did it perfectly, and Nick was grinning from ear to ear as he landed the plane, but so was Cassie. She had never had so much fun in her life, and her only complaint was that she had wanted to try barrel rolls and he wouldn't let her. He felt they had done enough for one day, and he'd told her they had to save something for next time. She wanted to learn a dead stick landing too, his specialty, which had earned him his nickname, but there was time for that too. There was time for everything. She was a fantastic student.

He sat in the plane for a moment, looking at her, unable to believe how much she had picked up over the years, just by watching. All those times Pat had taken her up with him, or that Nick had flown her somewhere, every moment, every gesture, every procedure had been absorbed, and somehow, by watching them, she had learned how to do it. She really was what he had suspected she was all along, the ultimate natural. A pilot who was born to fly, it would have been a sacrilege to keep her from it.

"How was I?" She turned in her seat after they'd stopped, and he killed the engine.

"Terrible," he grinned at her, still unable to believe what he'd seen. She had a natural sense of their altitude, an uncanny sense of direction, an instinct for guiding the plane almost as much with her mind as with her hands. She had known exactly what she was doing. "I don't think I could ever fly with you again," he teased, but his face told her all she wanted to know, and she let out a whoop of joy on the silent airstrip. She had never been as happy in her entire life. And Nick was the best friend she had ever had. He had given her her life's dream, and this was only the beginning. "You're good, kid," he said quietly, and handed her another Coke he had brought with him. She took a long swig, saluting him, and then handed it back to her new instructor. "But don't let that go to your head. Those can be dangerous words. Never be overconfident, never over trust yourself, never assume you can do anything you want to. You can't. This bird is only a machine, and if your head gets too big, the ground will get too close, and you'll wind up with a tree between your ears. Don't ever forget that."

"Yes, sir." But she was too happy to care about his warnings. She knew how careful she'd have to be, and she was prepared to be, but she also knew that she had been born to fly and now Nick knew it too, and maybe one day he'd convince her father. And in the meantime, she was going to learn every single thing she could and be the best pilot who had ever lived. Better than Jean Batten or Louise Thaden or any of the others. "When can we do this again?" she asked anxiously. All she wanted to do was go up again, and she didn't want to wait long to do it. Nick was paying for the fuel, and she didn't want it to cost him too much. But like an addict, she wanted more soon, and he knew it.

"You want to do this again tomorrow, right?" He grinned at her. He had been the same way when he was her age. In fact, he had been almost exactly her age when he floated all over the country, after the war, trying to get jobs at airports, and finally came to Illinois to fly for his old friend Pat O'Malley.

"I don't know, Cass." Nick thought about it for a moment. "Maybe we could do this again in a couple of days. I don't want Pat to start wondering why I'm taking out the Jenny. I don't exactly fly her much." And he definitely didn't want Pat to suspect them. He wanted her to get plenty of good solid lessons under her belt first, before they confronted him with her skill, of which there could be no question. She was a thousand times the pilot her brother was, a thousand times the pilot most people he had taught were. But they had to convince Pat of that, and they both knew that wasn't going to be easy.

"Couldn't you tell him you're giving someone lessons out here. He doesn't have to know it's me. Then you'd have an excuse to take her out whenever you want to."

"And where's the money, miss? I wouldn't want your dad to think I'm cheating him." They took a cut on each other's profits, when they used each other's planes, or sometimes if Nick took charters or taught on time he would have otherwise used flying for O'Malley.

Cassie looked crestfallen at this. "Maybe I could pay you . . . a little bit from my savings . . ." She started to look seriously worried and Nick touched the bright red hair and ruffled it.

"Don't worry. I'll get her out. We'll do plenty of this. I promise." Cassie smiled gently up at him, and his heart did a little flip. It was all the payment he needed.

He helped her step from the plane, and noticed that there was a shady tree nearby. "Did you bring anything to eat?" She nodded, and they went to sit under it. She shared her sandwich with him, and he shared his Coca-Cola. He drank a lot of it, and unlike Pat, who liked a good whiskey now and then, Nick had never been much of a drinker. He spent too much time in the air to be able to afford to do much drinking. He was always getting hauled out of bed for an emergency somewhere, or a special mail flight, or a long distance cargo flight for anywhere from Mexico to Alaska. He couldn't have flown those runs if he'd been unexpectedly drunk or even hung over. And Pat was careful too. He never drank if he knew he'd be flying.

They talked about flying for a long time, and her family, and how much they had meant to him when he first came to Illinois. He said he had come out from New York just to work for her father.

"He was good to me during the war . . . I was such a kid . . . I was a damn fool too. I'm glad you'll never have to get into something like that, dueling it out at ten thousand feet with a bunch of crazy Germans. It was almost like a game, sometimes it was hard to remember it was real . . . it was so damn exciting." His eyes shone as he talked about it. For many of them, it had been the perfect time, and everything afterward had paled in comparison. Sometimes she thought her father felt that way, and she suspected Nick did.

"It must make everything else seem awfully dull . . . flying the

Jenny . . . or cargo runs to California in the Handley can't exactly be exciting."

"No, it's not. But it's comfortable. It's where I need to be. I never feel as good on the ground, Cass, crazy as that sounds. That's my life up there." He glanced up at the sky as he said it. "It's what I do well," he sighed, and leaned back against the tree trunk where they were sitting, "the rest of it, I'm not so good at."

"Like what?" She was curious about him; she had known him all her life, but he had always treated her as a child, and now that they were sharing the secret of her flying, for the first time, they seemed almost equals.

"I don't know. I'm not so great at marriage, people . . . friends . . . except other pilots and the guys I work with."

"You've always been great to us." She smiled innocently up at him, and he marveled at how young seventeen was.

"That's different. You're my family. But I don't know . . . sometimes it's hard to relate to people who don't fly, it's hard to understand them, harder for them to understand me . . . particularly women." He grinned. It didn't bother him. It was the way his life was, and he was satisfied with it. There were ground people, those confined to earth, in their bodies and minds . . . and then there were the others.

"What about Bobby?" he asked her unexpectedly. He knew about her boyfriend. He had seen him often enough at the house when he stopped by there to see Pat, or came to dinner. "How would he feel about you flying like you do? You're good, Cass. If you learn right, you could really do it." But do what? That was the problem. What could a woman do, except maybe set records? "What would he say?" Nick persisted.

"What everyone else says. That I'm nuts." Cassie laughed at him. "But I'm not married to him, you know. He's just a friend."

"He won't be 'just a friend' forever. Sooner or later, he'll want to be a lot more, or at least that's what your father thinks." It was what everyone thought and she knew it.

"Is that so?" She sounded cool suddenly and Nick laughed at how prim she was.

"Don't go getting all icy at me over it. You know what I'm saying. It's going to be odd if you want to be another Earhart. You're going to have to live with it. That's not always easy." He knew that only too well. He knew a lot of things he suddenly wanted to share with her. The new dimension of their friendship both excited and frightened him. He couldn't imagine where it might lead them.

"Why is it such a big deal?" she said plaintively, thinking of Nick's questions about Bobby. It didn't make any sense to her. What was so wrong about flying?

"I guess it's a big deal because it's different," Nick explained. "Men are made to walk around on the ground. If you want to fly around like a bird all the time, maybe they figure you should have feathers, or maybe they just figure you're weird. What do I know?" He smiled easily at her, and stretched his long legs out ahead of him. It was fun talking to her, she was so bright and young and alive, so excited about the life she had before her. He envied her that. Her life was filled with challenges to be met and fresh beginnings. Even at thirty-five, a lot of the excitement in his life seemed to be behind him.

"I think people are stupid about flying. They're just planes, and we're just people," she said simply.

"No, we're not," he said matter-of-factly. "We're superheroes in their heads because we do something they can't do, and that most of them are afraid of. We're like lion tamers, or high-wire dancers . . . it's all very mysterious and very exciting, isn't it?" He made her think about it for a minute and she nodded, and handed his Coke back to him again. He took a swig and lit a cigarette, but he didn't offer her one. She might be learning to fly, but she wasn't that grown-up yet.

"I guess it is kind of exciting and mysterious," she conceded as she watched him smoke. "Maybe that's why I love it. But it feels so good too . . . it's so free . . . so alive . . . so . . ." She couldn't find the right words and he smiled. He knew just exactly what she meant. He still felt that way too. Every time his plane lifted off the ground, whichever one he was flying at the time, he always felt the same wild thrill of freedom. It made everything else seem bland and uninteresting. It had affected his whole life, what he did, who he saw, what he wanted to do. It had affected all his relationships, and one day it would affect hers too. He felt he should warn her somehow, but he wasn't sure what to say. She was so young and so filled with hope, it seemed almost wrong to warn her.

"It'll change your life, Cass," was all he could bring himself to say. "Be careful of that."

She nodded, thinking she understood what he had said, but she didn't. "I know"—and then she looked up at him, with eyes so wise it almost scared him—"but that's what I want. That's why I'm here. I can't live on the ground . . . like the others." She was one of them, she was telling him, and he knew it was true. It was why he had agreed to teach her.

They spent a long time talking that day, and he hated to leave her there all alone, to walk two miles back down the country road to where she'd catch the bus to home, but he had no choice. He watched her go, with a long wave, and a moment later he took off, and did a slow roll for her, to signal his leaving. She watched him fly for a long time, still unable to believe what he had done for her. He had changed her whole life in a single afternoon, and they both knew it. It was a brave undertaking for both of them, but one which neither of them could resist, for different reasons.

The long hot walk back to the bus seemed like dancing to her; all she could think about were the feats she had done, and the feel of the plane . . . and the look in Nick's eyes afterward. He was proud of her. And she had never felt better in her life.

She boarded the bus with a huge grin for the bus driver, and almost forgot to pay her fifteen cents. And when she got home, it was too late to go to the airport. She went home to help her mother instead, and suddenly even helping her didn't seem so terrible. She had fed her soul, and whatever price she had to pay seemed worth it.

She was quiet at dinner that night, but no one seemed to notice it. Everyone had something to say; Chris was excited about his job at the newspaper, her father had landed a new mail contract with the government, and Colleen's baby had finally come the night before, and her mother wanted to tell them all about it. Only Cassie was unusually quiet and she had the biggest news of all, but couldn't share it.

Bobby came by after dinner, as usual, and they talked for a while, but Cassie didn't seem to have much to say to him. She was lost in her own thoughts, and the only thing she really said to him was that she could hardly wait till the air show. It would be just after the Fourth of July that year, and Bobby had never been, but he thought this time he might come, and Cassie could explain all the planes to him. But to her, the prospect of going with a novice and explaining it all didn't seem very exciting. She would much rather have gone with Nick, and listened to him. But it never dawned on her then that the changes had already begun. That afternoon, she had set sail on a long, long, interesting but lonely voyage.

CHAPTER

5

The lessons continued through July, in total secrecy. But the air show, and Cassie's elation over it, was definitely not a secret. They all went to the air show together, her entire family, Nick, some of the pilots from the field, and Bobby and his younger sister. It was exciting for all of them, but nothing was as important to Cassie as her lessons with Nick, not even the Blandinsville Air Show. By the end of July she had mastered a very impressive dead stick landing. She had also learned barrel rolls, splits, and clover leafs, and some even more complicated maneuvers.

Cassie was every flying instructor's dream, a human sponge desperate to learn everything, with the hands and mind of an angel. She could fly almost anything, and in August, Nick started bringing the Bellanca instead of the Jenny, because it was harder to fly and he wanted her to have the challenge. It also had the speed he needed to show her the more complicated stunts and maneuvers. Pat still didn't suspect anything, and in spite of the long bus rides and the long walk, their flying lessons were frequent and easy.

In August, Cassie and Nick were both deeply upset when one of the pilots who flew for her father was killed when his engine failed on a flight back from Nebraska. They all went to the funeral, and Cassie was still depressed about it when she and Nick had their next lesson. Her father had lost a good friend, and one of his two D.H. 4s. And everyone was subdued at O'Malley's Airport.

"Don't ever forget that those things happen, Cass," Nick reminded her quietly as they sat under their favorite tree, having lunch after a lesson on the last day of August. It had been a wonderful summer for her, and she had never felt as close to him. He was her dearest friend, her only real friend now, and her mentor. "It can happen to any one of us. Bad engine, bad weather, bad luck . . . it's a chance we all take. You've got to face that."

"I have," she said sadly, thinking of the most wonderful summer of her life, which was almost over. "But I think I'd rather die that way than any other. Flying is all I want to do, Nick," she said firmly, but he knew that by now. She didn't need to do anything to convince him. He was sold on her abilities, her natural skill, her extraordinary facility to learn, and her genuine passion for flying. He was sold on a lot of things about her.

"I know, Cass." He looked at her long and hard. She was the only person he had been truly comfortable with in years, other than Pat and the men he flew with. She was the only woman who seemed to share his views and his dreams, it was just his bad luck that she was only a baby, and his best friend's little girl. There was no hope of her ever being more than that. But he enjoyed her company, and talking to her, and it had meant a lot to him to teach her how to fly. He had long since had her solo. "What do you want to do about lessons once you start school?" he asked as

WINGS

they finished lunch. She was going back the following day for her
last year of high school. It seemed hard to believe that she was
already a senior. She had always been such a little girl to him,
except that he had come to know her better than that now. In
many ways, she was more adult than most of the men he knew,
and she was very much a woman. But there was a child in there
too. She loved to play pranks and to tease, she had an easy laugh,
and she loved playing with him. In some ways, she was no different from the way she had been when she was a baby.

"What about Saturdays?" she asked pensively, "or Sundays?"
It meant they would fly together less frequently, but at least it
would be something. They had both come to rely on these long
quiet hours together, her unwavering faith in him, her trust in all
he told her, and his pleasure at teaching her the wonders of flying.
It was a gift they shared, each one enhancing it for the other.

"I can do Saturdays," he said matter-of-factly, and his tone
didn't tell her that nothing could have stopped him from it. She
was his star pupil now, but more than that, they were best friends,
and partners in a much loved conspiracy that they both held dear.
Neither of them could have given it up easily, nor did they intend
to. "I don't know about you walking two miles to the bus once
the weather gets bad though." He worried about her walking two
miles alone sometimes, though she would have been annoyed at
his concern. She was an independent spirit and she was convinced
she could handle anything. But the thought of her alone on a
country road made him faintly nervous.

"Maybe Dad'll let me borrow his truck . . . or Bobby . . ."
Nick nodded, but the thought of Bobby bothered him too, and he
knew that it shouldn't. He had no right to object to any of her
suitors, but Bobby just didn't seem right for her. He was so dull,
and so damn landlocked.

"Yeah. Maybe so," he said noncommittally, reminding himself
that he was twice her age, and Bobby wasn't.

"I'll work it out." She smiled at him without a care in the
world, and it was hard not to be dazzled by her beauty.

65

They both wondered sometimes how they could go on like this, meeting at the deserted airstrip for lessons. It had certainly worked so far, but they both knew it would be more difficult through the winter. If nothing else, the weather would be an enormous problem.

But surprisingly, it worked remarkably well, and they met regularly every Saturday. She told her father that she had a friend from school she was meeting to do her homework with, and he let her have the truck every Saturday afternoon. No one seemed to mind, and she always came back on time, with her arms full of books and notebooks, and in high spirits.

Her flying skill had improved still further by then and Nick was justifiably proud of her. He said repeatedly that he would have given anything to put her in an air show. Chris was already preparing for the next one, and he was precise and reliable, but unexciting, and he had none of the instinctive, natural skills of his sister. They both knew that if Pat hadn't been pushing him, Chris would never fly at all. He had admitted to Nick more than once that he didn't really like it.

Cassie and Nick sat and ate their lunch in the truck once the weather got cold, and sometimes if the weather was bright, they went for walks near the airstrip.

In September, they talked about Louise Thaden being the first woman to enter the Bendix Trophy race, and in October about Jean Batten becoming the first woman to fly from England to New Zealand. They talked about a lot of things. They sat on fallen trees and talked for hours sometimes, and as the months wore on, they only got closer. They seemed to agree about everything, although she thought he was too conservative politically, and he thought she was too young to go out with boys and he said so. She made fun of him, and he cherished her irreverence, and she told him that the last girl she had seen him with was the ugliest woman she had ever seen, and he told her that Bobby Strong was clearly the dullest. If he was a little more than serious, Cassie never knew it. They just loved to fly and talk, and share their views of life. Everything seemed so much in synch, their interests, their worries, their shared passion for all things that flew, even their almost identical sense of humor. It was always bittersweet when they left each other late on Saturday afternoon, because they knew they'd have to wait a week before they could meet again like this. And sometimes, he couldn't be there at all if he had a long cargo flight and couldn't get back in time. But that was rare, he had come to organize his flying schedule around their lessons.

On Thanksgiving, he joined her family, as he always did, and Cassie teased him without mercy. They always laughed at each other a lot, but their exchanges seemed a little sharper and more intimate than they had before their lessons. Pat told them they were an uncivilized pair, but Oona wondered if she was noticing something different. It seemed hard to believe after all these years, but they seemed closer than they'd ever been, and when Oona mentioned it to Colleen, she only laughed and said Cassie was just having fun. Nick was like her big brother. But Oona wasn't wrong. The time they had spent, and the things Cassie had learned, and their endless talks under the tree at the airstrip for the past six months, had inevitably brought them closer together.

Nick was lying on the couch, claiming that he was going to die from eating so much good food, and Cassie was sitting next to him, teasing him and reminding him that gluttony was a sin and he should go to confession. She knew how he hated to go to church, and he was pretending to ignore her, but smiling appreciatively at her, when Bobby appeared in the doorway, and came in brushing the first snow from his hat and shoulders. He was a tall, handsome boy, and just watching him, Nick felt a thousand years older.

"It's bitter cold out there," Bobby complained, and then smiled warmly at everyone, though cautiously at Nick. There was something about him that made Bobby uncomfortable, though he wasn't sure what it was. Maybe it was just that he was always so familiar with Cassie. "Did everyone have enough to eat?" he asked the room at large, proud of the fact that he had sent them a twenty-five-pound turkey. And everyone groaned in answer. They had invited him to come to dinner too, but he had wanted to be with his parents and sister.

He invited Cassie to go out for a walk, but she declined, and stayed to listen to her mother play the piano. Glynnis sang, and Megan and her husband joined in. Megan had just told them all that she was having another baby. Cassie was happy for her, but it was the kind of news that always made her feel alien and different. She just couldn't imagine herself getting married and having babies. Not for light-years anyway. It wasn't what she wanted to do with her life for a long time, if ever. But then what would she do with her life, she wondered. She knew she'd never be Amelia Earhart either, or Bobbi Trout or Amy Mollison. They were stars, and she knew she never would be. There seemed to be no middle ground out there. You either did what her sisters did, married right out of school, had kids, and settled down in a dreary life, or you ran away and became some kind of superstar. But there was no money for her to buy planes, or enter races and set records. Even if her father had been sympathetic to her cause, his planes were old and serviceable, but certainly not what you'd use to become world-famous.

More than usual lately, she had talked to Nick about what she was going to do with her life. In six months, she would finish school. And then what? They both knew there was no job waiting for her at the airport, and there never would be. She had talked to one of her teachers too, and she was coming closer to knowing what she wanted. If she couldn't fly professionally, and for the moment, she couldn't see how that was even remotely possible, at least she could go to college. She was thinking of becoming a teacher and much to her delight, she had learned that several teachers' colleges offered both engineering and aeronautics. In particular, Bradley College in Peoria. She was hoping to apply for the fall, and if she could get a scholarship, which her teachers thought was possible, she would major in engineering, with a minor in aeronautics. It was as close to flying as she could get for the moment. If she couldn't fly an airplane for a living, like a man, she could at least teach all about them. She hadn't told her parents yet about her plan but to her it seemed like a good one. Only Nick knew, but her secrets were always safe with him. He glanced at her warmly as he stood up to leave that night, with a disparaging look at Bobby, who was talking about his mother's prizewinning pumpkin pie. Somehow, Bobby Strong never failed to annoy him.

Nick kissed Cassie on the cheek, and left, and Bobby relaxed considerably once Nick was gone. The older man always made him nervous. But Cassie seemed distracted once Nick was gone. She looked like she had a lot on her mind, and she brushed Bobby off when he started to talk about graduation. She hated talking about it now. Everyone else had concrete plans, and she didn't. All she had were hopes and dreams, and secrets.

It was late when Bobby finally went home, and Chris teased her once he was gone, and asked her when they'd all be going to her wedding. Cassie only made a face and she made a gesture as though to hit him.

"Mind your own business," she growled, and her father laughed at them both.

"I don't think the boy's wrong, Cassie. Two years of coming by almost every night must mean something. I'm surprised he hasn't asked you yet." But Cassie was relieved he hadn't. She didn't know what she'd say to him. She knew what she was supposed to say to him, but it didn't fit into her larger plans for herself, which now included college. Maybe after that, if he stuck around that long. But waiting four more years seemed a lot to ask of him. At least she didn't have to worry about it for the moment.

She and Nick did plenty of flying for the next three Saturday afternoons, despite some fairly dicey weather. And two days before Christmas, they went up in the Bellanca and within minutes had ice on their wings. Cassie thought her fingers would freeze in her gloves as she held the stick, and then suddenly she heard the engine start to go, and felt it stall as they went into a dive, and everything happened incredibly quickly.

Nick had the controls, but it was obvious that he was struggling with them, and she held them firm along with him. They recovered from the dive, which was no small feat, but then the propeller died and she knew instantly what that meant. They were going to have to do a forced landing. The wind was shrieking in their ears, and there was no way for him to say anything to her, but she knew instinctively what he was going to do. All she could do was back him up, but suddenly she realized they were dropping too quickly. She turned and signaled him, and for an instant he started to disagree with her, but then he nodded, deciding to trust her judgment. He pulled up as best he could, but the ground came at them too quickly. For a second, she was certain they were going to crash, but at the last minute, he brushed the top of the trees, and somehow broke their fall. They landed hard, but were unhurt, and all they damaged was one wheel. They had been extraordinarily lucky and they both knew it, as they sat shaking, realizing full well how close they had come to dying.

Cassie was still shaking when they stepped from the plane, but it was as much from the cold as from the emotions, and Nick looked down at her, and pulled her hard into his arms, with a wave of relief. For several minutes he had been certain that no matter what he tried, he was going to kill her.

"I'm so sorry, Cass. We never should have gone up in this. There's a lesson for you. Never learn to fly with an old fool who thinks he knows better than the weather. And thanks for signaling me when we were going down." Her uncanny sense about altitude and speed had saved them. "I won't do that to you again, I swear." He was still shaking too as he held her. It was hard to ignore what she meant to him, as he looked down at her and felt his heart beat. All he had wanted was to save her life, not his own. He would readily have given up his life for her.

And then she looked up at him and grinned, still folded in his

70

embrace. "It was fun," she giggled and he wanted to strangle her as he held her.

"You're a lunatic. Remind me never to fly with you again!" But she was a lunatic who meant everything to him, as he slowly released her.

"Maybe I should give you a lesson or two," she teased. But instead she helped him tie the Bellanca to a tree, and put rocks under the wheels, and she gave him a ride back to her father's airport. No one there seemed to question their arriving together, and he told her to go home and get warm. He was afraid she'd get sick from the bitter chill. He was on his way inside to have a stiff drink of Pat's stash of Irish whiskey. Knowing that he had almost killed her that afternoon had still left him shaken.

"What have you been up to this afternoon?" her father asked when she got home. He had just come home with their Christmas tree, and her nephews and nieces were going to come and help decorate it and stay for dinner.

"Not much," she said, trying to look casual, but she had torn her gloves towing the plane, and there was oil on her hands.

"You been out to the airport?"

"Just for a few minutes." She suddenly wondered if he was on to her, but he only nodded, and stood the Christmas tree up in the corner with her brother's help. He seemed in good spirits, and not inclined to question Cassie further.

She took a hot bath, and thought about their close call. It had been frightening, but the odd thing was that she didn't think she'd mind dying in a plane. It was where she wanted to be, and it seemed a better place to die than any other. But nonetheless, she was very glad they hadn't.

And so was Nick. He was still deeply upset over what had almost happened. And at ten o'clock that night, he was dead drunk, as he sat in his living room, wondering how Pat would have ever survived it if his oldest friend had killed his daughter. It made him suddenly think twice about flying with her again, and yet he knew he couldn't stop. He just had to do it, not only for her sake. It was almost as though he needed to be with her now, needed her wit and humor, her wisdom, her big eyes, and the incredible way she always looked the first time he saw her. He loved the way she flew, the way she knew so much instinctively, and worked so hard to learn what she didn't. The trouble was, he had realized that afternoon, he loved too much about her.

The Christmas tree at the O'Malleys' was beautiful. The children had decorated it as best they could, and their aunts and uncles and grandparents had helped. They had strung popcorn and cranberry beads, and hung all their old handmade decorations. Oona made a few new ones each year, and this year the star of the show was a big handmade silk angel she hung near the top of the Christmas tree, and Cassie was staring up at it admiringly when Bobby arrived with a load of homemade gingersnaps and cider.

Her mother made a big fuss over him, and her sisters left shortly afterward to put their children to bed. Pat and Chris went outside to get more firewood, and Cassie found herself suddenly alone with Bobby in the kitchen.

"It was nice of you to bring us the gingersnaps and the cider," she said with a smile.

"Your mom said you were crazy about gingersnaps when you were a little girl," he said shyly, his blond hair shining and his eyes almost like a child's. And yet, in an odd way, he was so tall and so serious that there was something manly about him. He was just eighteen, but you could begin to guess what he might look like at twenty-five or thirty. His father was still a handsome man at forty-five, and his mother was very pretty. Bobby was a fine boy, and exactly the kind of person her parents wanted her to marry. He had a solid future, a decent family, good morals, good looks, he was even Catholic.

Cassie smiled, thinking of the gingersnaps again. "I ate so many once, I was sick for two days and couldn't go to school. I thought I was going to die . . . but I didn't." But she almost had that afternoon . . . She had almost been killed in a plane with Nick, and now she and Bobby were standing there talking about cookies. Life was so odd sometimes, so absurd and so insignificant, and then suddenly so thrilling.

"I . . . uh . . ." He looked at her awkwardly, not sure what to say to her, and wondering if this was a good idea. He had talked it over with his dad first, and Tom Strong had thought it was. But this was a lot harder than Bobby thought, especially when he looked at Cassie. She looked so beautiful, standing there, in a pair of dark slacks, and a big pale blue sweater, her bright red hair framing her face like one of her mother's white silk angels. "Cass . . . I'm not sure how to say this to you, but . . . I . . . uh . . ." He moved closer to her, and reached out and took her hand in his, and they could both hear her father and brother stirring in the living room, but they carefully left the two young lovers alone in the kitchen. "I . . . uh . . . I love you, Cass," he said, suddenly sounding stronger and older than he was. "I love you a lot . . . and I'd like to marry you when we graduate in June." There, he had said it. He looked remarkably proud of himself, as Cassie stared at him, her face suddenly paler than it had ever been, and her blue eyes wide in consternation. Her worst fears had come true. And now she had to face them.

"I . . . er . . . thank you," she said awkwardly, wishing she had crashed that afternoon. It would have been simpler.

"Well?" He looked at her so hopefully, wanting her to give him the expected answer. "What do you think?" He was so proud of himself he could have shouted. But his excitement was not contagious. All Cassie felt was dismay and terror.

"I think you're wonderful"—he looked instantly ecstatic at what she'd just said to him—"and I think you're really nice to ask me. I . . . uh . . . I just don't know what I'm going to do in June." June was not the issue, marriage was, and she knew that. "I . . . Bobby, I want to go to college." She said it as she exhaled, terrified that someone else would hear her.

"You do? Why?" He looked startled. None of her sisters had,

and her mother certainly hadn't before her, or even her father. His question was reasonable, and she wasn't even sure she had an answer. "Because I can't fly professionally" hardly seemed like a good answer. And marriage right out of school had never seemed like a particularly appealing option.

"I just think I should. I was talking to Mrs. Wilcox about it a few weeks ago, and she really thinks I should. I could teach after that, if I wanted to." And I wouldn't have to get married right away, and have babies.

"Is that what you want?" He seemed surprised; he had never counted on her wanting to go to college, and it altered his plans for her a little bit, but she could be married and go to college too. He knew people who had done that. "You want to be a teacher?"

"I'm not sure. I just don't want to get married right out of school, have kids, and never do anything with my life. I want more than that." She was trying to explain it to him, but it was so much easier to explain it to Nick. He was so much older and wiser than Bobby.

"You could help me with the business. There's lots you could do at the store. And my father says he wants to retire in a few years." And then suddenly he had an idea; it struck him as brilliant. "You could study accounting, and then you could do the books. What do you think, Cass?"

She thought he was a nice boy. But she didn't want to do his books. "I want to do engineering," she said, and he looked even more confused. She was certainly full of surprises, but she always had been. At least she hadn't told him she wanted to be Amelia Earhart. She hadn't said a word about flying, only about school, and now about engineering. But that was a little crazy too. He wasn't sure what to tell his father.

"What'll you do with an engineering degree, Cass?" Understandably, he sounded puzzled.

"I don't know yet."

"Sounds like you have some thinking to do." He sat down at the kitchen table, and pulled her into the chair next to his. He was holding her hand, and trying to excite her about their future. "We could get married, and you could still go to school."

"Until I get pregnant. And how long would that be?" He blushed at her openness, and he clearly didn't want to discuss it with her any further. "I'd probably never finish the first year. And then I'd wind up like Colleen, always talking about going back to school, and too busy having babies."

"We don't have to have as many as they do. My parents only had two." He still sounded hopeful.

"That's two more than I want for a long time. Bobby, I just can't . . . not now . . . not yet. It wouldn't be fair to you. I'd always be thinking about what I'd missed, or what I wished I had done. I can't do that, to either of us."

"Does flying have anything to do with any of this?" he asked suspiciously, but she shook her head. There was no way she could tell him all that she had been doing. And that was a problem too. She couldn't imagine herself married to a man she couldn't confide in. Nick and she were just friends, but there was nothing she couldn't tell him.

"I'm just not ready." She was honest with him.

"When will you be?" he asked her sadly. It was disappointing for him, and he knew his parents would be disappointed, too. His father had already offered to help him pick out and pay for the ring. But there would be no ring now.

"I don't know. Not for a long time."

"If you'd already been to college, do you think you'd marry me?" he asked her bluntly and she was startled by the question.

"Probably." She wouldn't have any excuse not to. It wasn't that she needed an excuse, and she did like him. She just didn't want to marry anyone. Not yet, and not now, and probably not for a long time, but suddenly Bobby looked hopeful.

"I'll wait then."

"But that's crazy." She was embarrassed at having encouraged him. How could she possibly know how she'd feel when she finished college?

"Look, I'm in love with you. It's not like I'm looking for a mail order bride to pick up in June. If I have to wait, I will. But I'd rather not wait the whole four years while you go to college. Maybe we could compromise in a year or two, and you could finish school once we were married. At least think about that, it doesn't have to be so terrible. And," he blushed furiously, "we don't have to have a baby right away. There are things you can do about that," he said, almost choking. She was so touched by what he'd said to her, and by the generosity of his feelings that she put her arms around him and kissed him.

"Thank you . . . for being so fair . . ."

"I love you," he said honestly, still blushing from the things he had just said to her. It was the hardest thing he had ever done, proposing to her, and being rejected.

"I love you too," she whispered, overwhelmed by guilt and tenderness and a maelstrom of emotions.

"That's all I need to know," he said quietly. They sat and talked in the kitchen for a long time, about other things. And when he left, he kissed her on the porch, feeling they had come to an agreement. The decision was not now, as far as he was concerned, but definitely later. And all he had to do now was convince her that sooner was better than later. It seemed a small task to him in the heat of the moment.

CHAPTER

6

T he class of 1937 walked slowly down the aisle of the auditorium of Thomas Jefferson School, the boys and the girls hand in hand, two by two, the girls carrying bouquets of daisies. The girls looked so lovely and pure, the boys so young and hopeful. Watching them, Pat was reminded of the boys who had flown in the war for him. They had been the same age, and so many of them had died, and to him they had all looked like children.

Together, the entire class sang the school song for the last time, and the girls all cried, as did their mothers. Even their fathers had tears in their eyes as the diplomas were handed out, and then suddenly, the ceremony was over and there was pandemonium. Three hundred kids had graduated and would go on to their lives, most of them to get married, and have babies. Only forty-one of a class of three hundred and fourteen were going on to college. Of the forty-one, all but one were going to the state university at Macomb, and only three of these were women. And of course one of them was Cassie, who was the only student going as far as Peoria, to attend Bradley. It would be a long haul every day, well over an hour each way in her father's old truck, but she was convinced it was worth it, just for the chance to take the aeronautics courses they offered, and some engineering.

Cassie had had to fight tooth and nail for it. Her father thought it was a waste of time, and she'd be a lot better off married to Bobby Strong. He was furious with her for turning him down, and he only backed off because Oona had insisted to him quietly that she was sure they would get married eventually, if they didn't push her. Cassie just needed time. It was Oona who had prevailed on him, and talked Pat into letting her go on to college. It certainly couldn't do any harm, and she had agreed to compromise and major in English, not engineering. If she graduated, she'd get a teaching degree, but she had still applied for a minor in aeronautics. No woman had ever applied for the course, and she had been told that she'd have to wait to see if the professor felt she was eligible for the class. But she was going to talk to him as soon as she got to school in September.

There was a reception at the high school after graduation, and of course Cassie had already gone to her senior prom with Bobby. He had seemed to accept his fate for the past six months, but the night they graduated, he talked to her about it again, just in case she'd changed her mind, and had second thoughts about college.

"No, I haven't," she said with a gentle smile. He was so faithful to her, and so earnest, that sometimes he made her feel very guilty. But she had made a commitment to other things, and she didn't want to lose sight of them now, no matter how sweet he was, or how kind, or how guilty he made her feel, or how much her father liked him.

He left early that night, his grandmother was in town, and he had to go home and visit with her. Pat growled at Cassie after

Bobby left. She was still wearing the white dress she had worn under her black gown, and she looked very pretty.

"You'll be a damn fool, Cassie O'Malley, if you let that boy slip through your fingers."

"He won't, Dad." It was the only thing she could think of to say to him. It sounded conceited, but it was better than saying she didn't care, which would really have enraged him. And the truth was, she did care. There were times when she thought she really loved him, especially when he kissed her.

"Don't be so sure," her father railed at her. "No man can be expected to wait forever. But maybe once you have your teaching degree, you won't care. Maybe you have it in mind to become an old maid schoolteacher. Now there's something to wish for." He was still annoyed with her about this business of going to college. Instead of being proud of her, as the other two girls' fathers were, he thought it was foolish. But Nick was pleased for her that she was going. He had realized long since how bright she was, and how capable, and it didn't seem fair, even to him, to just push her into getting married and having babies. He was relieved too that she hadn't decided to marry Bobby Strong fresh out of school. That would have changed everything, and he couldn't have borne it. He knew that eventually things would have to change, but at least for now their sacred Saturdays were safe, and they would still have their precious hours of flying.

Cassie sat by the radio that night after everyone had left. She had been dying to do that all afternoon, but she knew how much it would have annoyed her father. Amelia Earhart had taken off from Miami that afternoon, with Fred Noonan, in a twin-engine Lockheed Electra. She was flying around the world, and the expedition had been highly publicized by her husband, George Putnam. Her trip had been oddly plotted because of the threat of war, and there were areas she clearly had to avoid. They had chosen the longest route around the world at the equator, and the most dangerous, overisolated, and underdeveloped countries, which offered few airfields and fewer opportunities for fuel. She had not set an easy task for herself, and Cassie was enthralled with all of it. Like many other girls her age, and half the world, Cassie was in love with the courage and excitement of Amelia Earhart.

"What are you doing, sweetheart?" her mother asked as she wandered past her into the kitchen. It had been an emotional day for her, and she thought Cassie looked tired too.

"Just listening to see if there's any news about Amelia Earhart."

"Not at this hour," her mother smiled. "There will be plenty of it in the news tomorrow. She's a brave girl." She was more than a girl obviously, she was a month shy of forty, which to Cassie seemed fairly ancient. But in spite of that she was still exciting.

"She's lucky," Cassie said softly, wishing she could do something just like Earhart was doing. She would have liked nothing better than to tour the world, setting records, and flying incredible distances over strange lands and uncharted waters. It didn't frighten her at all, all it did was excite her.

And she said as much to Nick the next day, after they'd flown turns around a marker over their secret airstrip.

"You're as crazy as she is," he said, dismissing Earhart's folly with a casual wave. "She's not the great pilot Putnam sets her up to be. She's crashed more than half the women who fly, and I'll bet you a dollar that in that Electra of hers she overshoots every runway. It's a heavy machine, Cass, and it's got the heaviest Wasp engine Lockheed would give it. That's more than a handful for a woman of her size and build. This trip is just a stunt to make her the first woman to fly around the world. It's been done by men, and it's not going to do anything to advance aviation, only to advance Amelia Earhart." He seemed unimpressed, but Cassie was undaunted.

"Don't be a jerk, Nick. You're just mad because she's a woman."

"I'm not. If you told me Jackie Cochran was doing this, I'd say great. I just don't think Earhart has the stuff to do it. And I talked to a guy in Chicago who knows her, and he says she wasn't ready, and neither was the plane. But Putnam wants to squeeze all the publicity he can out of it. I feel sorry for her actually. I think she's being used. And I think she's being pushed into some lousy decisions."

"Sounds like sour grapes, Nick," Cassie teased, as they shared a Coca-Cola. Their flights together had become a beloved ritual neither of them would have missed for anything in the world. They had been going on for exactly a year now. "You'll eat your words when she breaks all records," Cassie said confidently as he shook his head.

"Don't hold your breath." And then he smiled at her, his eyes crinkling in the corners, as they did when he was staring into the sun when he was flying. "I'd rather put my money on you in a few years." He was playing with her, but he also meant it.

"Yeah, sure. And my father will be taking the bets, right?" They still hadn't figured out how to tell him about Cassie's flying, let alone that Nick thought Cassie was one of the best pilots he knew. But he had promised her that one of these days, when the time was right, they would do it.

The Peoria Air Show was in two weeks, and he was working with Chris, who was as steady as ever, and as uninterested as he had always been. He was entering the air show only to please his father. He was going to try and set an altitude record, though he didn't think he really could. Stunts were not his strong suit, and the hotshot flying still scared him. But they had strengthened the structure of Nick's Bellanca, and put a turbo supercharger on the engine to increase its power.

"I wish I could fly in it too," Cassie said longingly, and Nick wished the same thing right along with her.

"So do I. Next year," he promised her, and when he said it, he meant it.

"Do you really think I could?" She looked overwhelmed with excitement. Though it was a year away, it was something to look forward to, even more than college.

"I don't see any reason why not, Cass. You fly better than any of the guys there. It would make quite an impression, dazzle 'em a little bit. Believe me, they need it."

"There are some pretty good guys at the air show," Cassie said respectfully. She had seen some great flying over the years, but she also knew that she could fly as well as, or better than, most of those men now. Cassie had seen some terrible tragedies over the years too. It was not unusual to have fatalities at the air show. Oona had finally forced Pat to give it up, because flying stunts at the air show was just too dangerous. But he loved to see it.

"Want to take me back up and give me some cheap thrills?" Nick asked after their lunch. Sometimes they went back up for another spin, if the weather was good and they had time, as they did that afternoon. "You could use a little work on your takeoffs and landings in crosswinds." They had also been working on takeoffs with power cutbacks.

"The hell I do. My landings are better than yours are," she disagreed with a grin.

"Don't be so modest." He ruffled her hair, and let her sit behind him this time, and as usual, she didn't disappoint him. She was fabulous. It was as simple as that. And he was sorry all over again that he couldn't put her in this year's air show.

But two days before the air show, Cassie was sitting glued to her radio, unable to believe what she was hearing. Amelia Earhart had gone down, somewhere near Howland Island in the South Pacific. It seemed incredible to her, and to everyone else who heard the news. All except her father, who repeated constantly for everyone to hear that women belonged in the kitchen, and not in planes, except maybe as Skygirls, and even that didn't seem suitable to him. But Cassie was reminded of what Nick had said too, that Earhart wasn't good at handling heavy planes, and there were several people who knew her well who said she hadn't been ready. It seemed like a terrible tragedy, and the government cooperated immediately with the search for her. But on the day of the air show, two days later, they still hadn't found her.

It dampened Cassie's spirits terribly, as she watched all the trick flying and the stunts at the air show.

"Cheer up." She heard a familiar voice behind her. "Don't look so gloomy." It was Nick. He had a hot dog in one hand, and a beer in the other, and he was wearing a paper Fourth of July hat. The air shows were always festive.

"I'm sorry," she apologized with a tired smile. She had been up for two days, listening for reports of Amelia Earhart. But there were none. Nothing at all had been found. She had totally vanished. "I was just thinking about . . ."

"I know what you were thinking about. The same thing you've been thinking about since she took off. But it's not going to do you any good, getting sick over her. Remember, I told you a long time ago. There are chances we all take. We all know it. We accept them. So did she. She was doing what she wanted." He offered her a bite of his hot dog, and she took it, looking pensive. Maybe he was right. Maybe she had a right to die that way. Maybe if she'd been given a choice of a ripe old age in a rocking chair, and a quick exit in a Lockheed, she would have preferred this. But Cassie still hated to think of her going down. It was the death of a legend.

"Maybe you're right," Cassie said quietly. "It just seems so sad."

"It is sad," he agreed. "No one ever said it wasn't. It's sad when anyone goes down. But it's a risk we all take, and some of us love. You too." He put a hand under her chin and reminded her silently of how much she loved to fly and how willing she was to take chances. "You would do the same thing, given half a chance, you little fool. You ever try to go on one of those damn world tours, and I'll set fire to your plane. Count on it."

"Thanks." She grinned up at him, and then he tugged at her arm in excitement.

"Hey . . . take a look at this . . . there goes Chris . . . come on . . . come on . . . head up there . . ." He was heading for an altitude trophy in Nick's plane, and he almost disappeared as they watched him. He had good steady hands, and a seriousness that made him perfect for this kind of competition. He had none of Cassie's excitement or sheer grit; all he really had was endurance. And when he landed, Nick was amazed by how far he'd gone. They hurried over to where Pat and Oona and some of Cassie's sisters were standing with their children. Glynnis and Megan were both hugely pregnant again, and Colleen had been looking a little green around the gills of late, which had made Oona suspect she was pregnant again too, but hadn't yet said it. They were a prolific group. This would be the fourth for Megan and Colleen, the fifth for Glynnis.

"Good thing too," Cassie whispered under her breath as she chatted with Nick, "if I'm never going to have any. They can have all the kids they want, as far as I'm concerned." Lately she had begun to think she never wanted a husband or children.

"You'll have kids too, don't kid yourself. Why shouldn't you?" Nick never believed her when she said she'd never marry or have children. She didn't really believe it herself. But she knew she didn't want any of that for a long, long time, if ever. All she wanted was airplanes.

"What makes you so sure I'll have kids, Nick?" she challenged him.

"Because you come from a family that multiply like rabbits."

"Oh thanks a lot." She was still laughing when Bobby Strong found her, and glanced at Nick awkwardly. He always had the feeling that Nick didn't like him. Moments later, having said very little to either of them, Nick went off to hang out with the other pilots.

Half an hour later, they announced that Chris had won a prize for setting the altitude record. And her father was beside himself with excitement. He went off to find Chris, and Oona went to find drinks with the girls, and the younger children. Bobby stood watching the show with her, as tiny red and blue and silver planes did stunts and rolls, and lazy spins in the air, crazy eights, and double eights, and a few tricks Cassie had never heard of. Just watching them took your breath away, and more than once the crowd gasped as disaster seemed imminent, and then cheered when there was a last minute save. She was used to it, but it was always exciting.

"What were you thinking just then?" Bobby had begun watching her face. It had been filled with light and an expression of total rapture as she watched a plane do an outside loop; it was a stunt Jimmy Doolittle had invented ten years before, and it really impressed her. The pilot then finished with a flourish by doing a low-level inverted pass, away from the crowd, so no one was endangered. Bobby watched the look on her face with fascination. And then she turned and smiled at him, almost sadly.

"I was thinking that I wish I were up there doing that," she said honestly. "It looks like so much fun." All she wanted was to be one of them.

"I think I'd get sick," he said with equal honesty, and she grinned at him, as a vendor wandered by with cotton candy.

"You probably would. I almost have a couple of times." She had almost spilled the beans then, and had to remind herself to be careful. "Negative G's will do it to you. You get those in a stall, just before you recover. It feels like your stomach is going to fly right out of your mouth . . . but it doesn't." She grinned.

"I don't know how you can like all this, Cass. It scares me to death." He looked handsome and blond and very young as he stood admiring her, and she was growing, day by day, to be more of a woman.

"It's in my bones, I guess."

He nodded, worried that that was true. "That's too bad about Amelia Earhart."

She nodded too. "Yes, it is. Nick says that all pilots accept those possibilities. It can happen to anyone." She looked up at the sky. "Anyone here too. I guess they figure it's worth it."

"Nothing's worth risking your life," Bobby disagreed with her, "unless you have to, like in a war, or to save someone you love."

"That's the trouble"—Cassie looked at him with a sad smile—

"most pilots would risk anything to fly. But other people don't understand that."

"Maybe that's why women shouldn't, Cass," he said quietly and she sighed.

"You sound like my father."

"Maybe you should listen to him."

She wanted to say "I can't," but she knew she couldn't say that to him. She could only say that to Nick. He was the only human being who knew the whole truth about her, and accepted it. No one else really knew her. Especially not Bobby.

She saw Chris walking toward them then, and she ran to him. He was carrying his medal, his face was glowing with pride, and Pat was walking on air right behind him.

"First medal at seventeen!" he was telling anyone who would listen. "That's my man!" He was handing out beers, and slapping everyone on the back, including Chris and Bobby. Chris was basking in his father's love and approval. Cassie was watching them, fascinated by how desperate her father was for Chris's success in the air, yet at the same time how adamant he was that she never get there. She was ten times the flier Chris was, or better still, but her father would never acknowledge it, or even know it.

Nick came over to shake hands with Chris, and the boy was elated by his victory, and then he went off with Nick to meet some of the other pilots. It was an exciting day for him, and a day Pat O'Malley had waited fifty-one years for. And as far as he was concerned, this was only the beginning. Instead of seeing that this was the top of Chris's skill, he wanted more. He was already talking about next year, and Cassie felt sorry for Chris then. She knew how much their father meant to him, and that no matter what it cost him, he would do anything to please him.

The O'Malley clan were in high spirits. They were almost the last ones to leave, and Bobby went home with them for dinner. Nick went out to celebrate with his flying friends, and he looked pretty well oiled by the time he left the field. But he knew Chris was flying the Bellanca back to O'Malley Airport, and he could hop a ride in Pat's truck, so he didn't have to worry about flying or driving.

Oona had cooked platters of fried chicken for them in the morning before they left, and there was corn on the cob, and salad and baked potatoes. There was a ham too, and she had baked blueberry pie and made ice cream once back at the house. It was a real feast, and Pat poured Chris a full glass of Irish whiskey.

"Drink up, lad, you're the next ace in this family!" Chris struggled with the drink, and Cassie watched them, feeling sad. She felt left out somehow. She should have been flying with them, and basking in her father's praise, and she knew she couldn't. She wondered if she ever would. But the only fate that seemed open to her was that of her sisters, having another baby every year, and condemned to their kitchens. It seemed a terrible life to her, although she loved them all, and her mother, but she would have rather died than spend her life the way they had.

Cassie noticed too that Bobby was very sweet to all of them. He was kind to her sisters, and adorable to all their children. He was a gentle man, and he would make a wonderful husband. Her mother pointed it out to her again when she was helping clean up in the kitchen. And afterward, she and Bobby went for a long walk, and he surprised her when he talked to her about flying.

"I was watching you a lot today, Cass, and I know what all that means to you. And you may think I'm crazy, but I want you to promise me you'll never do any of that crazy stuff. I really don't want you to fly. It's not that I don't want you to have fun. But I don't want you to get hurt. You know . . . like Amelia Earhart." It seemed reasonable to him, and she was touched, but Cassie laughed nervously. The idea of promising anyone that she wouldn't fly made her shudder.

"I'm not going to fly around the world, if that's what you're worried about," she said with an anxious smile. But he shook his head, he meant a lot more than that, and she knew it.

"That's not what I mean. I mean I don't want you flying at all."

He had only seen a glimmer of how dangerous it was, but watching the stunts at the air show had convinced him. There was no question that there were risks in flying, and two years before there had been a terrible tragedy at the same air show. Bobby was no fool, and he knew the magic it held for her. Simply put, he didn't want to lose her. "I don't want you learning to fly, Cass. I know you want to. But it's just too dangerous. Your father is right. And it's much too dangerous for a woman."

"I don't think that's a reasonable thing to ask," she said quietly. She didn't want to lie to him, but she also didn't want to tell him that she'd been flying regularly with Nick for over a year now. "I think you have to trust my judgment on that."

"I want you to promise me you won't fly," he said, showing a strength and stubbornness she had never seen before. She was impressed, but she wasn't going to promise.

"That's unreasonable. You know how much I love to fly."

"That's why I'm asking you to promise, Cass. I think you would be just the one to take chances."

"Believe me, I wouldn't. I'm careful . . . and I'm good . . . that is, I would be. Look, Bobby, please . . . don't do this . . ."

"Then I want you to think about it. This is very important to me." So is flying to me, she wanted to scream. It was the only thing she cared about, and now he wanted to take it from her. What was wrong with all of them? Bobby, her father, even Chris. Why did they want to take something away from her that she loved so much? Only Nick understood. He was the only one who knew, and cared how she felt about it.

Though at that exact moment, Nick Galvin was passed out cold in the arms of a girl he had met at the air show. She had bright red hair, and brightly painted lips, and as he nestled close to her, he smiled and whispered, "Cassie."

CHAPTER

7

Cassie's schedule at Bradley was more demanding than it had been as a senior in high school, but she managed to juggle it anyway, and now she and Nick met twice a week, always on Saturdays, and sometimes on a weekday morning. Her father wasn't aware of her schedule, and it was easy for both of them. And she had started working as a waitress in order to repay Nick for the fuel, even if she couldn't afford to pay him for the lessons. But he had never expected any payment from her. He did it for sheer love and pleasure.

She was getting better each time they flew, refining some fine points, and flying every plane she could so as to learn their differences and their quirks. She flew the Jenny, the old Gypsy Moth, Nick's Bellanca, the de Havilland 4, and even the lumbering old

Handley. Nick wanted her to fly everything she could, and he had her perfecting all her techniques and honing her skills with great precision. He had even taught her some rescue techniques, and told her all the details of some of his more illustrious forced landings and near misses while fighting the Germans. There was very little she didn't know about flying the Jenny or the Bellanca or even the Handley, which Nick had brought with him because it was so much heavier and harder to fly, and had two engines.

She spent less time at her father's airport now, since she had farther to go to school, but she still hung around whenever she could, and she and Nick would exchange a conspiratorial smile, whenever their paths crossed.

She was working on an engine one day, in a back hangar, when she was surprised to see her father walk in with Nick. They were talking about buying a new plane, and her father thought it might be too expensive. It was a used Lockheed Vega.

"It's worth it, Pat. It's a heavy plane, but it's a beautiful machine. I checked one out the last time I was in Chicago."

"And who do you think is going to fly it? You, and me. And the others are just going to bring it down in the trees. It's a damn fine machine, Nick, and there aren't five men here I'd trust to fly it. Maybe not even two."

But as her father said the words, Cassie saw Nick looking at her strangely, and then she felt terror run up her spine. She knew instinctively what he was going to do. She wanted to tell him to stop, but another part of her wanted him to do it. She couldn't hide forever. Sooner or later her father would have to know. And Nick kept talking to her about flying in the next air show.

"There may not be five men around here who can fly it, Pat. But I can tell you one woman who can, with her eyes closed."

"What's that supposed to mean?" Her father growled at him, already annoyed at the mention of a woman who could fly anything, let alone a plane he wouldn't trust his own men with.

Nick said it very quietly, and calmly, as Cass watched them, terrified, praying that her father would listen. "Your daughter is the best pilot I've ever seen, Pat. She's been flying with me for more than a year, a year and a half to be exact. She's the best damn pilot you and I have seen since seventeen. I mean that."

"You *what*?" Pat looked at his old friend and associate in total outrage. "You've been flying with her? Knowing how I'd feel about it? How dare you!"

"If I didn't dare, she would. She would have killed herself a year ago, terrorizing her brother into taking her up and letting her fly anything she could lay her hands on. I'm telling you, she's the best damn natural pilot you've ever seen, and you're a fool if you don't let her show you what she's got, Pat. Give the kid a chance. If she were a boy, you would, and you know it."

"I don't know what I know!" he raged at both of them, "except that you're both two damn lying fools, and I'm telling you right now I forbid you to fly, Cassandra Maureen." He looked straight at her as he said it, and then at Nick. "And I'm not going to put up with any nonsense from you, you damn fool, Nick Galvin, do you hear me?"

"You're dead wrong!" Nick was insistent, but Pat was too livid to listen.

"I don't give a damn what you think. You're a bigger idiot than she is. She's not flying my planes at my airport. And if you're fool enough to fly her in your own, somewhere else, then I lay the responsibility on your head if you kill her, and it's your own damn fault, if she kills you, which she will undoubtedly. There isn't a woman alive who can fly worth a damn, and you know it." He had just knocked out, with a single blow, an entire generation of extraordinary women, and among them his own daughter. But he didn't care. That was what he believed, and no one was going to tell him any different.

"Let me take her up and show you, Pat. She can fly anything we've got. She's got a sense of speed and height that relies on her gut and her eyes, more than on anything she sees on the controls. Pat, she's terrific."

"You're not going to show me anything, and I don't want to see

91

it. Couple of damn fools . . . I suppose she's bamboozled you into all this." He looked at his daughter with total fury. As far as he was concerned, it was all her fault. She was a stubborn little monster, determined to kill herself with her father's planes and right at his own airport.

"She didn't bamboozle me into anything. I saw her scud running a year ago, in that storm she got herself into with Chris, and I knew damn well he wasn't flying the plane. I figured if I didn't step in, she'd kill both of them, so I started teaching her then."

"That was Chris flying in that storm last year," her father argued defiantly.

"It was *not!*" Nick shouted back at him, furious now himself at how unreasonable Pat was prepared to be, and all to support an outdated position. "How blind can you be? The boy's got no guts, no hands. All he can do is run straight up and down, like an elevator, just like he did for you at the air show. What on God's earth makes you think he could have gotten them out of that storm? That was Cassie." He looked at her possessively, and he was surprised to see that she was crying in the face of her father's fury.

"It was, Dad," she said quietly. "It was me. Nick knew. He confronted me when we came down, and—"

"I won't listen to this. You're a liar on top of everything else, Cassandra Maureen, trying to take the glory from your own brother." The force of his accusations took her breath away, and told her again how hopeless it was to try to convince him. Maybe one day, but not now. And never seemed more likely.

"Give her a chance, Pat." Nick was trying to calm him down again, but it was useless. "Please. Just let her show you her stuff. She deserves that. And next year, I'd like to put her in the air show."

"You're both daft, is what you are. Two brazen fools. What makes you think she wouldn't kill herself, and me, and you, and a dozen other people at the air show?"

"Because she flies better than anyone you've ever seen there."

Nick tried to stay calm, but he was losing control slowly. Pat was not an easy man, and this was a very volatile subject. "She flies better than Rickenbacker, for chrissake. Just let her show you." But he had uttered the ultimate sacrilege this time, in invoking the name of the commander of the 94th Aero Squadron. Nick knew he'd pushed too far, and Pat stalked off and left them, and went back to his office. He never looked back at them, and he never said another word to his daughter.

She was crying openly by then, and Nick came to put an arm around her.

"Christ, your father is a stubborn man. I'd forgotten how impossible he can be when he gets something in his teeth. But I'll get him yet on this one. I promise." He gave her a squeeze and she smiled through her tears. If she had been Chris, her father would have let her show him anything at all. But not now, not ever, not her, because she was a girl. It was so unfair, but she knew that nothing would change him.

"He'll never give in, Nick."

"He doesn't have to. You're eighteen. You can do what you want, you know. You're not doing anything wrong. You're taking flying lessons. So what? Okay? Relax." And very shortly she'd have her own license. She was more than qualified for it. When Pat had started flying in 1914, he hadn't even needed a license to fly then.

"What if he throws me out of the house?" She looked terrified and Nick laughed. He knew Pat better than that, and so did she. He made a lot of noise, and he was limited in his ideas and beliefs, but he loved his children.

"He's not going to do that, Cass. He may make you miserable for a while. But he's not going to throw you out. He loves you."

"He loves Chris," she said glumly.

"He loves you too. He's just a little behind the times, and stubborn as hell. Christ, sometimes he drives me crazy."

"Me too." She smiled and blew her nose, and then she looked up at Nick with worried eyes. "Will you still teach me?"

"Of course," he grinned, looking boyish and full of mischief, and then he pretended to look at her sternly. "And don't let everything I said go to your head. You don't fly like the leader of the great 94th," he scowled at her, and then grinned. "But you could be better than he was one day, if you'd clean up some of those turns and listen to your instructor."

"Yes, sir."

"Go wash your face, you look terrible . . . I'll see you at the airstrip tomorrow, Cass." He smiled at her. "Don't forget, we have an air show to prepare for." She looked gratefully at him, as he strode away, wondering what it would take to bring Pat O'Malley to his senses.

He had certainly not come to them that night when he refused to say a word to her at their dinner table. He had told Oona what she'd done, and her mother cried when she heard it. Pat had convinced her long since that women were not constitutionally or mentally cut out to fly airplanes.

"It's just too dangerous," she tried to explain to Cassie later that night in her room. With her sisters married and gone, Cassie had long since had her own bedroom.

"It's no more dangerous for me than it is for Chris," Cassie said through tears again. She was exhausted from fighting with them, and she knew she'd never win. Even Chris had said nothing in her defense. He hated getting into arguments with their parents.

"That's not true," her mother countered what she'd said. "Chris is a man. It's less dangerous for a man to fly," her mother said as though it were gospel truth, because she'd heard it from her husband.

"How can you say that? That's nonsense."

"It's not. Your father says that women don't have the concentration."

"Mom, that's a lie. I swear. Look at all the women who fly. Great ones."

"Look at Amelia Earhart, dear. She's a perfect example of what your father says. She obviously lost her direction, or her wits, somewhere out there, and she took that poor man with her."

"How do you know their disappearance wasn't his fault?" Cassie said persistently. "He was the navigator, not Earhart. And maybe they were shot down," Cass said sadly. She knew she wasn't getting anywhere. Her mother was completely convinced of everything her husband had always told her.

"You have to stop behaving this way, Cassie. I should never have let you loll around at the airport all these years. But you loved it so, and I thought it would be nice for your father. But you have to give up these foolish dreams, Cassie. You're a college girl now. One day you'll be a teacher. You can't go flying around like some silly gypsy."

"Oh yes, I can . . . dammit, yes I can!" Cassie raised her voice to her, and a moment later her father was in her room, berating her again, and telling her that she had to apologize to her mother. Both women were crying by then, and Pat was at his wit's end, and clearly livid.

"I'm sorry, Mom," she said mournfully.

"And well you should be," her father said before he slammed the door again. A moment later her mother left, and Cassie lay on the bed and sobbed, from the sheer frustration of dealing with her parents.

When Bobby Strong came by later that night, Cassie had Chris tell him that she had a terrible headache. He drove away looking concerned, after leaving her a note, telling her that he hoped she felt better soon, and he'd be back tomorrow.

"Maybe tomorrow I'll be dead," she said glumly as she read the note her brother handed her. "Maybe that would be an improvement."

"Relax, Sis. They'll get over it," Chris said calmly.

"No, they won't. Dad never will. He refuses to believe women can fly, or do anything except knit and have babies."

"Sounds great. So how's your knitting?" he teased, and she threw a shoe at him, as he closed the door to escape her.

But by the next day she felt better again. She felt like herself, once she and Nick took off in the Bellanca. He didn't feel he should let her fly any of her father's planes now. She handled it skillfully as usual, and just being in the air with Nick lifted her spirits. Afterward, they sat in the old truck for a while, talking, and Cassie seemed subdued. She was still obviously upset about her father's reaction to her flying.

"As good as Rickenbacker, huh?" she teased Nick after their flying.

"I told you not to let it go to your head. I was just lying to impress him."

"He sure looked impressed, don't you think?" Cassie grinned ruefully, and Nick laughed. She was a good sport, and sooner or later they'd wear Pat down. He couldn't keep his head in the sand forever, or could he?

Their flying schedule scarcely changed. The only time it did was when Nick had long cargo runs, or she had too much homework. But neither of them was anxious to miss their lessons, so they always worked their other obligations around them. And interestingly her father never asked either of them if they were continuing their lessons.

Nick joined them at Thanksgiving as usual; Pat was cooler than he normally was, to both of them. He hadn't forgiven either of them yet for what he considered their betrayal. At the airport, Nick was walking on eggs, and at home, Pat had scarcely said two words to Cassie since October. It was getting more and more difficult, but by Christmas he seemed to have relaxed again. And then finally, he relented totally when Bobby Strong handed Cassie a tiny diamond engagement ring on Christmas Eve.

Bobby said he knew it would be a long wait for her, but he'd feel better if they were engaged. He had been courting her for three years, and he didn't think it was too soon. He looked so earnest and so in love with her that Cassie just didn't have the heart to turn him down. She wasn't sure what she felt, other than confused, as she let him slip the ring slowly onto her finger. She had felt so guilty and so unhappy about everything, since her parents had made such a huge fuss about her flying. But the engagement seemed to mollify them, and restore her to their good graces.

They were very pleased. They announced her engagement to the rest of the family the next day at Christmas dinner. Nick was there too, and he looked surprised at the news, but he didn't say anything. He only looked at Cassie, wondering if this would change everything between them. But oddly, she didn't behave differently. She seemed no closer or more comfortable with Bobby now. And she was as easy with Nick as she ever had been. In fact, very little changed, Bobby only lingered a little longer on the porch before he left, but it wasn't what Cassie herself would have expected of an engagement. But Nick was still wondering about it the next time he saw her at their deserted airfield.

"What does that mean?" He pointed to the ring, and she hesitated for a moment and shrugged her shoulders. She didn't want to be mean, but she never seemed to react to anything the way people expected.

"I'm not sure," she said honestly. She didn't feel any differently about him from the way she had before he put the ring on her finger. She liked him, she cared about him, but she couldn't imagine being more to him than she was now. She had gotten engaged mostly because it seemed to matter so much to Bobby and her parents. Most of all, it seemed to make a difference to him, and she understood that. "I didn't have the heart to give it back to him." She looked sheepishly at Nick as she kept an eye on the Bellanca. They had had a good flight that day, and she had learned some fine points about landing in crosswinds. "He knows I want to finish college," she said helplessly. But college wasn't really the problem.

"Poor guy. This is going to be the longest engagement in history. What is that? Another three and a half years?"

"Yes." She grinned mischievously at him, and he couldn't help but laugh as he resisted an urge to kiss her. He was so relieved by what she'd said. He had felt sick when he first saw the engagement ring. He hated the idea of her being married to anyone, or even engaged, but Bobby wasn't much of a threat actually. Sooner or later Cassie would have to figure that out for herself, but then someone else would be. And he knew how much it would bother him when that happened.

"Okay . . . get your ass in gear, O'Malley . . . let's see another dead stick landing." He was going to take her up again.

"You must think I'm going to spend half my life on the ground instead of in the air. Can't you teach anything else, *Stick*?" She emphasized the word. "Or is that the only trick in your repertoire?" She loved teasing him, loved being with him, loved being with the only person in the world who really understood her. And better yet, if they could be flying.

This time he sent her up alone, and watched her land perfectly, dead stick, then again without a hitch, and finally, without flicking an eye or a wing in the crosswinds.

It really was a shame, he found himself thinking again, that her father refused to watch her fly. It would have given him so much pleasure.

"Ready to call it a day?" he asked, as they walked back to her truck, so she could drive home to Good Hope.

"Yeah, I guess so," she said sadly. "I always hate to come down. I wish I could go on forever."

"Maybe you should be a Skygirl when you grow up," he teased her again, and she swatted him with her gloves, but she looked sad. She really had no options. And if it weren't for Nick, she couldn't fly at all.

"Take it easy, kid," he said gently. "He'll come around."

"No, he won't," she said, knowing her father.

Nick touched her hand, and her eyes met his. She was grateful for all that he had given her, and his kindness. They had the kind of friendship that neither of them had ever found with anyone else. She was a great girl, and a good friend, and they had fun on their stolen afternoons at their airstrip. Nick only wished it could go on forever. He couldn't imagine not meeting her like this anymore, or not having her to fly with, and share his thoughts with. In all the important ways, she was the only person he really talked to. And he was her only friend too. The only tragedy, for both of them, was that there was nothing more ahead for them in the future.

She drove home alone late that afternoon, thinking of him, and it started to snow just after she got back. She went into the house and helped her mother cook dinner for the four of them, but her father was late. And an hour later, he still hadn't come home. Oona finally sent Chris out with the truck to find Pat at the airport.

Chris came back twenty minutes later to grab something to eat for him and Pat. There was a train wreck two hundred miles southwest of them, with hundreds of injuries, and they were asking for rescue teams from everywhere. Pat was organizing rescue teams at the airport, and he wanted Chris to help him. Nick was there too, and they were calling all their pilots in to fly. But three were home sick, and too ill to come in, and they hadn't been able to reach some of the others. They were still waiting for a few more to come in. Pat had told Chris to tell his mother they wouldn't be back all night. Oona nodded, used to this, and packed some food for them to eat at the airport.

"Wait!" Cassie said, as Chris started to go back to him. "I'll come with you."

"You shouldn't . . ." Oona started to object, but at the look on her daughter's face, she shrugged. There was no harm in it. All she could do was sit at the airport. "All right. I'll pack something for you to eat too."

She gave them a basket filled with food, and Cassie and Chris drove off, skidding on and off the old road on the property to the airport. It was an icy night, and the snow had been falling for two hours. She wondered if they'd even be able to take off. Conditions did not look good, and her father looked worried when she and Chris walked into his office at the airport.

"Hi, kids." He pushed aside the food. He and Nick were talking anxiously about the planes they could use, and the men they needed. They were trying to send four planes with supplies and rescue teams. Everything and everyone were assembled, except for the pilots. And so far, they were still two men short, and they were trying to reach them. Pat was going to fly the new Vega himself with Chris. Although, if he'd had to, Pat could have flown solo. Another of their best men had come in, with his co-pilot, and they had each been assigned planes. But they needed two more men to fly the old Handley. It was tricky to fly and because of its age and size, it was wiser to have two men flying it in this kind of weather. Nick could have flown it alone but it wouldn't have been a wise decision. And he wanted someone good to fly it with him. Silently, he looked over at Cassie, but he said nothing.

They heard from two more men shortly after that. One was bone-tired after a sixteen-hour flight around the country, delivering mail in terrible weather, and the other was quick to admit that he'd been drinking.

"That leaves one," Nick said unhappily. One man left they needed to hear from. He called in finally around ten, with a ferocious earache. "End of the line, O'Malley," Nick said pointedly. They were one man short for their mission. Pat read his mind easily, and began shaking his head, but this time Nick wouldn't listen.

"I'm taking Cassie with me," he said quietly, as Pat started to sputter. "Don't waste your time, Ace. There are hundreds of injured people waiting for help and supplies, and I'm not going to argue with you. I know what I'm doing, and she's coming with me." The only other choice would have been to let her co-pilot the Vega with her father, and Nick knew he wouldn't let her do it. Nick grabbed his jacket and started moving toward the door, and he held his breath as Pat stared at him angrily, but made no objection.

"You're a damn fool, Nick," Pat growled at him, but he said

nothing more as they gathered their things, and he called Oona and asked her to wait for them at the airport.

Cassie followed Nick quietly out to the familiar plane, feeling something deep inside her tremble, and for just an instant she saw her father look hard at her with eyes full of anger and betrayal. She wanted to say something to him then, but she didn't know what to say, and a moment later, he was gone, with Chris, in the Vega.

"He'll be all right," Nick said as he helped her to her seat, but she only nodded. Nick had stuck up for her, as usual; he believed in her, and he hadn't been afraid to say so. He was an amazing man, and she just hoped she wouldn't let him down as they flew the old plane in bad weather all the way to Missouri.

They did the usual check on the ground, and then checked inside carefully. She knew the plane well, thanks to Nick, and as she strapped herself in, she was suddenly excited at what they were doing and she forgot all about her father. They were carrying emergency supplies that had been brought to them at the airport. The other planes were also carrying supplies, and two doctors and three nurses. Help was coming from four states. There were nearly a thousand people injured.

Nick took off cautiously but smoothly. There had been no ice on the wings, and the snow had thinned. It had almost stopped as they reached their final altitude of eight thousand feet and flew southwest toward Kansas City. It was a two-and-a-half-hour flight for them, although her father and Chris would make it in a little over an hour in the Vega. It was turbulent most of the time, but it didn't bother Cassie or Nick. Cassie was stunned by the beauty of the night, and how peaceful it was to be at the controls in a night sky full of stars now. It was like being on the edge of the world, in an endless universe. She had never felt so small or so free or so alive as at that moment.

Nick let her fly the plane much of the time, and when they reached a good-sized field near the train wreck, he brought it in for a landing.

There were wounded everywhere when they got to the train, supplies being brought in, medical personnel trying to help people lying on the ground, children crying. Nick and Cassie and the others stayed to help until dawn, and by then the state police seemed to have everything under control. Ambulances and medical personnel had come from all over the state. People had driven, flown, they had come as soon as they could. And in the morning, Nick and Cass flew home with the others. She had scarcely seen her father all night, as they did everything they could to help the rescue workers.

The sun came up just as they took off, and on the way back Nick let her fly it herself, and she brought it in for a textbook landing in spite of heavy winds and slippery conditions on the runway. Nick shook hands with her as she turned the engines off, and congratulated her for a job well done. She was grinning broadly as she stepped off the plane, and she was surprised to almost collide with her father. He was standing right next to the plane, and he looked at Nick with tired eyes, as he barked a question.

"Who landed this plane?" It was his plane, and Cassie instantly sensed trouble.

"I did," Cassie said quietly, ready to take the blame for any mistake she'd made. She took her flying seriously and calmly.

"You did a damn fine job," he said awkwardly, and then turned and walked away. She had proven everything Nick had said, and they both wondered what Pat would do about her now. It was hard to say. There was no predicting Pat O'Malley. But as she watched him walk away, there were tears in her eyes. It was the only praise he had ever given her that had meant anything. And she wanted to shout she was so excited. Instead, she just grinned at Nick, and saw that he was smiling broadly. And they walked arm in arm back to the office.

Her mother had brought in coffee and rolls for all the men, and Cassie sat quietly drinking her coffee and talking to Nick about what they'd seen at the train wreck. It had been a long, rough night, but at least they'd been useful.

"So, you think you're a hotshot." She heard her father's words as he stood next to her, and she looked up at him, but he didn't look angry anymore when their eyes met.

"No, Dad, I don't. I just want to fly," she said softly.

"It's unnatural is what it is. Look at what happened to that poor fool Earhart." Cassie had heard it all before and she was prepared for it, but she was in no way prepared for what he said next, and her jaw dropped as she glanced at Nick to make sure she'd heard him correctly. "I'll give you some work out here, after school. Nothing big. Just the little jobs. I can't have Nick flying around all the time, wasting fuel and time, giving you lessons." She grinned as she looked at him, and Nick let out a whoop as the other men glanced over at them in confusion.

She threw her arms around her father's neck, and Nick pumped his hand, as Chris walked over to his sister and hugged her. She had never been happier in her life. He was going to let her fly . . . her father was going to let her fly, and give her flying jobs to do at the airport . . .

"Just wait till the air show in July!" she whispered to Nick as she hugged him tight, and he laughed. Her father was in for a big surprise. But this was certainly a good beginning.

CHAPTER
8

For the next six months, Cassie's days seemed to fly by. She drove to Bradley every day, worked at the restaurant three afternoons a week to pay for fuel when she flew with Nick. And she tried to get to the airport as soon as she could before nightfall. She did whatever she could to help there, but most of her work for her father, and flying, was done on weekends. And those were her happiest days. Nick even took her on some cargo runs to Chicago, Detroit, and Cleveland.

Her life had never before seemed as perfect. She missed her secret flying lessons with Nick sometimes, and the time they'd shared alone. But he taught her openly now, when they both had time, taking off from her father's airport. And although Pat never said anything to her, it was obvious that he approved of her style, and secretly he admitted to Nick once that she was a damn fine little flier. All of his obvious praise went to Chris, who tried hard, but really didn't deserve it. But it didn't bother Cassie anymore. She had everything she wanted.

The only problem she had was with her fiancé, who was aghast that her father had relented. But since he had, there was little Bobby could say, except to remind her constantly of his disapproval. Her own mother thought it was only a passing phase, something she would lose interest in once she and Bobby were married and had children.

The biggest news that spring was when Hitler took over Austria in March. For the first time, there was serious concern about war, although most people still believed Roosevelt. He said there would be no war, and America would never step in again if there was. Once had been enough. America had learned her lesson.

But Nick didn't think it was quite that simple. He had read about Hitler and didn't trust him. He also had friends who had volunteered to fly in the Spanish Civil War two years before, and he believed that soon all of Europe would once again be in terrible trouble. Nick could easily envision America getting involved again despite Roosevelt's promises and protests.

"I can't believe we'd get into it again. Can you, Nick?" Cassie asked seriously after they'd practiced for the air show.

"I can," he answered honestly. "I think we will too, eventually. I think Hitler is going to go too far, and we'll have to step in to support our allies."

"That's hard to believe," Cassie said. It was harder still to believe that her father was actually going to let her fly in the air show. Nick had talked him into it, and more than anything, Pat was afraid of being embarrassed. He had already seen that she was safe, had good hands, and had been well taught, but what if she did very badly? What if she did so badly he couldn't hold his head up?

"Chris won't let you down," Nick had encouraged him, and Pat had naively bought it. Nick was a lot surer of Cass, but he wouldn't have dared to say so to her father. Pat still wanted to believe that Chris had a great future in the air, and he refused to see how little Chris cared about flying. In all fairness, Chris didn't let him see his true feelings. He was afraid to.

And when at last the big day came, all of Nick's beliefs and predictions proved to be prophetic. Chris won the prize for altitude again, but Cassie took second for speed, on a straightaway, and first for a race on a closed-circuit course. As they announced the winners in the afternoon, Pat couldn't believe his ears, and neither could Cassie. She and Nick were dancing around like two children, hugging and kissing, and letting out whoops and screams. The local paper took a picture of her, first alone, and then standing next to her father. And Chris didn't begrudge her any of it. He knew how much it meant to her. It was her whole life. Pat couldn't believe what she'd done. But Nick could. He had always known it. And he wasn't surprised either when one of the turn judges said he'd never seen a pilot as good at high-speed pylon turns as Cassie.

"Well, you did it, kid." Nick smiled at her, as he drove her home at the end of the day, after they had flown all her father's planes back to the airport.

"I still can't believe it," she said, staring at him, and then looking into the distance out the window.

"Neither can your dad." He smiled.

"I owe it all to you," she said seriously, but he only shook his head. He knew better.

"You owe it to yourself. That's the one you owe it to. I didn't give you the gift, Cass. God did that. I only helped you."

"You did everything." She turned to look at him, feeling suddenly sad. What if he stopped teaching her now? What if they no longer spent time together? "Will you still take me up sometimes?"

"Sure. If you promise not to scare me." He told her what the turn judge had said then, with real pride in her.

She guffawed, and then she almost groaned when she saw

Bobby Strong waiting on their front porch. He had been so afraid of what might happen to her, he had refused to come to the air show. There were things she had to reckon with there, but she never had the courage, and he never wanted to hear it. He didn't want to believe how much flying meant to her, how badly she wanted other things than being his wife and having babies. What she really wanted right now was to relive every moment of the air show with Nick and have him assure her that their time together wasn't over. But instead now she'd have to deal with Bobby.

"There's your friend," Nick said quietly. "You gonna marry him one of these days?" It was something he always wondered.

"I don't know," she said honestly with a sigh. She was always honest with him. But her honest answers were not what Bobby wanted. She was nineteen years old and she didn't feel ready to tie herself to anyone, and yet it was what they all wanted for her. "Everyone keeps telling me I'll change, that being married and having kids changes everything. I guess that's what I'm scared of. My mom says it's what all women want. So how come all I want is what I had today and a hangar full of airplanes?"

"I can't say I've ever felt any different," he grinned, and then grew thoughtful. "No, that's not true. I did feel differently when I was about your age. I tried like hell, but it didn't work. And I've been scared to death ever since. There's no room for both a family and planes in my life. But, Cassie, maybe you're different." In a way he wanted her to be, but not for Bobby.

"My dad seemed to do okay at it," she grinned back at him. "Maybe we're both weird, you and I. Maybe we're both just cowards. Sometimes it's easier to love airplanes than people." Except that she knew she loved him. He was the dearest friend she had, and she knew he had loved her since she was a child. The trouble was, she wasn't a child now.

"You know," he nodded thoughtfully then, responding to her calling herself a coward, "that's exactly what I said to myself today when I watched you do that triple loop followed by the inverted spin before you flipped into the barrel roll in the aerobat-

ics race. I said to myself, gee, I never realized Cassie is a coward."
She burst into laughter at the expression on his face, and pushed
him where he sat behind the wheel in his old truck.

"You know what I mean. Maybe we're cowards about people,"
she said cautiously.

"Maybe we're just not stupid. I think being married to the
wrong person is about as bad as it gets. Believe me, I tried it."

"Are you telling me he's the wrong person for me?" Cassie
asked him in an undertone as Bobby waited for her patiently on
the porch. He had already heard that she'd been a two-time winner at the air show.

"I can't tell you that, Cass. Only you know that. But don't let
anyone else tell you he's the right one either. You figure it out. If
you don't, you'll be awfully sorry later." She nodded at the unexpected wisdom of his words, and then hugged him again for all
he'd done for her.

"I'll see you at work tomorrow." She was going to be working at the airport all summer. Her father was going to let her
quit her job at the restaurant and work for him, for a pittance.
She wondered if her father would let her do cargo runs alone.
She wondered if her performance in the air show was going to
change things.

She hopped lightly out of the truck, with a last look at Nick,
and then went to talk to Bobby. He had waited a long time for
her, and he was pleased that she had won, but he looked annoyed
as she hurried over. He had been worried sick all afternoon,
working in his father's store, and terrified he would hear of a
disaster at the air show. And now she looked as breezy as could
be, as though she'd gone into town to go shopping with her sisters.

"It's not fair to me, Cass," he said quietly. "I was worried
about you all afternoon. You don't know what it's like, thinking
of all the horrible things that could happen."

"I'm sorry, Bobby," she said quietly, "but it was a special day
for me."

109

"I know," he nodded, but he didn't look pleased. None of her sisters flew, what was she trying to prove? He really didn't want her to keep on flying, and he said so. But now was not the time, and Cassie suddenly looked as angry as he did.

"How can you say that to me?" She had come too far now, the air show, her father, all those years of lessons with Nick. She wasn't coming down ever again now. She was up there. And she was staying, whether Bobby liked it or not. He figured that eventually he'd change her. But by the end of the summer he had come to understand that he had allied himself with a family of fliers, and blood ran thicker than engagements. For the moment, all he could do was ask her to be careful. And she was, of course, but not because of Bobby. She was just good at what she did. And she flew constantly. By fall, when Jackie Cochran won the Bendix Trophy race from Burbank to Cleveland, Cassie was starting to fly mail runs for her father. He was sure of her flying by then, and had had her fly him all over the state herself. He had finally admitted to Nick that he was right. It was a coincidence of course, and you couldn't really trust a female the way you could a male, but she was a damn good pilot. Of course, Pat never said as much to Cassie.

She stayed on at Bradley for her sophomore year, and worked at the airport all through the winter. She helped out on several emergencies, flew with Nick whenever she could, and by spring she was an accepted member of the team at the airport. She flew everywhere, short runs, long, and of course she was practicing again for the summer air show. She went out to practice sometimes with Nick, and their time together reminded her of their years of lessons. But now they had time to talk at the airport, while they worked, and more than once, she joined him flying cargo or mail runs.

She was still engaged to Bobby Strong, but his father had been sick all year, and he had more responsibilities at the store now. He seemed to be visiting Cassie less and less often. And she was so busy, sometimes she didn't even notice.

Hitler occupied the rest of Czechoslovakia in March, and became more of a threat than ever. Once again, there was talk of war, and fear of an American involvement. Roosevelt continued to promise that it wouldn't happen this time. And Nick continued not to believe him.

When Charles Lindbergh returned from Europe in the spring of 1939, he was the most outspoken champion of America staying out of the war. And Pat was glad to hear it. He believed whatever the famed aviator had to say. To Pat O'Malley, the name of Lindbergh was still sacred.

"We don't belong in the next one, Nick. We learned our lesson in the last one." Pat was adamant. He was sure the United States would never get pulled into another war in Europe. But there was already trouble between the Chinese and the Japanese. Mussolini had taken Albania. And Hitler seemed to be looking toward Poland.

But all Cassie could think of by then was the summer air show. She was hard at work learning rolls and turns, and some new aerobatics she'd seen at a small airstrip in Ohio where she'd gone with Nick. She was working on her speed, and practicing whenever she could spare the time. By June, she had finished her sophomore year, and she thought she was ready for the air show.

Bobby was annoyed about her participating in the air show again, but he had his own problems at the grocery store, and he had long since understood how impossible Cassie was about flying. They went to see the new Tarzan movie when it came out in June, and it was the only respite they shared as she prepared for the air show.

Finally, at long last, the big day came, and Cassie was at the airstrip in Peoria with Nick at four o'clock in the morning. Her brother was coming in later with Pat, but he wasn't particularly enthused about flying in the show this year. He had been so excited about starting college at Western Illinois University at Macomb that he had hardly practiced. Pat was still pinning all his hopes on him, and despite Cassie's impressive wins the year before, he scarcely ever mentioned her entering the air show.

Nick helped her fuel the plane and check everything, and at six o'clock he took her out for breakfast.

"Relax," he smiled at her, remembering how he himself had been the first time he'd flown in an exhibition show, after the war. Pat had gone with him and Oona had brought the kids to see him. Cassie had been there too of course, she was only two then. And remembering that suddenly made him feel old. The two had become so close since he had started teaching her to fly years before. They had developed a bond that they would never lose now. But the painful thing for him sometimes was forcing himself to remember that he was old enough to be her father. She was twenty now, and there were eighteen years between them. He still felt like a kid, and he looked far younger than his years, and Cassie accused him constantly of acting like a child. But the fact was, he was thirty-eight . . . and she was only twenty. He would have given anything to cut in half the difference between them. Not that she seemed to care. But he did. But then again, she was still the daughter of his closest friend, and nothing would ever change that. Pat would never have understood the bond or the closeness between them. Nick knew it was a hurdle they would never overcome, unlike her flying. Pat had gone that far, but he would go no further.

Nick ordered her a plate of eggs, some sausages, a side of toast, and a cup of black coffee. But she waved it away as soon as it appeared at the table.

"I can't, Nick. I'm not hungry."

"Eat it anyway. You'll need it later. I know what I'm talking about, kid. Otherwise, you're going to go weak in the knees when you're doing loops and negative G's out there. Be a good girl and eat it, or I'll have to force it down your throat, and the waitress might not understand it." He looked at her in a way that said how much he cared, and she grinned up at him happily.

"You're disgusting."

"You're cute. Especially when you take first prize. I like that in a girl. In fact, I'm kind of counting on you to do that."

"Be nice. Don't push. I'll do what I can." But she wanted to win first prize too, maybe even several of them. For him, for herself, and more importantly, to impress her father.

"He loves you anyway, you know. He just can't stand admitting he was wrong. But he knows how good you are. I heard him tell a bunch of guys at the airport last week. He just doesn't want to tell you, that's all." Nick understood him better than Cass did. For all his gruff ways and seeming outrage over women fliers, her father was desperately proud of her, and just as embarrassed to show it.

"Maybe if I stacked a bunch of prizes up today, he'd have to admit, finally, that I fly okay . . . to me, I mean, not just to a bunch of guys." She still sounded angry when she talked about it sometimes. Her father was always bragging about Chris, who didn't even like to fly. It drove her crazy.

"Would it really make that much difference to hear the words?" Nick asked her, eating fried eggs and steak with her. He wasn't going to be doing loops, but he had ordered himself a healthy breakfast.

"Maybe. I'd like to hear them just for the hell of it. Just to see how it feels."

"And then what?"

"I go back to flying for you, and him, and myself, no big deal, I guess."

"And you finish college and become a teacher." He liked to say the words, but they both knew that she didn't believe that.

"I'd rather teach flying like you," she said honestly, taking a sip of hot coffee.

"Yeah, and fly mail runs. That's a great life for a college girl."

"Don't be so impressed. I haven't learned a thing, except from you." And she meant it. But they were interrupted before he could deflect her praise, by a group of young men who had just finished

113

breakfast. They seemed to hesitate somewhere near their table, circling like young birds, glancing at Nick and eyeing Cassie.

"You know those guys?" Nick asked in an undervoice, and she shook her head. She had never seen them, and then finally one of them approached Cassie's table. He looked down at her, and then at Nick, and he looked suddenly very young as he got up the nerve to address them.

"Are you . . . Stick Galvin?" he asked hesitantly, and then he glanced at her, "And Cassie O'Malley?"

"I am," she answered before Nick did.

"I'm Billy Nolan. I'm from California . . . we're flying in the air show. I saw you there last year," he blushed furiously, "you were terrific." He looked about fourteen and Nick almost groaned. He was actually twenty-four, but he didn't look it. He was blond and young, his hair stood up in a cowlick like a kid's, and his face was covered with freckles. "My dad knew who you were," he said to Nick. "He flew in the 94th with you, he got shot down. You probably don't remember him . . . Tommy Nolan."

"Oh, my God," Nick grinned as he stuck out his hand, and invited Billy to sit down with them. "How is he?"

"Pretty good. He's had a bad limp since the war, but it doesn't seem to bother him much. We have a shoe store in San Francisco."

"Good for him. Does he fly anymore?" Nick remembered him well, and the funny thing was that Billy looked just like him.

But Billy said he hadn't flown in years, and he was none too thrilled that Billy had caught the bug from him. His friends were standing watching him then, and Billy beckoned them over. There were four of them, all about his age, and all from various parts of California. For the most part, they looked like cowboys.

"Which races are you in?" they asked Cass, and she told them. Speed, aerobatics, and a number of others, which Nick thought was a little ambitious. But it meant so much to her, and she loved being in the air show so much, he hadn't wanted to dampen her spirits. She had waited a long time for this, and she really enjoyed it.

Billy introduced them to everyone, they were a nice bunch of guys, and for the second time that morning, Nick Galvin felt ancient. Most of the boys were fifteen years younger than he was. They were all closer to Cassie's age, and by the time they all left the restaurant, everyone was laughing and chatting, and talking about the air show. They were like a bunch of kids, going to the school fair, and having a great time.

"I ought to let you kids go play," Nick grinned at them, "but then again maybe Cassie might forget to fly. Maybe I'd better stick around to see that you all behave and remember the air show." They all laughed at him, and most of them had a thousand questions about the 94th and the war, and the Germans he had shot down before it ended. "Hey, hold on a minute, guys . . . one at a time," and he told them another story. They treated him like a hero, and they were all in high spirits when they got to the fairground. This was what flying was all about, the camaraderie, and the fun, and the people you met at times like this, the experiences you shared. It wasn't just about the long flights and the solitude, and the sky at night when you felt as though you owned the world. It was all of those things, the highs and the lows, the terror and the peace of it, the incredible contrasts.

They wished Cassie luck, and went off to check their plane. They were all taking turns flying it, and they were enrolled in different events. But only Billy was going to be flying against Cassie.

"He's nice," she said easily, once they were gone, and Nick glanced at her over his shoulder.

"Don't forget you're engaged," he said politely, and she laughed at the pious look on his face, which was very unlike him. Most of the time he had no interest at all in Bobby Strong, or her fidelity to him.

"Oh for heaven's sake. I just meant he was 'nice,' you know, as someone to talk to. I wasn't planning to run off with him." She was fueling the plane, and wondered suddenly if Nick could be jealous. It was a ridiculous idea, and she brushed it off as soon as she thought it.

"You could run off with him, you know," he persisted. "He's the right age. And at least he flies. That might be refreshing," he said innocently.

"Are you finding guys for me now?" She looked amused. "I didn't know that was part of the service you provided," she said calmly.

"The service I will provide will be to chain you to the ground if you don't prepare your plane right. Don't fool around, Cass. You're going to be putting a lot of stress on the plane, and yourself. Pay attention."

"Yes, sir." The games were over now, but for a fraction of an instant, she could have sworn that he was jealous, although he certainly had no reason to be. She was engaged to someone else, and they were just friends, and always had been. She wondered if it annoyed him to see her making friends with other pilots. He was very proud of all she'd done, and maybe that was what had been bothering him. It was hard to tell as he helped her check the plane. And then a few minutes later they saw her father and her brother. It was nearly eight o'clock by then. And the races started at nine. Although her first event wasn't until nine-thirty.

"All set, Cass?" her father asked nervously. "Did you check everything?"

"I did," she said defensively. Didn't he think she was capable of doing it? And if he cared so much, why hadn't he come out to help her, instead of Chris? He could have been attentive to both of them, but he wasn't. All his concern was for Chris, who looked more than anything as though he wished he didn't have to be there. He was in only one event this year, and Cassie hoped for his sake that he'd win it.

"Good luck," her father said quietly, and then left her to join Chris across the airfield.

"Why does he bother?" she muttered as he walked away, and Nick answered gently.

"Because he loves you, and he doesn't know how to say it."

"He has an odd way of showing it sometimes."

"Yeah? Maybe it's because you kept him up all night when you were born. Maybe you deserve it." She grinned at the answer he gave her. Nick always made her feel better about everything, and it was comforting to know that he'd always been there.

She saw Billy Nolan and the boys again before her first event. They were hooting and laughing and raising hell. It was hard to believe they were serious, but they had entered all the toughest races.

"I hope they know what they're doing," Nick said quietly. They looked like a bunch of kids, but it was hard to tell sometimes. He had known some real aces who had looked like cowboys. But no one wanted to watch a tragedy, and that usually happened when people overestimated their skill, or didn't know their planes' limits.

"They must be okay," Cassie said confidently, "they qualified."

"So did you," he teased, "what does that mean?"

"Jerk . . ." she laughed at him, and half an hour later she was on her way. It was almost her turn. There had already been some pretty impressive stunts in the air, some great gasps, a few screams. It was all in a day's work at the air show.

"Give 'em hell!" Nick called as he left her and she taxied off down the short runway in the Moth for the aerobatic event. And for the first time in years, he found himself praying. He hadn't been nearly as nervous for her last year, but this year he was afraid she might push too hard, just to prove something to him, or her father. She wanted to win more than anything, and he knew it.

She began with a few slow loops, then a double, and a barrel roll. She went through the whole repertoire backward and forward, including a Cuban eight, and a falling leaf, and as he watched her, each exercise was completed to perfection, and then she did a triple, and a dive, and somewhere near him a woman screamed, not realizing that in an instant, Cassie would recover . . . and of course she did. Perfectly. It was the most beautiful demonstration he had ever seen, and she finished it off with an outside loop, which delighted everyone. And Nick was beaming at her when she landed.

"Not bad for a start, Cass. Pretty clean." His eyes shone right into hers as he praised her.

"That's all?" Her excitement and adrenaline turned instantly to disappointment, but he gave her a tight hug and told her she'd been terrific. "You were the best," he said honestly, and half an hour later, the judges confirmed it. Her father congratulated her politely when their paths crossed. But his praise was more for Nick than for Cassie. He was proud of her. But it still irked him that she was showing up the men with her flying.

"You must have had a very good teacher."

"I had a very good student," Nick corrected him, and the two men smiled, but her father said nothing more to Cassie.

Chris's race was next, and he tried hard, but he lost. He didn't even place this time, and the truth was he didn't really care anymore. For him, his flying days were over. He was much more interested in his classes at school, and all things separate from planes and airports. He just didn't have the bug, and the only thing he hated about it was disappointing his father.

"I'm sorry, Dad," he apologized after he parked the plane. "I guess I should have practiced more." He'd been flying Nick's beefed-up Bellanca, which Cassie was going to fly too.

"Yes, you should have, son," Pat said sadly. He hated to see him lose when, with a little effort, he could have been a great flier, or so Pat thought. But Pat was the only one who thought of Chris that way. Everyone else knew the truth, even Chris, that he just wasn't a flier. But Cassie congratulated him anyway.

"Good job, baby brother. That was a pretty piece of flying."

"Not pretty enough apparently," he grinned at her, and then congratulated her for taking first prize in the previous event.

And a few minutes later she saw one of Billy Nolan's friends take second place. He had done some very fine flying.

Cassie's next race was at ten o'clock and it was more difficult this time. It involved speed, and she was worried that the Vega couldn't do it. It was fast, but some of the racing planes were faster.

"She'll do it if you play her right," Nick promised as he talked to Cassie right before takeoff. The Vega was a great plane and Cassie flew it well. Nick knew that for this race it was better than the Bellanca. "Just keep cool, Cass. Don't let it scare you." She nodded and said not a word as she taxied off, and a moment later she was in the air, and flying remarkably. Nick had never seen anyone more precise or faster, and she managed some extraordinarily complicated maneuvers. He couldn't take his eyes off her, and he noticed that Pat was watching her intently too. And so was a tall blond man in a blazer and white trousers. He was watching her very carefully through binoculars, and talking to a man who was taking notes. He was out of place and Nick figured he was probably from one of the Chicago papers.

Cassie won second prize that time, but only because she hadn't had a faster plane. She had overcome every handicap the Vega had, and Nick still couldn't believe it. He had never expected her to win that race, and she had placed handsomely. When she was down again, Billy came over and congratulated her. He had won third against her. They were a great bunch of fliers, and Nick liked what he had just seen of Billy. He was careful and sure, and he had won in spite of an inferior plane. Like Cass, he had pushed it to the limit.

She had two more races to fly that day. One at noon, which went well, and the last one in the afternoon, which was a race Nick would have preferred she hadn't entered. She and Nick had had lunch with Billy Nolan and his friends, Chris had joined them eventually, and when her father wandered by, she introduced them to the famous Pat O'Malley. He liked all the young boys, and Billy spent some extra time talking to him, telling him about his father. Pat remembered him well, and was sorry he had lost track of him in the past twenty years. He had genuinely liked him.

And then it was time for Cassie's race. When Pat heard that she had entered, he was furious, and his eyes blazed as he berated his partner.

"Didn't you tell her not to?" he barked at Nick, who looked annoyed and unhappy at Pat's reaction. He felt guilty enough for letting her enter it and Pat wasn't helping.

"She takes after her old man, Pat. She does what she wants."

"She's got the wrong plane for that, and she doesn't have the experience to do it."

"I told her that. But she's practiced a lot, and I think she's smart enough to let it go if she can't make it. She's not going to push it to the edge, Pat. I told her that myself." He only prayed that she had listened.

The two men stood staring up at the sky unhappily, with Chris, and Billy and his friends, and the man in the white trousers. It was a daredevil event, usually entered only by old stunt pilots with aerobatic planes, which Nick's Bellanca wasn't. But she had desperately wanted to try her hand at this event. It allowed her to show off all the stuff she did best, and pull off a miracle or two, if she could get the plane to cooperate with her at low altitudes. She knew it was going to be scary, but she was prepared to scrub the race if she really had to.

There were over a dozen moves she had to do, all of them impressive and frightening, and she went through the first half dozen of them without being a hair off. Pat was even beginning to smile as he watched her. And then on the final dive, she seemed to lose control. Her plane dove with its wings askew, and Nick wondered if she was panicking and had forgotten everything he had taught her, or maybe she had fainted. But she was doing absolutely nothing to save herself, nothing at all, and no one moved as they stared in horror at what was going to become a tragedy in a single instant. But suddenly, with a roar, she throttled the hell out of it, and pulled up, barely higher than the heads of the horrified crowd, and pulled out of it, soaring high and completing a triple roll that took everyone's breath away. She completed every move and did a final loop that won her the race hands down, without even hearing from the judges.

Nick had a lump in his throat the size of an egg and Pat looked gray, but as he realized what she'd done, Nick wanted to throttle her for scaring him so badly. How could she terrify them that way? Even first prize wasn't worth it. He ran to where she taxied the plane and almost yanked her out of the cockpit.

"What the hell were you doing up there, you damn fool? Trying to kill yourself showing off? Don't you realize that another foot and you couldn't have pulled up?"

"I know that," she said calmly, startled to realize that he was shaking. She had done everything intentionally and with flawless calculation.

"You're a lunatic, that's what you are! You're not human, and you have no right to be in a plane."

"Did I lose?" She looked agonized and more than ever he wanted to shake her, as her father watched from the distance with a look of fascination. And as he watched Nick's face, he realized that he was seeing something there he had never seen before. He wondered if Nick even knew it.

"Did you *lose*?" Nick raged on, holding firmly to her arm. "Are you *nuts*? You almost lost your life up there, and killed about a hundred people."

"I'm sorry, Nick." She looked suddenly contrite. "I thought I could get away with it."

"You did. Damn you. And it was the finest piece of flying I've ever seen, but if you ever do anything like that again, I'm going to kill you."

"Yes, sir."

"Good. Now get out of that damn plane, and go apologize to your father."

But surprisingly, he was much kinder to her, although he had been as scared as Nick, and he was grateful that Oona wasn't there to see it. She had stayed home with Glynnis, who was pregnant again, and all five of her young ones had the measles. But Pat had seen what Nick had done, and he thought there had been enough said. Instead, he complimented her on her style and her courage.

"I guess Nick was right after all," he said almost humbly. "You're quite a flier, Cass."

"Thank you, Dad." He gave her a hug, and it was the greatest moment of her life as he held her.

They watched Billy Nolan fly again after that, and he won first prize in his last race too. Cassie had won a second and three firsts, which was better than she'd dreamed. And the newspaper kept taking her picture.

They were all standing around drinking beer and watching the last event, when suddenly Cassie saw Nick's jaw tighten as he stood beside her. She followed his eyes high into the sky, and saw smoke, and suddenly, like everyone else there, she looked frightened.

"He's in trouble," Nick whispered to her. They all knew who it was. It was a young pilot named Jim Bradshaw. He had two babies and a young wife, and a plane that wasn't worth spit, but more than anything in life, he loved air shows.

"Oh, my God," Cassie mouthed the words, as they all watched in horror, as he began to spiral lazily, just as she had, but this was for real, and the plumes of smoke from his fuselage told them all that this was no stunt. This was a disaster. The crowd began to run away from where the plane appeared to be, and people started screaming. But Cassie found she couldn't move, all she could do was stare at it, the lazy bird falling head over heels, into the ground, and then suddenly it hit with a tremendous crash and an explosion. People ran from everywhere, and Nick and Billy were among the first there, trying to pull Jim from the wreckage, but it was too late. He was inhumanly burned, and it was obvious that he had died on impact. His wife was sobbing hysterically, and two of the women held her, as her mother held onto the children.

The ambulances were already there, but it was a somber end to an exciting day, a reminder to all of them of the danger they constantly courted.

"I guess we'd better go home," Nick said quietly, and Pat nodded. Earlier that day, Pat had feared that Cassie might meet the same fate and he was ashamed to admit now how grateful he was that it had been someone else and not his daughter.

Billy came to say good-bye to them, as they loaded their three planes onto flatbeds, and tied them up firmly.

"I'd like to come out and see you at the airport before I go," he said to Pat after they shook hands.

"Anytime. You going back to San Francisco?"

"Actually, I was wondering . . . I was kind of hoping maybe you could use another pair of hands . . . I . . . I wouldn't mind sticking around and doing some flying."

"We could use a flier like you, lad. Come by and see me tomorrow morning."

Billy thanked him profusely, and they all said good-bye again. His friends were all going home the next day, and Billy looked thrilled to be staying.

"What do we need another hotshot kid for?" Nick asked Pat, with a look of annoyance.

"You planning to spend the rest of your life flying nights?" Pat asked with a look of amusement. "Don't worry. I don't think he's her type." Her father grinned ruefully and for the first time in years, Nick blushed, and turned away from his old friend. "I might remind you though, Nick Galvin, she's engaged to the Strong boy, and she'll marry him eventually, if I have anything to say about it. She needs a man firmly planted on the ground, not up in the sky, like the two of us." He meant what he said, but what he'd seen in Nick's eyes that day intrigued him. There was something very powerful there, between the two of them, though he suspected that Cassie was too young to know it. But he also knew that Nick was wise enough not to be carried away by his own emotions.

They headed for the O'Malley home then, where Oona had promised to cook them dinner.

She was amazed to hear of Cassie's wins when they got home. In most ways, it had been a good day. But the death of Jim Bradshaw had spoiled it for all of them, and then in the midst of dinner, Bobby had arrived, looking crazed. He burst into their living room, and apologized when he saw them all eating dinner. His eyes went to Cassie first, and he looked as though he were going to burst into tears. He looked so distressed that Oona rose as though to go to him, but he backed out of the room apologetically and stood in the doorway.

"I'm sorry . . . I . . . they told me there was an accident . . ." His eyes filled with tears again, and they all felt sorry for him. It was easy to see what he'd thought, and Cassie got up and went to him.

"I'm sorry. It was Jim Bradshaw," she said softly.

"Oh, my God. Poor Peggy." She was a widow at nineteen and alone with two children. Bobby seemed overcome at the thought of it, but what had upset him so terribly was the fear that it could have been Cassie who was killed. And no one he talked to seemed to know what had happened.

They went out to sit on the porch quietly, and Cassie closed the door. You couldn't hear anything from inside the room, but they could still see how distressed he looked, as he talked to her. And she just sat there and nodded.

He was telling her that he couldn't live like this anymore, just being engaged to her, not going anywhere, not getting married, and never being entirely sure if they even had a future. He knew that she wanted to finish school, but he wasn't sure he could wait two more years. His father was so ill now, and his mother was so dependent on him. He seemed overwhelmed by all of it, and it was obvious to her that he needed her to help him. But it was equally obvious to both of them that she wasn't prepared to give up everything, and be what he needed.

"And this flying thing." He looked at her, his eyes filled with anguish. "I can't live like this. I keep thinking you're going to be killed . . . and today . . . you could have been . . . you could have been . . ." He started to cry and she put her arms around him and held him.

"Oh, poor Bobby . . . poor Bobby . . . it's all right . . . shhh . . ." It was like consoling one of her nephews. But she understood now that there was too much on his shoulders and she was only part of that burden. He desperately needed someone to help. He was only twenty-one, barely more than a boy himself, and he deserved so much more than she had to give, and they both knew it. As she comforted him, she gently slipped his ring off her finger, and pressed it into his hand. "You deserve so much," she whispered to him, "you deserve everything, and I have a long, long road ahead of me. I know that now. I was never sure of it before, but I am now." She wanted life and freedom and flying. And now that her father accepted her, maybe she could have all those things. But she couldn't give Bobby Strong what he deserved, and in truth it was the last thing she wanted.

"Are you going to keep flying, Cass?" he asked miserably, sniffing like a small child, while the members of her family in the main room tried to ignore them.

"I am," she nodded at him. "I have to. It's my life."

"Don't get hurt . . . oh God, Cassie . . . don't get hurt . . . I love you . . . I thought you were dead today." He was sobbing again and she felt terrible for him. She could only imagine what it must have been like. Just as it had been for Peggy Bradshaw.

"I'm okay . . . I'm fine . . ." She smiled up at him with tears in her own eyes. "You deserve wonderful things, Bobby, not someone like me. Find yourself a good wife, Bobby Strong. You deserve it."

"Will you stay here?" he asked curiously, and it seemed an odd question to her. She had nowhere else to go, and she had always lived there.

"Where else would I go?"

"I don't know," he smiled sadly, holding her ring. He missed her already. "You seem so free to me. Sometimes I hate our damn grocery store, and all the problems that go with it."

"You're going to do great things," she said confidently, sure that it was a lie, but he deserved all the encouragement she could give him.

"Do you really think so, Cass?" He sighed then, thinking of his life. "The funny thing is I just want to be married and have kids."

"And I don't." She grinned. "That's the trouble."

"I hope you do one day. Maybe we'll find each other again," he said hopefully, wanting to pursue the dream again. She had always seemed so exciting to him, maybe even too much so.

But she shook her head as she looked at him. She was wiser than he was.

"Don't wait for that. Go get what you want."

"I love you, Cass."

"I love you too," she whispered as she hugged him again and then stood up. "Do you want to come inside?" she asked, but he shook his head, tears bright in his eyes.

"I guess I better go." She nodded, and he slipped the ring into his pocket. He stopped for a long moment, and looked at her again, and then he turned and hurried off the porch before he started crying again. And Cassie went back inside and sat down. No one asked her anything, but they could all guess what had just happened. Nick glanced at her finger, and he wasn't surprised not to see the ring. In fact, he was relieved not to see it. Now all he had to worry about was Billy Nolan.

CHAPTER
9

The next morning, as Cassie lay in bed, thinking of the day before, she realized with a start that she was no longer engaged. She wasn't sure it changed anything, but suddenly she felt as though she didn't belong to anyone. It was partially very exciting, and in some ways suddenly very lonely.

But she had known all along it was wrong, she just hadn't had the courage to say it. But that night, it had seemed so cruel to go on torturing him, to make him wait another two years, and then tell him she still wasn't ready. She didn't think she ever would be, not for a life like his or for him, and now she really knew that.

She made herself breakfast, and saw a note from her mother, saying she had gone to take care of Glynnis's kids again, and she doubted if she'd be home in time to make dinner. Chris had left another note saying he'd be out with friends, and half an hour later, Cassie had showered, dressed, and gotten herself to the airport. She put on a clean pair of overalls and fueled some planes, and it was noon before she saw either Nick or her father.

"Sleeping till noon these days, Cass?" Nick teased. "Or just resting on your laurels?"

"Oh don't be such a smartass. I was here at nine. I was just doing some work in the back hangar."

"Yeah? Well, I've got a run for you today, if you want it."

"Where to?" She was intrigued.

"Indiana. A little cargo, and some mail, and a quick stop in Chicago on the way back. It shouldn't take too long. You should be home in time for dinner. You can fly the Handley."

"Sounds good to me," she grinned. He told her where to pick up the log, and her father came out of his office just then, and told Billy to load the cargo. He had appeared out of nowhere, and he had been working hard all day. And her father surprised her by telling him to go with her.

"I can go alone, Dad."

"Sure you can. But he needs to learn our routes, and I don't like the idea of your flying into Chicago." She rolled her eyes at him, and he made a face, but at least he wasn't objecting to her flying. Things were looking up, and Nick looked warningly at her and Billy, as though they were both naughty children.

"Behave yourselves, you two. No stunts, no rolls." He turned to Billy then, "And watch out for her double loops."

"If she tries anything, I'll toss her out on her ear," Billy grinned, looking more than ever like everyone's brother.

And as they took off toward the plane, Nick stood for a minute and watched them. They looked as though they were enjoying themselves, but they looked like two kids. He couldn't imagine her falling for him, but stranger things had happened. And in fact, even if she didn't, it didn't change anything for him. He had no right to be chasing a girl her age, and he would never have done it. She deserved a lot more than life in a lean-to shack at O'Malley's Airport, and he knew it.

They had just taken off when a brand-new green Lincoln Zephyr pulled up, and a man in a gray double-breasted suit stepped out and looked around the airport. He looked pleasantly at Nick, and at the small building which housed their offices and was the airport.

"Do you know where I might find Cassie O'Malley?" he asked smoothly. He had wavy blond hair, and movie-star good looks. And suddenly, Nick wondered if someone was going to offer Cassie a movie career. This was the man he'd seen the day before at the air show, in the blazer and white trousers. And he didn't look like a reporter now. He looked like a businessman of some kind, or maybe an agent.

Nick pointed up at the sky. "She just took off on a mail run. Can I help you?"

"I'd like to talk to her. Do you know when she'll be back?"

"Maybe seven or eight hours. Not before. I'd say she'll be back sometime tonight. Can I give her a message?"

He handed Nick a card. His name was Desmond Williams. And the card said "Williams Aircraft," with an address in Newport Beach, California. Nick knew exactly who he was. He was the young tycoon who had inherited a fortune and an aircraft company from his father. And he wasn't all that young, Nick decided, looking at him. He was pretty close to his own age. In fact, he was thirty-four. A lot too old for Cassie, according to Nick anyway.

"Will you be sure and give her my card? I'm staying at the Portsmouth." It was the finest hotel in town, which wasn't saying much. But it was the best Good Hope had to offer.

"I'll tell her," Nick assured him, dying of curiosity. "Anything else?" Williams shook his head, and looked Nick over with interest. "How did you like the air show?" Nick couldn't resist asking him. "Not bad for a small town, eh?"

"Very interesting." Williams conceded with a smile, and then sized Nick up again, and decided to ask him a question. Williams's whole style was very cool, everything about him was perfect and manicured, totally calculated and planned. He was a man who never made mistakes, or allowed himself to be swayed by emotions. "Are you her instructor?"

Nick nodded with pride. "I was. She could teach me to fly now."

"I doubt that," Desmond Williams said politely. He had an Eastern accent despite his Los Angeles address. And twelve years before, he had graduated from Princeton. "She's very good. She's done you proud."

"Thank you," Nick said quietly, wondering what this man wanted with her. There was something faintly ominous about him, incredibly cool, and strangely exciting. He was very good-looking and very aristocratic, but everything about him said that he meant business.

He didn't say another word to Nick then, but got back into the car he'd just bought in Detroit a few days before, and drove swiftly away from the airport.

"Who was that?" Pat asked as he came outside. "He certainly kicked up enough dust. Can he go any faster?" The car was the latest wonder by Ford, with a V-12 engine.

"That's Desmond Williams." Nick answered his question with a look of concern at his old friend. "They're after her, Pat. I never thought it would happen, but I think it may now. She made just enough noise at the air show."

"I was afraid of that." Pat looked unhappily at Nick. He didn't want her exploited or used, and he knew how easy it would be for that to happen to her. She was beautiful and young and innocent, and an incredible flier. It was a dangerous combination, and they both knew it. "Where is she?" Pat asked.

"She's gone. She and the Nolan kid took off just as he got here," Nick explained.

"Good." Pat glanced at the card in his hand, took it and tore it in half. "Forget him."

"You're not going to tell her?" Nick looked at him in amazement. No matter what he thought, he wouldn't have had the guts to do that. But on the other hand, he wasn't her father.

"No, I'm not," Pat answered him, "and neither are you. Right, Stick?"

"Yes, sir." Nick saluted with a grin, and they both went back to work with a vengeance.

On the way back from Chicago Cassie turned the controls over to Billy, to see how he handled them. She was impressed by how good he was. He said his father had taught him at fourteen, and he had flown for ten years now. And from the way he flew, it was easy to believe him. He had sure hands, and a good eye, he flew steadily and well, and she knew her father would be pleased. Billy was going to be a great asset to the airport. And besides that, he was a nice guy, easygoing and intelligent, and very pleasant to be with. They'd had a good time that day, on the flight, trading stories.

"I noticed yesterday that you were engaged," he mentioned conversationally on the leg home. "But I don't see the ring today. You getting married soon?"

"Nope," she said, thinking of Bobby. "I'm not engaged anymore. Gave back the ring last night." She wasn't sure why she was telling him, but he was there, and they were almost the same age, and she liked him. Besides, she didn't get the feeling he was interested in her. He just wanted to be friends, and that seemed comfortable and easy.

"Are you upset? Think you'll get back together?"

"Nope," she said again, almost feeling sorry for herself now. "He's a great guy, but he hates my flying. He's in a hurry to get married, I want to finish school. I don't know . . . it wasn't right, never was, I just never had the guts to say it."

"I know what that's like. I've been engaged twice, scared the hell out of me both times."

"What did you do about it?"

"The first time I ran," he admitted honestly with his boyish grin and his face full of freckles.

131

"And the last time? You got married?" Cassie looked surprised, he didn't look like someone who'd been married.

"No," he said quietly, "she died, at the San Diego Air Show last year." He said it very calmly but she could see the pain in his eyes.

"I'm sorry." There was nothing else to say. They had all lost friends at air shows. And it was terrible, but worse for him if he had loved her.

"So am I. But I've learned to live with it, more or less. I haven't really gone out with anyone since, and I don't think I want to."

"Is that a warning?" she grinned.

"Yeah," his eyes were full of mischief, "just in case you thought you could jump me at ten thousand feet. I've been scared to death the whole trip." The way he said it made her burst into laughter, and five minutes later they were both laughing again. By the time they got home, they were as easy with each other as old friends. As far as Cassie was concerned, there was nothing romantic about Billy Nolan, Cassie just liked him, and he was a terrific pilot. Her father had lucked out, and she thought Nick would like him too.

They landed at the airport about nine and Cassie offered him a ride to the boardinghouse where he was staying. His friends had gone back to California with their truck and their plane, and he had to save enough money to buy a car, which wouldn't be any time soon with the wages she knew her father paid. "How long do you think you'll stay?" she asked him.

"I don't know . . . thirty, forty years . . . like forever?" He grinned.

"Sure." She laughed at his answer.

"I don't know. Awhile. I needed to get away. My mom died, and with Sally last year, I just figured I needed to get away from California. I miss my dad, but he understands."

"Lucky for us," she smiled warmly at him. "It was fun today. See you tomorrow." She waved, and drove home. Her mother was home by then, and she made Cassie a sandwich. Her father was sitting in the kitchen, drinking a beer. He asked her how the flight was, and she told him how impressed she was with Billy's

132

flying. She told him why, and Pat nodded, pleased by her report, though he'd have to see for himself. He told her to get some sleep after she'd had something to eat, and he never mentioned Desmond Williams's visit to the airport.

CHAPTER
10

C assie was lying under an Electra the next day, with grease all over her face after working on the tail wheel, when she looked up and noticed an immaculate pair of white linen trousers. She couldn't help smiling as she looked at them, they looked so incongruous here, and so did the handmade spectators where the trousers ended. She looked up in curiosity, and was surprised to see an attractive blond man looking down at her with a puzzled air. She was almost unrecognizable, with her hair piled up on her head, grease all over her face, and a pair of old blue overalls that had been her father's.

"Miss O'Malley?" he asked with a frown, and she grinned. She looked like a bad joke from vaudeville as her white teeth shone in the black face, and the polished-looking man couldn't help smiling.

"Yes, I'm Miss O'Malley." She was still lying on her back, looking up at him, and she suddenly realized she'd better get up and see what he wanted. She sprang easily to her feet, and hesitated to shake hands with him. He looked so clean and so exquisitely groomed, everything about him was perfection. She wondered if he wanted to charter a plane from them, and she was about to direct him to her father. "Can I help you?"

"My name is Desmond Williams, and I saw you at the air show two days ago. I wanted to speak to you, if I may." He looked around the hangar and then back to her. "Is there anywhere we could go and talk?" She looked startled at the question. No one had ever come to visit her that way, and the only place to talk privately would have been her father's office.

"If you don't mind the noise of the planes, we could walk over near the runway, I guess." She didn't know what else to offer him.

They began walking side by side, and she almost laughed thinking of how incongruous they must have seemed, he so beautifully clean, and she so incredibly dirty. But she forced herself to look serious. She had no idea if he had a sense of humor. She saw that Billy had caught sight of them by then. He waved, but she only nodded.

"You were very impressive at the air show," Desmond Williams said quietly to her as they walked along the edge of the fields, and his shoes began to get very dusty.

"Thank you."

"I don't think I've ever seen anyone win so many prizes . . . certainly not a girl your age. How old are you, anyway?" He was watching her very carefully, and he sounded serious, but he was quick to smile at her. She still didn't know what he wanted.

"I'm twenty. This fall I'll be a junior in college."

"I see," he nodded, as though that made a big difference. And then he stopped walking and looked at her pointedly before he

136

asked his next question. "Miss O'Malley, have you ever thought of a future for yourself in aviation?"

"In what sense?" She looked completely baffled, and all of a sudden she wondered if he had come here to ask her to be a Skygirl, but even to her, that didn't seem very likely. "What do you mean?"

"I mean flying . . . as a job . . . as your future. Doing what you love best, or at least I think it is. You certainly fly as though you love it better than anything." She nodded with a smile, and he watched her face relentlessly, but so far, he liked it.

"I'm talking about flying remarkable planes, planes that no one else has . . . testing them . . . setting records . . . becoming an important part of modern-day aviation . . . like Lindbergh."

"Like Lindbergh?" She looked amazed. He couldn't mean it. "Who would I be flying for? You mean someone would just give me these planes, or would I have to buy them?" Maybe he was trying to sell her a new plane, but Desmond Williams smiled at her innocence. He was glad that no one had gotten to her before him.

"You'd be flying for me, for my company. Williams Aircraft." As soon as she heard the name, she realized who he was, and she couldn't believe he was talking to her and comparing her to Charles Lindbergh. "There's a wonderful future out there for someone like you, Miss O'Malley. You could do great things. And you'd be flying planes that otherwise you'd never be able to lay your hands on. The best there is. That's quite a thrill. Not like these." He looked around him disparagingly, and for a moment she felt hurt on behalf of her father. These planes were her friends, and her father's proudest possessions. "I mean real planes," Williams went on. "The kind that world records are made in."

"What would I have to do to get the job?" she asked suspiciously. "Would I have to pay you?" No one had ever offered her anything like this, and she had no idea how it worked. She had always thought that important pilots had their own planes, it had never occurred to her that they were given or loaned by aircraft companies like his. She had a lot to learn, and he was more than willing to teach her. She was the first fresh face he had seen since he had taken over his father's business.

"You wouldn't have to pay me anything." He smiled at her. "I would pay you, and handsomely. You'd get your photograph taken all the time, you'd get a lot of publicity, and if you're as good as I think you are, you could become a very important figure in aviation. Of course," he looked at her carefully, "you might have to wash your face a little more often than you do now," he teased and she suddenly remembered that she was probably covered with grease. She wiped her face on her sleeve, and was astonished at what she saw there. But he was even more impressed by the face he could see better now. She was exactly what he had been looking for. She was the girl of his dreams. All he had to do now was get her to sign a contract.

"When would I start?" She was curious, it was the most exciting thing she had ever heard, and she couldn't wait to tell Nick and her father.

"Tomorrow. Next week. As soon as you can get to Los Angeles. We would pay your way out of course, and give you an apartment."

"An apartment?" Her voice almost squeaked as he nodded.

"In Newport Beach, where Williams Aircraft is. It's a beautiful spot, and you can get into the city in no time. What do you say? Do you want the job?" He had brought the contract with him, and he was hoping she would sign without waiting another moment. But she hesitated briefly as she nodded.

"Yes. But I have to ask my father. I'd have to give up school. He might not like that." Particularly not for a flying job. Although he'd never been overly excited about her going to college. But he might not like this either.

"We could arrange for you to take classes, whenever you're free. But most of the time, you'll be pretty busy. There's a lot of good will involved, a lot of photography. And frankly, a lot of flying."

It sounded utterly fantastic. "Actually, I came by yesterday, but the man in the office said you were flying. I left my card with him, and asked for you to call me. You probably got back too late, but I thought I'd better come out here again just in case he lost my card." He smiled a winning smile at her, as Cassie looked at him pensively.

"You gave it to a man?" It had to be Nick or her father.

"I did and I told him I was staying at the Portsmouth. Did you call me there? Maybe I just didn't get the message."

"No, I didn't," she said honestly. "I never got the card or the message."

"Well, there's no harm done. I'm glad I found you today. Here's the contract for you to go over with your father."

"What does the contract say?" she asked innocently.

"It commits you to a year of test flights and publicity for Williams Aircraft, nothing more than that. I don't think you'll find anything wrong with it," he said confidently. He somehow managed to convey, just looking at her, that this was a great opportunity and she would love it.

She held the contract nervously in her hands, wondering what it all meant and why he had really come here. It couldn't really be this simple.

"I'll show my father," she said quietly. She wanted to ask him about it too. Why hadn't he and Nick told her anything about Desmond Williams's visit? To give them the benefit of the doubt, maybe they had just forgotten. But something told her it was more than that. They had kept it from her. But why? It sounded so perfect.

"Why don't you think it all over, and we'll meet again tomorrow morning. How about breakfast at my hotel at eight-thirty? After that, I've got to head back to the West Coast. But hopefully you'll be there too in a few days." He smiled, and she noticed that there was something very persuasive about him. He was very handsome and very cool, and he somehow made it sound as though she couldn't possibly resist him, and surely wouldn't want to. "Eight-thirty tomorrow morning then?" he asked pointedly, and she nodded. They shook hands on it, and a moment later, he had walked back to his car and driven away. As she stood staring, the Lincoln disappeared into the horizon. She tried to remember everything she'd ever heard about Desmond Williams. He was thirty-four; he was one of the richest men in the world, and he had inherited an empire from his father. His company made some of the finest planes, and he was supposedly ruthless in his business dealings, she had read somewhere. She had seen a photograph of him with some movie stars. And in her wildest dreams, she couldn't imagine what he wanted with Cassie O'Malley.

She walked slowly toward the small building where Nick and her father worked, thinking of everything he had said, and what it might mean to her. It was an opportunity that clearly would never come again. She couldn't even bring herself to believe that it had come this time.

She walked in, in her father's old overalls, and he glanced up at her, with her streaked face, and disheveled hair, and asked her if there was a problem with the de Havilland, because if there wasn't they needed it at noon for a long run. But she wasn't paying any attention to him, as she stared at him. And in her hand she was holding the contract.

"Why didn't you tell me someone came to see me yesterday?" she asked, and he looked suddenly startled.

"Who told you that?" He was going to have Nick's head if he had betrayed him. But Nick was staring at them. He had seen the look on her face when she walked into the office.

"That's not the point. A man came here yesterday and left a card for me. And neither of you ever told me." She turned angry eyes to Nick then, accusing him as well, and both men looked uncomfortable beneath her gaze. "That's like lying to me. Why?"

Her father tried to look unconcerned. "I didn't think it was important. I probably just forgot."

"Do you know who he is?" She looked from one to the other of them, unable to believe that they had been that ignorant. "He's Desmond Williams, of Williams Aircraft." It was one of the largest manufacturers of airplanes in the world, the second biggest in the States. Desmond Williams was certainly what one could call important.

"What did he want?" Nick asked casually, watching her, but he already sensed what Williams must have said, from the way she was behaving.

"Oh . . . just to give me a bunch of remarkable planes to fly, you know, to test fly, set records in, check out for him. Nothing much. Just a little job like that for a whole lot of money, and an apartment." The two men exchanged a dark look. This was exactly what they'd been afraid of.

"Sounds nice," Nick said easily, "what's the catch?"

"There is none."

"Oh yes, there is," Nick laughed at her. She was still a child, and he knew that he and Pat would have to do everything they could to protect her. Desmond Williams was flying around the country looking for publicity props, and once he had her, he would use her till she dropped, not just for test flights, but for everything else he could, newsreels, advertisements, endless photography. In Nick's opinion, she was just going to be another kind of Skygirl. "Did he give you a contract?" Nick asked casually, and she was quick to wave it at him.

"Of course he did."

"Mind if I have a look?" She handed it to him, and Pat glared at both of them. This was exactly what he had never wanted.

"You're going to say no to him, Cassandra Maureen," her father said quietly as Nick pored over the contract. Nick was no lawyer, but it looked pretty good. They were offering her a car, an apartment, for her use of course, not as a gift; she was to fly anything they thought appropriate, doing test flights for them; and the second part of the contract said that she would be available for unlimited publicity in connection with their planes. She had to make herself available for social, state, and even national events, for photography at the drop of a hat. She would be counted on as a spokeswoman for Williams Aircraft, and they expected her to act accordingly. She couldn't smoke at all, or drink excessively, there was an allowance for wardrobe costs, and they were going to supply her with uniforms she could fly in. Everything was clearly spelled out. The contract was for one year, and they were offering her fifty thousand dollars for the year, with a renewable option for a second year, if both parties agreed, at a higher rate to be negotiated, within reason. It was the best contract Nick had ever seen, and an opportunity few men would have turned down. But the contract also made it clear, Williams Aircraft was looking for a woman. It could be an opportunity that would be hard to miss, in spite of the fact that she was going to be part pilot, part model. But he was still deeply suspicious of Desmond Williams.

"What do you think, Pat?" Nick looked up at him, curious about his reaction.

"She's staying right here. That's what I think. She's not going anywhere, and certainly not to California to live in an apartment."

Cassie looked at him, blinded by anger over his not even telling her that Desmond Williams had come to see her. "I haven't decided yet, Dad. I'm going to meet with him tomorrow morning."

"No, you're not," Pat O'Malley told his daughter firmly, and Nick didn't want to argue with him in front of Cassie. He thought there were plenty of possibilities for exploitation in the deal but it was still worth exploring. It would be fun for her, and she would fly incredible planes for the next year. It was very exciting. They were even testing planes for the military, and openly competing with the Germans, and the money she would make would take care of her for a long time. It seemed unfair to him to keep her from it, or not to at least consider it carefully.

"What about college?" Nick asked her quietly as her father stormed back into his office and slammed the door behind him.

142

"He said I could take classes there when I have time."

"It doesn't sound like you will, at least not most of the time. When you're not flying, you'll be doing publicity." And then, cautiously, "Cassie are you sure you want to do this?"

She looked at him thoughtfully. She had never wanted to leave home, but her life wasn't going anywhere. She liked hanging around the airport, and she had had a good time at the air show. But she didn't want to teach. She didn't want to marry Bobby Strong, or any of the other boys she'd gone to school with. What was she going to do with the rest of her life? She wondered sometimes. And even she knew that there was more to life than greasing and gassing her father's planes, and making short runs to Indiana with Billy Nolan.

"What am I going to do here?" she asked honestly.

"Hang around with me," he said sadly. If only she could, forever. He would have loved it.

"That's the bad part of it, leaving all of you here. It would be perfect if I could take you all with me."

"It says in the contract they'll lend you a plane to come home with now and then. I can hardly wait for that. How about bringing home an XW-1 Phaeton for a quiet weekend."

"For you, I'd bring home a Starlifter if you wanted me to, I'd even steal one."

"Now there's a thought. That might soften up your old man. We could use a few new planes around here. Maybe they'd like to give us one or two," he joked, but he was feeling devastated at the thought of her leaving. She was so much a part of his everyday life, and they had done so much flying together in the past three years, he couldn't bear to think of her going to L.A. He had never expected anything like that to happen to her.

And neither had Pat. He had no intention of losing his little girl. It was bad enough that Chris had been talking about going to Europe to study architecture for a year or two. But that was still a few years away. This was now. And it wasn't Chris, it was Cassie.

"You're not going anywhere," he reiterated again that afternoon, "and that's final." But in her mind, she was still going to make the decision. She talked to Nick about it again, and he could definitely see opportunities for them to take advantage of her, but there were so many benefits to her in the process that he wasn't at all sure it mattered. The money, the fame, the planes, the test flights, the records she could set, the benefits to her seemed almost endless. It would be impossible to turn them down. But he had no idea how she was going to convince her father.

She talked to Billy about it too, and he knew Desmond Williams from the West Coast, though only by reputation. Some people said he was a fair man, others clearly didn't like him. He had offered a job to a girl Billy knew from San Francisco and she had hated it. She had said it had been too much hard work, and she felt as though they owned her. But Billy confided to Cass that she had also been a miserable pilot. For someone like Cassie, it could be the opportunity of a lifetime.

"You really could end up another Mary Nicholson," he said, citing one of the stars of the day. But Cassie couldn't imagine ever being that famous.

"I doubt it," she said gloomily. The difficulty of the decision was driving her crazy. She didn't want to leave her home and family, but she also knew that she had very little else to stay for. And if she wanted to fly, Williams Aircraft was the place to be, no matter hów many dumb photographs they took of her in her uniform, or how many interviews she had to give. She wanted to fly airplanes. And Williams had the best ones.

"Give it some thought, kid. You may not get another chance," Billy advised her solemnly, and in their offices, Nick was telling Pat much the same thing. She was a brilliant pilot, and there was nowhere for her to go from here. She'd be hanging around the airport all her life, and flying dusty routes around the Midwest with a bunch of guys who would never fly as well as she did.

"I told you not to teach her to fly!" Pat roared at him, suddenly angry at everyone, Nick, Cassie, Chris, all of them. It had to be someone's fault. And the worst culprit of all was the devil himself,

Desmond Williams. "He's probably a criminal . . . going after innocent young girls, looking to rob them of their virtue." Nick felt sorry for him. After all these years, and with almost no warning at all, he was about to lose his little girl. And Nick knew how he felt. He hated it as much as Pat did. But he also knew they had no right to hang onto her. She had to fly . . . like a bird . . . and it was time for her to soar with the eagles.

"You can't stop her, Pat," Nick said quietly, wishing he could say how much it hurt him too. "It's not fair. She deserves so much better than we have to give her."

"That's your fault," Pat boomed at him again. "You shouldn't have taught her to fly so damn well." Nick laughed at the reproach, and Pat helped himself to a slug of whiskey. He knew he wouldn't be flying that day, and he was deeply upset over losing Cassie. And he still had to tell Oona about Cassie's visit from Desmond Williams.

And when he did, that night, Oona was shocked. She imagined all sorts of terrible immoral things. She couldn't imagine Cassie living anywhere but home, certainly not in Los Angeles, living alone as a test pilot and a publicity spokeswoman for Desmond Williams.

"Do girls do that kind of thing?" she asked Pat unhappily. "Pose for pictures and all that? Do they wear clothes?"

"Of course, Oona. It's not a striptease parlor, the man builds airplanes."

"Then what do they want with our little girl?"

"Your little girl," he said miserably, "is probably the best pilot I've ever seen, including Nick Galvin, or Rickenbacker. She's the best there is, and Williams is no fool. He can see that. She put on a hell of a show two days ago, at the air show. I didn't want to worry you, but she almost killed herself, the little fool, pulled herself right out of a spin no more than fifty feet off the ground. I damn near died. But she did it, and never turned a hair. Did a lot of other crazy stunts too. But she did them perfectly. And he knew it."

"Does he want her to fly stunts?"

"No, just to test planes, and set some records if she can. I read the contract, and it sounds fair. I just don't like the idea of her going away, and I knew you wouldn't either."

"What does Cassie want?" her mother asked, trying to take it all in, but there was a lot to absorb in a short time. And they all knew that Cassie had to make a decision before morning.

"I think she wants to go. She says she wants to go. Or she says she wants the freedom to decide her own fate."

"And what did you say?" Oona asked with wide eyes, and her husband grinned sheepishly.

"I forbade her to go, just like I forbade her to fly."

"That didn't get you very far," Oona smiled, "and I don't suppose it will this time."

"What should we say?" He turned to his wife for advice. He relied on her judgment more than he realized, and sometimes more than he wanted to. But he trusted her, particularly about their daughters.

"I think we should let her do what she wants. She will anyway, Pat, and she'll be happier if she feels she can make her own decisions. She'll come back to us, no matter how many planes she flies in California. She knows how much we love her." They called her into their bedroom then, and Oona let her father tell her what they had decided.

"Your mother and I want you," he hesitated and glanced at Oona for a second, "to make your own decision. And whatever you decide, we're behind you. But if you go," he warned, "you'd better come back, and damn often." There were tears in his eyes when he hugged her, and she clung to him and kissed her mother, who was crying.

"Thank you . . . thank you . . ." She hugged them both, and sat down at the foot of their bed with a sigh. "It's been a hard decision."

"Do you know what you're going to do?" Oona asked. Pat didn't dare ask her, but he already suspected what Cassie had decided as she nodded and looked at them with a shiver of excitement.

"I'm going."

But leaving them was harder than she'd feared. She met with Desmond Williams at the Portsmouth the next morning, and signed the contract with him. She had black coffee and toast, she was too nervous to eat anything else, and the details of what he was telling her were so exciting that she kept getting confused. They were going to arrange a flight for her from Chicago to Los Angeles. There was an apartment, a car . . . uniforms . . . a chaperone when they felt she needed one . . . a wardrobe . . . escorts, a weekend place in Malibu she could use. A plane for her personal use, whenever she wanted to fly home. And the kinds of planes she had always dreamed about flying.

Her schedule began in five days. There would be a press conference, a newsreel, and a test flight of a new Starlifter right off the bat. He wanted her to show America just how good she was. But first he wanted to show her what his planes could do. He was going to spend the first two weeks with her, mostly flying.

"I can't believe it," she said to Billy as they lay in the sun on an old unused piece of runway later that morning.

"You sure did get a big break," he said enviously. But he was happy here, and for the moment he had no desire to go back to California.

"I'll be home in two weeks for a visit, no matter what," she promised him and everyone else.

Her parents gave a big dinner for her the night before she left, with all her sisters and brothers-in-law, their kids, Chris, Nick, and Billy. Bobby wasn't there of course, although she had seen him two days before at Jim Bradshaw's wake. He had been talking quietly with Peggy, and holding one of her babies.

But it was Nick she stood next to all night, whom she couldn't bear to leave. She derived so much comfort and support from him, and had for so many years, that now she didn't know how she would survive without him.

The next morning everyone was at the airport when she left. Nick was flying her to Chicago in the Vega, and after she kissed her mother and sisters and Chris good-bye, she went over to her father. They both had tears in their eyes as he looked at her. He wanted to ask her to change her mind, but he would never do it.

"Thank you, Dad," she whispered into his neck as he held her close to him.

"Be careful, Cassie. Pay attention. Don't ever get sloppy in one of those fancy planes. They won't forgive you for an instant."

"I promise, Dad."

"I wish I believed you," he smiled, "damn female pilot." He was laughing then through his tears, and gave her another bear hug and then sent her off with Nick. Chris and Billy were waving from the runway too, when they took off, and Cassie heaved an enormous sigh. It had been harder leaving home than she had ever dreamed, and all she could think of were the people she was leaving there, instead of the places where she was going. And as she turned to look at Nick, her heart felt heavier still. She wanted to hold onto every moment she had with him.

"You're a lucky girl," Nick reminded her on the way up, to take her mind off her family, who were still waving at her, "but you deserve it. You've got what it takes, Cass. Just don't let those city slickers use you." Desmond Williams was indeed pretty slick, but he also seemed both fair and honest. He had made no bones about what he wanted from her. He wanted the best pilot in the world, the best-looking, best behaved woman he could find to represent his product, he wanted new records set, and his planes unharmed and well viewed by the American public. It was a tall order, but she was capable of filling it for him, and he was smart enough to sense that. She was the best pilot he had ever seen, and good-looking too, and for him, that was a beginning. For Nick it was an end. But he was more than willing to sacrifice himself for her future. It was his final gift of love to her. First flying, and then finally, her freedom.

"Don't let them push you around," Nick reminded her; "you're a great girl, and if they're too tough on you, tell them to go to hell, and come straight home. All you have to do is call, and I'll fly out to get you." It sounded crazy, but it was actually reassuring.

"Will you come out to see me?"

"Sure. Whenever I have a run out there, I'll take a little detour."

"Don't give the California runs to Billy then," she reminded him, "be sure you do them yourself." He smiled at her admonition. She was suddenly looking very nervous.

"I kind of thought you might like to see more of him," Nick said, speaking of Billy as nonchalantly as he could, which meant not very. "Was I wrong?" He was relieved at what she had just said. But he had already begun to suspect that Billy was a friend and not a romance, just as her father had predicted. But it was nice to hear her confirm it. What he wanted from her was celibacy and total adoration, and he knew how crazy that was. One of these days she'd have to find a husband, and have kids, and he knew it wouldn't be him, but he wished it could be.

"Billy and I are just friends," she said quietly. "You know that."

"Yeah. Maybe I do."

"You know a lot of things," she said wisely. "About me, about life, about what matters, about what doesn't. You've taught me a lot, Nick. You've made my whole life mean something to me. You've given me everything."

"I wish I had, Cass, but I haven't done all that well myself. And no one deserves it all more than you do."

"Yes, you have given me everything," she said, her admiration obvious, her love for him even more so.

"I'm no Desmond Williams, Cass," he said honestly. He had no pretense about him.

"Who is? Most people aren't that lucky."

"You might be one day, Cass. You might become someone really important."

"From being in newsreels and getting my picture taken? I doubt it. That's show-offy stuff, it's not real. I know that much."

"You're a smart girl, Cass. Stay that way. Don't let them spoil it."

They landed in Chicago after a little while, and he walked her to her plane, carrying her bag for her. She was wearing a navy blue suit that had been her mother's. It looked a little out of date, and it was too big for her, but it was hard to make Cassie O'Malley look anything but lovely. At twenty years of age, she took your breath away, with her shining red hair, her big blue eyes, her full bust and long legs, the tiny waist he loved to put his hands around when he helped her to the ground. But she was looking up at him now, like a child, and all he wanted to do was take her back to her mother. Her eyes were filled with tears, but she wasn't crying for them, she was crying for him. She didn't want to leave him.

"Come and see me, Nick . . . I'll miss you so much. . . ."

"I'll always be there for you, kid . . . don't you forget that."

"I won't," she sniffed, and he put an arm around her and held her. He didn't say anything else to her. He just kissed the top of her head, and walked away. There was nothing else he could say, and he knew if he did, his voice would betray him, and he'd never leave her.

CHAPTER

11

Whthis the flight from Chicago landed in Los Angeles, there were three people waiting to meet her, a driver, a representative from the company, and Mr. Williams's secretary. Cassie was a little surprised to see them. He had told her she would be met at the plane, but she hadn't expected to be met so officially, or by so many people.

On the drive to Newport Beach, the company representative gave her a list of appointments for the week, a review of their latest planes, a test flight in each of them, a press conference with all the most important members of the local press, and a newsreel. The secretary then gave her a list of social events she was expected to attend with and without any of several escorts, and a few with Mr. Williams. It was more than a little overwhelming. But she was even more overcome when she saw the apartment they had rented for her. It was in Newport Beach, and it had a bedroom, a living room, and a dining room, all overlooking the ocean. It had spectacular views, and a terrace which surrounded it. The refrigerator was stocked, the furniture was beautiful, there were Italian linens in the drawers. And she was told that a maid would attend to her needs if she wished to entertain, and she would clean the apartment daily.

"I . . . oh, my Lord!" Cassie exclaimed as she opened a drawer full of lace tablecloths. Her mother would have given her left arm to have any one of them, and Cassie couldn't begin to imagine why she had them. "What are these for?"

"Mr. Williams thought you'd like to entertain," his personal secretary, Miss Fitzpatrick, said primly. She was twice Cassie's age, and she had gone to school at Miss Porter's in the East. She knew very little about planes, but she knew everything there was to know about all things social, and the proper decorum.

"But I don't know anyone here," Cassie laughed as she spun around, looking at the apartment. She had never dreamed of anything even remotely like it. She was dying to tell someone, or show them. Billy, Nick . . . her sisters . . . her mom . . . but there was no one here. Just Cassie, and her entourage. And when she looked in the bedroom, she found all her new clothes neatly arranged for her. There were four or five well-cut suits in an array of somber colors, several hats to match, a long black evening dress and two short ones. There were even shoes and some handbags. Everything was in the sizes she had given them. And in a smaller closet in the room, she found all her uniforms. They were navy blue, and looked extremely official. There was even a small hat that had been designed for it, and regulation shoes. And for a moment, she almost felt her heart sink. Maybe Nick was right. Maybe she was going to be a Skygirl.

Everything was so regimented and prearranged, it was all like a very strange dream. It was like being dropped into someone else's life, with their clothes, and their apartment. It was hard to believe this was all hers now.

There was a young woman waiting for Cassie too. She was neatly dressed in a gray suit, with a matching hat. She had a warm smile, lively blue eyes, and well-cut dark blond hair that hung to her shoulders in a smooth page boy. And she appeared to be in her early thirties.

"This is Nancy Firestone," Miss Fitzpatrick explained. "She will be your chaperone, whenever Mr. Williams feels that one is needed. She can help you with whatever needs you have, handle the press, escort you to meetings and luncheons." The young woman introduced herself to Cass, and gave her a warm smile as she showed her around the apartment. A chaperone? What would she do with her? Leave her on the runway when she tested planes? After seeing all of it, Cassie was beginning to wonder if she'd even have time to fly one.

"It's all a little overwhelming at first," Nancy Firestone said sympathetically. "Why don't you let me unpack for you, and then we can talk about your schedule over lunch?" Nancy said, as Cassie glanced around, feeling lost. She had noticed a maid in the kitchen making sandwiches and a salad. She was an older woman in a black uniform, and she seemed perfectly at home there. Far more than Cassie felt at the moment. She couldn't help wondering what she was going to do with all these people. It was obvious that they were there to help, and Desmond Williams had certainly provided every possible creature comfort. He had done more than that. He had provided a dream for her. But suddenly all she felt was desperately lonely among all these strangers. And Nancy Firestone seemed to sense that. That was why Williams had hired her. He knew her well, and had assessed instantly that she was just what Cassie needed.

"Are we going out to look at the planes today?" Cassie asked mournfully. At least that was something she understood, and she was a lot more interested in planes than in what she'd seen in her closet. At least the planes were familiar to her, and this glamorous lifestyle wasn't. She hadn't come to California to play dress-up. She had come to fly airplanes. And amid all the hats and shoes and gloves, and people who were there to take care of her, she wondered if she'd ever get a chance to fly one. Suddenly, all Cassie wanted was her simple life in Illinois, and a hangar full of her father's airplanes.

"We'll go out to the airfield tomorrow," Nancy said kindly. She knew instinctively, and from everything Desmond had said, that she had to treat Cassie gently. This was a whole new world for her, and he had warned Nancy that she would be new to all this and probably a little startled at first, but she was also headstrong and independent. He didn't want her suddenly deciding that this wasn't for her. He wanted her to like it. "Mr. Williams didn't want to wear you out on the first day," she smiled warmly, as they sat down and helped themselves to sandwiches. But Cassie wasn't hungry.

"You have a press conference at five o'clock. The hairdresser is coming here at three. And we have a lot to talk about before that." She made it sound as though they were just two girls getting ready for a party, and Cassie's head was spinning as she listened. Williams's secretary, Miss Fitzpatrick, left the apartment then, after pointing to a stack of briefing papers Mr. Williams wanted her to have about his planes. And she said tersely that Mr. Williams would come by to pick her up between four and four-thirty.

"He's taking you to the press conference," Nancy explained as the door closed behind Miss Fitzpatrick. She made it sound like a great honor, and Cassie knew it was. But it terrified her anyway. They all did. All Cassie could do by then was stare at Nancy Firestone in dismay and amazement. What was all this? What did it mean? What was she doing here? And what did any of it have to do with airplanes? Nancy read her face easily and tried to reassure her.

"I know it's a little startling at first," Nancy smiled calmly. She was a pretty woman, but there was something sad in her eyes that

154

Cassie had noticed the moment she saw her. But she seemed determined to make Cassie feel at ease in these unfamiliar surroundings.

"I don't even know where to start," Cassie admitted to her, suddenly feeling an overwhelming urge to cry, but she knew that she couldn't. They were all being so good to her, but there was so much to absorb and understand, the clothes, the appointments, what they expected of her, what she had to say to the press. All she really wanted to do was learn about the planes, and instead she had to worry about how she looked and dressed, and if she sounded intelligent or grown-up enough. It was terrifying, and even Nancy Firestone's warmth was of very little comfort.

At first glance, it almost seemed as though they had brought her out for show and not for flying. "What do they want with me?" Cassie asked her honestly as they sat looking out at the Pacific. "Why did he bring me out here?" She was almost sorry she'd come now. It was just too scary.

"He brought you here," Nancy answered her, "because I hear you're one of the best pilots he's ever seen. You must be terrific, Cassie. Desmond doesn't impress easily. And he hasn't stopped talking about you since he saw you at the air show. But he brought you here because you're a woman too, and not just an amazing pilot. And to Desmond, that's very important." In some ways, women were important to him. In others, they mattered not at all. But Nancy didn't explain that to Cassie. Desmond Williams liked to have women around when they served his purposes, but he attached himself to no one. "He thinks that women sell planes better than men because they're more exciting. He thinks that women—women like you, that is—are the future of aviation. You're a terrific press bonus for him, and a great boost for public relations." She didn't tell Cassie it was also because of her looks, but that was part of it. She was a real beauty, and if she hadn't been, she wouldn't have been there. Nancy knew he had been looking for someone like her for a long time, and he had talked to a lot of female pilots, and gone to a lot of air shows before he found her. This was an idea he had had for years, even before George Putnam discovered Amelia Earhart.

"But why me? Who cares about me?" Cassie asked innocently, still looking overwhelmed in spite of Nancy's encouragement and explanations. She still didn't understand it. She wasn't stupid, she was naive, and it was difficult for most people to conceive of a mind like Desmond Williams's. Nancy knew a lot about him, from her husband, before he died, testing one of Williams's planes, from the other pilots he knew, and from her own experiences since Skip had died. Desmond Williams had done a lot to help her. In many ways, he'd been a godsend. Yet there were things about him that were unnerving. There was a single-mindedness about him that was frightening at times. When he wanted something, or when he thought something would be good for the company, he would stop at nothing to get it.

He had been very good to her when Skip died, and he had done everything possible for her and her daughter. He had told her that she and Jane were part of the "family," that Williams Aircraft would take care of them forever. He had opened a bank account for them, and all of their needs would be provided for. Jane's education was assured, and Nancy's pension. Skip had died for Desmond Williams, and he would never forget it. He had even bought a small house for them. And drawn up a contract. She was to remain an employee of Williams Aircraft for the next twenty years, doing projects such as these, nothing too unreasonable, or terribly wearing. But projects that required intelligence and loyalty. He reminded her subtly of how much he'd done for them, and suddenly she knew she had no choice but to do what he wanted. Skip had left them nothing but debts and sweet memories. And now, after all he'd done for her and Jane, Desmond Williams owned her. He kept her in a pretty little gilded cage, he made good use of her, he was fair, or at least he seemed to be, but he never let her forget that he owned her. She couldn't go anywhere, she couldn't leave; if she did, they'd have nothing again. She had no real training for anything, she'd be lucky to get a job, and Janie would never go to college. But if she stayed, she could keep what he'd given her. And Williams saw something useful in her, just as he did in Cassie. And what he wanted he got. He bought it, fair and square, and he paid a high price for it. But there was no mistaking his ownership once the contract was signed, and the purchase complete. He was a smart man, and he always knew what he wanted.

"Everyone will care about you eventually," Nancy said quietly. She knew more about his plans than she intended to share with Cassie. He was a genius at dealing with the press, and creating a huge concept from a very small one. "The American public will come to love you. Women and planes are what's ahead of us now. Williams Aircraft makes the finest planes that fly, but to have that brought home to the public through your eyes, through *you*, is a very powerful thing. To have you identified with his planes will give them a special appeal, a special magic." And Desmond Williams knew that. It was that that he wanted from Cassie. He'd been looking for years for a woman who embodied the American dream, young, beautiful, a simple girl with great looks, a good mind, and a brilliant flier. And much to everyone's amazement, he had finally found her in Cassie O'Malley. And what better fate for her? What more could she possibly have wanted? Nancy knew Cassie was a lucky girl, and even if there were strings attached eventually, even if he wanted lifetime fealty, he would make it up to her. She'd be famous and rich, and a legend, if she played her cards right. Even in Nancy's eyes, knowing just how tightly those strings could be tied, she thought that Cassie O'Malley was to be envied. Desmond was going to make her a star like no other.

"It's so strange though, when you think of it," Cassie said, looking thoughtfully at Nancy. "I'm no one. I'm not Jean Batten, or Amy Johnson, or anyone important. I'm a kid from Illinois who won four prizes at the local air show. So what?" she asked modestly, finally taking a bite of a perfectly made chicken sandwich.

"You're not 'just a kid' anymore," Nancy said wisely, "or you won't be after five o'clock today." She knew just how carefully Desmond had begun laying the groundwork from the moment she'd signed the contract. "And just how do you think those other women got started? Without someone like Desmond to publicize them, they'd never have happened." Cassie listened, but she didn't agree with her. Their reputations were built on skill, not just on publicity, but Nancy clearly believed in what Williams was doing. "Earhart was what George Putnam made of her. Desmond has always been fascinated by that. He always felt that she was a lot less of a pilot than Putnam made her out to be, and maybe he was right." Skip had thought so too, and as Nancy thought of it, she looked at Cassie sadly. Cassie was intrigued by Nancy, though there was a lot she liked about her, and yet there was a part of her that seemed very removed. She seemed both enthusiastic about what lay ahead for Cassie, and maybe even a little bit jealous. She made it all sound like such a great deal, and she spoke of "Desmond" as though she knew him better than she would ever have admitted. Watching her, Cassie couldn't help wondering if there was anything between them, or maybe she just admired him a great deal, and wanted to be sure that Cassie appreciated everything he had done for her. It was all a lot to absorb and analyze in one afternoon, as they sorted through Cassie's things, and Nancy tried to explain the importance of "marketing" to her. Like Desmond, Nancy thought it was everything. It was what made people buy the products other people made. In this case, planes. Cassie was part of a larger plan. What she was, what she would be, was a tool to sell airplanes. It was an odd concept to her, and when the hairdresser arrived, she was still trying to understand it.

Nancy had told her about her husband by then, and Jane. She had explained, simply, that Skip had died in an accident the year before during a test flight over Las Vegas. She spoke about it very calmly, but there was something ravaged in her eyes when she spoke of him. In a way, her life had ended when he died, or she felt that way. But in a number of ways, Desmond Williams had changed that.

"He's been very good to me," she said quietly, "and to my daughter." Cassie nodded, watching her, and then the hairdresser distracted both of them with her plans for Cassie's bright red mane. She wanted to give it a good trim, and have her wear it long, like Lauren Bacall. She even said she saw a similarity, which made Cassie guffaw. She knew Nick would have really laughed if he'd heard that, or at least she thought so. But Nancy took the hairdresser very seriously, and approved of everything she wanted.

"What exactly is it they want from me?" Cassie asked with a nervous sigh, as the hairdresser clipped and snipped with determination, and Nancy watched her.

She managed to glance at her new charge with a smile, and answered her as best she could.

"They want you to look pretty, sound smart, behave yourself, and fly like an angel. That about sums it up." She smiled again and Cassie grinned at the description. Nancy made it sound surprisingly simple.

"That shouldn't be too hard. The flying part anyway; the behaving ought to be okay if it means don't fall down drunk or run around with guys. I'm not sure what 'sound smart' is going to mean, that could be rough, and 'pretty' could be hopeless," Cassie grinned at her new friend. When she stopped feeling terrified over it, it was all very exciting. How did things like this happen? It was almost like being in a movie. There was a feeling of unreality to it that she just couldn't escape now.

"I get the feeling you haven't looked in the mirror in a while," Nancy said honestly, and Cassie nodded.

"No time. I've been too busy flying and repairing planes at my father's airport."

"You'll have to learn to look in the mirror now." This was why Williams had so much faith in Nancy. She was tactful, ladylike, intelligent, she did what she was told, and she knew what was expected. Desmond Williams knew his people well and he always knew exactly what he was buying. He had never doubted for a

159

moment that Nancy would be useful to him when they had signed their contract. "Just smile and think that a few photographs won't hurt you. And the rest of the time you can fly anything you want. It's an opportunity almost no one gets, Cassie. You're very lucky," Nancy encouraged her. She knew just what flying fanatics liked, and how to cajole Cassie into doing the things she didn't. Like the press conferences she was scheduled for, the interviews, the newsreels, and the parties Desmond wanted her to be seen at. Miss Fitzpatrick had even provided a list of escorts.

"Why do I have to go to those?" Cassie asked suspiciously about the parties.

"Because people have to get to know your name. Mr. Williams went to a lot of trouble to have you included, and you really can't disappoint him." She said it surprisingly firmly.

"Oh," Cassie said, looking more than a little daunted. She didn't want to seem ungrateful, and she was already beginning to trust Nancy's opinions. It was all happening so quickly, and Nancy was her only friend here. And what Nancy said was true, Williams was doing a lot for her, and maybe she owed it to him to accept his invitations. Nonetheless, to Cassie, looking at the list, the social obligations seemed endless. But Desmond Williams knew exactly what he was doing. And so did Nancy.

When the hairdresser was finished, they all liked Cassie's hair. She suddenly looked more sophisticated, but it was both elegant and simple. And then the hairdresser helped Cassie to do her makeup. At three-fifteen she took a bath and at three forty-five, she put on her own underwear, and the silk stockings that had been left for her. And when she put on a dark green suit at four o'clock, she looked like a million dollars.

"Wow!" Nancy said, adjusting Cassie's blouse carefully and checking that the shoes matched her suit and handbag.

"Silk stockings!" Cassie beamed. "Wait till I tell Mom!" She was grinning like a kid and Nancy laughed and asked if she had any earrings. Cassie looked blank and then shook her head. Her mom had a pair that had been her mother's, but Cassie had never owned any. Nor had her sisters.

"I'll have to tell Mr. Williams." Nancy made a note to herself. She needed a string of pearls too. He had told Nancy exactly the look he wanted. No greasy overalls or work clothes. They could save that for one rare shot, maybe for *Life*, as part of a bigger shoot. But the look he wanted for her on the ground was pure Lady. Although all Nancy could think of as she looked at her was Rita Hayworth.

Desmond Williams arrived promptly at four o'clock, and he was very pleased with what he saw. He handed Cassie some photographs and details of the Phaeton and Starlifter she was going to fly that week, just so she could familiarize herself with them. And the following week she had some important tests to do on a high-altitude plane he was trying to convert for the Army Air Corps. But as she looked at the photographs, she couldn't help thinking of Nancy's husband. What if Desmond's planes were too dangerous, or the risks he wanted her to take were too great? Like all good test pilots, she tempered blind courage with caution. She wasn't afraid to fly anything, she decided, as she looked longingly at a photograph of the experimental Phaeton.

"You're going to let me fly *that*?" She beamed at him, and he nodded. "Wow! How about right now? Forget the press, let's go fly." She beamed at him happily, and suddenly all her earlier concerns and hesitations were forgotten.

He laughed. He loved the way she looked, and Nancy had let him know as he came in that Cassie had been completely cooperative with her. He was very pleased with both of them. This was the best publicity plan he had ever had, and he knew it. "Never forget the press, Cassie. They can make or break your business. Or mine at any rate. We want to be very nice to them. Always." He looked at her pointedly, and she nodded, still feeling completely in awe of him. He was wearing an impeccably cut dark blue double-breasted suit, and brilliantly shined handmade black shoes. His blond hair was perfectly combed and everything about him was starched, ironed to perfection, and spotless. He was the most beautifully groomed man she had ever seen. And she watched him with utter fascination. Everything about him was calculated and preconceived, thought out to the nth degree. But she was too young to understand that. What she saw was the finished product, what he wanted her to see. And that was what he wanted to teach her, to show the world just exactly the face he wanted. The smiling, sunny, small-town girl, who flew better than any man, and dared everything, and then came tumbling out of the cockpit with a big grin, and a shock of perfectly combed red hair. She was going to have every man in the country in love with her in six months, if it even took that long, and she was going to be every woman's idol. In order to do that, she had to behave perfectly, look spectacular, and fly planes that made the toughest pilots tremble. He had studied everyone else's mistakes, and he didn't intend to make any of the same ones. Desmond Williams was not going to fail, nor was Cassie, if he had any control over her at all. She was going to become the biggest name the country had ever seen. He was going to completely create her. And in her own small way, just by making her comfortable and keeping an eye on her, Nancy Firestone was going to help him. He wasn't going to have all his dreams shot down, by having Cassie get drunk, or swear at someone, or look like hell after a long flight or get involved with some bum. She was going to have to be perfect.

"Ready for the big time?" he smiled at her. She looked fine, better than that actually, but he could still see room for improvement. She had her own remarkable looks, but the suit was a little too big for her, and later Nancy would have to arrange for alterations. She was just a fraction thinner than he'd remembered, and her looks were stronger. She needed something just a little more glamorous, a little bit younger. And he hadn't realized when he'd met her in Good Hope that she had such a spectacular figure. He wanted to play to that without cheapening her, or even approaching the vulgar. But there was a look he wanted to achieve, and they were not quite there yet. But for a first run . . . she was doing fine.

And she did far better than he had expected at the press conference, in the large conference room next to his office.

Twenty members of the press had been handpicked by him, the impressionable ones. The men who liked girls a little too much, the women. None of the great cynics. And then he introduced her. She came in looking frightened and a little pale, and feeling a little strange in her new clothes and bright red lipstick. But she looked terrific in her new haircut and the green suit. And her natural good looks and warm nature sparkled.

She enchanted them. He had given them the information about the air show, and she was very humble about it. She explained that she had hung around her father's airport all her life, working on engines and fueling planes.

"I spent most of my childhood covered with grease. I only found out I had red hair when I got here," she quipped, and they loved her. She had an easy style, and once she got used to them, she treated them like old friends, and they loved it. Desmond Williams was so ecstatic he couldn't stop grinning.

In the end, he had to tear her away. They'd have sat with her all night, listening to her stories. She had even told them about her father not wanting her to fly, and only convincing him after the night she flew in the snowstorm with Nick, to rescue the wounded at the train wreck.

"What did you fly, Miss O'Malley?"

"An old Handley of my father's." There was an appreciative look from the knowledgeable members of the crowd. It was a hard plane to fly. But they knew she had to be good, or Williams wouldn't have brought her out here.

By the time she left them, they were calling her Cassie. She was totally unpretentious and completely ingenuous. And when she made the front page of the L.A. *Times* the next day, the picture of her was sensational, and the story told of a redheaded bombshell that was about to hit L.A. and take the world by storm. They might as well have written a banner headline that said, WE LOVE YOU, CASSIE! because it was obvious that they did. The campaign had begun. And from then on, Desmond Williams kept her very busy.

Her second day in L.A., Cassie "visited" all his planes, and of course the press was there, and so were the Movietone people for a newsreel.

When the newsreel was released, her mother took all her sisters and their children to see it. Cassie wanted Nick and her father to see it too, but all she got was a postcard from Nick that said, "We miss you, Skygirl!" which annoyed her. She knew what she looked like in the newsreel, in the uniform she had to wear, but she knew he had to be impressed by their planes too. They were nothing short of fantastic.

Her first flights were in the Phaeton they were working on, and then the Starlifter he had shown her. After that, he let her fly a high-altitude plane he was working on, to take extensive notes for their designers. She had gone to forty-six thousand feet, and it was the first time she'd ever had to use an oxygen mask, or an electrically heated flight suit. But she had been able to gather some very important information. Their goal was to convert the plane into a high-level bomber for the Army. It was hard work. And she scared herself once or twice, but she impressed the hell out of Desmond Williams. His engineers and one of his pilots had gone up with her, and they had described her flying as better than Lindbergh's. She was prettier too, one of them had pointed out. But that much Williams knew. What he was pleased to hear was that her flying skill was beyond expectation.

She set an altitude record her second week there and a speed record in the Phaeton three days later. Both were verified by the FAI and they were official. These were the planes she had always dreamed of.

The only thing that slowed her down was the constant press conferences and the photographs and the newsreels. They were incredibly tedious, and sometimes the press really got in her way.

She'd been in Los Angeles for three weeks by then, and the press were already starting to follow her everywhere she went. She was becoming news. And although she tried to be pleasant to them, sometimes it really annoyed her. She had almost run over one of them the day before on takeoff.

"Can't you keep them off the runway for chrissake?" she shouted from the cockpit before takeoff. She didn't want to hurt anyone and they'd frightened her by getting so close to the plane. But the men on the ground only shrugged. They were getting used to it. There was a frenzy about her like none they had ever seen. Items were printed about her constantly, and photographs. The public ate her up, and Desmond Williams kept feeding them exactly what they wanted. Just enough of her to excite them and keep the love affair alive, but never so much that they tired of her. It was a fine art, and he was brilliant at it. And Nancy Firestone was feeding him all the little personal details they needed. And she continued to be a huge help to Cassie.

She was scheduled to do a commercial for a breakfast cereal for kids, and an ad for her favorite magazine, and when Nick saw it at the airport one day, he tossed it in the garbage. He was furious and railed at her father.

"How can you let her do that? What is she doing, selling breakfast cereal, or flying?"

"Looks like both to me." He didn't really mind. He didn't think women belonged in serious aviation anyway. "Her mother loves it."

"When does she find time to fly?" Nick groused at him, and Pat grinned.

"I wouldn't know, Stick. Why don't you fly out and ask her?" Pat was surprisingly calm about all of it, now that she was out in California. The only thing he was sorry about was that she didn't have time to go to school, but she was flying some damn gorgeous airplanes. And he couldn't help being proud of her, though he never actually said it.

Nick had thought of flying out to see her several times, but he

165

hadn't had time to get away. With Cassie gone, he seemed to be doing more flying than ever, in spite of the useful presence of Billy Nolan. But business was booming at O'Malley's. And Pat recognized more than anyone that his daughter's sudden stardom probably hadn't hurt them. The reporters had turned up there a few times too, but there wasn't much fodder for them, and after a few photographs, and a shot of the house where she'd grown up, the wire-service guys had gone back to Chicago.

Cassie's life on the West Coast seemed to move even faster than her planes. She could hardly keep up with herself, between test flights, and short runs to check out new instruments on planes, and meetings with engineers to explain their aerodynamics to her. She had gone to a few development meetings too, to better understand what direction Williams Aircraft was striving for, and Desmond himself couldn't believe the extent of her involvement. She wanted to know everything there was to know about his planes. He was flattered and impressed, and he was enormously proud of his good judgment. He had inherited an empire, which he had doubled in size in an incredibly short timespan. At thirty-four, he was one of the richest men in the country, if not the world, and he could have had or done almost anything he wanted. He had been married twice, and divorced both times, had no children, and the only thing he cared about, or loved with any passion at all, was his business. People came and went in his life, and there was always plenty of talk about his women, but the only thing that mattered to him were his planes, and being at the very top of the aviation business. And for the moment, Cassie O'Malley was helping him get what he wanted.

He loved Cassie's remarkable understanding about planes, and her naive but clear perceptions about his business. She wasn't afraid to express herself, or even, when necessary, to confront him. He liked seeing her at meetings, liked the fact that she cared enough to be there. He was thrilled with the flying records she'd set too. She dared almost anything, within reason. The only thing she seemed hesitant about, and often balked at going to, were the social events, which he insisted were critical, and Cassie thought were nonsense.

"But *why?*" She argued constantly with Nancy Firestone. "I can't stay out all night, and fly intelligently at four o'clock in the morning."

"Then start later. Mr. Williams will understand. He *wants* you to go out in the evening."

"But I don't want to." Cassie's natural stubbornness hadn't been left in Illinois, and she had every intention of winning. "I'd rather stay home and read about his airplanes."

"That's not what Mr. Williams wants," Nancy said firmly, and so far she had usually won the argument, but there were a few times when Cassie escaped her. She preferred walking on the beach, or being alone at night, writing letters to Nick, or her sisters, or her mother. She missed her family terribly, and the familiar people she had grown up with. And even writing to Nick made her heart ache. Sometimes she felt as though the air was being pressed out of her as she wrote to him and told him what she was doing. She missed flying with him, and arguing with him and telling him how wrong he was, or what a fool. She wanted to tell him how much she missed him, but it always sounded strange to her in a letter. And more often than not, she tore it up, and just told him about the planes she was flying.

She never mentioned her social life to him, or to anyone, it didn't mean anything to her, no matter how much they wrote about it in the papers. Nancy had found a lot of young men to escort her, most of whom knew nothing about planes, and some of them were actors who needed to be seen too. It was all about being "seen," and where she went, and who you were "seen" with. She didn't want to be seen with any of them, and most of the time, they just posed for photographs and then took her home, and she would collapse into bed, relieved to be rid of them. The only thing she really loved about her new movie-star life was the flying.

And the flying was incredible. Sailing into the dawn in the Phaeton, breaking all records for speed, was the sweetest thing she had ever done, and probably the most dangerous. But much to her own surprise, with the incredible machines, she was honing her skills here. She was learning how to handle very heavy planes, learning how to compensate for any problems they had, signaling them to the engineers, and correcting them right along with them. Her input was valued here, her views, they admired the way she flew, and they understood everything she wanted. It was every pilot's dream to be in the seat she was in, and as long as she was in the air, there was no question about it. She loved it.

She was stepping out of an Army pursuit plane with a Merlin engine on it for more speed, one afternoon, after a short flight over Las Vegas to make some notes for the design team, when a hand reached up to her and helped her down, and she was surprised to see it was Desmond Williams. He was as impeccable as ever, and his hair blew a little off his face in the soft breeze and he looked suddenly less rigid, and much younger than the other times she'd seen him.

"Did you have a good flight?"

"I did. But the Merlin engine was disappointing here. It still didn't give us what we wanted out of this plane. We have to try something else. But I've got some ideas I want to kick around with the design team tomorrow. The plane was pulling to port on takeoff too, which is a real problem." She always thought of his planes, and the problems they needed to conquer. At night she dreamed of them, and by day she pressed them to their limits. And as he glanced at her, he was more impressed than ever with what he was hearing. She was a gold mine.

"Sounds like you need a break." He smiled at her, as she pushed her hair out of her eyes and smoothed her uniform. She still longed for her overalls sometimes, and the old days of never caring how she looked when she flew. To Cassie, it didn't matter. "How about dinner tonight?"

She was surprised at the invitation, and wondered if he had something on his mind. Maybe he was unhappy with her. He had never invited her out before, and their dealings with each other had been strictly business.

"Is something wrong, Mr. Williams?" She looked worried and he laughed at the question. She wondered if maybe he was firing her, and he shook his head and looked at her in amusement.

"The only thing wrong is that you work too hard, and have absolutely no idea what a miracle you are. Of course nothing's wrong. I just thought it might be nice to have dinner."

"Sure," she said shyly, wondering what it would be like to have dinner with him. He was so handsome and so perfect and so smart, and so rich, that he scared her. Nancy always said what good company he was, and how pleasant, and she seemed to know him well. But he still frightened Cassie more than a little.

"What do you like? French? Italian? There are some wonderful restaurants in Los Angeles. I imagine you've been to them all by now."

"Yes, I have." She looked him right in the eye, overcoming her shyness for a moment. "And I wish I hadn't."

"So I hear." He smiled at her. "I understand you've been chafing at your social schedule." He looked almost fatherly for an instant, despite his age, and Cassie could see why Nancy liked him.

"That's putting it mildly. I just don't see why I have to go out every night if I'm going to fly for you at four o'clock the next morning."

"Maybe you should get a later start." He said practically, but she groaned in answer.

"That's what Nancy said. But flying is the important part. Going out doesn't matter."

He stopped walking with her then, and looked down at her, and she was totally surprised to realize how much taller he was. In more ways than one, he was a man of great stature. "It's *all* important, Cassie. All of it. Not just the flying. But the going out too. Look what the papers say about you . . . what the public thinks now . . . how much they love you . . . Look how much

169

that means, how much access that gives you to them, how much weight you carry with the public after only a month here. They want to know what you eat, what you read, what you think. Don't ever underestimate that. It's the power of the American public."

"I don't get it," she said, looking like a kid, and he smiled at her. He already knew her better than that. He had an uncanny sense about people.

"Yes, you do," he said quietly. "You just don't want to. You want to play the game on your terms. But you'll get a lot more out of it in the end, if you play my way. Trust me."

"Having dinner at the Cocoanut Grove, or Mocambo, isn't going to make me a better flier."

"No, but it will make you exciting . . . glamorous . . . someone people want to know more about. It will make them listen to you, and once they're listening, you can tell them anything you want to."

"And if I'm asleep at home in bed, they won't listen?" She grinned, but she had gotten his point, and she was intrigued by it, and he knew it.

"All they'll hear then, Miss O'Malley, is you snoring."

She laughed at him, and he left her at the hangar a few minutes later. He had promised to pick her up at seven o'clock, and said he would tell her later where they were going.

She told Nancy who she was having dinner with when she got home, but she had already heard from Miss Fitzpatrick what her dinner plans were. There were no secrets at Williams Aircraft. And she suspected where he would take her, probably Perino's. Nancy helped her pick out a particularly sophisticated dress, and assured Cassie that it was just the sort of thing he really liked.

"Why do you think he wants to have dinner with me?" Cassie asked worriedly. She was still wondering if he was secretly displeased with her about something. Maybe he really was annoyed that she complained about going out at night, and wanted to scold her.

"I think he wants to take you out because you're so ugly," Nancy teased. She had begun treating Cassie like her daughter. In some ways, Cassie was still a child, not unlike Janie. In fact, Jane and Cassie had hit it off splendidly on the two occasions Nancy had invited her to dinner. She would have invited her more frequently, but Cassie never had time for a private evening. "Now go wash your face and stop worrying. He's a perfect gentleman." He always was, no matter what he wanted, business or pleasure. Desmond Williams had a brilliant mind and impeccable manners. What he did not have was a heart, or at least, that was what women said. If he did, no one had found it yet. But Nancy knew it was not Cassie's heart Desmond wanted. He wanted her loyalty, and her life, her mind, her judgment about planes, and her courage. It was what he wanted from everyone. He wanted everything, except what was really important. And in return, he would take care of her, in the ways he understood, with contracts and money.

Cassie was ready right on time, and he appeared downstairs in a brand-new Packard. He was a man who liked machines, and he had bought every exciting car there was to own, at one time or another. The Zephyr she'd seen him in back home had already been shipped to California.

She was wearing a slinky black dress Nancy had picked out for her, and black silk stockings and black satin platform shoes that made her look even taller. But he was still taller than she was, and her figure looked fabulous in the black dress. Her hair was piled high on her head in loose curls, and in the month since she'd been in L.A. she had learned to do her makeup to perfection.

"Wow! If I do say so myself," Desmond beamed at her, as they headed toward the city, "that's quite an outfit."

"I was going to wear my overalls," she grinned mischievously, "but Nancy sent them to the cleaners."

"I can't say I'm disappointed," he teased back. They chatted easily all the way into town, about a new plane she knew he was designing. There were questions she had about the fuselage, and her queries about the design, as usual, impressed him deeply.

171

"How did you ever get to know so much about planes, Cass?"

"I just love them a lot. You know, like dolls, for some kids. I've just played with planes all my life. I put my first engine back together when I was nine. I've been doing it since I was a little kid. My father put me to work when I was five, but then he had a fit when I learned to fly. Engines were okay, but flying was for guys, not for women."

"It's hard to believe." He looked amused. To him, it sounded like the dark ages.

"I know." She grinned, thinking fondly of her father. "He's an adorable old dinosaur and I love him. He threw your card away that day, you know. The first time you came to the airport."

"I thought he'd do something like that, he and his partner. That's why I came back." He glanced over at her as they reached L.A. "I'm glad I did. When I think what I would have missed. What this country would have lost. It would have been a tragedy." He made it sound very dramatic, and she laughed. What he said was very frightening, but it always sounded like nonsense to Cassie. She knew her own worth, or she thought she did. She was a pretty good pilot, but she wasn't the oracle he pretended she was, or the genius . . . or the beauty . . . but Americans were already beginning to know different. They agreed with Desmond Williams.

"Where are we going tonight?" she asked with mild curiosity. She recognized the neighborhood, but hadn't guessed what restaurant. He told her they were going to the Trocadero.

And when they stepped inside, she saw instantly how glamorous it was, and how luxurious. The lights were dim, and the band was playing a rumba.

"You haven't been here yet, Cassie, have you?"

She shook her head, visibly impressed by her surroundings, and by being there with him. She was twenty years old, and she had never seen anything like that. "No, sir," she said, and he leaned closer to her and touched her arm.

"You could call me Desmond." He smiled at her, and she

blushed. It was odd being so friendly with him. He was so important, he was her boss, and he was so much older.

"Yes, sir . . . I mean, Desmond . . ." She was still blushing in
the darkness as they were led to an important table.

"Of course Sir Desmond has a certain ring to it. I hadn't
thought of that before." He made her laugh easily, and he helped
her order. He made her feel surprisingly comfortable, even though
everything she was experiencing was new. But he never made her
feel ignorant or foolish. He treated it all as a great opportunity for
her, and for him. He always let her know how lucky he felt to be
there with her. He was a master at the fine art of putting her at
ease, and before their dinner came, he had her laughing and dancing, and completely comfortable with him. So much so that she
danced in his arms as though she had been doing it for a dozen
years, and when the photographers appeared after dinner, they
got a wonderful photograph of her smiling up at him, as though
she adored him.

She was uncomfortable about it the next day, when she saw the
newspaper on her way to work. The photograph somehow managed to convey the impression that she was involved with him,
which she certainly wasn't. But there was something very intimate
about the way he looked at her, as she stood next to him, and yet
nothing inappropriate, or even faintly romantic, had ever happened. He was her boss, the man who had "discovered" her, and
given her a great opportunity. And she was grateful to him for
that. But there was absolutely nothing else between them. She
wondered if anyone at work would make a comment about it, but
no one did, until three days later when she got a call from Nick.
He was flying a mail run to San Diego that night, and he could
come up to see her the following morning. It would be Saturday
and she was free to spend the day with him. She was supposed to
go to a charity ball with one of Nancy's young friends that night,
but for Nick, she'd gladly cancel.

"So, is Williams giving you the rush, or are you falling for him?" he asked bluntly after he told her he'd meet her at her apartment as soon as he came up from San Diego.

"What's that supposed to mean?" She was annoyed at his assumption.

"I was in Chicago yesterday, Cass. I saw the picture of you two in the paper. Looks pretty cozy." There was an edge to his voice she'd never heard there before, and she didn't like it.

"I happen to work for him. And he took me out to dinner. That was it. He has about as much interest in me as he has in his engineers, so knock it off."

"I think you're being naive. And those didn't look like work clothes." He was angry and jealous, and sorry her father had ever let her come out here. The flying she was doing for Williams was too damn dangerous. But it wasn't just the flying he was upset about. It was the look on Desmond's face as he looked at her in the photograph in the paper.

"It was just a business dinner, Nick. He was just being nice taking me out. He was probably bored to death. And believe it or not, those are my work clothes." She was referring to the slinky black dress she'd been wearing. "My chaperone buys me everything, and they send me out every night like a trained dog to show off and get my picture taken. They call it public relations."

"Doesn't sound like work to me. Or flying." He was consumed with annoyance, and the loneliness of not having seen her in over a month. He had been aching to see her. But she hadn't had time to get home yet. It had shocked him to discover how much he missed her. He felt as though he'd lost a limb, or his best friend. And he didn't like the idea of Williams taking her out to dinner.

"We'll talk about it when you're here," she said quietly, sounding more grown-up than she had at home. She had already changed, but she didn't know it. And she had already acquired a lot of big-city polish. "How long can you stay?"

"I've got to be out by six o'clock. I've got to get back with some mail." She was instantly disappointed, and she would have no excuse to cancel her "date" to go to the ball to benefit children with infantile paralysis.

"Well, we'll make the best of it. Try and get here early."

"As early as I can, kid. I'm not flying the fancy stuff you are."

"You don't need 'em. The way you fly, you could fly egg crates and get more out of them than anything I see here," she said warmly.

"Stop flattering an old man," he said, sounding mellower than he had at the beginning of the call. "I'll see you tomorrow."

She could hardly wait, and she was up as usual at three-thirty, anxious for him to arrive. It seemed endless, before he rang her bell at seven-fifteen that morning. She flew down the stairs and threw herself into his arms so hard she almost knocked him down. He was stunned by the sheer beauty of her, and the force of her affection. She had missed him too, even more than she'd realized. She missed their confidences, and their long talks, and their flying.

"Hey, wait a minute, you . . . give a guy a chance, before you knock the wind out of me . . ." She was kissing him and hugging him, she was like a lost child who had finally found her parents. "Hey, it's okay . . . it's okay . . ." There were tears in her eyes as she clung to him, and he held her so close he wanted never to let her go. She had never looked as good to him, or felt as good in his arms, and he had to force himself to step back and release her. He would have liked to stay that way forever. "Wow . . . don't you look fine." He smiled. He noticed the new haircut, and the makeup, and she was wearing beige slacks and a white sweater. She looked surprisingly like Hepburn or Hayworth. "You don't look like you've been suffering," he teased, and then he whistled when he saw the apartment. "My, my . . . talk about hardship . . ."

"Isn't it great?" she beamed at him, and showed him around. He was very impressed, and he had to remind himself that this was the little girl he had known since she was a baby. This was not some movie star he had just met. This was Pat O'Malley's daughter.

"Looks like you got lucky, Cass," he said fairly. But he also thought she deserved it. There was no reason for her not to have all this. But he still worried about her. "Do they treat you right?"

"They do everything for me. Buy me clothes, feed me, I have a maid, she's the nicest woman you've ever met. Her name is Lavinia. I have a chaperone named Nancy, who buys me clothes and sets up everything for me, like all the events I have to go to, my escorts, the people I see." She chatted on and Nick looked at her strangely.

"Your *escorts*? They set you up with men?" He looked startled, and none too pleased, as she served him the breakfast she had made for him, and fried some eggs while he waited.

"Sort of. But not really. Some of them aren't really . . . I mean . . . they don't really like women, you know . . . but they're friends of Nancy's, or she knows who they are. Some of them are actors who need to be seen, and we . . . I . . . we go to events, or parties and get our photographs taken together." She looked embarrassed as she explained it to him, it wasn't the part of her work she liked best by any means, but after Desmond's explanation the other night, she was trying to accept it. "I don't like doing it, but it's important to Desmond."

"Desmond?" Nick raised an eyebrow as he ate the eggs she had made him. They were delicious. But the sudden mention of Williams in such familiar terms made him stop eating.

"He thinks public relations is the most important thing in business."

"What about flying? Is that important to him, or do you even get to do that?"

"Come on, Nick, be fair. I have to do what they ask me to. Look at all this." She waved around at the spacious modern kitchen and the rest of the apartment beyond it. "Look what they're doing for me. If they want me to go out and have my photograph taken, I owe it to them. It's not such a big deal." But he looked angry as he listened.

"That's bullshit, and you know it. You didn't come out here to be a model, or go to finishing school, Cass. And the only thing you *owe* them is to risk your ass testing their planes, and break any record you can. That's what you *owe* them. The rest is up to you, or at least it should be. Williams doesn't own you, for chrissake. Or does he?" He looked at her ominously, and she shook her head. He made her feel ashamed for going along with the plan. But she *did* feel she owed it to them, and she could also understand what Williams wanted. He wanted her to become a star, in order to further her career in aviation, and publicize his planes. That wasn't totally wrong, and the other women in aviation had done their share of it too. You did what you had to.

"I don't think you're being fair," she said quietly.

"I think you're being used, and it makes me mad as hell," he said, pushing his plate away, and then taking a sip of his coffee. "He wants to use you, Cass. I can smell it."

"That's not true. He wants to help me, Nick. He's already done a lot for me, and I just got here."

"Like what? Take you out dancing the other night? How often has he done that?"

"Just that once. He was being nice. And he was trying to explain to me how important it is to do the social things too, because Nancy told him how much I hate it."

"Well, at least I know you haven't been completely snowed by him. How often have you been out with him?" he asked pointedly, and she looked him square in the eye when she answered.

"I told you just that once. And he was totally polite and respectful. He was a perfect gentleman. He danced with me twice, and it just so happened that the second time he danced with me they took our picture."

"And that was an accident, I suppose." He marveled at her innocence. It was all so obvious to him. He had thought it a great opportunity at first, but only if their main focus had been on her

177

flying. All this social nonsense, and going out, and courting the press told him something very different. It told him Williams was using her in a much broader sense. And he knew she was too young to understand it. And what more did Williams want from her? Did he want her for himself? As young and naive as she was, she would be inevitably dazzled by him and Nick suddenly realized he didn't like the prospect of that either. She was too young to be involved with a man like him. And besides, Desmond Williams didn't love her. Nick had said all this to Pat, and even suggested that Williams might have unsuitable designs on her, and he had tried to rile Pat up about it. But her father was under Oona's spell and she was completely enthralled to be seeing her daughter in newsreels. And Pat wouldn't have done anything to interfere with it. She was safe, she was well, and from what she said in her letters, they were treating her like royalty. She even had a chaperone, so how unsuitable could that be? And they were paying her a ransom on top of it. What more could she ask for?

"Don't you realize," Nick went on, pressing her, "that either the guy has the hots for you, or he set it up to look that way by taking you someplace where you'd be seen, and photographed. He probably tipped them off that he'd be taking you there. So now America has more than just a pretty face to fall in love with, they have a romance. Dashing tycoon Desmond Williams courts America's sweetheart from the Midwest, girl next door and flying ace, Cassie O'Malley. Cassie, wake up. The guy is using you, and he's great at it. It's working. He's going to make you the biggest name there is, just to sell his goddamn planes and then what?" That was what worried Nick. What if he married her? The thought of it made him feel sick, but he didn't say that.

"What difference does it make? What's wrong with it?" Cassie didn't see all the dangers he did.

"He's doing it for himself, for his business, not for you. He's not sincere. He doesn't give a damn. This is business to him. He's exploiting you, Cass, and it scares me." Everything about Williams, and his plans for Cassie, scared him.

178

"Why?" That was what she didn't understand. Why was he so against it? And why was he so suspicious of Desmond Williams? He had done only good things for her, but Nick saw other dangers.

"Look what happened to Earhart. She got too big for herself, she did something she never should have . . . a lot of people thought she wasn't capable of that last trip, and she obviously wasn't. What if he sets you up for something like that? What if that's what he's leading up to? You'll get hurt, Cass . . ." He felt his heart squeeze as he thought of it, and all he wanted to do was take her back to Good Hope where he knew she'd be safe forever.

"He's not doing that, Nick. I swear. He has no plans for me. At least not that I know of. And I'm a better flier than she was anyway." It was an outrageous thing to say, and she laughed as she said it. But Nick took her seriously, as he sat there and watched her. She had gotten still lovelier in the month she'd been away and she didn't even know it.

"You are faster, as a matter of fact. And you don't know what his plans are. This guy isn't doing it for small potatoes. He's got his eye on the big time."

"Maybe you're right," she said, doubtfully. Maybe he did have a world tour in mind. "If he mentions anything about one, I'll tell you. I promise."

"Be careful." He frowned at her, still worried about her, and lit a cigarette, as she closed her eyes and sniffed the familiar fumes of his Camels. They reminded her of her father's airport . . . and of Nick . . . and the old days, of meeting at the airfield in Prairie City. Just sitting there with him made her desperately homesick, for him, and all the people she loved there. But she had missed him almost more than anyone.

In the end he relaxed, and enjoyed the fact that he was finally with her again. Being away from her for so long had almost driven him crazy. And day after day, he had thought of new plots that Williams might be hatching to exploit her. He finally stopped nagging her about Williams's plans for her, and the fact that she was being used, and they had a nice afternoon. They went for a long walk on the beach, and sat on the sand in the August sun, looking out at the ocean. It felt good just sitting side by side again, and they sat for a long time together in silence.

"There's going to be a war in Europe soon," he said prophetically, when they started chatting again. "The signs are as clear as that sun up there," he said unhappily. "Hitler won't be controlled. They're going to have to stop him."

"Do you think we'll get into it eventually?" She loved talking to him about politics again. She had no one to talk to here. She was too solitary and too busy. Nancy talked to her about clothes, and her "escorts" just posed for pictures.

"Most people think we won't get into it," he said quietly. "But I think we'll have to."

"And you?" She knew him well. Too well. She wondered if that was what he was telling her. That he felt the same pull he had felt twenty years before. She hoped not. "Would you go?"

"I'm probably too old to go." He was thirty-eight, and not old by any means. But he could have stayed home if he'd wanted to. Pat was too old to fight another war. But Nick still had choices. "But I'd probably want to." He smiled at her, his hair flying in the salt air, as hers did. They were sitting side by side on the sand, their shoulders touching and their hands. It was so comforting to have him near her. She had relied on him for so long, and learned so much from him. She missed him more than anyone at home, and he had found that her absence was like a physical ache that still had not abated.

"I don't want you to go," she said unhappily, looking into the blue eyes she knew so well, with the small crow's-feet beside them. She couldn't bear the thought of losing him. She wanted to make him promise he wouldn't go to another war in Europe.

"I couldn't bear it if anything happened to you, Nick." She said it so softly he could hardly hear her.

"We take the same risks every day," he said honestly. "You can run into trouble tomorrow, so can I. I think we both know that."

"That's different."

"Not really. I worry about you out here too. Flying those planes is risky business. You're dealing with high speeds, and heavy machines, and altered engines at unusual altitudes. You're looking for problems and trying to set records. That's about as dangerous as you get," he said grimly. "I keep worrying that you're going to crash somewhere in one of his damn test planes." He looked at her seriously and they both recognized the danger. "Besides, your dad says women pilots can't fly worth a damn." He grinned and she laughed.

"Thanks."

"I know what a lousy teacher you had."

"Yeah." She smiled up at him, and touched his face with her fingers. "I miss you a lot . . . I miss the days when we used to hang out and talk on our runway."

"So do I," he said softly, and curled her fingers into his. "Those were some special times." She nodded, and neither of them said anything for a long time, and then they walked along the beach for a while and talked about family and friends back home. Her brother hadn't flown since the air show, and her father didn't seem to mind. Chris was busy with school now. Colleen was pregnant again. To Cassie, it seemed endless. And Bobby had started seeing Peggy Bradshaw. She was widowed and alone with two small kids, and Nick had seen him more than once, driving his truck to her little cottage.

"She'd be good for him," Cassie said fairly, surprised at how little she felt for him. It was only amazing that they had been engaged for a year and a half. They never should have been. "And now she'll hate flying as much as he does," she said sadly, thinking of the horrifying accident at the air show. It had been so awful.

"You'd have been miserable with him," Nick said, looking down at her possessively. He wanted to stay right here and protect her, from being used, or endangered.

"I know. I think I even knew that then. I just didn't know how to get out of it without hurting his feelings. And I really thought I was supposed to marry him. I don't know what I'm going to do," she said, looking out at the horizon. "One of these days everyone's going to want me to grow up and get out of the sky, and then what am I going to do, Nick? I don't think I could stand it."

"Maybe you can figure out a way to have both one day. A real life, and flying. I never have, but you're smarter than I am." He was always honest with her. Most of them made a choice. He had made his. And so had she, for the moment.

"I don't see why you can't have both. But nobody else seems to believe that."

"It's not much of a life for the other guy, and most people are smart enough to know that. Bobby was. So was my wife."

"Yeah," she nodded, "I guess so."

They went back to her apartment after that, and talked some more. And he promised to tell her mother all about where she lived. And afterward she drove him to the airport. She got into the familiar Bellanca with him, and she almost cried. It was like going home. She sat there with him for a long time, and then finally, she got out, once he was on the runway.

He looked down at her with the smile she had known and loved all her life, and she wanted to cry and beg him to take her with him. But they had their lives to lead. He had to get back to Illinois, and she had signed a contract with Desmond Williams. Most people would have died for what he had given her, but a part of her wanted to throw it all away and go home to where life was simpler.

"Take care of yourself, kid. Don't let them take too many pictures." He smiled at her. He still didn't trust what Williams had up his sleeve. But he felt better about Cassie now that he had seen her. She had her head on her shoulders. And she wasn't being snowed by anyone. She also didn't appear to be in love with Desmond Williams.

"Come back soon, Nick."

"I'll try." His eyes held hers for a long time. There was so much he wanted to say to her, but this wasn't the time, or the moment. "Say hi to everyone . . . Mom . . . Dad . . . Chris . . . Billy . . ." She was lingering, wishing he would stay. But she knew he couldn't.

"Yeah." He looked down at her, wishing he could swoop her up with him. He had wanted to do that for a long time, but he knew now he never would. It wasn't in their destinies. All he had to do was learn to accept that. "Make sure you don't run off with Desmond Williams. I'll come after you, if you do. Course your mama might shoot me for destroying your big chance."

"Tell her not to worry," Cassie laughed. That was one thing that she was sure would never happen. "Tell her I love her." And then as he revved up his engines, she had to shout at him. "I love you, Nick . . . thanks for coming."

He nodded, wanting to tell her he loved her too, but he didn't. He couldn't. He saluted her, signaled her to step back, and a few minutes later he was circling lazily and dipping his wings over the Pasadena Airport. She watched him as long as she could, until he disappeared, a tiny speck on the horizon.

CHAPTER

12

Exactly two weeks after Nick's visit to L.A., Germany invaded Poland, and the world was aghast at the destruction Hitler wrought there. And two days after that, on September third, Britain and France declared war on Germany. It had happened at last; there was war in Europe.

Cassie called home to the airport when she heard, but Nick was out, and her father was taking some passengers to Cleveland. She had lunch with Desmond that day, and he had spoken to the President only that morning. There was no question, the United States was planning to stay out of the war in Europe. And it was a relief to hear that.

She told him she wanted to go home anyway, and Desmond lent her one of his personal planes for the weekend. She had been planning to go home for a weekend since July, and she never had any free time. So this was the perfect opportunity, and no one objected.

She landed at her father's airport late Friday night. She had left L.A. at noon, and got to Good Hope at eight-thirty local time. There was no one there, but it was still light as she came in on the long east-west runway, and taxied to a slow stop. She tied down her plane, and walked to the old truck she knew her father kept there. She hadn't told anyone she was coming. She wanted to surprise them. And she did. She slipped into the house after nine o'clock that night. Her parents were already in bed, and her mother almost fainted when she walked out of her room in her nightgown the next morning.

"Oh, my God!" her mother screamed, "Pat!" He came running out of their room and grinned when he saw her.

"Hi, Ma . . . Hi, Dad . . . I thought I'd drop in and say hi." She beamed at them.

"You're a sly one." Her father hugged her with a broad smile, and her mother cooed and clucked, made her an enormous breakfast, and woke Chris, who was pleased to see her.

"What's it like being a movie star?" her father teased. He still wasn't completely sure he approved of it, but everyone in town seemed to think it was great stuff, and it was hard to ignore that.

"Nick said you live in a palace," her mother said, as she looked Cassie over carefully. She looked healthy and well, and other than a good haircut and beautifully manicured red nails, she didn't look any different.

"It's a pretty nice place," Cassie conceded with a grin. "I'm glad to hear he liked it."

They sat around talking about her life in Los Angeles for a while, and finally she got dressed and rode with her father to the airport. She was happy to see all her old friends, and Billy gave a huge whoop of glee as soon as he saw her. She put on a pair of old overalls, and walked out to work on one of the planes with him, and half an hour later she heard Nick's old truck drive in. And

186

she looked up and grinned. But he didn't come out to the hangar to see her until lunchtime. She figured he was busy, and she'd see him in a while, but she was happy just knowing that she was near him.

"You guys sure start work late around here," she teased when she first saw him. "I'm at fourteen thousand by four A.M. every morning."

"Yeah? How come," he grinned, obviously elated to see her, "you meet your hairdresser up there?" His eyes danced, and his heart was pounding as he looked at her. His feelings for her were beginning to worry him. Maybe it was just as well she was living in California. Lately, it was getting harder and harder to control what he felt about her.

"Very funny."

"I hear the Movietone guys will be here at three"—he grinned at Billy and two of the other men—"better get clean clothes on."

"That'll be a nice change for you, Stick," she shot back at him, and he leaned against the plane she'd been working on with Billy, and gave her an appraising look. She looked better than ever.

"Did you bring your chaperone with you?" he teased.

"I figured I could handle you myself."

"Yeah," he nodded slowly, "you probably could. Want to go have something to eat?" He invited her in an undertone, which was unusual. It was rare for him to take her anywhere. Usually, they just hung out together at the airport.

"Sure." She followed him to his truck, and he drove her to Paoli's dairy. They had a lunchroom in the rear, and they made good sandwiches and homemade ice cream.

"Hope this'll do. It's not exactly the Brown Derby."

"I'll manage." She was just so happy being with him, she'd have gone anywhere and loved it.

He ordered roast beef sandwiches for them both, and a chocolate milk shake for her. All he wanted to drink was black coffee.

"It's not my birthday, you know," she reminded him. She was

187

still impressed that he had taken her out to lunch. She couldn't even remember the last time he'd done that. If ever.

"I figure you're so spoiled now, eating beef jerky in the back hangar wouldn't do it." He shrugged, but he looked desperately happy to see her. They were halfway through lunch, and she noticed he wasn't eating much, when she realized there was more to it than just taking her out to eat. He looked uncomfortable suddenly and a little worried.

"What's up, Stick? You rob a bank?"

"Not yet. But I'm working on it." But the jokes ended there. He looked into her eyes and the moment she looked at him, she knew. And she said the words even before he did.

"You're going?" The words caught in her throat, and her milk shake soured instantly in her stomach when he nodded. "Oh, Nick . . . no . . . but you don't have to. We're not in it."

"We will be eventually, whatever they say. And I'll bet Williams knows it too. He's probably counting on it. He'll sell a lot of airplanes. I don't believe all this stuff about the U.S. staying out of it. And it doesn't matter if we do. They need help over there. I'm going to England to join the RAF. I made some inquiries, and they need all the guys they can get. I've got what they need, and no one really needs me here. They don't need a genius to fly mail runs to Cincinnati."

"But they don't need you to get shot down in a war that's not yours." Tears filled her eyes as she said it. "Does Dad know?"

He nodded. He hated telling her. But he had wanted to tell her himself. He had told Pat that the minute he knew she was home, and Pat had agreed to let him tell her. "I told him yesterday. He said he knew anyway." And then he looked at her strangely. "I'll be back, Cass. I've got a lot of years left to do this kind of thing. And who knows? Maybe I'll grow up this time. There's a lot of things I never did with my life after the last one."

"You can do them here, you don't have to risk your life in order to change what you don't like in your life here."

"I don't like how lazy I've been, how easy I've made it on

myself. I just cruised for the last twenty years, because it was easy. It went by so fast I forgot where I was. Now I'm here, I'm halfway through, or thereabouts, and I've wasted a lot of time. I'm not going to do that next time." She wasn't sure what he meant, but it was obvious he had regrets about things he hadn't done, relationships he hadn't bothered with. He always thought he had time. And he did. But in some ways he had lacked courage. He had never wanted to get married again, or to care too much about anyone, or get too involved, or have kids of his own. He never wanted to risk anything on the ground. He didn't want to lose. But he didn't mind dying. It was an odd kind of cowardice peculiar to most of them; they were brave in the air, but on land they were terrible cowards.

"Don't go . . ." she whispered over the remains of their lunch. She didn't know what to say to stop him, but she wanted to more than anything. She didn't want to lose him.

"I have to."

"No, you *don't*!" She raised her voice at him, and people turned around at other tables. "You don't have to do anything!"

"Neither did you," he suddenly raged back, "but you've made choices with your life. I have a right to that too. I'm not going to sit here while they fight a war without me." They took their battle outside and shouted at each other in the September sunshine.

"Are you so important then? You're the only flier who can do it right for them? For God's sake, Nick, grow up. Stay here . . . don't get yourself killed in a fight that's not yours, or even ours . . . Nick . . . please . . ." She was crying, and before he knew it, he was holding her and telling her how much he loved her. He had promised himself he never would, and now he couldn't stop himself any longer.

"Baby, don't . . . please . . . I love you so much . . . but I've got to do this . . . and when I come back, things'll be different. Maybe you'll be through playing Skygirl for Desmond Williams by then, and I'll have learned something I never figured out

189

the first time. I want so much more than I have now . . . And, Cassie, I never figured out how to get it."

"All you have to do is reach out and take it . . . that's all . . ." She was clinging to him, and he was holding her, and all she wanted suddenly was to go away somewhere with him and forget the war, but there was nowhere to run now.

"It's not as simple as all that," he said slowly, looking down at her. There was so much he wanted to say to her, so much he didn't dare. And maybe he never would. He just didn't have the answers.

They walked back to his truck hand in hand, and when they got to the airport he drove to the hangar where they kept the Jenny. It was the plane he had taught her in, and she knew without a word where they were going. She got into the front seat, out of deference to him, since the instructor always sat in the rear seat, and a few minutes later they had done all their checks, and were taxiing down the runway. Her father saw them take off and he didn't say anything. He knew Nick must have told her he was going.

They reached the old airstrip, and Nick let her land, and they sat beneath their familiar tree. She laid her head against him, and they sat in the soft grass, looking up at the sky. It was hard to believe that there was a war somewhere, and Nick was really going.

"Why?" she said miserably after a while, the tears rolling slowly down her cheeks, and then her eyes met his and he thought his heart would break as he touched her face, and gently wiped her tears away with his fingers. "Why do you have to go?" After all this time, he had told her he loved her, and now he was leaving, maybe even forever.

"Because I believe in what I'm doing. I believe in free men, and honor, and a safe world, and all those things I'm going to defend in the skies over England."

"You did that once. Let someone else do it this time, Nick. It's not your problem."

"Yes, it is. And I've got nothing important to do here. Even though that's my own fault."

"So you're going because you're bored." There was always a little bit of that in all men, that and the spirit of the hunter. But there were good motives there too, and she knew that. She just thought it was foolish of him to go now, and she didn't want him to get hurt. But he swore he wouldn't.

"I'm too good to get hurt," he said, teasing her.

"You fly like shit when you're tired," she said, not entirely believing it, but he laughed.

"I'll be sure to get lots of sleep. What about you?" he said, frowning. "You're flying those damn heavy planes over the desert, don't think I don't know the chances you take testing them. Plenty of guys have gotten killed doing it, and they probably flew better than you do." It reminded her of Nancy's husband when he said it and she nodded. She couldn't deny the dangers of her job, but she was good at what she did, and there were no Germans shooting at her over Las Vegas.

"I'm careful."

"We all are. Sometimes that's not enough. Sometimes you just have to be lucky."

"Be lucky . . . please . . ." she whispered to him, and he looked at her for a long time, and then without a word, he did what he had wanted to for so long, and never dared. What he had never let himself do, and thought he never would. But now he knew he had to. He couldn't leave without letting her know how much he loved her. He leaned down ever so gently, and kissed her. And she kissed him back as she had kissed no man before him. There had been no man . . . only a boy . . . and now, Nick, the man she had loved since she was old enough to remember.

"I love you," he whispered into her hair, breathlessly, wishing there could be more, but he knew there couldn't. "I always have . . . I always will . . . I want to give you so much, Cass . . . but I have nothing to give you . . ."

"How can you say that?" He broke her heart with his words. "I've been in love with you since I was five . . . I've always loved you. That's all we need. I don't want anything else."

"You should have lots more than that . . . you should have a house and kids . . . you should have a lot of things, like all the things they've given you in California. But they should come from your husband."

"My parents never had fancy things, but they didn't care. They had each other, and they built my father's business from a pile of dirt. I don't care if we start with nothing."

"I couldn't let you do that, Cass. And your father would kill me. I'm eighteen years older than you are."

"So what?" She was unimpressed, all she could think of now was the fact that he loved her. And she didn't want to lose him. Not after all they'd been through.

"I'm an old man," he tried to object unconvincingly, "compared to you at least. You should marry someone your age and have a mob of kids like your parents."

"I'd probably go crazy if I did. And I don't want a mob of kids. I never did. Just one or two kids would be fine." With Nick, even the prospect of children wasn't as daunting as she had once thought it.

He smiled down at her tenderly as he listened to her, trying to talk him into something impossible. He was going to war, and she had a contract to fly planes in California. But he had to admit, he liked the sound of what she was saying. Maybe someday though he doubted it. He'd never be that lucky or that foolish. She deserved so much more than he could ever give her. "I'd love to give you kids, Cassie . . . I'd love to give you everything I have to give. But I'm never going to have anything but a bunch of old planes, and a shack at the end of your father's airport."

"He'd give you half of everything, and you know it. You've earned it. You built the business with him. You know he's always wanted you to be his partner."

"It's funny, I was so young when I started out that I never

wanted to be more than a hired hand, and now I'm sorry. Maybe you're doing the right thing with that crazy job of yours, Cass. Make a bunch of money, save it up, and come back where you belong with something to show for it. I don't have zip, and I never cared . . . until you grew up, and I realized everything I didn't have to give you. That and the fact that I'm almost twice your age, and your father would probably kill me for this."

"I doubt it," Cassie said wisely. She was smarter than he was about her father. "I've always thought he wouldn't be surprised. I think he'd rather I was happy than married to the wrong man and miserable."

"You should be married to a man like Desmond Williams," he said unhappily and she laughed at him. He hated the thought of it, but Williams had so much to give her.

"And you should be married to the Queen of England. Don't be stupid, Nick. Who cares?" She smiled at him, but he was unconvinced.

"You'll care, when you're older. You're just a kid. You think your sisters are so happy being poor, or your mother?"

"My mother never complains about anything, and I think she is happy. And maybe if my sisters stopped having babies every year they wouldn't be quite as poor." Cassie had always thought they had too many children. One or two seemed sensible to her. But Glynnis was expecting her sixth, and Colleen and Megan their fifth, respectively. To Cassie it had always seemed excessive and a little scary.

He kissed her again then, thinking of the babies he would have liked to have with her, and never would. He would never allow himself the self-indulgence or the selfishness of marrying Cassie. No matter how much he loved her, or maybe because he did. She deserved so much better.

"I love you, Nick Galvin. I'm not going to run away. Or let you run away from me. I'll come over and find you, if I have to." And she would too. He knew it.

"Don't you dare. I'll have you kicked right out of England if I

193

have to. And don't you dare let Williams talk you into some goddamn world tour. I just smell that's what he has in mind for later. Just like Earhart. But with the war in Europe now, you won't be safe anywhere, not in the Pacific, and not in Europe. Stay home, Cass. Promise me . . ." He looked desperately worried and she nodded.

"You too," she said softly, and then kissed him, and he had to control himself as he felt her passion meeting his own. He lay on the ground next to her, holding her, wishing he could have her forever. "When are you going?" she finally asked him hoarsely, as he lay next to her and held her.

He hesitated for a long time and then he answered. "In four days."

"Does Dad know?" She knew it would be hard on her father, and she was sorry now that she wouldn't be there to help him.

"He does. Billy said he'd take care of things. He's a good kid and a tremendous pilot. I think he just needed to get away from his father. Old flying aces sometimes make life difficult for their kids, but I guess you wouldn't know about that, would you?" She smiled, thinking of how impossible her father had been, but lately he seemed to have mellowed.

She sat up and looked down at Nick then, wanting to know where things stood between them. "What does all this mean, Nick? We find out we love each other, and now you go? Now what? Now what am I supposed to do without you?"

"Same thing you did before," he said firmly; "go out and smile pretty for the cameras."

"What does that mean?"

"Exactly what it sounds like. Nothing's changed. You're free. And I'm going to England."

"Bullshit." She raged at him. "That's it? I love you, you love me, and nothing, so long, good-bye, I'm going to war, have a nice life, and see you when I get back. Maybe."

"You got it." He looked suddenly hardened, but he had made

up his mind a long time ago, and he was not going to change it. For her sake.

"And then what? You come home, and if we're lucky we find each other again and start over?"

"Nope," he said sadly. "If you're lucky, we find each other again, and you introduce me to your husband and kids, if I'm gone that long, and if I'm not, then you just introduce me to your husband."

"What are you? Crazy, or sick?" She looked outraged as she stared at him, suddenly wanting to hit him. What kind of game was this? But this was no game to him. Nick Galvin had promised himself years before that he wasn't going to let himself ruin Cassie's life just because he loved her.

"Haven't you been listening to me?" He was shouting at her in their secret place, but there was no one to hear them. They were safe here. "I have nothing to give you, Cass. That's not going to change while I'm gone, and it's not likely to improve when I get back, unless I rob a bank or hit it lucky in Las Vegas. You're a lot likelier to make some money than I am."

"Then go work for Desmond Williams," she said angrily. How could he be so stupid!

"My legs aren't good enough. Look, you're a commodity to him. You're a genius in the air, and look good. You're a dolly who can fly; you're gold in the bank for him, Cass. I'm just another flyboy."

"Why is that my fault?" she said angrily. "Why are you taking it out on me? What did I do, aside from get lucky?" She was crying now, and shaking with rage and frustration. Why were men so unfair sometimes? It was exhausting being a woman.

"You didn't do anything. The trouble is neither did I for the last twenty years, except fly a bunch of old planes and hang out with your father. I had a good time, we did some good things, the best of which was teach you how to fly, or teach you not to crash maybe more like it, you taught yourself to fly. But that's not enough,

Cass. I'm not going to marry you with nothing in the bank and empty pockets."

"You're a jerk!" She shouted at him through her tears. "You own three planes, and you built my father a goddamn airport."

"I may never come back, Cass," he said quietly. That was part of it too. He was not leaving her hanging there, waiting for him. It wasn't fair, not at her age. "That's a fact. I may be gone for five years. I may be gone forever. You gonna wait for that? With the life you have now, and the opportunities, that's what you want? To wait for a guy twice your age, who may leave you a penniless widow before you start? Forget it. This is my life, Cass. This is what I've made of it. This is what I want. I want to fly. No strings. No promises. That's it . . . forget it . . ."

"How can you say that?" she raged at him, but he looked at her very calmly.

"Easy. Because I love you so damn much. I want you to go out there and hit the jackpot. I want you to get everything you can get, fly everything you can lay your hands on, as long as you're safe, and I want you to be happy forever. I don't want to worry about your doing that, when I'm flying my tail off after some Kraut over the English Channel."

"You're incredibly selfish," she said angrily.

"So are most people, Cass," he said honestly, "especially fliers. If they weren't, they wouldn't do it. They wouldn't scare the hell out of the people they love, risking their lives every day, and killing themselves right under their loved ones' noses at air shows. Think of that. Think of what we do to the people we love."

"I have. A lot. But you and I both know that, that's an advantage right there. We're even."

"No we're not. You're twenty years old, for chrissake. You have a whole life ahead of you, and a great one. But I don't want you waiting for me. If I get back, and I win the Irish sweepstakes while I'm there, I'll call you."

"I hate you," she stormed, unable to move him or change his mind. Nick was as stubborn as she was.

"I figured that. I especially figured that when I kissed you." He kissed her again then, and all her fury and her rage and her sorrow exploded through her in a wave of passion that he felt with equal flame. He would have wanted to change a lot of things, but he knew he couldn't. He wanted to hold her and make love to her till they both died of pleasure. But he forced himself to let go of her before it was too late to stop. And for both of them, that moment was coming closer.

"Will you write to me?" she asked breathlessly, a little while later.

"If I can. But don't count on it. Don't worry if you don't hear from me. That's just what I don't want. I don't want you waiting for me. It's the shortest love story in the world. I love you. The End. That's it. I probably should never have told you."

"Then why did you?" she asked unhappily.

"Because I'm a selfish sonofabitch and I couldn't stand not saying it anymore. I had to fight myself not to say it each time we came here. And it almost killed me when I left you in California. I've needed to tell you for a long time. But it doesn't change anything, Cass. It's nice to know. Maybe for both of us. But I'm still going."

They went round and round about it for a long time, but she couldn't convince him not to go. And eventually, they flew back to the airport after kissing each other for a long time and nearly tearing each other's clothes off.

It was a long, sad weekend for her, and she spent a lot of time with him. And on Sunday afternoon when she left, it tore her apart as nothing before in her life had. Her father had sensed what was happening and he had talked to her before she left, but it hadn't really helped her. It made her feel closer to him, but it didn't change what was happening with Nick. She was in love with him, and he with her, and he was telling her to forget it. She didn't tell her father that in so many words, but he understood it.

*　*　*

"It's the way he is, Cass. He has to be free to do what he believes in."

"It's not our fight."

"But he wants it to be his, and he's good at it. He's a good man, Cassie."

"I know that." And then she looked unhappily up at her father. "He thinks he's too old for me."

"He is. I used to worry about him falling for you," Pat admitted, "but I think he'd do you a lot of good too. But you can't convince a man of that. He has to find it out for himself."

"He thinks you'd be angry at him."

"He knows that's not the truth . . . nor the problem . . . the problem is in his mind, what he believes, what he wants for you. You won't find the answers now, Cass. If you're lucky, he'll come back, and you can both work it out later."

"And if he doesn't?" she asked sadly.

"Then you've been loved by a fine man, and you've been lucky to know him." She clung to her father then, finding the lessons to be learned to be almost beyond bearing.

She said good-bye to her family at the house, and Nick drove her out to the airfield. He helped her untie her plane, and do all her ground checks, admiring the extraordinary machine she had brought with her, but as she revved her engines, he pulled her close to him and just held her.

"Take care of yourself . . ." she said, in anguish. "I love you."

"I love you too. Now be a good girl, and do some good flying. I can see now why they keep a chaperone with you," he teased, to help lighten the moment. They had come very close to losing their heads more than once over the weekend.

"Write to me . . . let me know where you are . . ." she said, as tears ran down her cheeks like rivers.

He pointed to the sky with a sad smile. His eyes told her everything she needed to know, and he could no longer say to her. He was leaving her, and if he came back, who knew what the future held. There were no promises, no sure things. There was only now. And right now, at this very moment, he loved her as he had never loved anyone and never would again.

"Take it easy, Cass," he said softly, as he stepped away from her. "Keep it high." He was smiling, but there were tears in his eyes too. "I love you," he mouthed, and then left the plane. She looked at him for a long painful moment, and her eyes were so full of tears she could hardly see as she taxied down the runway. It was the only time in her entire life when there was no thrill as she left the ground, and she slowly dipped her wings to him, and then headed west, as he watched her.

CHAPTER

13

The first weeks after Nick was gone were difficult for Cass. Her mind was constantly on him, but she had to force herself to concentrate on other things when she was flying. She seemed to fly all the time, from morning till night, and in the month of September she set two more records in the Phaeton. By October, Poland had fallen completely into German hands. And Cassie knew that Nick was at Hornchurch Aerodrome, and assigned to a unit of fighter pilots as an instructor. He was training young pilots to do what he had done in the last war, and for the moment he wasn't flying missions himself. Her father claimed that his age might keep him out of it, but with his extraordinary reputation, he thought it unlikely. But at least for the moment, he was safe. He hadn't written to her, but he had gotten word to her father through another pilot, which was something.

Her life in Los Angeles was as hectic as usual, and the photographers and social events seemed to be thicker than ever. But Desmond kept insisting on the importance of it, and he took her to lunch from time to time, to discuss his planes and her observations of them, which always astounded him, but also to encourage her about the importance of public relations. Their conversations were almost always about his planes, and he was always very businesslike with her. There was a mutual respect there too, and at times he seemed a little more friendly. But the only thing that ever really interested him was his business. And for someone who had such a strong interest in publicity, she was surprised that she so seldom saw anything personal about him in the papers.

He continued to be very generous with her, giving her a large bonus each time she set a record. And he encouraged her to fly all his planes. On Thanksgiving she went home in a Williams P-6 Storm Petrel; she was sleek and painted black and the sheer beauty of her totally amazed her father. She took him up in it, and offered Chris a ride too, but he said he was too busy. He had a new girlfriend in Walnut Grove, and he didn't want to waste any time at the airport. But Billy was more than eager to go with her. He had heard from Nick. It seemed as though everyone had, except Cassie. It was almost as though he were proving a point. But she had long since understood the message. It was just as he had said it would be in spite of all her pleas and protests. "I love you. So long. End of Story." And there was nothing she could do about it now, if ever. She talked to Billy about it late one night, and he told her Nick was the greatest guy he'd ever known, but the epitome of a loner.

"I think he's crazy about you, Cass. I saw it the first time I met you. I figured you knew it too, and I was surprised you didn't. But he's scared, I guess. He's not used to taking anyone with him. And he figured maybe he wouldn't come back this time. He didn't want to do that to you."

"Great. So he tells me he loves me, and then dumps me."

"He figures you should marry some hotshot in L.A. He said so."

"Nice of him to decide that," she complained, but there was nothing she could do. Talking to Billy helped. He was like another brother, except one who liked to fly as much as she did. He was planning to come out and see her in L.A. sometime before Christmas.

And when she left again, she promised to come home for the Christmas holidays. Until then, she had a lot to do. Williams was introducing two new planes, and she was an important part of those introductions. She was going to be doing test flights, and interviews, and posing for photographs. But she figured that by Christmas the worst of it would be all over. Desmond had already agreed to give her a week off between Christmas and New Year's.

The Russians invaded Finland the day she went back after the Thanksgiving holiday, and it was obvious that things were not going well in Europe. It worried her for Nick, but with her grueling schedule, she scarcely had time to keep up with the news.

She was relieved to know that, for the moment, Nick was just an instructor.

When Billy came out to visit her in mid-December, she took him up in their best planes. He was stunned by what she'd been flying.

"You've got some great stuff out here, Cass." His eyes had lit up like Christmas when he saw the maritime patrol variant developed by Williams from an earlier transport, borrowing innovations from Howard Hughes's fabulous racer.

"They'd probably give you a job as a test pilot if you ever wanted it," she suggested to him, but her father would probably be outraged by her luring him away. Pat was relying on him now, and Billy knew that.

"I couldn't leave him," Billy smiled. "Just bring one of these gals home for a visit now and then, and that'll keep me happy."

But she introduced him to Desmond Williams anyway, and told

him what an extraordinary pilot Billy was the next time they had lunch in his office. He showed some interest in him, but his real interest was in Cassie. He couldn't imagine another pilot who flew as well as she did. They talked a lot about the war in Europe these days too. He was hoping to sell planes abroad, and like Nick, he assumed America would get involved eventually.

"I think we'll get shamed into it by our allies," he said calmly. It was exactly what had happened last time.

"I've got a friend over there now," she admitted to him one day. "He signed up as a fighter instructor for the RAF. He's stationed at Hornchurch." It was one of those rare days when they talked about something more than business.

"He sounds like a noble man," Desmond commented as a waiter poured coffee for them in his private office.

"No, just another fool like the rest of us," she said ruefully and he laughed. They both knew that fliers were a special breed of people.

"And what about you, Cass? No grandiose ideas of noble plans? You've accomplished a great deal since you've been here. Does that give you any bigger ideas?" She wasn't sure what he had in mind, but he seemed to have an idea he wasn't ready to discuss yet.

"Not for the moment," she said honestly, "I'm happy here. You've been very good to me, Desmond."

He couldn't help notice that she had grown up a lot in the five months since she'd been in Los Angeles. She looked very sophisticated, and very polished, in part thanks to Nancy's help. But Cassie had her own ideas about clothes now. She handled herself beautifully with the press, and the public adored her. Not enough of them knew her yet, for his taste, but in the spring, he wanted her to start doing a tour of local air shows. She wondered sometimes what difference that kind of publicity made and if it really sold airplanes. Most air shows seemed so local and small scale. But it was important to him, and he reminded her that he expected her to make a tour of several hospitals and orphanages for a Christmas newsreel.

"You should have time to do that before you go home," he said firmly.

"Don't worry, I'll take care of it." She smiled at him and he laughed. Her eyes were always full of mischief, and he found it very appealing. He knew how much she disliked his publicity ideas, and he always wondered if she would balk at them. But in the end, she always did what was expected of her.

"In January, we're flying to New York, by the way," he said casually, but this time with a glimmer in his own eye. "For a meeting between the queen of the cockpit, Cassie O'Malley, and the illustrious Charles Lindbergh." She knew her father would be thrilled with that piece of news when she told him. Even she was impressed by that one, as she listened to Desmond explain it to her.

They were taking Desmond's brand-new plane, and Cassie was to fly a brief demonstration for Lindbergh, and then he would give both her and the plane his endorsement. He had already promised it to Desmond, and they were old friends. Like Desmond, Charles Lindbergh knew the value of public relations. And besides Lindy was interested in meeting Desmond's legendary young pilot.

She managed to do her hospital tour as planned, and Desmond was extremely pleased with what they got of it on the newsreel. And then she went home on schedule, for a week. Her mother had influenza, but she managed to be up and around long enough to cook Christmas dinner for all of them, and her father was in fine form. Billy had gone home too, to see his dad in San Francisco. And Chris was all wrapped up in Jessie, his new girl in Walnut Grove, so there was no one for her to play with. But she was happy anyway. She went for a long walk on Christmas Eve, and to church that night with her sisters. She stopped at the airfield on the way back, to check on her plane. She always felt even more responsible for the ones she brought home, they were so valuable and they weren't hers. But it was fun to fly them.

She checked that no one had disturbed anything, that the windows were closed, and the engine was protected. Her father had cleared his best hangar for her, and she knew that all his friends would come to see the plane she'd flown home. Little by little, she was becoming a legend.

After she'd checked on the plane, she walked slowly back into the night air. It was cold and brisk, and there was snow on the ground. It reminded her of Christmases when she was a little girl, and she had come to the airport with Nick and her father. It was hard not to think of him here. There were so many memories that Nick was a part of. She looked up at the sky, thinking of him, and almost jumped out of her skin when she heard a voice behind her whisper "Merry Christmas." She wheeled to see who it was, and gave a gasp when she saw him standing there in uniform, like a vision.

"Oh, my God . . ." She stared at him in disbelief. "What are you doing here?" she asked Nick breathlessly as she flung herself toward him and he caught her.

"Should I go back?" he asked with a grin, looking handsomer than ever, as he held her and she hugged him.

"No. Never," she answered as he clung to her as powerfully as she held him. He had never been happier than at this moment as he kissed her.

They were golden days. They talked, they laughed, they flew, they went for long walks, they even went ice skating on the pond, and to see *Ninotchka* with Garbo at the movies. It was all like a dream. Their time together was so precious and so short, it was idyllic. And although they sat and kissed and held each other for hours sometimes, he was adamant that no one know what had changed between them.

"My father knows anyway. What difference does it make?" She was always so matter-of-fact, but as usual he was insistent, and convinced he was right.

"I don't want to ruin your reputation."

"By kissing me? How old-fashioned can you get?"

"Never mind. The whole world doesn't need to know you've fallen in love with an old man."

"I'll be sure not to tell them your age."

"Thanks." But as usual, he was very stubborn. There were no ties, no promises, no future held out to her. There was only now, and the infinite exquisite beauty and pain of the moment. They kissed constantly whenever they were alone, and they were hard-pressed not to go any further. But the last thing he wanted to do now was leave her pregnant.

The day before he had to leave, he brought up the subject of the war. He said conditions in England were good, and so far he hadn't flown a single mission.

"They'll probably never put me out there at my age, and you'll get me back like a bad penny at the end of the war. And then you'll be sorry, my friend," he warned her. But that was all she wanted.

"And then what?" She tried to pin him down, but he wouldn't let her.

"Then I talk you into marrying Billy, which you should be doing yourself, not an old goat like me." At thirty-eight, he was hardly an old goat, but no matter what she felt, he was still convinced he was too old for Cassie. She wondered sometimes if he hadn't seen her in diapers if he might have felt different.

"I don't happen to love Billy, if you care," she explained with a grin, as they walked by the lake.

"That's absolutely immaterial. You'll have to marry him anyway."

"Thank you."

"Don't mention it."

"Should we warn him?" Cassie loved being with him, he always made her laugh, even when he made her cry, which he had done a lot lately.

"Eventually. Might as well let the boy relax for a while. Besides he might bolt if he knew."

"How flattering!" She gave him a shove and he almost tripped on the ice. He gave her a push then too, and a few minutes later they were rolling in the snow again and kissing.

They were perfect days, and over too soon, almost as soon as they had begun. She flew him to Chicago, and he took the train to New York, and from there he would return to England.

"Will you be able to come back again soon?" she asked as they stood waiting for the train in Union Station.

"I don't know. That was kind of a fluke. I'll have to see what happens once I'm back at Hornchurch." She nodded. She understood that.

There were no promises again, only tears, and the aching feeling of knowing that he might not come back and this could be the last time she ever saw him. He kissed her one last time before he left, and she ran beside the train for as long as she could, and then he was gone, and she stood alone in the station.

It was a lonely flight back to Good Hope, and the next day she flew back to L.A., and her apartment. She was desperately lonely for him this time, and tired of the ache of worry and not knowing if he was all right, if he'd be back, and if they'd ever find a way to be together. She wondered if he'd ever get over the objections to the difference in their ages, it was so hard to know what would happen.

In January, she flew to New York with Desmond and his new plane to demonstrate it for Charles Lindbergh. There were lots of photographs and newsreels too. And after that, it was a long, lonely spring for her, despite the long flights, the constant tests, the checking and rechecking of new equipment. She was racking up quite a reputation, for her skill and passion for flying. And she had begun meeting some of the women she had only read about for years, like Pancho Barnes and Bobbi Trout. They gave her whole life new dimension. She spent time with Nancy and Jane Firestone too. It was fun being with them, although she realized eventually that she never became as close friends with Nancy as she had hoped to. Maybe there was just too much difference in their ages.

She had dinner again with Desmond one night in April, and he surprised her by asking if she was involved with anyone. Given the businesslike relationship they shared, it struck her as an odd question, but she told him that she wasn't, and Nancy was still lining up her "escorts."

"I'm surprised," he said pleasantly.

"Just too ugly I guess," Cassie smiled at him, and he couldn't help laughing as she joked. And in truth, she looked more spectacular than ever. If anything, she had gotten more beautiful, and Desmond had never been as pleased with any of his plans or projects.

"Maybe you work too hard," he said thoughtfully, looking her straight in the eye. "Or is there someone at home?"

"Not anymore," she smiled sadly. "He's in England. And he's not mine," she added quietly. "He's his own. Very much so."

"I see. That might change." Desmond was intrigued by her, she was as good as any man at what she did, better perhaps, and far more serious about her work. She didn't seem to care at all about her social life, and even less about becoming famous. It was part of her charm, and part of what the public sensed, and why they loved her. In spite of her astonishing success and visibility in the past nine months, she had somehow managed to stay modest. He didn't know many women like that. He liked a lot of things about her, and he was surprised he did. It was rare for him to take a personal interest in his employees, except for unusual cases, like Nancy's.

"War does funny things to men," he said. "Sometimes they change . . . sometimes they realize what's important to them."

"Yes," Cassie said with a wistful smile, "their bombers. I think fliers are a different breed of men. At least all the ones I know are. The women too. They're all a little crazy."

"It's part of the charm." He smiled at her, suddenly looking more relaxed than she'd ever seen him.

"I'll have to remember that," she said, sipping her wine, and watching him. She wondered what made him tick, but there was no way of knowing. Even when he was being friendly, he was completely guarded. There was really no way of knowing him. He was careful to keep his distance. Nancy had told her that about him, and Cassie finally understood it.

"And then there are the rest of us." He smiled at her again. "Those who live on the ground. So simple, and so lowly."

"I don't think I'd say that," she said quietly, as he watched her. "More sensible perhaps. More reasonable about what life is all about, more directed toward their goals. There's a lot of merit to that, I think."

"And you? Where do you fall in all that, Cass? Up in the sky, or on the ground? You seem to live very successfully in both worlds, from what I've noticed." But the sky was her preference, she lived to fly, and he knew that. All she did on the ground was pass time until she could get back in the air, and fly with the birds again.

And then he decided to spring his idea on her. It was still too soon, but not for the seed to be sown, like a precious baby. "What would you think of a world tour?" he asked cautiously, and she looked up, startled. Nick had warned her of that, and its dangers. He had said that that was what Williams had in mind all along. But how could he have known? She looked puzzled as she struggled for an answer.

"Now? Wouldn't it be awfully difficult?" The Germans had already invaded Norway and Denmark, and they were advancing toward Belgium and the Netherlands at that moment. "A lot of Europe would be inaccessible to us, and the Pacific is awfully sensitive." It had affected Earhart's route, and that had been three years before. Things were so much worse now.

"We could probably get around it. It wouldn't be easy, but we could do it, if we had to. But I've always thought that was the ultimate. The round the world trip. If you did it right. It has to be carefully planned and brilliantly handled. And it's not for now of course. It would take at least a year of planning."

"I've always thought it would be fantastic, but right now or even a year from now, I can't imagine how we'll do it." She was intrigued by the idea, but nervous about it too, and mindful of Nick's warnings. But Desmond seemed so sure of what he wanted.

"Let me worry about that, Cass," he said, touching her hand, looking excited for the first time since she'd known him. It was his dream. And he had shared it with her. "All you'd have to do is fly the very best plane in the sky. The rest is mine to worry about. If you'd ever want to do it."

"I'd have to give it some thought." It would certainly change her life. Her name would be a household word forever, just like Cochran or Lindbergh, Elinor Smith, or Helen Richey.

"Let's talk about it again this summer." They both knew her contract would be up for renewal then. And there was no reason why she wouldn't want to renew with them. She made no secret of the fact that she loved what she was doing. But the world tour was something else. It was her dream too, but Nick had been so adamant about her not doing it for Williams. ". . . He's using you . . ." she could still hear his words . . . "Cassie . . . don't do it . . . it scares me . . ." But why not? What was wrong with it? And why shouldn't she? Nick was doing what he wanted, wasn't he? And most of the time, he didn't even bother to write her. She had only had two letters from him since Christmas. And they only told her what he was doing, and not what he felt for her. He was doing nothing to maintain his relationship with her. He thought it wasn't right for her, and he refused to encourage her, or ask her to wait for him. His letters were like bulletins from flight school.

Desmond had taken her dancing that night, and all he talked about as they whirled around the floor at Mocambo was his world tour. Now that he had shared it with her, he couldn't stop talking about it, and he felt sure that she would be as excited about it as he was.

He mentioned it to her again the following week, not to press her about it, but just in passing, as though it were a secret they shared, a goal they both longed for. It was obvious that this was something that meant a great deal to him, and now that he had shared it with her, he felt closer to her.

And given how busy he was, Cassie was startled when he asked if he could take her out for her twenty-first birthday. She was surprised he knew, but he had armies of people to remind him of minor details. Details were important to him, the smallest element of anything fascinated him, and he thought it was the key between the ordinary and perfection.

Not having anyone special to celebrate with, Cassie was pleased he remembered. He took her to the Victor Hugo Restaurant, and then dancing at Ciro's afterward for an evening which touched her deeply. He had a birthday cake for her at the restaurant and served champagne both there and at Ciro's. He had obviously checked with Nancy Firestone about all of Cassie's favorite things, and the entire meal was planned around them. Her favorite dinner, her favorite cake, her favorite songs. She felt like a little girl having a magical birthday. And afterward he gave her a diamond pin in the form of a plane, with the number twenty-one on its wings, and the word Cassie on its side. He had had it made months before by Cartier. He told her that after she opened it, and she couldn't believe the trouble he'd gone to.

"How could you do that?" She blushed as she looked at it. She had never seen anything as beautiful, and somehow felt she didn't deserve it.

But he was looking at her very seriously. She had only seen him look that way at a plane that he was studying before he redesigned it. "I always knew you'd be very important to me someday. I knew that the first day I met you." He said it with total seriousness but Cassie laughed, remembering the moment.

"In the overalls with the grease all over my face? I must have

212

made quite an impression." She was laughing and holding the pin that seemed so remarkable to her. Even the propeller moved when she touched it.

"You did," he admitted. "You're the only woman I know who looks good in blackface."

"Desmond, you're awful." She laughed, feeling close to him. It was odd, but despite the distance between them, she felt friendly toward him. He was one of the few friends she had here. Other than Desmond, there was only Nancy, and one or two of the other pilots. But there was no one she spent any real time with. She respected Desmond enormously and all he stood for and worked so hard for. He believed in excellence, at any cost, to him, or to his company. He never settled for anything less than perfection. Just like the little plane she held in her hand as a gift from him. It was perfect.

"Am I awful, Cass?" he asked seriously after her lighthearted comment. "I've been told that by experts and they're probably right." But he said it so disarmingly, she felt sorry for him. She realized he was a lonely man, in spite of his importance, and all the luxuries he had. He had no children, no wife, few friends, and according to the newspapers at the moment, not even a girlfriend. All he had were his airplanes and his business.

"You know you're not awful," Cass said softly.

"I'd like to be your friend, Cass," he said honestly, and held a hand out to her across the table. She wasn't quite sure what he meant, but she was deeply touched by all he'd done for her, and the gesture of friendship.

"I am your friend, Desmond. You've been very kind to me . . . even before this . . . I never really felt that I deserved it."

"That's why I like you," he smiled, "you don't expect anything, and you deserve it all, even better than that." He gestured to the tiny diamond plane in her hand, and then took it from her, and pinned it on her dress from across the table. "You're a special girl, Cass. I've never known anyone like you." She smiled at him, touched by what he had said, and grateful for his friendship.

He took her home that night, and walked her upstairs. He didn't ask to come in, and he never mentioned the world tour. But he surprised her by sending her flowers the next day, and calling her on Sunday and inviting her to go for a ride. It had never even occurred to her before what he might do on the weekends. She usually flew if she had time, or Nancy booked her into social events where she had to be seen with her long list of escorts.

Desmond picked her up at two o'clock, and they drove out to Malibu, and walked on the beach. It was a glorious day, and the beach was almost deserted. He talked for a while about his youth, his years in boarding school, and then at Princeton. He hadn't been home a lot during that time. His mother had died when he was very young, and his father had plunged himself into his business. He had built an empire, but in the process of building it, he had forgotten his only child. He had never even bothered to have Desmond home for vacations. He stayed at his various schools, first Fessenden then St. Paul's, and then finally Princeton. By then, he didn't really care anymore, he went away on his own or with friends for his vacation.

"Didn't you have any family at all?" Cassie looked horrified at the story of his desperately lonely childhood.

"None. Both of my parents were only children. All of my grandparents were dead before I was born. I never had anyone except my father, and actually, I never really knew him. I think that's why I've never wanted any children of my own. I wouldn't have wanted to inflict that kind of pain on anyone. I'm happy as I am, and I wouldn't want to disappoint a child." There was something very bleak and sad about him, and she understood him better now. It was the loneliness she had sensed, the isolation that had gone on for years. He had put it to good use, but how painful for him. And he still seemed so lonely.

"Desmond . . . you wouldn't disappoint anyone . . . you've been so kind to me." He had been. Her contacts with him had been nothing but pleasant. He was the perfect gentleman, the perfect friend, the perfect employer. There was no reason why he

214

couldn't be the perfect husband or parent. She knew he had been married twice previously and she also knew he had no children. Magazines she'd read made a big point of saying that there was no heir to his gigantic fortune. But now she knew why. He didn't want one.

"I married very young," he explained, as they sat on the sand finally, looking out at the water. "I was still at Princeton. And it was incredibly stupid. Amy was a lovely girl, and completely spoiled by her parents. We came back here when I graduated, and she hated everything about it." He looked at Cass then with sudden amusement. "I was the same age you are now, but with tremendous illusions about being grown up, and knowing what I was doing. She wanted me to move to New York, and I wouldn't. She wanted to be close to her family, and I thought it terribly strange. I took her to Africa instead, on safari, and then to India for six months. And then we went to Hong Kong, where she took the first ship back to her parents. She said I had tortured her and taken her to horrible places. She said she'd been held hostage with savages." He smiled at the absurdity of it and Cassie laughed. He made it all sound very funny. "By the time I got back, her father's lawyers had filed for divorce. I suppose I never understood that she wanted to be near her mother, and I wanted to show her something a lot more exciting.

"My next wife was a lot more intriguing. I was twenty-five, and she was a fascinating Englishwoman in Bangkok. She was ten years older than I was, and apparently she'd led a very busy life. It turned out that she was married to someone else, and he surfaced rather unexpectedly while we were happily living together. He was not pleased, and our marriage was annulled. And then I came back here and settled down eventually. I enjoyed some of it, but I'm afraid none of that sounds like real marriage. I've never really tried it right here, or done what was expected of me. And once I inherited the business, I had no time for all that nonsense. I had no time for anything . . . except the business. So here I am, ten years later, alone, and very boring."

"I wouldn't call all that boring . . . safaris . . . India . . . Bangkok. . . . It's certainly a long way from Illinois, where I come from. I'm the fourth of five children, and I've spent my whole life living on an airport, and I have sixteen nieces and nephews. You don't get much more mundane than that. I'm the first member of my family to go to college, the first woman to fly a plane, the first person to move away, although my father and mother came out from New York, and from Ireland before that. But it's awfully ordinary, and not in the least glamorous or exciting."

"You're glamorous now, Cass," he said quietly, watching her. He always seemed interested in her reactions.

"I don't think I am. I know I'm still the girl in the overalls, with grease all over her face."

"What other people see is very different."

"Maybe I just don't understand that."

"You couldn't say we have an awful lot in common," he said thoughtfully, "but sometimes that works," he said pensively. "Actually, I'm not sure anymore what works. It's been so long since I even tried to figure it out, I can't remember." She smiled, and suddenly she felt as though she were being interviewed, but she wasn't sure for what position. "What about you, Cass? Why is it exactly that at the ripe old age of twenty-one and two days, you're not married?" He was only half teasing. He wanted to know just how free she was. He had never been quite sure, although she didn't seem to be too tied to anyone, except maybe the RAF pilot in England.

"No one wants me," she explained easily and he laughed, and so did she. She was surprisingly comfortable with him.

"Try again." He lay back on the sand, looking at her, completely amused by her, and very relaxed in her unaffected presence. "Tell me something I'll believe." She was far too beautiful for no one to want her.

"I mean it. Boys my age are terrified by women pilots. Unless

216

they fly themselves, and then the last thing they want is competition from another pilot."

"And what about boys my age?" he asked cautiously, as she remembered that he was four years younger than Nick, who was thirty-nine now.

"They seem to get upset about the difference in age. At least some of them do, the ones say . . . four years older than you are."

"I see. They think you're immature?" But she wasn't that either.

"No, they think they're too old, but haven't come far enough in life and have nothing to offer me. They fly away to England and tell me to go play with kids my own age. No promises. No hope."

"I see. And do you play with boys your own age?" He was intrigued by her story. He wondered immediately if it was her father's partner at the airport, but he didn't ask her. He assumed it was, after the way the fellow had tried to protect her from him that first day at the airport.

"No," she said honestly. "I haven't had time for any boys of any age. I've been too busy flying for you, and going to all the social events you think are important." She also didn't want to be involved with anyone. She was too much in love with Nick to care about someone else, but she didn't say that.

"Social events are important, Cassie."

"Not to me," she smiled.

"You can't be easy to please, Miss Cassie O'Malley. You've been out five nights a week with a different man each night for close to a year now. And no one has struck your fancy?"

"I guess not. Too busy, no time, no interest. They all bore me." She didn't bother telling him that most of them were male models, or less than masculine actors. Not that it made a difference to her.

"You're spoiled." He wagged a finger at her, and she laughed at him.

"If I am, it's all your fault. Look what you've done for me, apartments, clothes, all the planes I could ever want to fly, including a diamond one"—she smiled gratefully, she had written him a thank-you note only that morning—"cars . . . hotels . . . fancy restaurants . . . who wouldn't be spoiled after all that?"

"You," he said simply, telling the truth, and then he pulled her to her feet and they walked further down the beach in their bare feet telling each other silly stories. They had dinner at a little Mexican restaurant near her apartment, and he told her the food was terrible, but she loved it, and then he took her home and promised to call her the next morning.

"I go to work at four," she said, "I won't be here."

"So do I," he smiled, "we must both work for the same tyrant. I'll call you at three-thirty." She was surprised when he did. He was the oddest person. And so lonely. His stories of his childhood made her heart ache. It was no wonder he had never loved anyone, no one had ever loved him. It made her want to protect him, and undo it all, and yet at the same time he was always doing things for her. He was an unusual combination of warm and cold, invulnerable, and deeply wounded.

He picked her up at the airport that afternoon, and drove her home, but he didn't come in. And from then on, he called her every day, and took her to dinner several times a week in quiet places. He never did anything more than that, and Cassie never felt they were more than friends, but within a short time they were very good ones. He had never mentioned the world tour again, but she thought of it sometimes when she flew, and all of Nick's warnings. She thought he was crazy to have been so worried. Desmond had no desire to do anything that would harm her or push her. He wanted only the best for her. She was sure of that. More than anything, he was her friend now. He turned up at the oddest times, as she climbed out of a plane, or left for work at four in the morning. He was there for her, if she needed him, he never intruded on her, or asked for more than she wanted to give. He seemed to want so little from her, and yet she always sensed his presence.

He brought her new contract to her himself at the end of June, and this time she was amazed at what she saw in it. Most of the terms were the same, except that some of the social events were optional, and the money was doubled. He promised to let her test all their best planes, and wanted her to guarantee that she would do a minimum number of commercials per year. But then the last clause in the contract was the one that stunned her. It stated that for an additional hundred and fifty thousand dollars, plus any additional fees and benefits that accrued from it, he was offering her a world tour within the year, in the best plane they had, on the safest route that could be devised, to be embarked on, on the second of July 1941, almost exactly a year from then, on the anniversary of the day Amelia Earhart disappeared four years before. It was to be the publicity tour of all time, and she would undoubtedly set new records. The prospect of it was enormously tempting, but she thought she ought to discuss it with her father. She was going home that week anyway, for the air show.

"Do you think he'll disapprove?" Desmond asked her nervously before she left, looking like a boy who was terrified someone would take his favorite toy from him. And she smiled and tried to reassure him.

"I don't think so. He may think it's dangerous, but if you think it could be done safely, I believe you." He had never lied to her, never cheated her, never fooled her. He had never disappointed her as a friend, or as an employer. And they spent a great deal of time together. Theirs was a strange relationship for a girl her age, and a man his, it was based only on business and friendship. Nothing more. He had never even tried to kiss her and yet he had wanted to know that she was free. And he had relaxed visibly when he heard she was, with the exception of Nick, who hadn't written to her in months. She knew how violently he would have disapproved of this contract. "My father is pretty reasonable," she reassured him.

"Cassie, I've always wanted to do this. But there was never anyone who could, or whom I would have trusted, or wanted to work with. I trust you completely. And I've never seen anyone fly a plane the way you do." She couldn't help being flattered by what he said about her.

"We'll talk about it when I get back," she promised him. She just needed a few days to think it out, but she was very tempted, and he knew it.

"You're not flying in the air show this year, are you?" He looked worried before he left her, but she was quick to shake her head. Her life was an air show every day, and she hadn't practiced. She just hadn't had time this year, although she was looking forward to going.

"No, but my brother is. God knows why. He doesn't really like to fly, he just does it to please my father."

"He's no different than the rest of us. I did wrestling at Princeton, because my father had. It's the most disgusting sport in the world, and I hated every minute of it, but I thought he'd be delighted. I'm not sure he ever even knew, and when I think of all the stiff necks and bloody noses I got, not to mention the bruises." She laughed at his description of it, and she promised him she'd call him from home and tell him about the air show.

"I'll miss you when you're gone, you know. I have no one else to call at three o'clock in the morning."

"You can call me," she said generously. "I'll get up to talk to you, it's five o'clock there."

"Just have fun," he smiled at her, "and come back and sign on for the world tour. But if you don't," he suddenly said seriously, "we'll still be friends, you know. I'd understand if you didn't want to do it." The way he said it made her want to throw her arms around him and tell him she loved him. He was such a solitary soul, and he wanted so badly to do the right thing, and to be fair. He also wanted the world tour so desperately. She really didn't want to disappoint him.

"I'll try not to let you down, Desmond, I promise. I just need some time to think about it." She was glad she didn't have to face Nick and listen to him erupt like a volcano.

"I understand." He kissed her on the cheek before she left, and told her to wish her brother luck from him, and she promised she would when she saw him.

She flew home in one of Desmond's twin engine transports and wondered what her father was going to say about the world tour when she asked him. There was no doubt that it was somewhat dangerous, even without the war, and the problems in the Pacific; flying long distance like that could be disastrous if you didn't know what you were doing, or had incredibly bad luck and hit unexpected storms. Nobody had ever figured out what had happened to Amelia Earhart. The disappearance had no rational explanation, except perhaps that she'd run out of fuel and gone down without a trace. It was the only sensible reason anyone could come up with. The wilder theories had their fans, but Cassie had never believed them.

But the world tour gnawed at Cassie all the way home. Dangerous or not, she was aching to do it.

CHAPTER
14

The Peoria Air Show was the same wonderful circus that Cassie remembered it to be. She had never been happier than when she stood there with Billy and her father. Her mother and the other girls were off somewhere with the children. And Chris was pacing back and forth nervously eating hot dogs.

"You're making me sick," Cassie scolded him, and he grinned and bought some cotton candy.

All of their old friends were there, her father's cronies, and the younger flyboys. Most of the flying fanatics from miles around had come to visit the day before, at her father's insistence. The Peoria Air Show was an important event in aviation. There were even a couple of girls this year, in one of the tamer events. And Chris was going for his usual prize for altitude in the last race of the afternoon. It wasn't much of a showstopper, but they both knew it would please their father.

"Don't you want to try something, Sis? Dad could lend you a plane." The one she had flown east in was far too big, and far too clumsy. And also worth far too much money. And it was Desmond's. She had tested it for him right after she had gone to work for him, and they had only recently perfected her recommended changes. For a girl of twenty-one, she had a remarkably important job; everyone here knew how famous she was now and there was a lot of talk about her being there. At Desmond's suggestion, the wire services had shown up in full force to greet her.

But Cassie was quick to tell her brother she wasn't going to be in the air show. "I'm not good enough anymore. I've been flying these boats all year long, Chris. Besides, I haven't practiced."

"Neither have I," he said with a grin. At twenty, he looked exactly like their father. He was doing well in school, and still intent on becoming an architect, if he could get a scholarship at the University of Illinois in another year or two. And for the moment, he spent every spare waking moment with Jessie. They were adorable and Pat said he wouldn't be surprised if they got married.

Billy looked no older than Chris did. He seemed to have even more freckles this year, but it was obvious from his performance in the first two races that, unlike her brother, he had practiced. He won first prize twice, and another one half an hour later, in three of the most difficult competitions.

"What have you been doing, practicing all year? Boy, you guys get a lot of time to fool around," she teased with an arm around him, as a photographer from the wire service snapped their picture. Cassie was careful to give them Billy's name and spell it correctly, and to remind him that Billy had taken first prize three times so far that morning.

"And the day's not over yet," he quipped with a wink at Cassie.

"What about you, Miss O'Malley?" one of the reporters asked her. "No performance today?"

"I'm afraid not. Today is my brother's show, and Mr. Nolan's."

"Any romantic ties between you and Mr. Nolan?" he asked pointedly and she grinned at him as Billy pretended to choke on his lemonade.

"Not a one," she answered coolly.

"And what about you and Mr. Williams?"

"We're the best of friends," she said with a smile.

"Nothing else?" the man pressed on as her father wondered how she stood it. But she was very patient with him, and very gracious. Desmond had taught her well, and she felt an obligation to him to behave with the press here, although a little mischief with them might have been tempting. They took themselves so seriously, and of course Cassie didn't.

"Not that he's told me," she said pleasantly, and then turned away to talk to some friends, and they finally left her.

"What pests they are," Billy said with a look of annoyance. "Don't they get on your nerves all the time?"

"Yes, but Mr. Williams thinks they're good for business."

"Was there any truth to that, by the way?" Billy asked when they were alone again. "Anything between you and Williams?"

"No," she said cautiously, "we're just friends. I don't think he wants to be involved. I'm probably as close to him as he is to anyone. He's a very lonely man. I feel sorry for him sometimes," she said quietly so no one else would hear her. But Billy was in no mood to be serious, and he was always irreverent about tycoons worth over a billion dollars.

"I feel sorry for him too. All that nasty old money he has to take care of. And all those movie stars he probably goes out with. Poor guy."

"Oh shut up." She gave him a shove, and Chris came over to join them. He was eating again, and Cassie made a face watching him. He'd been eating like that since he was fourteen, and he was still as thin as a scarecrow. Jessie was standing right next to him, beaming up at him in silent adoration. She worked at the local library. She was a serious girl, and she gave all the money she earned back to her parents to help support her four younger sisters. And it was obvious to everyone that she was crazy about Chris. She was very sweet to all the O'Malleys, especially the younger children.

"Don't you ever stop eating?" Cassie asked him, with feigned irritation.

"Not if I can help it. If you time it right, you can pretty much keep eating from the time you wake up till you go to bed at night. Mom says I eat more than the entire family put together."

"One day you're going to wind up a fat old man," Billy warned him, with a wink at Jessie, who giggled.

They were all in a good mood, and there were a few really glorious feats, but none that matched Cassie's of the year before, her horrifying dive and last second recovery.

"I hated it when you did that," Chris admitted to her; "it made my stomach roll over watching you. I thought you were going to crash."

"I'm too smart for that," she said smugly. But she was glad he wasn't doing anything dangerous. Altitude never got anyone into much trouble. It wasn't very exciting either, but she was happy knowing he was safe, and not taking any chances.

"So what's happening in L.A.," Billy asked during a lull, and she told him about her work and their new planes, but she didn't say anything about the world tour. She wanted to talk to her father about it first. And then she was going to mention it to Billy. She had been thinking about it a lot, and if she did it, she wanted him to fly with her. He was the best pilot she'd ever seen; even after a year in Los Angeles flying with some real greats, she still thought Billy was better.

He went back up after they chatted for a while, and won another first prize, to prove her point. And shortly after that, there was a near disaster when two planes almost collided, but there was a last minute save, and after some gasps and screams from the crowd, everything turned out all right. But it made everyone think of the year before, when Jimmy Bradshaw crashed at the air show. Needless to say, they didn't see Peggy there this year, but Cassie had already heard from Chris that she and Bobby Strong were getting married. She had no regrets about him at all. Her life had moved far past him. But she wished him well, and she was happy for Peggy.

Chris was standing with her just before his big event, and they were chatting about some old friends, and then they called his group to their planes.

"Well, here goes nothing." He looked nervous, understandably, and he looked at Cassie and grinned, and she reached out and touched him.

"Good luck, kid. When you come back, we'll get you something to eat. Try and hang on till then."

"Thanks." He grinned at her as Jessie went to find one of her sisters.

And as he walked away, for no particular reason except that she was proud of him, Cassie shouted after him, "I love you!" He turned and showed a sign that he had heard her, and then he was gone. And at last it was his turn in the small red plane as he climbed, and he climbed, and he climbed, and she watched him sharply. She thought she saw something then, and she narrowed her eyes against the sun, and she was about to say something to Billy. Sometimes she felt things even before she saw them. But before she could say anything, she saw what she had feared, a thin trail of smoke, and she found herself looking up at it, willing him to the ground as swiftly and as safely as he could get there. She wasn't even sure he knew what the problem was yet, but he did a moment later. His engine had caught fire, and a moment later he was plummeting to the ground faster than he had risen. There was no stopping him, no time to say anything. There were the familiar gasps that meant something terrible, as everyone waited. And Cassie was mentally willing him to pull up on his stick as he fell, and she clutched Billy's arm, but she never took her eyes off her brother's plane. And then he was down, in a column of flame, as she and every man at hand rushed toward him. But the flames were furious and the smoke pitch black. Billy reached him before anyone else and she was right beside him. Together they pulled him from the flames, but he was already gone, and every inch of him was burning. Someone ran toward them with a blanket to quench the flames, and Cassie was sobbing as she held him. She didn't even realize she had burned her arm very badly. She didn't know anything, except that Chris was in her arms, and he would never see again, or laugh, or cry, he would never grow up, or be rude to her, or get married. She couldn't stop crying as she held him, and she heard a guttural cry above her, as the plane exploded and threw shards of metal at the crowd. Billy was pulling on her to get her away, and she was still holding Chris as her father tried to take him from her.

"My boy . . ." He was sobbing . . . "My boy . . . oh, God . . . no . . . my baby . . ." They were both holding him, and people were running and screaming all around them, and then powerful arms lifted Chris from her, and her father was led away, and in the distance she could see Jessie crying, and all Cassie knew was Billy was holding her, and then she saw her mother sobbing in her father's arms. And everyone around them was crying. It had been that way the year before, but this was worse, because it was Chris . . . her baby brother.

She was never sure what happened after that, except that she remembered being in the hospital, and Billy was with her. The arm didn't hurt at all, but people were doing things to her. Someone said it was a third degree burn, and they kept talking about the accident . . . the accident . . . the plane . . . but she hadn't crashed. She hadn't crashed in her plane, and she kept saying as much to Billy.

"I know, Cass. I know, sweetheart. You didn't do anything."

"Is Chris okay?" She suddenly remembered that there was something wrong with him, but she couldn't remember what, and Billy just nodded. She was in shock. She had been since it happened.

They gave her something to sleep for a while, and when she woke up, the arm had started to hurt terribly, but she didn't care. She had remembered.

But Billy was still there, and they cried together. Her parents were there too by then. They had come back to see her. Her mother was almost hysterical, and her father was heartbroken, and Glynnis and her husband Jack were there, but everyone kept crying. Glynnis told her Jessie had gone home with friends of Chris's, and her parents had had to call the doctor.

Because Chris was so badly burned, the casket was closed, and the wake was the following night at the funeral home in Good Hope. And the funeral was the next day at St. Mary's. Everyone he had ever gone to school with was there, all his friends, and Jessie. She was in terrible shape, surrounded by her sisters, and Cassie made a point of going to kiss her. It was a terrible thing for a nineteen-year-old girl to live through.

Bobby Strong was there, and he came over and talked to Cass, but Peggy just couldn't. Some of Chris's friends from college had come too, and almost everyone who'd been in the air show, just as all of them had gone for Jim the year before. It seemed such an idle death, such a stupid way to die, climbing to the sky just to prove how far you could go, or worse yet, that you couldn't.

Cassie felt as though part of herself had died, and as she followed the casket out of the church, she and her father had to hold up her mother. It was the worst thing Cassie had ever seen, the worst thing she'd ever been through.

And it was only as they left the church that she looked up and saw Desmond Williams. She couldn't even imagine how he had known, and then she realized the wire services had been there and it was probably all over the papers. She was a star now, and her brother's death in an air show was big news. But she was glad he had come anyway. There was something comforting about seeing him there. And she reached out to him as they left the church, and thanked him for coming. She asked him to come to the house afterward, with their other friends, and once he arrived she could tell him how much his coming meant to her. He nodded, and then she started to cry, and he just held her in his arms, feeling awkward. He didn't know what to say or do, he just held her, hoping that was enough. And then he saw her arm, and moved her gently.

"Are you all right? How bad is it?" He had been very worried when he heard she'd been burned trying to save her brother.

"I'm okay. Billy and I pulled him out, and . . . and . . . he was still burning." The image she created was so horrible that it almost made him sick. But he was reassured when she told him the doctors weren't worried about her. He told her he wanted it checked out in L.A. when she got back. And he made a point of talking to her parents, and chatting with Billy for a while. And then he left. He said he was flying back that night. He had just wanted to be there for her, and she was glad he'd come. It meant a lot to her, and she told him.

"Thank you, Desmond . . . for everything . . ." He didn't mention the world tour, but she knew it was on his mind. And she was still planning to talk to her father. But she had already told Desmond she wanted to stay home for a week or two, with them, and he told her to stay as long as she wanted.

She walked back outside with him, and he hugged her, and then he left, looking very somber. And when she went back inside, her father was crying and said that Chris had done it for him, and he should never have let him.

"He did it because he wanted to, Dad," Cass said quietly, "We all do. You know that." It was true in her case, but not in Chris's, but she felt she at least owed her father that. "He told me before he went up that he wanted to do it. He liked it." It was a lie, but a kind one.

"He did?" Her father looked surprised, but relieved as he dried his eyes, and took another shot of whiskey.

"That was a nice thing you did for him," Billy said to her later, and she only nodded, thinking of something else.

"I wish Nick were here," she said quietly. And then Billy decided to tell her what he'd done.

"I sent him a telegram the night it happened. I think they're pretty reasonable about granting leave to volunteers. I don't know, I just thought . . ." He wasn't sure if she'd be mad at him, but it was obvious now that she wasn't.

"I'm glad you did," she said gratefully, and stood around looking at their friends.

It was a miserable reason to get together. She wondered then if Nick would come, if he could get away, or they would let him.

She sat for hours with her parents that night, talking about Chris, and the things he'd done as a child. They cried and they laughed, and remembered the little things that meant so much to them now that he was no longer with them.

The next morning Cassie dropped by the hospital, to have them look at her arm. They changed the dressings for her and then she went back to the house to sit with her father.

He hadn't gone to the airport since the accident, and Billy was taking care of things for him. Cassie stopped there on the way, and Billy asked her how her dad was.

"Not so great." He'd been drinking that morning when she left him after breakfast. He just couldn't face what had happened yet. He only drank in moments of great stress or celebration, and when she went back, he was sitting alone in the living room and crying.

"Hi, Dad," she said as she came in. She had lain awake all night, thinking of how she had resented Chris, of how often she had thought her father liked him better. She wondered if Chris had ever known it. She hoped not. "How're you feeling?"

He just shrugged and didn't bother to answer. She talked about some of their visitors then, and about stopping to see Billy at the airport. But for once, her father didn't ask how things were there.

"Did you see Desmond Williams here yesterday?" she said, groping for things to say to him as he looked up at her blankly. But at least this time he answered.

231

"Was he here?" She nodded, and sat down next to him. "That was nice of him. What's he like, Cass?" Her father had talked to him briefly, but he didn't remember in the agony of the day.

"He's very quiet, very honest . . . hardworking . . . lonely." They were odd things to say about the man she worked for. "Driven, I guess, would be the right word. He lives for his business. It's all he has."

"That's sad for him," he said, looking at her, and then he started to cry again, thinking about the air show. The poor kid had been only twenty. "It could have been you, Cass," he said through his tears. "It could have been you last year. I was never so scared as when I watched you."

"I know," she smiled, "I scared the pants off Nick too, but I knew what I was doing."

"That's what we all think," he said gloomily. "Chris probably thought so too."

"But he never did know, Dad. He wasn't like us."

"I know," he agreed. They all knew it too. Chris had really never known what he was doing. "I just keep thinking of how he looked when you and Billy pulled him out." He looked sick as he thought about it, and not knowing what else to do, she poured him another drink. But by lunchtime, he was slurring and half asleep. And then finally, he dozed off, and she just let him sit there. Maybe the best thing for him was to sleep. Her mother came back that afternoon with two of Cassie's sisters, and by then her father was awake and had sobered up again. Cassie made them all something to eat, and then they sat talking quietly in the kitchen.

It was odd being with all of them, and Cassie realized that they seemed to be waiting for something. It was as though the reality of Chris's being gone hadn't sunk in yet, and everyone was waiting for him to come home, or for someone to tell them it hadn't happened. But it had. It had been as bad as it could have been. It couldn't have been much worse, except if he had suffered.

Glynnis and Megan left when Colleen arrived, with all her kids, and the brief chaos did them all good, and then finally they were alone again. Cassie cooked dinner for her parents, and she was glad she was there with them. She had no idea yet when she'd be leaving. Her mother cried again at the end of the meal, and Cassie put her to bed, like a child, but her father seemed better that night. He was calmer and very clear-headed, and he wanted to talk to her after Oona had gone to bed. He asked her about her work, and if she liked it, what kind of planes she'd been flying, and about her life in L.A. He knew the year was up and he wondered if Cassie would stay in L.A. or come home now. With Chris gone, his concerns were more poignant.

"I've been offered a new contract." Cassie answered his question directly.

"What's he giving you?" he asked with interest.

"Double what he paid me last year," she said proudly, "but I was going to send the difference to you and Mom. I really don't need it."

"You might," her father said gruffly. "You never know what can happen. Your sisters have their husbands to take care of them, but you, and Chris . . ." And then he caught himself and his eyes filled with tears again as she touched his hand and he held hers tightly. "I forget sometimes," he said through his tears.

"I know, Daddy . . . so do I . . ." She had been thinking about Chris that afternoon, and wondered if he was in Walnut Grove with Jessie, and then she remembered. It was as though their hearts and minds just didn't want to accept it. She had talked to Jessie on the phone that afternoon, and she felt that way too. She said she kept listening for his truck. They all did.

"Anyway, I want you to keep the money," Pat said firmly.

"That's silly."

"Why is he paying you so much?" he asked with a worried frown. "He's not making you do anything dishonest, is he, Cass? Or too dangerous?"

"No more dangerous than any other test pilot who works for him, and probably less so. He's got a big investment in me. I think

233

he just thinks I'm useful to the company, because I'm a woman, and all the publicity . . . the speed records I've set are important for his planes." And then she looked at him, wondering if it was too soon to tell him. But she wanted to tell him now. She wanted to sign the contract as soon as she went back. She had thought about it a lot in the last few days, in spite of Chris, and she knew what she wanted.

"He wants me to do a world tour, Dad," she said quietly, and for a moment, there was a long silence while he absorbed it.

"What kind of world tour? There's a war on, you know."

"I know. He said we'd have to work around it. But he thinks it could be done safely, if we plan our route carefully."

"So did George Putnam," her father said grimly. He had just lost one child, he didn't want to lose another. "There's no way to do a world tour safely, Cass, war or no. There are too many variables, too many dangers. Your engines could fail. You could navigate wrong. You could hit a storm. A million unexpected things could happen."

"But less so in one of his planes, and if I took the right man with me."

"Did you have anyone in mind?" He thought instantly of Nick, but he couldn't go now.

Cassie nodded. "I thought maybe Billy." Pat hesitated while he thought about it, and then he nodded.

"He's good," he agreed. "But he's young," and then he reconsidered. "Maybe you have to be. No one older than you kids would be crazy enough to want to do it." He almost smiled then, and Cass suddenly felt better. It was almost as though he had approved. And she wanted him to. She wanted to do it with his blessing. "Is that why they're paying you so much?"

"No," she shook her head. "They'd pay me even more for the world tour." She didn't even dare tell him how much. A hundred and fifty thousand would sound like the world to him, and it was. And she didn't want him to think she was doing it out of greed, because she wasn't. "And there would be bonuses, and other contracts resulting from it, and endorsements. It's a pretty good deal," she explained modestly. But even talking about those amounts of money scared her.

"It's not a good deal if you're dead," Pat said bluntly, and she nodded. "You'd better think about it carefully, Cassandra Maureen. It's not a game. You'll take your life in your hands if you do it."

"What do you think I should do, Dad?" She was begging for his approval and he knew it.

"I just don't know," he said, and then he closed his eyes, thinking about it. He opened them again, and reached for her hands and held them. "You have to do what you need to do, Cass. Whatever it is your mind and heart tell you. I can't stand between you and a great future. But if you get hurt, I'll never forgive myself . . . or Desmond Williams. I'd like you to stay here, and never risk anything again . . . particularly after what just happened to Chris. But that's not right. You have to follow your heart. I said as much to Nick when he decided to go to England. You're young, it could be a great thing if you make it. And a terrible heartbreak for us, if you don't." He looked at her long and hard, not sure what else he should say to her. It was her decision in the end. She'd been right to go to Los Angeles the year before, but he just didn't know now.

"I'd like to do it, Daddy," she said quietly, and he nodded.

"At your age, I would have too. It would have been the greatest opportunity in my life, if anyone had offered it. But they didn't." He smiled, and looked more like himself again. "You're a lucky girl, Cass. That man has given you a great chance to become someone very important. It's a gift . . . but a dangerous one. I hope he knows what he's doing."

"So do I, Daddy. But I trust him. He's too smart to take chances. He believes totally in what he's doing."

"When does he want you to go?" Pat asked cautiously.

"Not for another year. He wants to plan it perfectly."

"I like that," Pat said. "Well, think about it, and let me know

235

what you decide. I wouldn't tell your mother for a while, if you decide to do it." She nodded, and a little while later they turned out the lights and went to bed, but she was immensely relieved to have talked to him, and even more so that he hadn't gotten angry. He seemed to have finally accepted who she was, and what she was doing. He'd come a long way since he'd forbidden her to fly or take lessons. The memory of that made her smile now.

She talked to Billy about it the next day, and he went wild when she told him she had suggested him as her navigator and co-pilot.

"You want *me*?" he shrieked and then threw his arms around her neck and kissed her. "Zowie!!!!"

"Would you do it?"

"Are you kidding? When do we leave? I'll pack now."

"Relax," she laughed at him, "not for another year. July 2, 1941, to be exact. He wants to do it on the anniversary of the day Earhart went down. It's a little spooky but he likes that." It had to do with publicity, and in that, she trusted Desmond's judgment.

"Why so long?" Billy sounded disappointed.

"He wants to plan it carefully, build it up, test the right plane. He's thinking about our using the Starlifter, which would be tremendous publicity for it, for distance and endurance." That was really what it was all about, but if they made it, their lives would never be the same again. And she already knew that there was fifty thousand dollars in it for Billy, and she told him.

"I could sure have a good time with that, couldn't I?" But like Cassie, it wasn't the money that appealed to him, it was the excitement and the challenge. It was the same thing that appealed to Desmond, and had even sparked a flicker of excitement in her father. "Well, let me know what you do." And like her father, he suspected that she had already made the decision. She had, but she was trying it on for size, thinking about it, trying to be sure she wanted to make the commitment. Working for Desmond for another year was one thing, that was an easy choice, but agreeing to do the world tour was entirely different, and she knew it. She knew how great the risks were, and the benefits, if she made it.

Imagine what Earhart would have been if she had succeeded. It was hard to imagine her legend being even stronger than it was, but it would have been. If only . . .

Billy left on a quick hop to Cleveland that afternoon, and her father was still at home, so Cassie volunteered to stick around and close the office. She put some papers away for them, and then she put on a familiar pair of overalls and went out to gas some planes. She had nothing else to do, and it would save Billy some work in the morning.

She had just finished the last of them, and put away some tools, when she saw a small plane coming in on the main runway. The little plane didn't seem to hesitate. It came right in, and then taxied toward the far hangar. She wondered if it was a regular, it had to be. She didn't know all of them anymore. He seemed to know exactly where to go, and what to do. She watched him for a minute, but the sun was in her eyes. And then she saw him. It couldn't be . . . it couldn't . . . but it was. He had come home to them. It was Nick. And she was crying as she ran toward him. She flew into his arms and he held her there, careful of her bandaged arm. It brought it all back to be there with him, the sorrow and the pain, and the shock of losing Chris mingled with the pleasure of seeing Nick now. He kissed her long and hard, and she felt safe and at peace suddenly, knowing he was home now.

"They let me go as soon as I heard," he explained when they came up for air. "But I had a hell of a time getting to New York. I had to fly out of Lisbon, I got in last night, and I chartered this crate in New York this morning. I never thought I'd make it. The damn thing barely got off the ground in New Jersey."

"I'm so glad you're here." She hugged him again, so relieved to see him. And he looked incredibly handsome in his RAF uniform. But also very worried.

"How's your dad?"

"Not great," she said honestly. "He'll be glad to see you. I'll drive you over now. You can stay with us." And then she almost choked on the words, "You can have Chris's room . . . or mine

237

. . . I'll sleep on the couch." Billy was living in Nick's old shack, and it would have been close quarters with both of them there.

"I can sleep on the floor," he grinned. "It's not a problem. The British aren't known for their comfortable barracks. I haven't had a decent night's sleep since last September."

"When are you coming home?" she asked, as she drove him to her parents' house.

"When it's over." But it wouldn't be over soon. Now that France had fallen three weeks before, Hitler had control of an even larger chunk of Europe. And the British had their hands full keeping him from trying to take what was left of the French fleet in North Africa. Their problems were far from over.

Nick inquired about her arm, and she admitted it hurt, but was getting better.

They had arrived at the house by then, and her father was sitting in a chair on the porch looking doleful.

"Got a cot for a soldier, Ace?" Nick said quietly as he stepped onto the porch and walked swiftly to his old friend and embraced him. The two men cried, sharing each other's pain, and Cassie left them alone to talk and fix them some dinner. Her mother had gone to bed with a terrible headache. She was still taking it very hard, understandably, he had been her baby, and so young. He was only twenty.

Cassie made them both sandwiches and poured them beer, and her mother had made a big salad in case they wanted it. It was enough. None of them were very hungry. And as they ate, Nick told them about what was happening in Europe. He had heard tales of the fall of France three weeks before, and the heartbreaking fall of Paris. The Germans were everywhere, and the British were afraid Hitler would try to take them next, and there was some fear that he might succeed, although no one said it.

"Are they letting you fly missions yet?" Pat asked, smiling at the memories of their days together at the end of the last war.

"They're too smart for that, Ace. They know I'm over the hill."

"Not at your age. Give 'em time. When things get hot for them, they're going to throw your behind into a fighter and kiss you good-bye in a hot minute."

"I hope not." It made Cassie angry listening to them. They all loved war so much, and as far as they were concerned, it was all right to take chances, as long as they were the ones who did it.

She left them talking on the porch late that night. She would have liked to talk to Nick too, but she knew her father needed him more. And she had time. Nick was there for three days. She would see him in the morning.

Her father finally went to his office the next day, and he was pleased to find everything in good order. Billy had taken good care of the planes. Cassie had taken good care of his desk, and his pilots were all standing by waiting for directions. It did him good to come back, and halfway through the morning, Cassie was surprised when Desmond called her. He asked if it was okay to talk, and she stepped in and closed the door to her father's office.

"It's fine. You're nice to call."

"I've been worried about you, Cass. But I didn't want to intrude at a time like this. How's the arm?"

"I'll be fine." She didn't want to worry him by telling him how bad it really was, but so far it was healing nicely. "Is everything all right there?" she asked, feeling guilty for staying away for so long. She had been gone almost a week now, but he had told her not to rush back. She apologized again, and he told her to stay as long as she wanted.

"How are your parents?"

"Not great. But my dad came to work today. I think it'll do him good, especially once someone makes him mad about something. It'll take his mind off his troubles." He laughed at what she said, and asked if she'd given the world tour any more thought, and she smiled and said she had. "I talked to my father about it."

"I imagine he was thrilled to hear about it right now. Your timing wasn't exactly the best, Miss O'Malley." He almost groaned at the thought of her telling him now. He could just imagine what he must have said. But she surprised him.

239

"Actually, he wasn't all that opposed to it, after we talked about it for a while. I think he's worried about a lot of things, but he was surprisingly reasonable. I think he sees it as a great opportunity for me. He told me I had to make up my own mind."

"And have you?" he asked, holding his breath. He had been frantic about her since she left. And he was surprised at how much he missed her. And he was even more worried she might not come back to L.A. or renew her contract after her brother's death. She was an important part of his life now.

"Almost," she told him tantalizingly. "I just want to think it out while I'm here. I'll tell you the minute I get back, Desmond, I promise."

"I can't stand the suspense." And he meant it. It was driving him crazy.

"I think you'll find the answer worth waiting for," she teased and he grinned. He liked the way she sounded. And he couldn't help thinking of how she looked, as he talked to her. She had even looked beautiful at the funeral with her ravaged face and heavily bandaged arm, but it seemed wrong to think so.

"Promises, promises. Hurry up and come home, I miss you."

"I miss you too." She said it as she would have to a friend, as she would have to Chris, or to Billy. She missed talking to him at the crazy hours when they were both awake, and about the things they both cared about, his airplanes.

"I'll see you soon, Cass."

"Take care. Thanks for calling." She hung up and went back outside to her father and Nick. Her father asked her who had called and she told him Desmond Williams.

"What did he want?" Nick asked, looking annoyed.

"To talk to me," she said coolly. She didn't like the way Nick had asked the question. He was acting as though he owned her. And for a man who hadn't even bothered to write in three months, that was pushing his luck, or so she thought.

"What about?" Nick persisted.

"Business," she said bluntly and changed the subject.

Pat smiled then and walked away. He could see a storm gathering, and he could only smile. She was definitely an O'Malley.

"How's the arm?" Nick asked when they were alone again.

"So-so," she said honestly. "It's starting to hurt like hell, which they claim is a good sign." She shrugged and looked up at him then, and invited him to take a walk with her. He agreed and they strolled to the far edges of the airport.

"What are you doing these days, Cass?" He sounded gentler than he had a few minutes before, and her heart melted again the minute he came near her, and put an arm around her.

"The same stuff. Flying planes, pushing limits. My contract is up this week. They've offered me a new one."

"Same terms?" he asked bluntly.

"Better." So was she.

"Are you going to do it?"

"I think so."

And then Nick asked a question she hadn't expected. "Are you in love with him, Cass?" He looked worried as he asked, and she smiled at the bluntness of the question.

"Desmond? Of course not. We're friends, but that's all. He's a very lonely person."

"So am I, in England." But he didn't sound sorry for himself as he said it. He sounded angry about Desmond, and jealous.

"Apparently not lonely enough to be bothered writing to me," she said tartly. She hated not hearing from him, especially since he wrote to her father sometimes, and to Billy.

"You know how I feel about that. There's no point stringing you along, or our getting tied up with each other, Cass. There's no future in it for you."

"I still don't see why not. Unless you don't love me. That I could understand. This I can't. This is crazy."

"It's very simple. I could be dead next week."

"So could I. So what, we're fliers. I'm willing to take my chances on you. Are you willing to take them on me?"

"That's not the point and you know it. If I do get lucky and

241

survive, which would be lucky for me, and maybe not so lucky for you, then what? You live in a shack and starve for the rest of your life? Congratulations to the big winner. I'm a flier, Cass. I'm never going to have a hill of beans. I never minded till now. I never paid attention, just like Billy isn't. He's having a good time. So was I. I still am. Then what? It's no future for you, Cass. I won't do that. And your father would kill me if I let you do that to yourself."

"He may kill you sooner if you don't wind up with me. He thinks we're both crazy. Me for loving you, and you for running."

"Maybe he's right. Who knows, but that's the way I see it."

"And what if I save some money?" It was an interesting question.

"Good for you. Enjoy it. I hope you do. You're practically a movie star these days. Every time I see a newsreel from home now, you're in it more than Hitler."

"Gee, thanks."

"Well, it's true. Williams sure knows what he's doing. So what are you asking me? If you get rich thanks to him, am I willing to live off of you? The answer is no, if that's the question."

"You don't make anything easy, do you?" She was beginning to get annoyed. He made everything impossible. Heads I win, tails you lose. He had loaded the dice, and she just couldn't win a round, and she was getting sick of it. "Are you saying that if you'd saved some money over these past few years, then you'd come home and marry me. But since you didn't, if I make some money, that's not okay. Is that it?"

"You've got it," he said smugly. He had decided not to ruin her life, and he was determined to do everything he had to to stick by it. "I don't live off women."

"You don't make much sense either. You're the only man I've ever met who's more stubborn than my father. And he's at least beginning to make sense in his old age. Just how long do I have to wait with you?" She said impatiently.

"Till I get soft upstairs," he said with a grin, "and it won't be long now." He was tired of arguing with her. All he wanted was to put his arms around her and kiss her. It drove him up the wall when he saw her in the newsreels. He wanted to shout, "Hey, that's my girl!" But she wasn't. He wouldn't let her be. She was his best friend's daughter, and the girl he'd been in love with since she was three. Try explaining that to a bunch of guys in the RAF. It had knocked him off his feet to realize that. Two or three of them had her on their walls as pinups.

"Get over here," he said gruffly, as she stood several feet away with her arms crossed, tapping her foot at him. "And don't look at me like that."

"Why not?" She scowled at him.

"Because I may be a complete jerk, and I may want you to marry someone half my age and have ten kids, but I still love you, Cass . . . I always will, baby . . . you know that."

"Oh, Nick." She melted at the sight of him, and as he pulled her into his arms all she wanted was him. They stood together and kissed for a long time, forgetting all the words and the arguments and the problems. And then they walked slowly back to the airport. Her father saw them from where he sat in his office, and he figured they had worked things out. He wondered when they were going to get smart and figure out that they had something rare and important. But they were both stubborn as hell, and he wasn't going to get into it with them. He wondered if she had told Nick about the world tour yet, and what he would say. But it was only the next day that it came up, as they were all three sitting in Pat's office.

"What are you talking about?" Nick looked confused. Pat had referred to it, and Nick had no idea what he was saying.

Pat looked at his daughter then and raised an eyebrow. "Aren't you going to tell him?"

"Tell me what? Oh great. So what's the big secret?" He knew she wasn't in love with someone else or even seeing anyone, although he had told her to, and she had had a fit over his telling her that. And she certainly wasn't pregnant, since he pretty much knew she was a virgin. There had never been anyone in Cassie's

243

life except Bobby, and Nick. And all she and Bobby had ever done was a little light kissing on the porch. And Nick would never have touched her. "So what's the deal here?"

She decided to tell him herself. It wasn't a fait accompli yet. But she was as good as sure. And she was going to tell Desmond when she went back to L.A. that she was going.

"I've had a very interesting offer from Williams Aircraft."

"I know. For another year. You told me," he said smugly, but Cassie only looked at him and then slowly shook her head as Pat watched her.

"No. For a world tour. A year from now. I've been thinking about it, and I talked to Dad about it before you got here. But I wanted to make up my own mind before I told you."

"A *world tour?*" He exploded onto his feet with a look of outrage.

"That's right, Nick," she said calmly. She didn't tell him the price attached to it, because that wasn't why she wanted to do it. And saying it sounded vulgar.

"I told you that's what that sonofabitch had in mind right from the beginning. Goddammit, Cassie, don't you ever listen?" He raged at her, swinging at the air with a pointing finger. "That's what the newsreels are all about, and the constant publicity. He wanted to make you into a name, and now he's going to exploit the hell out of you, and risk your life. There's a war going on, how the hell do you think you're going to do it? Even if you do figure out some insane route, which I doubt. Goddammit, Cass, I won't let you do it!"

"That's my decision, Nick," she said quietly. "It's not up to you. Any more than your joining the RAF was mine. We make our own decisions."

"Oh great. So what is this? Revenge? Because I volunteered? Or because I don't write you? Don't you understand what this guy is doing? He's using you, Cass. For God's sake, wake up, before he kills you." Nick was in a total rage over what Williams was doing, and Cass refused to see it.

244

"He's not going to kill me. That's ridiculous."

"Are you crazy? Do you know how dangerous that trip is, with or without the war? It's suicide. And you won't make it. You don't have the endurance or the experience."

"I do now."

"Bullshit, all you do is fly test flights. That's nothing like it. When was the last time you flew long distance?"

"Last week when I came here. I do it all the time, Nick."

"You'll kill yourself, you damn fool. And what about you?"

He turned to Pat with a look of fury. "You're willing to let her do this?"

"I'm not happy about it," Pat said sadly. He had just lost a son after all, but he had learned a lot in recent years, and much of it from Cassie. "But she's old enough to make up her own mind, Nick, for better or worse. I don't have a right to make her decisions for her." Cassie wanted to cheer when she heard him.

"What happened to you?" Nick looked stunned. "How can you say that?"

"Because I've grown older and wiser, and maybe you need to too. On the one hand you tell her she's on her own, you won't marry her because you're too old for her or God knows why and then you want to tell her what to do. It doesn't work that way, Nick. And even if you marry her, she may not let you tell her what to do. It's a new generation of women out there. I'm learning fast. And I'm damn glad I got Oona when I did, I can tell you. They're a complicated lot, these newfangled women."

"I don't believe you. You sold out. You've let her talk you into this."

"No." Pat was adamant. "She hasn't even told me if she's going yet. This is her decision, Nick. All hers. Not yours, or mine. I don't want to be the man who kept her from it, if I stop her, and you shouldn't either."

"And if it kills her?" Nick asked bluntly.

"Then I'll never forgive myself," Pat answered honestly. "But I still have to let her do it." There were tears in his eyes as he said the words, and she walked over and kissed him.

Nick was staring at her when she turned to him again. "Well, *are* you going to do it?" Both men held their breath while they waited, and then she nodded, and Nick looked as though he might cry.

"Yes, I am. But I haven't told Desmond."

"No wonder he called yesterday," Nick groaned in anguish. He couldn't believe she was going to do it. He had taught her himself. He knew that she was capable of great things, but not this . . . not yet . . . not now . . . and maybe never.

"He called to see how I was, and how Dad was."

"How touching." And then he looked at her in fresh rage. "And that'll be the next thing, won't it?"

"What will?" She didn't understand him and neither did Pat, but Nick was off on a new tangent.

"More publicity. More stunts. It was no accident last year when he took you to that restaurant to go dancing and had his picture taken with you. It kept things exciting in the press, mysterious . . . but he'll have to go a lot further than that now, to make things interesting, to keep it going. How much do you want to bet he'll ask you to marry him?" Nick said in a complete rage over it, and Cassie looked at him in disgust, and her father in amusement. He had never seen his old friend have a jealous fit before but that was clearly what this was, and it amused him.

"That's the most disgusting thing I've ever heard," Cassie accused him, but he was sure of it.

And Pat shared wise words with him. "If you've told her you won't marry her under any circumstances when you get back, and you won't even write to the girl now, what exactly do you expect? For her to enter a convent for the rest of her life, or stay a virgin? She has a right to a life, Nick. If not with you, then with someone else. And he seemed a decent man, if you ask me, whatever commercial motives he might have over this trip, or about his publicity. He's selling airplanes. He has to do what he can to make them

246

interesting, and if having them flown by a pretty girl, who happens to be a damn fine pilot, I might add, works for him, then more power to him. And if you don't want to marry her and he does, then I don't think you've got much to say about it, do you?" Cassie had to hide a smile as she listened to him. She had never heard her father make a speech like that, and the best part of it was that he was right. But Nick didn't want to admit it.

"He doesn't love her, Pat . . . I do."

"Then marry her," Pat said quietly, and walked out of the room, to give them some time alone. They needed it more than any two people he knew, but an hour later they were still fighting and had gotten nowhere. He was accusing her of either being naive or leading Desmond on, and she was accusing him of being infantile. It was a hell of an afternoon, and by the end of the day, both of them were exhausted. And Nick had to fly back to New York in the morning.

They talked almost all night, and nothing was resolved. He kept reminding her that he was a thirty-nine-year-old man and he was not going to marry a child, and destroy her life.

"Then leave me alone!" she shouted at him, and went to bed finally, and the next morning before he left they were both still angry at each other.

"I forbid you to fly on the world tour," he told her before he took off in his chartered plane, and she begged him to be reasonable and not give her ultimatums.

"Why can't we forget it for right now? It's not for another year, and you're leaving and going back to England."

"I don't care if I'm flying to the moon, I don't want you to sign that contract."

"You have no right to say that. Stop it, Nick!"

"No, I won't, goddammit, until you agree not to do it!"

"Well, I'm going to!" She shouted at him, her red hair flying in the wind, as he grabbed her and yanked her toward him.

"No, you're not." He kissed her hard on the lips, but they both came up fighting.

"I am."

"Shut up."

"I love you."

"Then don't do it."

"Oh for God's sake." He kissed her again, but nothing was resolved by the time he left, predictably, and as he took off, she stood crying next to the runway. And five minutes later, she stormed into her father's office. "That man drives me nuts."

"You two are going to kill each other one of these days. It's a wonder you haven't yet," he said, smiling. "Stubborn as two mules. It really will be a shame if you don't get married one day. You deserve each other. Either of you would wear anyone else out." And then he looked at her seriously for a long moment. "Do you think he's right, that Williams might ask you to marry him for publicity for the trip?"

"No, I do not." She looked incensed. "The man is terrified of getting involved with anyone. He's had two disastrous marriages. And I think if he ever did marry again, it would have to be for love."

"I hope so." But he felt better to have heard her say it. "Has he shown any particular interest in you, Cassie?" Other than coming to Chris's funeral, which he had thought was damn fine of him, and he said so.

"Not really. We're just friends. Nick doesn't know what he's talking about."

"Well, you could do a lot worse, if you don't marry that lunatic on his way back to England. I swear, he'll be the death of me one day. He and I used to have rows like that in the old days. Stubbornest sonofabitch I ever met." Cassie didn't disagree with him, as she went back to the house to check on her mother.

She left Illinois the following week, and returned to Newport Beach, to her apartment, and to work, and to sign her new contract for another year at twice the money. And on her first day back, she went to talk to Desmond alone in his office.

"Is something wrong?" he asked nervously, standing up quickly as she came in. He always did that for her when she entered the room, and she liked it. "Fitzpatrick said it was urgent."

"That depends on how you look at it," she said quietly. "I thought you'd want your answer about the world tour." But he suddenly sensed from the look on her face that she didn't want to do it, and he could feel his heart sink.

"I . . . I understand, Cass . . . I thought probably after your brother . . . I don't suppose your parents were pleased . . . it wouldn't be fair to them . . ." He was trying to accept her decision gracefully, but it was a huge disappointment for him, and very painful. He wanted this so badly. He wanted to be part of it, and to help her do it.

"No, it wouldn't be fair to them," she agreed. "And my dad wasn't pleased." They had agreed not to tell her mother yet. "But he said it was my decision entirely, so that's how I made it." He didn't say a word as he looked at her, and she came a step closer. "I'll do it, Desmond."

"What?" he whispered.

"I'll do the tour. I want to do it for you."

"Oh, my God." He sank back into his chair with his eyes closed, and then he looked up and saw her. He leaped to his feet and came across his desk to kiss her. It was a chaste kiss, but it held all the fervent gratitude that he felt for her. Nothing had ever meant more to him. And nothing would ever again be as important. He would see to that. He had a thousand plans, and he was going to share all of them with her. They had an incredible year ahead of them. And as he sat down and started telling her, he held tightly to her hand, and kept thanking her. And she was happier than ever that she had decided to do it. To hell with Nick. This was her life.

CHAPTER
15

The publicity for the world tour began almost at once, with a huge announcement at a press conference in Newport Beach. This was followed by a series of announcements and brief lectures given by Cassie, all orchestrated and organized by Desmond. She spoke to men's and women's groups, political associations, and clubs. She was interviewed on radio, and there was a special newsreel just about her. Within two weeks the press was saturated with news of her coming tour. And then suddenly in mid-August Cassie was forced right off the front pages, by the escalation of the war in Europe. The Battle of Britain had begun, the blitz as it was called. The Luftwaffe was pounding England, in the hope of destroying it. And she knew without any doubt, just by being there, that Nick was in danger. No matter how angry at him she was, the news terrified her, and all she could think of now was Nick.

She called her father to see if he'd heard from him, but of course he hadn't, even by the end of August.

"I don't see how anything could get out, Cass. You just have to know he's all right. I'm listed as his next of kin. I'll hear if anything happens." It was small encouragement, and her father had agreed with her that he was sure that by now they had pressed Nick into active service. He wouldn't be teaching anymore, he'd be flying bombers or fighters. The Luftwaffe's entire goal was to destroy the RAF, so Cassie knew Nick had to be fighting to defend it. And knowing that worried her constantly. It seemed even more awful now to have left each other on such bad terms. She only hoped that he would be safe. Nothing else mattered.

Despite the war, Desmond continued to plan the tour very carefully, and with incredible precision. They had agreed on the plane she would take, and it was already being prepared and equipped with extraordinary new instruments, extra fuel tanks, and long-range tracking devices. With Desmond's meticulous attention to detail, Cassie felt sure that they were proceeding safely.

The only real difficulty they had, and major change, was with their route, because of the war in Europe. By 1940, the war had spread to too many places. There were areas of the Pacific that weren't safe, large parts of North Africa, and of course all of Europe. It had become impossible to think of circling the globe now. But there were still extraordinary records to be set, and enormous distances to cover. And with Desmond's heightened interest in warplanes, he was anxious to prove the reliability of his aircraft over vast expanses of ocean. In essence, they were going to circle the Pacific, doing eight legs in ten days, and covering fifteen thousand five hundred and fifty miles. Their plane was to fly from Los Angeles to Guatemala City, and from there to the Galápagos. From the Galápagos to Easter Island, and then on to Tahiti. From Tahiti to Pago Pago, and then on to Howland Island, where Desmond already had a brief ceremony in mind, to honor

Amelia Earhart, and from Howland they would head for Honolulu. There would be celebrations there, of course, and he planned
to meet them, and then he would fly back with them to San Francisco, for the final triumphant leg of their tour. He was disappointed not to have her circle the globe, but the Pacific tour, as he
called it now, accomplished many of the same things. The world
tour would just have to come later, after the war in Europe was
over. And flying nearly sixteen thousand miles would establish
almost all the same things for Cassie's reputation, and that of his
airplanes. Cassie was impressed too by how sensibly he'd made
the adjustment. In some ways, it disproved all the terrible things
Nick had said about Desmond. He was not a madman, determined to kill her. Certainly that year, no one, mad or otherwise,
would have attempted to fly through Europe.

Desmond arranged more press conferences for her in the fall,
and saw to it that she was always in the news. He wanted all the
attention possible focused on her. It was also a good diversion for
people from the war in Europe. This was something wholesome
and hopeful and exciting, and she looked so beautiful in every
photograph that everyone was in love with her and wanted her to
make it. People stopped her on the street now, and men hung out
of cars to wave to her. People asked her to sign autographs. Nick
was right in that sense, she was being treated like a movie star.
But Desmond had slowed down her social life lately too. He
seemed to want to keep her "pure" and free of romantic gossip.
Nancy Firestone was still working with her, but she no longer
arranged for escorts. If Cassie went anywhere important now, she
went with Desmond. He said he could keep better control of
things if he was there. They went to openings and premieres in
Hollywood, they went out dancing at night, and to the theater.
He was good company, and she enjoyed being with him, and since
he got up as early as she did every day, he was happy to go home
early. It was the perfect arrangement.

Meanwhile, Britain was still being pounded mercilessly by the
Luftwaffe. And Cassie knew that her father had finally heard

from Nick, and he'd been safe as recently as early October. He was flying Spitfires in the 54th Squadron, and he was still stationed at Hornchurch Aerodrome. He almost sounded as though he was enjoying it, and he promised that if he had anything to do with it, the Brits would soon be kicking the shit out of the Germans. His only mention of Cassie was to tell Pat to give his love to his very unreasonable daughter. So the battle between them was not yet over, but at least he was alive, which was a huge relief to all the O'Malleys.

Even Desmond had been kind enough to inquire about his welfare, and she told him what she knew. But at least by November, the Luftwaffe seemed to be easing up a little bit. Until then, the bombings had been incessant and relentless. Children had begun arriving in the States to be cared for until after the war, and her sister Colleen had taken in two of them, which touched Cassie deeply. They were adorable, and the poor things were still completely terrified when Cassie saw them over Thanksgiving. Funnily enough they were both redheads just like she was. Annabelle was three and Humphrey was four. They were brother and sister, and their parents had lost their home in London, and had no relatives in the country. The Red Cross had arranged for them to come to New York, and Billy had flown there to get them. And he was shocked when the children asked him, on the way back, if he was going to bomb the airport.

Like everyone else, Cassie had fallen completely in love with them. Having the two children there gave her mother something to worry about and caring for them took her mind off missing Chris. It was particularly hard over Thanksgiving for everyone, but somehow they got through it, thankful for each other. Cassie went to see Jessie then too, while she was home for Thanksgiving, and she seemed to be getting over it better than the O'Malleys. She was young and eventually, for her, there would be someone else, but Cassie would never have another brother.

She ran into Bobby and Peggy too. And Cassie had correctly guessed that Peggy was pregnant. She congratulated them, and

Bobby looked as though he had grown up and flourished since he'd gotten married. His father had died, and the grocery store was his now. He was still dreaming of a chain of stores across Illinois, but for the moment he was more excited about the baby.

"And what about you, Cass?" he asked hesitantly. He didn't want to pry, and he'd heard about the tour, but he wondered what else she was doing with her life, other than flying.

"I'm pretty busy getting ready for the Pacific tour," she said honestly. And he felt sorry for her. He had long since decided that she would probably never get married, or know the happiness he now had with Peggy.

The tour didn't seem like much to him, but it was amazing how many hours of every day it consumed, reading reports, checking out the plane, and double-checking every little change the engineers made. She was also making long-range trips to get ready for the actual tour, and familiarizing herself with the details of their route across the Pacific.

She explained it to her father while she was there, and he was fascinated by all the preparations. He was anxious to see her plane, and she invited him to California to visit her, and see it. But he insisted he didn't have time, he was too busy at the airport. And he was about to get a lot busier. Billy had to be in Newport Beach right after Christmas to start preparing for the trip too. He was so excited it was all he talked about, and Pat growled constantly about what an inconvenience it would be to have him go away for seven or eight months. They were expecting the trip to take less than a month to complete but there would be press conferences and interviews afterward, if he ever came back at all. Like Cassie, he would become a hero and he would get much bigger offers than O'Malley's Airport. And Pat hated to lose him.

In December, Cassie tried to do a thousand things, before she went home again for Christmas. The days were never long enough, and finally she had to send Nancy out to buy toys for all her nieces and nephews and Annabelle and Humphrey. She bought her sisters' gifts herself, and for her brothers-in-law, and her parents. It made her sad to realize there was no gift for Chris this year, and there never would be. When he was a little boy she used to give him cars that she traded her dolls for. She would have done anything for him then, and now he was gone. She still couldn't believe it.

It was going to be a rough Christmas this year, she knew, but they were expecting it, and she was touched when Desmond came by the night before she left, to bring her a present. She had bought him a beautiful navy cashmere scarf that she'd picked out for him at Edward Bursals in Beverly Hills, and a handsome new briefcase from the Beverly Hills luggage shop where Nancy said he bought his luggage. She couldn't imagine giving him anything frivolous, like a loud tie or a baggy sweater. The very idea made her laugh. And she was thrilled when he liked his presents. They weren't personal, but they were useful, and he liked that.

The gifts he had given her reminded her, as always, of how thoughtful he was. He had given her the book *Listen! the Wind* by Anne Morrow Lindbergh, the famed aviator's wife, and a licensed pilot in her own right, and a lovely watercolor of the beach at Malibu, because he knew she loved it there. And then he handed her a smaller box, and she smiled as she unwrapped it.

"I'm not sure you'll like this one," he said anxiously, which was unlike him. And then he stopped her and took her hand. "But if you don't, Cass, just give it back, and I'll understand. You don't have to feel obliged to accept it."

"I can't imagine giving anything back that you gave me," she said kindly, and he let her start unwrapping it again. Beneath the red paper, there was a small black box, and she couldn't imagine what was in it. It was very small, and she guessed it had to be a very tiny object. And then he stopped her again and took both her hands in his own. He looked so pale, she was worried about him. This was so unlike him. It was almost as though he regretted giving her the gift at all, or was afraid of her reaction.

"I've never done anything like this," he said, looking very nervous. "You may think I'm crazy."

"Don't worry," she said gently. Her face was very close to his, and for the first time in a year and a half, she felt a strange current run between them. "Whatever it is, I'm sure I'm going to love it," she promised, speaking very softly, and he looked relieved, but still uncertain. He was a powerful man, but for this one moment, he looked so vulnerable. She couldn't imagine what was happening or why. She wondered if the holidays were hard for him, because he was alone. She felt sorry for him, as she thought of it, and then she smiled at him.

"Everything is okay, Desmond. I promise." She wanted to reassure him. They were friends now. The long preparations for the Pacific tour had already brought them closer together.

"Don't say that until you look at my present."

"All right, then let me open it," she said calmly. He took his hands away then, and she opened the box finally, and all she could do was stare at the contents. It was a perfectly round, extremely large fifteen-carat diamond engagement ring, and as she stared at it in total disbelief, he slipped it on her finger.

"Desmond, I . . ." She didn't know what to say to him. She hadn't expected this. He had never even really kissed her.

"Whatever you do, don't be angry at me," he begged. "I never intended to do this . . . not this way . . . but . . . Cass—" He looked at her imploringly, so vulnerable suddenly, so open. "I've fallen head over heels in love with you. I never expected to do that. I thought we'd just be friends, and then . . . I don't know what happened. But if you don't want to marry me, I'll understand. We'll just go on as we did before, we'll do the tour . . . Cass . . . please . . . say something . . . oh God, Cassie . . . I love you." He buried his face in her hair, and she was overwhelmed with tenderness for him. She didn't love him as she loved Nick, that would have been impossible, but she loved him as one would a dear friend, or someone who needed you very badly. She wanted to make things right for him, to be there for him, to help him. Even to erase the pain of the past for him, if she could. But not for an instant had she ever thought of their getting married.

"Oh, Desmond," she said softly, as he pulled away to look at her face and see what she was really saying.

"Are you angry at me?"

"How could I be . . . ?" She looked stunned more than anything. She had no idea what to say now.

"Oh, Cassie, God how I love you," he whispered and then kissed her for the first time, without waiting to hear if she would keep the ring, and she was startled by the extent of his passion. He was deeply emotional, in a way she had never even suspected. Everything was bottled up inside, and had been for years probably. He kissed her again, and she was surprised at herself when she responded, and was breathless when she pulled away from him. The entire experience was dizzying and she was confused by everything she was feeling. He was a far more powerful person than she was.

"I think this is supposed to be the engagement, not the honeymoon," she said hoarsely, and he grinned, looking boyish and a little wild-eyed.

"Is it? Is it the engagement, Cass?" He couldn't believe what he was hearing. He wanted it to be, but she wasn't sure yet. This was all so unexpected.

"I don't know . . . I . . . I didn't expect this . . ." But she didn't look angry at him, and she hadn't said no yet.

"I don't expect you to love me immediately. I know about your friend in the RAF . . . if . . . if you think that . . . Cassie, you have to do what's right for you . . . what about him?" He had to know now. And she wanted to be honest with him.

"I still love him." She couldn't imagine loving anyone but him. She had always loved him, as far back as she could remember. "He says he'll never marry me . . . he left in a rage about the tour the last time I saw him, and I haven't heard from him since. I don't think I will." She looked at him a little forlornly, remembering the last time she'd seen Nick. But everything with Desmond was so different.

"Where does that leave us?" he asked her gently. She looked at him and shivered. He was so good to her, so understanding. And she knew she couldn't abandon him now after all he'd done for her. But it didn't seem right to love one man and marry another. It wasn't fair to Desmond, more than anyone, but he seemed willing to accept the situation. And Nick would never marry her, that she was sure of. He was the stubbornest man alive. And she and Desmond had so much in common. They shared his business and the tour. Together they could do great things. And if she couldn't have Nick, then maybe all she needed was to be married to a good friend. It didn't seem possible to find another man she loved as she did Nick in one lifetime. And in time, she might come to love him as she did Nick, though she couldn't imagine it. But in many ways, she already cared about Desmond deeply. Marriage would be the ultimate bond between them. But it hurt to think of marrying anyone other than Nick Galvin.

"I'm not sure." She looked at Desmond honestly. "I don't want to short-change you. You've already had two marriages that cheated you out of what you should have had. I . . ." She looked into his eyes then, and saw all his desperate hope there. He was pleading with her, without saying a word, and all she wanted to do was please him. She wanted to help him, and be there for him . . . and maybe that meant she loved him.

"I know how much he must mean to you," he said understandingly. "I don't expect to replace him overnight, Cass . . . I understand . . . I just love you."

"I love you too," she said softly. And she did. She valued his friendship, and his loyalty. She respected and admired everything about him. He had done nothing but good things for her. Right from the moment they met he had been wonderful to her. And now he wanted to give her everything. He wanted her to become Mrs. Desmond Williams. She couldn't help smiling at the idea. It was more than a little overwhelming.

259

"If it doesn't work for you, we'll get divorced," he said, as though to reassure her. But she looked horrified at the suggestion.

"I would never do that." She had her parents' marriage as an example. "I don't mean to seem . . . ungrateful . . . or hesitant." She was groping for the right words, as he watched her. His eyes never left hers, and she felt the power of his wanting bore through her. She was surprised at the sheer force of him, as he held her hand and sat next to her. She could feel the strength of his need for her, and everything he wanted to give her.

"I'll never hurt you, Cass. And I'll always leave you free to be your own person. You're too important to me to try and clip your wings. You can do, and be, anything you want if we get married."

"Would you ever want children?" She was almost embarrassed to ask him. The question was so intimate, and their relationship never had been.

"They're not important to me," he said honestly. "But maybe some day, if that's what you really want, and you're not too busy flying. But I think that's something you really have to think about. You have a lot of important things to do with your life. Having children might be more appropriate for women like your sisters. That's their job. You have yours, and it's a very important one. But I'm not telling you I wouldn't have one. I just wonder if that's really what you want."

"I've never been sure. I used to think I didn't." And then with Nick, she had begun to think she would love to have his babies. She didn't feel ready to give up the idea forever. It was too soon, and she was too young to decide that, and he knew it.

"You've got plenty of time to make those decisions later. At twenty-one, it's really not all that important. And you've got the tour to think of." It was that that brought them together. And now she could imagine feeling even closer to him, if they were married.

"Desmond, I don't know what to say to you." She was near tears as he pulled her closer.

"Say you'll marry me," he said, putting an arm around her

shoulder and bringing her closer. "Say you trust me . . . say that even if you're not sure now, you believe that one day you could really love me. I already do, Cass. I love you more than anyone or anything in my life until this moment."

How could she deny that? How could she let him down, or run away from him? How could she spend a lifetime waiting for Nick when she knew he wouldn't marry her? Her father had told him as much the last time he'd been home. If Nick wouldn't marry her, he had no right to interfere with her future, or her decisions.

"Yes . . ." The word was barely more than a whisper as he stared at her in amazement. "Yes," she said it very softly, and without another sound, he kissed her. It seemed hours before he let her go again, and Cassie was trembling with emotion.

"My parents are going to be stunned," she said, looking like a child suddenly, and then she had a thought. Everything was going to be so different.

"Why don't you come home with me for Christmas?" She wanted to take him home to her family. If they were going to be married, it was important to her that he meet them and spend time with them. Her parents didn't even remember meeting him when Chris died. And their announcement would certainly make for an unexpectedly happy Christmas for the O'Malleys.

But he looked uncomfortable at the invitation. He hadn't had a family Christmas in years. He no longer even missed them. "Cass, I don't want to intrude, sweetheart. Especially not this year. It may be a lot for your parents to absorb. And holidays aren't my strong suit."

But she looked terribly disappointed. "Desmond, please. They'll think I made it up, and stole the ring."

"No, they won't. I'll call you three times a day. Honestly, I have a ton of work to do. You know that better than anyone. And when you come back, we'll go skiing for a weekend." The last thing he wanted to do was spend Christmas in Illinois with the O'Malleys. The thought of it made him desperately uncomfortable and nothing she said would persuade him.

"I don't want to go skiing. I want you to come home with me," she insisted with tears in her eyes. She was suddenly overwhelmed by events and emotions. She was *engaged* to Desmond Williams. It was amazing. And through it all she tried to force herself not to think of Nick Galvin.

"I promise we'll go next year," he said firmly.

"Well, I should hope so," she said, shocked at the idea that they wouldn't. "You're not just getting me, you're getting my family. And there are lots of us." She beamed, warming up to the idea of announcing her engagement.

"There's only one of you," he said intensely and then he kissed her again. And for a flash of an instant, she thought of Nick, and knew she had betrayed him. And as she thought of him, she remembered his warnings about Desmond. But he'd been wrong about him. Desmond was a decent man. He loved her and she knew that in time she would love him, and they would have a great life together.

"When shall we set the date for?" Desmond broke into her thoughts again as he poured her another glass of champagne. "Let's not wait too long. I'm not sure I can stand it, now that you've said yes. You'll have to keep Nancy around to protect you." He smiled knowingly at her and she blushed as she smiled up at him.

"I'll be sure to warn her," Cassie said softly. She was happy with him, she always had been, even now they were more like friends than lovers, except for the sudden fervor of his kisses.

"What about Valentine's Day?" he suggested. "It's sort of corny, but I like it. What do you think?" He sounded as though he were planning the tour, but she didn't mind that. She was used to Desmond being in control of things, but she also knew that he respected her opinions.

It was all so romantic. She was marrying a man that any woman in the world would have given her right arm to be married to, and he wanted to marry her on Valentine's Day. How much more perfect could it get, she asked herself. Not much . . .

except if Nick had felt any different . . . But she wouldn't let herself think that. She couldn't. She would hold onto the dream of him forever, but that's all it was now.

"Valentine's Day is less than two months away," she said, looking startled. "Will we have a big wedding?" She was looking down at her ring, and flashing it. It looked like a headlamp. Everything seemed so unreal. It had been a remarkable evening.

"Do you like it?" he asked, as he pulled her closer again and kissed her.

"I love it." She had never even seen a diamond that size, nor had anyone she knew. It was beyond amazing. And so was Desmond Williams.

"In answer to your question," he said, with a smile, as she flashed her ring at him again and sipped champagne, with a giggle, "no, I don't think we should have a big wedding. I think we should have a very small one, with only special people in attendance." He kissed her again, and explained, "This may be your first wedding, my love . . . but it's not mine. I think the third time one ought to be discreet, so as to generate a minimum of comment."

"Oh . . ." She hadn't thought of it, but he was right. And they couldn't be married in the church if he was divorced. She wondered if her parents would mind terribly, though her parents had never been very religious. "What are you, by the way?" she asked innocently. She had never even thought to ask him. "I'm Catholic."

He smiled. She was still a child sometimes, and he loved that. "I suspected that. I'm Episcopalian. But I think a nice friendly judge would do just fine, don't you?" Feeling herself swept away on his tides, she nodded. "And you'll need a beautiful dress . . . I'd say, something short but very elegant, in white satin. And a hat with a small veil. It's a shame we can't order something from Paris . . ." Hats from Paris, fifteen-carat rings . . . marriage to Desmond Williams on Valentine's Day. Suddenly she was staring at him, wondering if she had dreamed it all, but she hadn't. He was sitting there, talking about white dresses and hats with veils, and she was wearing the biggest diamond she had ever seen, as she looked up at him, and tears filled her eyes. She looked like a child as she sat there beside him.

"Desmond, tell me I'm not dreaming."

"You're not dreaming, my love. And we are engaged. And very soon, you'll be married to me, for better or worse, forever." He looked ecstatic and triumphant.

"Do you want to get married here?" she asked quietly, leaning against him. It was too much to absorb, she almost felt weak looking at him, and suddenly she realized more than she ever had before, how powerful he was, and how handsome. He had a quiet sexuality that he kept in control at all times, but now she could sense his nearness to her, and his interest. He hadn't stopped kissing her since he'd proposed, and she was almost feeling dizzy.

"I think we should get married here. It's not as though we can have a church wedding in Illinois, Cass. I think this is simpler, more discreet, and requires fewer explanations."

"I guess you're right. I hope my parents come."

"Of course they will. We'll fly them out for it. They can stay at the Beverly Wilshire."

"My mother will die." She grinned.

"I hope not." And then he took her in his arms again, and forgot all the arrangements. She was so young, so sweet, so pure, he almost felt guilty kissing her, and there was so much more he wanted now. But it was still too soon, and he knew it.

He seemed to have to force himself to leave that night, and he called her the moment he got home, and then again, as he always did, at three-thirty the next morning. They chatted like old friends, and it was exciting knowing that soon she would be his wife, and she would share his life forever. And together, they decided not to tell anyone, until she had told her parents. They both knew that the entire country would be very excited.

He took her to the airport himself and as usual, she had

checked out a plane to fly home. But this time, he told her repeatedly to be careful.

"It hasn't affected my brain, you know. Or maybe it has." She grinned, kissing him again. She noticed one of the ground crew watching them and smiling. "It'll be all over the papers if you don't watch out."

"Something more dramatic might end up in the papers, if you don't hurry up and marry me soon, Miss O'Malley."

"You only asked me last night! Give me a chance to get a dress and some shoes for heaven's sake. You don't expect me to get married in my uniform, do you?"

"I might. Or less. Maybe I should have come to Illinois with you." But he was only teasing. She knew he had too much to do to go anywhere, with all the plans for the Pacific tour. But she was still sorry he wasn't going.

"My parents are going to be disappointed that you didn't," she said sincerely. Especially when they heard the news. She still couldn't believe it herself, even when she saw his ring on her finger. And she would never forget how sweet he'd been when he'd asked her.

"Fly safely, my love," he warned her again, and a few minutes later he left the plane, and waved as he watched her from the runway. She took off easily, and the flight was smooth. She had plenty of time to think of him, and Nick, along the way. Her heart still ached for him, but he had made his choice, so had she. They both had to move on now.

The flight to Good Hope took exactly seven hours. She landed at dinnertime and the first person she saw at the airport was Billy.

"Ready to come to California with me next week?" she asked, but she didn't need to. He was ready to leave that night. For weeks now, it was all he could think of. And then as she signed her log, he noticed her ring, and stared down at it in amazement.

"What's *that*? A flying saucer?"

"More or less." She grinned up at him, feeling awkward suddenly. But she'd have to tell him sooner or later. "Actually, it's my engagement ring. Desmond and I got engaged last night."

"You *did?*" He stared at her in disbelief, knowing that was impossible. Or was it? "What about Nick?"

"What about Nick?" she asked coolly.

"Okay . . . sorry I asked . . . but does he know? Did you tell him?" She shook her head in answer. "Are you going to? Did you write him?"

"He doesn't write to me," she said unhappily. Why was Billy trying to make her feel guilty? "He'll find out sooner or later."

"Yeah I guess," Billy said, confused by what she'd done. Ever since he'd met them, he had known how much she and Nick loved each other. "He's going to be very upset, isn't he?" Billy said quietly and she nodded, fighting back tears. But she had made her decision, and she couldn't let Desmond down now. He wanted her to be his wife. Nick didn't. He had said so. But still, being back home made Nick all the more real, which only made it harder for her.

"I can't help Nick's being upset," she told Billy quietly. "He didn't want any ties to me when he left. He said he wanted me to marry someone else." She looked at him sadly.

"I hope he meant it," Billy said softly, and drove her home to her parents. Everyone was there waiting for her, and it was only a matter of moments before one of her sisters let out a scream, pointing at her finger.

"Oh, my God, what is it?" Megan asked, and Glynnis and Colleen pointed it out to their mother, who was playing with the children.

"I think it's a light bulb," Colleen's husband explained.

"I think it must be," Megan teased, as her parents exchanged a look. Cassie hadn't said anything when she called them.

"It's my engagement ring," Cassie said calmly.

"I figured that much out," Glynnis said. "Who's the lucky guy? Alfred Vanderbilt? Who is it?"

"Desmond Williams." Almost as soon as she said his name, as

though on cue, the phone rang. It was Desmond. "I just told them," she explained. "My sisters went into shock when they saw my ring."

"What did your parents say?"

"They haven't had a chance to say anything yet."

"May I speak to your father, Cassie?" Desmond asked gently, and she passed the phone to him, and after that, Desmond talked to her mother. Her sisters were all going wild by then, and her brothers-in-law were teasing her. She had just told them she was getting married in Los Angeles on Valentine's Day, and Desmond was going to fly her parents out for the wedding.

Her parents had come back from the phone by then. Her mother was crying softly, which she did a lot these days, and she hugged Cassie close to her. "He sounds like such a nice man. He promised me he'd always take care of you like a little girl." She kissed Cassie then, and Pat seemed pleased as well. The man had said all the right things to him. But when he was alone with his daughter that night, he asked her some questions, and he wanted to hear her answers.

"What about Nick, Cass? God willing, he's going to come back eventually. You can't stay mad at him forever, and you can't marry another man because you're angry at him. That's a childish thing to do and Mr. Williams doesn't deserve it." He had liked him on the phone that night, but he wanted to know that his daughter was being honest with him, and herself.

"I swear I'm not marrying him out of revenge. He just asked me last night, and he took me by surprise . . . but he's so alone . . . he's had such a rotten life. He's a decent person and he wants to marry me. And in a funny way I do love him, though not like Nick. We're friends and I owe him so much for all he's done for me."

"You don't owe anyone that much, Cassie O'Malley. He pays you a salary and you earn it."

"I know that. But he's been so good to me, Dad. I want to be there for him. And he knows about Nick. He says he understands. I think in time, Daddy, I could really come to love him."

"And Nick? What about him?" He looked her straight in the eye. "Can you tell me you don't love him?"

"I still love him, Dad," she sighed. "But nothing's going to change. He's going to come back and tell me why he can't marry me. He's too old, he's too poor. Maybe the truth is he doesn't love me. He hasn't written to me since he left. And before he left, he kept saying no strings, no ties, no future. He doesn't want me, Dad. Desmond does. He really needs me."

"And you can live with that? Knowing you love another man?"

"I think I can, Daddy," she said softly, but just thinking of Nick turned her knees to water. Being back here now made him all the more real to her. But she knew she had to put him out of her mind now. For Desmond.

"You'd better be rock sure before you marry this man, Cassie O'Malley."

"I know. I am. I'll be fair to him. I promise."

"I'll not have you running around here, cheating on him, and going off somewhere with Nick, when he comes back. A married woman is just that in this house."

"Yes, sir." She was impressed by what he said to her and the way he said it.

"Marriage is a sacred vow, no matter where you get married."

"I know, Daddy."

"See that you don't forget it, and that you bring honor to this man. He seems to love you."

"I won't let him down . . . or you . . . I promise."

Her father nodded, satisfied with her answers. But there was another thing he wanted to ask her now. Maybe it was unfair, but he had to ask the question. "Do you remember what Nick said before he left, about how Williams would try and marry you before the world tour, to publicize it? Do you think he's doing that now, or that he's sincere? I don't know the man, Cassie. But I want you to think about it for a minute and tell me." Nick's words had rung in his ears that night, the moment Cassie said she was getting married to Desmond Williams.

She was only twenty-one after all, and still naive. Williams was thirty-five and a man of the world. It would have been child's play for him to fool her. But she shook her head as she thought of it. This time Nick was wrong. She was sure of it.

"I don't believe he'd do that to me. I think it's just coincidence. We've worked so closely ever since I said I'd do the tour . . . and he's so solitary, I think it just happened by accident. And I think it's only coincidence that Nick said it would. It was a mean thing for him to say. I think he was jealous."

Pat nodded, anxious to believe her, and relieved, and then he had to smile at her in spite of himself. "That's nothing to the fit he's going to have when he comes home and finds you married. I warned him of that."

"I know you did. I don't think he wants to be tied to anyone . . . and certainly not me . . ." she said, but she seemed to accept her fate now. It was certainly a lucky one, and her father was pleased with what she'd told him.

He looked down at her tenderly on Christmas Eve, and held her hand in his own, and then he kissed her cheek. There were tears in his eyes when he spoke to her. And in hers when she heard him.

"Cassandra Maureen, you have my blessing."

CHAPTER

16

Cassie stayed at home until the morning of December 31, and then she and Billy flew back to Los Angeles together. It was emotional for everyone when they left. And this time, most of the family came to the airport, even little Annabelle and Humphrey. Cassie wanted to spend New Year's Eve with Desmond. And when she got back, he was waiting for her on the runway. He was wearing a navy blue coat, flapping in the breeze, and the sun was setting just behind him. He looked handsome, and tall, and very distinguished. He was an extremely aristocratic man, and together they made a striking couple.

Desmond climbed into the cockpit easily, and he startled her by kissing her on the lips, and smiling down at her before she had even left her seat. He barely even seemed to notice Billy, who looked away with a smile while they were kissing.

"Hello there, Miss O'Malley . . . I missed you . . ."

"Me too," she said with a shy smile. She had had dinner with her entire family the night before, and everyone had toasted her on her engagement. They were all excited about her wedding in six weeks, and everyone wanted to meet him. Suddenly she was the one who had done well. She was the shining star. And her engagement ring sparkled impressively on her left hand as though to prove it.

"I have a surprise for you," he said with a big smile, after finally greeting Billy. He was gathering up his things and ready to leave the aircraft.

"Not another surprise," she beamed, leaning back in her seat. "My life has been nothing but surprises for the past week." It was hard to believe that they had only gotten engaged a week before. It already seemed as though she had belonged to him forever. She was already getting used to it, and she really liked it. He was an exciting man to be engaged to.

Nick had come to mind a lot when she was in Illinois, but she had forced herself to remember that he had wanted her to marry someone else. He had given her up intentionally, and Desmond wanted and needed her very badly. And she had every intention of being a good wife to him. She smiled up at him as she thought of it, and he kissed her again, and gently touched her face with his fingers. The ground crew waited outside respectfully. The word was already out among them. O'Malley was to be the next Mrs. Williams.

"What's the surprise?" she asked excitedly while Billy watched them. Williams certainly seemed to be crazy about her, but Billy still felt sorry for Nick Galvin. It was going to destroy him when he found out he'd lost her.

"We've got some friends outside," Desmond explained, as he hung his head with a sheepish grin that made her smile. "I'm afraid I've been so excited I've been doing a little too much talking . . . Some of the boys from AP want to get a picture of us together. Everyone wants to be first. And I told everyone you were away, but they just thought . . . I told them you were coming back tonight, and when I got here . . . there they were . . . do you mind terribly, Cass? Are you too tired after the flight? I just couldn't help telling them we were engaged . . . I'm so proud . . ." He looked more boyish and more vulnerable than ever. There were times when he looked like a tycoon, or a relentless businessman, and there were others when he looked like a little boy, and she wanted to put her arms around him.

"It's okay. I'm excited too. I told everyone in Illinois. I guess if the press was there, they'd have been on our doorstep morning, noon, and night too." She stood up in the cramped cockpit, and picked up her flight bag with her log and her maps, and Desmond reached up and took it for her. And then he glanced at Billy, as though remembering him.

"You know, I don't suppose it would hurt to have your Pacific tour co-pilot on hand too. You're welcome to join us." He invited Billy with a smile, but the younger man looked embarrassed.

"I don't want to intrude."

"Not at all." He insisted on including him, as Cassie combed her hair and put on lipstick.

Desmond stepped out of the plane first, and Cassie came out right behind him. And as she did, what seemed like a hundred flashbulbs went off, and she was almost blinded. She and Desmond both waved gamely at them, and then he turned around and kissed her. And as she stepped onto the runway with him, she was stunned to realize that there must have been twenty photographers waiting for them. They didn't even notice Billy.

"When's the big day?" The *L.A. Times* shouted at them as the *Pasadena Star News* crowded in for another picture. The *New York Times* took two more, and the *San Francisco Chronicle* wanted to know about the Pacific tour *and* their honeymoon.

"Wait a minute, wait a minute . . ." Desmond laughed amiably at them. "The big day is Valentine's Day . . . the Pacific tour

273

is in July . . . and no, we're not spending our honeymoon on the *North Star*." It was the name she had chosen for her plane for the tour.

And then they asked a hundred more questions, and all the while, he stood close to her, smiling and laughing with the press, as she tried to catch her breath, and understand everything that had happened.

"I think that's all, boys," Desmond finally said good-naturedly. "My little bride has had a long flight. We've got to get home and get her rested. Thank you for coming."

They snapped a dozen more photographs as the couple got into his Packard, while one of the ground crew gave Billy a ride. And Cassie waved gamely as they drove away. Overnight she had become the bride of the year and America's sweetheart in a flight suit.

"It seems so weird, doesn't it?" Cassie asked, still struggling to absorb it. "They act as though we're movie stars. Everyone is so excited." People had stopped her on the street back home, just to ask about the Pacific tour, and they hadn't even known she was engaged yet.

"People love a fairy tale, Cass," he said quietly as he drove her home, and he patted her knee as she sat beside him. He really had missed her. "It's nice to be able to give it to them."

"I guess. But it feels weird to be one. I keep thinking to myself I'm just me . . . but they act as though . . . I don't know . . . as though I were someone else, someone I don't even know . . . and now they want to know everything, they want to be part of it." It was almost as though they wanted to own her. And the thought of that made her uncomfortable. She had tried to explain it one night to her father, and he had reminded her that it would get worse after the tour. Look at the price poor Lindy had paid . . . his infant son kidnapped and killed . . . the price of fame could be frightening. But Pat hoped that Desmond would protect her.

"You belong to them now, Cass," Desmond said, as though he

believed that. And stranger still, he seemed to accept it. "They want you. It's not fair to hold back. They want to share in your happiness. It's a nice thing to give them." Desmond always seemed to feel as though he owed a great deal to the public.

But she wasn't prepared for the intensity of their attention over the next six weeks until their wedding. She was followed everywhere, and photographed, at the hangar, in the office going over charts and maps with Billy, outside her apartment, on the way to work, in department stores, shopping for her wedding dress, and any time she appeared anywhere with Desmond.

She took Nancy Firestone with her everywhere now, and sometimes she even tried to hide, with a big hat, or a scarf and dark glasses. But the persistence of the press was astounding. They hung off fire escapes and ledges, dropped from awnings, lay under bushes and in cars. They popped out at her constantly, from everywhere, and by early February Cassie thought they would drive her crazy. And for once, Nancy was of fairly little help to her. With anything. As organized as she was, Nancy seemed to have a lot on her mind, and she seemed less interested than usual in the details of Cassie's wedding. Desmond had told Cassie not to worry about it, and he was having Miss Fitzpatrick and an assistant handle most of the details. Cassie had enough to do just dealing with the press, and getting ready for the Pacific tour. He didn't want her too distracted by having to organize her own wedding.

But when Cassie tried to talk to him about Nancy Firestone, he never took her seriously. She was trying to explain to him that she had the impression lately that Nancy was annoyed at her and she wasn't sure why. Nancy had been irritable and cool ever since she and Desmond had announced their engagement. And there was no rational explanation for it. Nancy herself seemed to spend less time with her, and on the one evening Cassie had invited her for dinner, she had insisted that she had to stay home and help Jane with her homework.

"I don't know what's wrong with her. I feel awful. Sometimes I get the feeling she hates me." They had never gotten as close as Cassie had once thought they might when they first met, but they had always been on good terms, and enjoyed each other's company when they worked together.

"The wedding probably upsets her," Desmond said sensibly, with the rationality of a man, analyzing the situation, "it probably reminds her of her husband. So she's backed off so as not to get too involved, or upset. It probably brings up painful memories for her," he said, smiling at his bride. She was so young, there were a lot of things she didn't think of. "I told you, just work with Miss Fitzpatrick."

"I will. And I'm sure you're right. I feel like a moron for not thinking of it." And the next time she saw her, she realized that Desmond's explanation fit completely. Nancy was short with her more than once, and a little brittle when Cassie asked her advice about some detail of the wedding. And from then on, for Nancy's sake, Cassie took Desmond's advice and kept her distance.

She did her best to cope with the press herself, but at times they were truly impossible to deal with.

"Don't they ever stop?" Cassie gasped one day, as she ran into Desmond's house through the kitchen, and collapsed into a chair, exhausted. She had been trying to move some of her things from her apartment, but someone must have tipped them off. They had arrived en masse before she ever got through the door, and from then on it was sheer circus.

Desmond came in the front door half an hour later, and they besieged him, and finally he convinced her to come out and pose for a few pictures with him and get it over with. He had a great way with them. He always gave them just enough to keep them happy.

"Are you nervous yet?" one reporter shouted at her and she grinned back at them and nodded.

"Only about you tripping me on my wedding day," she quipped back, and they laughed and shouted at her.

"We'll be there."

Desmond and Cassie went back inside a few minutes later, and after that the reporters went away, until the following morning.

Her parents arrived the day before her wedding day, and Desmond had arranged for a suite for them at the Beverly Wilshire. None of her sisters had come, finally. It was just too complicated with all of their children. And Cassie was especially touched that Desmond had asked Billy to be his best man. It was really going to be the home team at their wedding. Her father would give her away, even though the ceremony was being performed by a judge. And she had asked Nancy Firestone to be her matron of honor. Nancy had balked at first, claiming that one of her sisters really should be. But in the end, she'd relented after Desmond talked to her. They had selected a gray satin dress for her, and an exquisitely made white one for Cassie, by Schiaparelli. I. Magnin had made her a little hat to match, with a short white veil, and she was going to carry a bouquet of white orchids, lily of the valley, grown locally, and white roses.

Desmond had given her a string of his mother's pearls and a spectacular pair of pearl and diamond earrings.

"You'll be the bride of the year," her mother said proudly as she looked her over at the hotel. There were tears in Oona's eyes, as she thought she had never seen Cassie look so lovely. She looked radiant, and very excited. "You're so beautiful, Cass," her mother breathed, and then added proudly, "Every time I look at a newspaper or a magazine, we see your picture!"

And the next day was all that they had expected. Photographers, reporters, and newsreel crews waited outside the judge's home where they were to be married. Even the international press were there. They threw rice at her, and flowers as the wedding party left to return to the Beverly Wilshire, where Desmond had arranged a small reception in a private room. There were even crowds outside and in the lobby of the hotel, because someone had leaked to the press that that was where they were going.

Desmond had invited about a dozen friends, and several of his more important designers were there, particularly the man who had designed Cassie's plane for the Pacific tour. It was an impressive group, and the bride looked like a star in a movie. She was the most beautiful thing Desmond had ever seen, and he beamed as they danced a slow waltz to the "Blue Danube."

"You look ravishing, my dear," he said proudly, and then he smiled even more broadly. "Who would have ever thought that the little grease monkey I met under a plane less than two years ago would have turned out to be such a beauty. I wish I'd had a picture of you that day . . . I'll never forget it."

She rapped his shoulder with her bouquet and laughed happily as her parents watched her.

It was a perfect day, and after Desmond, she danced with her father, and then Billy. He looked very handsome in the new suit he had bought for the occasion. He was having a great time in L.A., particularly with all the money he was making. And he was enjoying some of the best flying he had ever done, in planes he had longed all his life to get his hands on.

"You have a wonderful daughter, Mrs. O'Malley," Desmond said warmly to his new mother-in-law. Cassie had bought her a blue dress the same color as her eyes, and a little hat to go with it, and she looked very pretty, and very much like her daughter.

"She's a very lucky girl," Oona said shyly. She was so impressed by Desmond's elegance and sophisticated air, she could hardly speak to him. But he was very polite to her and very friendly.

"I'm the lucky one here," he disagreed with her. And a little while later, Pat toasted them and wished them many happy years and many children.

"Not till after the Pacific tour!" Desmond qualified, and everyone laughed, "But immediately thereafter!"

"Hear! Hear!" her father said proudly.

Desmond had decided to let the press in for a round of pictures of them. They were in the lobby anyway, and he thought it was better to do it in a controlled situation. They arrived en masse, led by Nancy Firestone, and they got a very pretty picture of the bride dancing first with Desmond, and then her father. They made a big deal about his being a flying ace from the last war, and Cassie gave them all the details, knowing it made her father feel important.

And then, finally, they escaped to a waiting limousine in a shower of rose petals and rice. Cassie was wearing an emerald green suit, and a big picture hat, and the photographs of her afterward were spectacular, as Desmond lifted her easily in his arms, and put her in the limousine. They were both waving from the rear window as they drove away, and her mother was crying and waving. Her father had tears in his eyes as he stood beside her.

The newlyweds spent the night at the Bel Air Hotel, and the next morning they flew to Mexico, to a deserted beach on a tiny island off Mazatlan, where Desmond had rented an entire hotel just for them. It was small, but perfectly private. The beach was as white as pearls, the sun was brilliant and hot, there was always a gentle breeze, and at night they were serenaded by mariachis. It was the most romantic place Cassie had ever seen, and as they lay on the beach and talked, Desmond reminded her that some of the places she would go on her tour would be even lovelier and more exotic.

"But I don't suppose I'll be spending much time lying on beaches," she smiled at him, "or with you. I'll really miss you."

"You'll be doing something incredibly important for aviation, Cassie. That's more important." He said it firmly, as you would to a child who was not paying attention to her homework.

"Nothing is more important than we are," she corrected him, but he shook his head.

"You're wrong, Cass. What you're going to do has far, far-reaching importance. People will remember you for a hundred years. Men will attempt to follow your example. Planes will be named for you, and designed after yours. You will have proven that plane travel over vast expanses of ocean can be safe, in the right aircraft. A myriad of people and ideas will be affected. Don't think for a moment that it isn't of the utmost importance." He made it sound so serious, so solemn, that it didn't even sound like flying. And she wondered sometimes if he attached too much importance to it, like a game that had stopped being fun and had become so vital that people's lives depended on it. Hers did of course, and Billy's, but still . . . she never lost sight of the joy of it. But he did.

"I still think you're more important than anything." She rolled over on her stomach in her new white bathing suit, resting on her elbows. And he smiled down as he saw her.

"You're too beautiful, you know," he said, looking at the gentle cleavage between her breasts. She had a very exciting body. "You distract me."

"Good," she said comfortably. "You need it."

"Shame on you." He leaned down and kissed her then, and a little while later they went back to their room. He was amazed, and so was she, at how easily they had adjusted to each other. She had been afraid of him at first, and of what physical love might be, but he had surprised her by not forcing it, and spending their night at the Bel Air merely holding her, and stroking her, and talking about their lives, and their dreams, and their future. They had even talked about the tour and what it meant to them.

It had allowed her to feel at ease with him, just as she always did. And it was only when they reached the hotel in Mexico the following afternoon that he permitted himself to undress her. He peeled her clothes gently away from her, and stood looking at her astounding body. She was long and tall and lean, with high round breasts, and a tiny waist that curved into narrow but appealing hips, and legs almost as long as his. He had taken her slowly and carefully, and in the past week, he had shown her the exquisite ecstasies of their joined bodies. And as with everything he did, he did it expertly and well, and with extraordinary precision. And she had been ready for him. She wanted to be his wife, and to be there for him, and to make love to him, and prove to him that someone loved him. She was healthy and young and alive and vital and exciting. He was much more restrained, but she pushed him to heights he had forgotten for a long time, and he found himself enjoying the unexpected youth and abandon she brought him.

"I don't know about you," he said hoarsely, after they made love that afternoon, "you're dangerous." He enjoyed making love to her enormously, much more than he had expected. There was a warmth and sincerity to her, which added to her passion, surprised him and touched him.

"Maybe I should give up flying, and we should just stay in bed and make babies," she said, and then she groaned at herself, thinking that she was becoming just like her sisters. It made her wonder if this was what had happened to them; it was just so easy to be swept away, in the arms of a man you loved, and abandon yourself to the pleasures of the flesh, and their obvious rewards, in the natural order.

"I always thought they were missing so much by marrying so young, and having so many kids," she explained to him as they lay side by side on the bed, their bodies hot and damp and sated. "But I guess I can see now how it happens. It's just so easy to let things be, to be a woman, and get married and have babies."

But Desmond shook his head as he listened to her. "You can never do that, Cass. You're destined for far greater things."

"Maybe. For now." If he said so. Right now, she felt as though she were destined for nothing more than his arms, and she didn't want more. That was enough for her. Just to be his. Forever. Her sudden introduction to the physical side of him had swept her to a place she had never known, or understood before, and she liked it. "But one day I'd like to have kids." And he had said he would be willing if that was what she wanted.

"You have a lot to do first. Important things," he said, sounding like a schoolteacher again, and she grinned, and turned over to look at him and run a lazy finger enticingly around him.

"I can think of some very important things. . . ." she said mischievously, as he laughed and let her do as she wanted. The results were inevitable. And the sun was setting on their desert island when they fell from each other again like two bits of lifeless flotsam in the ocean.

"How was the honeymoon?" the reporters shouted at them from their front lawn as they got home. As usual, they had somehow learned when the Williamses would be arriving, and as the limousine drove up, the reporters rushed forward. Sometimes it made her wonder how they always knew where they would be and where they were going.

They could hardly get through the door into the house, and then as usual, Desmond stopped for a moment and spoke to them, and while he did, they snapped a thousand pictures. The one on the cover of *Life* the next week was of Desmond carrying Cassie over the threshold.

But from that moment on, for Cassie, the honeymoon was over. They had been gone for two idyllic weeks, and the first morning back, he woke her at three, and she was back in training in her *North Star* by four o'clock that morning.

Their schedule was grueling and she and Billy were put through their paces a thousand times. They simulated every disaster possible, taking off and landing with one engine, then two, flying in with both engines cut, and practicing landing on the shortest of runways and in ferocious crosswinds. They also simulated landings in all kinds of conditions, from the difficult to nearly impossible. They also simulated long distance flying for hours at a stretch. And whenever they weren't flying, they were poring over charts, weather maps, and fuel tables. They met with the designers and engineers, and learned every possible repair from the mechanics. Billy spent hours practicing with the radio equipment, and Cassie in the Link Trainer, learning to fly blind, in all conditions.

She and Billy flew hard and flew well; they were a great team, and by April, they were doing stunts that would have dazzled any air show. They spent fourteen hours together every day and Desmond brought her to work at four A.M., and picked her up promptly at six o'clock every night. He took her home, where she bathed, and they ate a quick dinner. Then he retired to his study with a briefcase full of notes and plans for the tour, and recently with requests for visas. He was also busy arranging for fuel to be shipped to each of their stops. And of course he was negotiating contracts now for articles and books afterward. Generally he brought papers for her to look over too, about weather conditions around the world, important new developments in aviation, or areas they would have to watch out for on the tour, given the sensitivities of the world situation. It was like doing homework every night, and after a long day of flying she was seldom in the mood to do it. She wanted to go out to dinner with him once in a while, or to a movie. She was a twenty-one-year-old girl, and he was treating her like a robot. The only times they went out at all were to the important social events that he thought were useful for her to be seen at.

"Can't we do anything that doesn't have to do with the tour anymore?" she complained one night when he had brought her a particularly thick stack of papers, and reminded her that they needed her immediate attention.

"Not now. You can play next winter, unless you've planned another record-setting flight. Right now, you have to get down to business," he said firmly.

"That's all we do," she whined, and he looked at her with disapproval.

"Do you want to end up like the *Star of the Pleiades*?" he asked angrily. It was Earhart's plane, and there were times when Cassie was sick of hearing him say it.

She took the papers from him, and went back upstairs, slamming her study door behind her. She apologized to him later on, and as always, he was very understanding.

"I want you to be prepared, Cassie, in every possible way, so there will never be a mishap." But there were elements they both knew he wouldn't be able to anticipate for her, like storms, or problems with the engine. But so far, he had thought of every-thing, down to the merest detail.

Even Pat was vastly impressed by what she told him of their preparations. The man was a genius at planning and precision. And more so at public relations. Even if he was compulsive about all his plans, he had her safety in mind, and her well-being.

And as a reward for her hard work, he took her to San Fran-cisco for a romantic weekend in late April, and Cassie thoroughly enjoyed it, except for the fact that he had set up three interviews for her when they got there.

Their publicity stepped up radically in May. There were press conferences every week, and footage of her flying in newsreels. She and Billy made appearances everywhere: on radio and at women's clubs. They did endorsements and posed for photo-graphs constantly. She felt sometimes as though she had no life of her own anymore, and in fact she didn't. And the harder they worked, and the closer they got to the tour, the less time she and Desmond spent together. He even went to his club a few hours at night sometimes, just to get a breather. And more often than not, by late May, he read papers in his study until he fell asleep there.

She was so sick of it that he suggested she go home for a week-end in May, for a break, and she was relieved to go. She was also happy to see her parents. This time it meant not being with Des-mond on her birthday, but he gave her a beautiful sapphire brace-let before she left and told her they'd be together for the next fifty. Even she didn't feel it was a tragedy to miss this one. She was too tense now before the tour to enjoy it much anyway. And she and Desmond seemed miles apart these days. All he cared about was the tour.

It was ridiculous; she was turning twenty-two years old, mar-ried to one of the most important men in the world. She was one of the most celebrated women herself, and she was feeling restless and unhappy. All Desmond talked about was the tour, all he wanted to do was read about it, all he wanted her to do was pose for pictures, and spend fifteen hours a day flying. There was more to life than that. At least she thought so, but he didn't seem to know she was alive these days. And in some ways, she wasn't. There was certainly no romance in their life. Just the tour and its myriad preparations.

"How much goddamned flying can we do?" she complained to Billy on the way home. He had decided to come with her for the long weekend. "I swear, sometimes I think I'm beginning to hate it."

"You'll feel better once we get under way, Cass. It's just rough waiting to go now." The tour was only five weeks away, and they were both getting tense about it. Cassie could feel it. And on top of it, she had been married for three and a half months, and she felt as though she were no closer to Desmond than before they got married. Their nights together certainly weren't romantic, she thought to herself as they flew east, but she didn't say anything to Billy.

Instead they talked about the press conferences Desmond had set up in L.A. and New York. And he wanted them to go to Chicago for an interview after the weekend, but so far Cassie hadn't agreed to do it.

"God, it's exhausting, isn't it?" She smiled at Billy when they were halfway there. She was glad she was going home. She needed to see her parents.

"I figure that later we'll think it was all worth it," Billy encouraged her, and she shrugged, feeling better.

"I hope so."

They flew on in silence for a while, and then he looked at her. She had looked particularly tired and unhappy lately. He suspected that the constant pressure from the press was getting to her. They were a lot easier on him. But they devoured Cassie, and Desmond never seemed to protect her from them. On the contrary, he liked them.

"You okay, Cass?" Billy asked after a while. She was like a younger sister to him, or a very best friend. They spent almost all their time together every day, and they never argued, or snapped at each other, or got tired of each other's company. She was going to be the perfect companion for the Pacific tour, and he was gladder than ever that he was going.

"Yeah . . . I'm okay . . . I'm feeling better. It'll be good to get home and see everyone."

He nodded. He had gone to San Francisco the week before, to see his father, who was so proud of him. He knew how much Cassie's family meant to her. She needed them right now, just as he had needed to see his father. And then, suddenly, alone in the plane, he found himself wanting to ask her something he had felt awkward asking her before. But she seemed very relaxed now.

"Do you ever hear from Nick?" he asked casually, and she stared out into the clouds for a long time and then shook her head.

"Nope, I don't. He wanted us both to be free. I guess he got what he wanted."

"Does he know?" Billy asked quietly, sorry that things hadn't worked out for them. Nick was a great guy, and Billy had always sensed how much Cassie loved him. Right from the first day he'd met them. It was as though they belonged to each other.

"About Desmond?" she asked, and he nodded. "No. Since he didn't want to write, I figured he'd just hear eventually. I didn't want to write and tell him." She also didn't want to write him and upset the balance. Something like that could make you just loose enough to make a fatal mistake in a fighter plane, and she didn't want that. "He must know by now. I know he writes to my dad sometimes." But she had never asked Pat if he had told him. It was still too painful to even think about, and she forced him from her mind as they flew over Kansas.

The press was waiting for them as they touched down in Illinois. They had spent the entire day waiting for them at her father's airport. And she knew there wasn't going to be any peace anymore, not until after the tour. It was just too close now.

She did what Desmond always wanted her to, gave them plenty of time, lots of photographs, satisfied them by answering some questions, and then she called it a day, and said she was anxious to go home to her mother.

Her father had been waiting for her, and he posed for photographs with her too, as did Billy. And then finally, the photographers left, and she heaved a sigh of relief, as she and Billy threw their things into her father's truck, and he looked at her with a long, slow smile. But she had noticed as soon as they'd arrived that her father didn't look well.

"You okay, Dad?" He looked kind of gray, and she didn't like it. But she figured maybe he'd had influenza. She knew her mother had when they returned from California. And he worked hard for a man his age. Harder now that Nick was gone, and she and Billy, and Chris. . . . He had to rely entirely on hired hands, and the usual nomadic crews of wandering pilots.

"I'm fine," he said unconvincingly. And then he looked anxiously at his daughter. Oona said he should have told her on the phone, but he wasn't sure what to say. But she had to know now. Pat hadn't told Nick either. And amazingly neither had anyone else. He had only arrived the night before though.

"Something wrong?" She had sensed his hesitation. Billy was unaware of it, as he looked at the familiar landscape out the window.

"Nick is here," he said all at one gulp, looking straight ahead.

"He is? Where is he staying?" she asked uncomfortably.

"At his own place. But I imagine he'll come by the house eventually. I thought I'd better warn you."

"Does he know I'm coming?" Pat shook his head, and Billy watched her eyes. He had just heard what her father had said, and he hoped it wouldn't upset her too much.

"Not yet. He got in last night. He's just here for a few days. I didn't have a chance to tell him." She didn't dare ask if he had told him she was married.

She said not another word, and a few minutes later she was in the arms of her mother. Billy carried in her things, and Pat took him into Chris's room. His things were still everywhere, and it was a shock to walk in and see it. It made Cassie's heart ache to look around. It was as though he would be home any minute.

She settled into her old room, and her mother had dinner waiting for them. It was a hot, simple meal of the things Cassie liked best, fried chicken, corn on the cob, and mashed potatoes.

"I'd be the size of this house if I lived here," Cassie said happily between mouthfuls.

"Me too," Billy grinned happily, and her mother was flattered.

"You've lost weight," Oona reproached her with a worried frown. But Billy was quick to explain it.

"We've been working pretty hard, Mrs. O'Malley. Test flights fifteen hours a day. Long distance runs all over the country, we're testing everything we can before July."

"I'm glad to hear it," Pat said.

And as Oona cleared the table and prepared to serve them apple pie with homemade vanilla ice cream, they heard footsteps on the porch, and Cassie felt her heart stop. She was looking at her plate, and she had to force her eyes up to look at him as he came through the door. She didn't want to see him, but she knew she had to. And when she did, he took her breath away. He was more handsome than he had ever been, with his jet black hair, brilliant blue eyes, and a dark suntan. She almost gasped when she saw him, and then she blushed bright red, and no one moved or said a word. It was as though they all knew what was coming.

"Did I interrupt something?" Nick asked awkwardly. He could sense the tension in the room, like another person. And then he saw Billy. "Hiya, kid. How's it going?" He strode around the room to shake his hand, and Billy stood up, grinning, his face still freckled, his eyes alight with pleasure to see him.

"Things are great. What about you, Stick?"

"I'm starting to sound like a limey." And then, inevitably, he looked down at her, and their eyes met. There was a world of sadness in hers, and a look of wonder in his. He had missed her more than he had ever wanted. "Hi, Cass," he said quietly. "You're looking good. Getting ready for the tour, I guess." The last newsreel he'd seen had talked about it, but it was five months old. They were a little behind the times at Hornchurch, for obvious reasons. He had done nothing but fly for the last year, every moment, every hour, every second. That and pull the bodies of dead women and children from burning buildings in London. It had been a tough year, but he felt as though he were being useful. It was better than sitting here, picking corn from his teeth and waiting for mail runs to Minnesota.

Oona offered him dessert, and he sat down cautiously. He could sense that he had interrupted something, or that they all felt awkward with him. Or maybe he just imagined it. He wasn't sure, but he chatted amiably with Billy and Pat, and Cassie said nothing. She went out to the kitchen to help her mother. But she had to come back eventually, while they all ate dessert. She didn't touch her apple pie, even though her mother knew she loved it. Pat knew what was wrong with her. And so did Billy. But Nick had no idea what had happened.

He lit a cigarette afterward, and stood up and stretched. He had lost a lot of weight too, and he looked young and firm and lean and very healthy.

"Want to go for a walk?" he asked her casually. But there was nothing relaxed about the question. He knew something was wrong, and he wanted to ask her himself. For a terrifying moment, he wondered if she'd fallen in love with Billy. Nick hadn't been home in almost a year, not since Chris had died. It was just an odd quirk of fate that he had come back when she was here. But as always, he was glad to see her. More than that, it filled his soul with light and air, and all he wanted to do was kiss her, but she was holding back purposely and he knew it. He figured she was probably mad at him. He had made a point of not writing to her all year. He didn't want to lead her on. He had meant what he said when he left her.

"Something wrong, Cass?" he asked finally, when they reached the stream that ran along the far edge of her father's property. She had said not a single word until then.

"Not really," she said softly, trying not to look at him, but she had to. She couldn't keep her eyes from him. No matter what she had told herself that year about being ready to move on, about caring for Desmond and his needing her, she knew without a doubt she was still in love with Nick, whether he loved her or not. That was the way it was between them. But she would never have betrayed Desmond. She remembered her father's words when she'd told him she wanted to marry Desmond. And she was going to honor her marriage, if it killed her. But it might, she realized, as she looked up at Nick. Just seeing him made her heart ache.

"What is it, sweetheart? . . . You can tell me . . . whatever it is, if nothing else, we're old friends." He sat down next to her on an old log, and took her hand in his, and then as he looked down, he saw it. The thin line of gold on her third finger, left hand. She hadn't worn her engagement ring home this time, just her wedding band, that said it all, as his eyes met hers and she nodded. "You're *married*?" He looked as though she had just hit him.

"I am," she said sadly, feeling, despite all her explanations to herself, and the fact that he had told her to move on, that she had betrayed him. She could have waited. But she hadn't. "I got married three months ago . . . I would have told you . . . but you never wrote anyway . . . and I didn't know what to say . . ." Tears rolled slowly down her cheeks, and her voice caught as she told him.

"Who? . . ." Billy had looked very uncomfortable with her, and they had come home together. Nick had always felt they were right for each other, and he was the right age. It was what he had wanted for her, but it hurt so damn much now thinking of it, it brought tears to his eyes. "Billy?" he asked in a choked voice, trying to sound noble, but this time she laughed through her tears, and took her hand away gently.

"Of course not." She hesitated for a long time, looking away, and then, finally, back up at him. She had to tell him. "Desmond."

There was an endless silence in the warm night air, and then a shout of disbelief, almost of pain, as he understood it. "Desmond *Williams?*" As though there were ten others with the same first name. He stared at her in outraged agony as she nodded. "For God's sake, Cassie . . . how could you be such a fool? I told you, didn't I? Why the hell do you think he married you?"

"Because he wanted to, Nick," she said with a tone of annoyance. "He needs me. He loves me, in his own way." Though she knew better than anyone that most of the time there wasn't room in his life for more than planes and papers.

"He doesn't need anything but a flight director and a newsreel crew and you know it. I haven't seen a newsreel that's less than five months old in a year, but I bet he's pumped the hell out of marrying you, and you've spent more time posing for pictures than Garbo."

"It's five weeks before the tour, Nick, what do you expect?"

"I expected you to have more brains, to see him for what he is. He's a charlatan and a bullshitter, and I've said it since the day I met him. He's going to use you until he's squeezed you dry, or fly you till you drop, or wind yourself around a tree somewhere in a machine that's too much for you. He cares about one thing: publicity and his goddamn aircraft company. The man is a machine, he's a publicity genius, and that's all he is. Are you telling me that you love him?" He was shouting at her, and she flinched as he stood right in front of her and cast aspersions on her husband.

"Yes, I do. And he loves me. He thinks of me constantly. He takes care of . . . sure he cares about his planes, and the tour, but he's doing absolutely everything to protect me."

"Like what? Sending you with waterproof cameras and a frogman crew? Come on, Cassie, come off it. Are you telling me he hasn't publicized the hell out of your marriage? I haven't seen any of it, but I'll bet they have here. I'll bet you tossed your bouquet right at the cameras."

"So what for God's sake?" He was closer to the truth than he knew, but Desmond was always telling her to cooperate and be patient, that the press was an important part of their life, and her tour. But she was sure he had not married her because of it. That was disgusting, and hearing Nick say that made her angry. What right did he have to criticize? He hadn't even written to her. "What do you care anyway?" she fought back. "You didn't want me. You didn't want to marry me, or write to me, or come home to me, or even offer me any hope if you did get back from the war. All you want to do is play ace in somebody else's dogfight. Well, go for it, flyboy. You didn't want me. You told me that. You just wanted to smooch around with me while you were here and then go off to your own life. Well, go for it. But I have a right to a life too. And I've got one."

"No, you don't," he said viciously, "you have a figment of your imagination. And as soon as the tour is over, and he doesn't need the illusions anymore to feed the press, he's going to dump you so fast your head will spin, or maybe he'll keep you around and ignore you." It was what he was doing now, but she knew it was because he had so much work to do before the tour. She wanted Nick to be wrong. Everything he said was unfair, because he was a sore loser and he was angry. And then he went on to make it worse as he took another step closer to her. He wanted to yank her right off the log and into his arms, but out of respect for her, he didn't. "I hear he keeps half a dozen mistresses quietly stashed away, Cass. Has anyone told you that, or have you figured it out for yourself yet?" He said it viciously, but he also looked as though he believed it.

"That's ridiculous. How would you know anyway?"

"Word gets around. He's not the saint he appears to be, or the husband," he said sadly. He wished he had married her himself, but it seemed so wrong to him when he left. It still did. But so did her being married to Desmond. "The guy's a bastard, Cass. He probably doesn't love you at all. Face it. He's a showman and a con man. You didn't marry him. All you did was join the circus." But hearing Nick say those things about Desmond frightened her so much all it did was make her want to strike out to stop him.

She reached back to slap him with all her strength, but he was faster than she was. He grabbed her arm and pulled it behind her, and then he couldn't help himself. He kissed her harder than he ever had, harder than he would have dared at any other moment, but she wasn't a little girl anymore, she was a woman. And without even thinking, she felt herself respond to him, and for an endless piece of time, the two clung to each other in unbridled passion. It was Cassie who finally pulled away, with tears rolling down her cheeks. She hated what was happening to them, hated herself for what she had done to him, but it had seemed so right at the time to marry Desmond. Maybe she was wrong.

But that wasn't the issue now. The issue was Nick, and what they no longer had a right to.

"Cassie, I love you," Nick said urgently as he held her in his arms again, but this time he didn't kiss her. "I always have, I always will. I didn't want to ruin your life, but I never thought you'd do anything this stupid . . . I thought you'd wind up with Billy." She laughed at the idea, and sat down next to him on the log again, thinking about the mess she'd created. She was in love with two men . . . or maybe only one . . . but she was obsessed with one, and married to another.

"Being married to Billy would have been like marrying Chris," she laughed sadly.

"And being married to *him?*" he asked in a choked voice. He wanted to know now.

"He's very serious," she sighed, "everything he does is for the tour right now. I think he's doing it for me. I don't know, Nick . . . I thought I was doing the right thing. Maybe I made a mistake. I just don't know."

"Cancel the trip," he said urgently. "Divorce him." He was panicking. He would do anything. He would marry her if that was what she wanted. But every fiber of his being told him she was in danger.

"I can't do that, Nick," she said honorably. "It wouldn't be fair. He married me in good faith. I can't walk out on him. I owe him too much now. He's got so much riding on this tour, he's invested so much in it, not just the plane . . ." It didn't bear thinking about.

"You're not ready for it."

But she was. And she knew it. "Yes, I am."

"You don't love him." He looked suddenly so young and so vulnerable. She wished she had waited for him, but she hadn't.

"I'm not in love with him. I never was. He knew that. I told him about you, and he accepted it. But I do love him. He's been too good to me for me not to love him. I can't let him down now, Nick."

"And afterward? Then what? You're stuck with him forever?"

"I don't know, Nick. There are no easy answers."

"They're as easy as you want them to be," he said stubbornly.

"That's what I said to you two years ago, Nick, before you left. And you didn't listen to me either."

"Sometimes things seem more complicated than they are. We make them that way, but we don't have to," he said wisely.

"I married him, Nick, for better or worse. Whether I loved you or not. I can't abandon him, just because you say so."

"Maybe not," Nick said tersely, "but he'll abandon you one day, emotionally if not otherwise, when this is over. It's all for publicity. You'll see, Cass. I know it."

"Maybe. But until then, I owe him something. And I'm not going to break my word, or betray him. He is my husband. He deserves better than the two of us defiling him. I won't do it."

He looked at her for a long time, and then seemed to sag as the force of her words hit him. "You're a good girl, Cass. He's a lucky man. I guess I've been a fool all along. I thought I was too old for you . . . and too poor . . . and too foolish. I was part right anyway." And then he couldn't resist a cheap shot, "How does it feel to be married to one of the richest men in the world?"

"No different than being married to you would have been," she came back at him quickly. "You're both spoiled boys who want everything your own way. Maybe all men are like that, rich or poor," she said, meeting his gaze, and he laughed at her. She hadn't lost her spirit.

"Touché. I wish I could be happy for you, Cass, but I'm not."

"Try. We don't have any other choice." She had to live up to the choice she'd made. For all their sakes. She was an honorable woman. He nodded then, and eventually they walked back slowly, holding hands in the starlit night and talking. He realized more than ever what a fool he'd been, but he had made his decisions for her, and look what had happened. Her father had been right. He had set her free, and she had married someone else. But Desmond Williams . . . he hated everything he knew about him. And he was convinced to his bones that he was using Cassie. And she was much too young and innocent to know it. He was forty years old and he could read Desmond like the front page of the *New York Times*. And so far, Nick didn't like the headlines.

Cassie said good night to him on the front porch, and they didn't kiss again. And it was only after she had gone inside that Nick saw his old friend, quietly sitting in a chair and watching.

"Keeping an eye on me, Ace?" Nick asked with a tired grin, and sat down in a chair near him.

"I am. I told Cassie months ago I'll not have her defiling her marriage."

"She's not going to. She's a good girl. And I'm a fool. You were right, Pat."

"I was afraid I would be." And then, in the partnership among men, he was honest with his old friend, the boy who had been his protégé in another war, a quarter of a century before. "The worst of it for her is that she still loves you. You can see it. Is she happy with him?" Pat asked him conspiratorially.

"I don't think so. But she thinks she owes him everything."

"She owes him a lot, Nick. There's no denying it."

"And if she gets hurt?" Nick didn't want to say "killed" to her father. But it could happen, and they knew it. "What do we owe him then?"

"It's the risk we all take, Nick. You know it. She knows what she wants and she knows what she's doing. The only thing she's not sure about is you."

"Neither am I. I still wouldn't have married her by now. I didn't want to leave her a widow." He laughed emptily then. "I thought I was too old for her, but hell, he's almost as old as I am."

"We're all fools. I almost didn't marry Oona thirty-two years ago. I thought she was too good for me, and my mother told me I was crazy. She told me to go for the brass ring. I was right. She is too good for me . . . but I love the girl . . . to this day, I've never regretted a single day of our marriage." It was more than he had ever said to her, and the advice was too late for Nick. For now anyway. But if Nick was right about Desmond tossing Cassie aside, maybe she'd be free again someday. It was hard to say now.

They sat on the porch together and talked for a long time, and Nick noticed when they stood up that Pat was a little breathless. That was something new for him, and Nick didn't like it.

"You been sick, Ace?"

"Ahh . . . nothing much . . . a little influenza, a little cough . . . I'm getting too fat, Oona's cooking's too good. I get breathless sometimes. It's nothing."

"Take it easy," Nick said with a worried frown.

"Tell yourself," Pat laughed at him, "shooting Jerries all day. I'd say you've got a lot more to worry about than I do."

Nick nodded, grateful for the things Pat had said to him about Cassie. "Good night, Ace. See you tomorrow."

Nick walked all the way back to his shack, and everything in it was dusty. He hadn't been home in a year, but it felt good to be there. Everything felt good to him, except the fact that Cassie was married. He still couldn't believe it. He lay in his familiar bed that night, aching for her, unable to believe that she belonged to someone else now . . . that sweet face . . . the little girl he had loved so much was no longer his, and never would be again. She was Desmond's. And as he fell asleep that night, the tears rolled slowly from his eyes and into his pillow.

CHAPTER
17

The weekend at home turned out to be difficult for both of them. Cassie made every effort to stay away from Nick, but their world was too small. And they kept running into each other everywhere, at the house, at the airport, even at the grocery store when she did some shopping for her mother. And he tried to be respectful of her, for her sake, if not for Desmond, but it was impossible. They wound up in each other's arms again the night before she left. It was the night of her twenty-second birthday. He'd had dinner with her and her family. And all through the meal, they were inexorably drawn to each other like magnets. They knew it was their last night to see each other, and there might never be another chance again. The very thought of that made them panic.

"We can't do this, Nick," she said after kissing him longingly. "I promised Dad I wouldn't. And I can't do it for me . . . or to Desmond." And the way the press followed her around, all she needed was a scandal. They had tried to get pictures of everyone at the airport today, but Nick had disappeared discreetly into his shack until the photographers left and then he emerged again, and she was grateful. She knew that Desmond would have been very upset to see Nick in the pictures. She hadn't told him Nick was home when she called him.

"I know, Cassie . . . I know." Nick didn't argue with her. He didn't want to hurt her. They sat on the porch and talked. Her parents had gone to bed an hour before but they hadn't said anything when Nick had stayed to talk to Cassie. She was leaving the next day and it was their last chance to be together.

"Are you sure you're ready for the tour? Billy says your plane is heavy as hell."

"I can handle it."

He didn't argue with her about it this time. "Is your route safe?"

"It better be. Desmond works on it every night until midnight."

"That must be fun for you," he said smartly, and then he smiled at her ruefully. "Damn fool. You could have had Bobby Strong and be selling onions, and what do you do? You marry the biggest tycoon in the country. Can't you do anything right, Cass?" he teased and she laughed. There was nothing laughable about it, but if they didn't laugh, they'd cry. Just in the few days that they'd both been in town, it was obvious to both of them that they were cursed with loving each other forever. Each time they met, or looked into each other's eyes, the power of what they felt for each other brought them closer. There was no escaping it. And Cassie realized now that it wasn't something time would change. She and Nick were part of each other. They always would be. There was no denying it anymore. She had never loved Nick more, and now she had to live with the agony of loving Nick and not wanting to betray Desmond.

But on this last night, they both knew this was their only chance to be together, and perhaps their last one. He was returning to the war to risk his life again, and she was taking every chance possible, flying across the Pacific. It was too late for games, or even anger anymore. They just had to live with what they'd done. They had both been foolish, and they knew it.

"What are we going to do, Cass?" he asked unhappily, as they looked at a full moon in a starry sky. It was a perfect night to be in love, but their story was no longer simple. They both longed for the early days when they had spent hours together at the deserted airstrip. They could have done anything then. And instead, they had made such stupid choices, he to fight another war, and she to marry a man she cared for, but didn't love. She knew only too well that despite all her loyalty to Desmond, Nick was the only man she loved or ever would. Maybe one day it would change, but it hadn't yet, and she didn't think it would for a long time, if ever. She'd been kidding herself when she married Desmond, and now that she saw Nick again, she knew it.

"I wish I were going back to England with you," she said sadly.

"So do I. There are no women flying in combat over there. Not yet anyway, but the limeys are pretty open-minded."

"Maybe I should run away and join the RAF," she said, only half serious. She couldn't see how she was going to live her life now. In a way, she was grateful for the tour. At least it would keep her busy, and away from Desmond.

"Maybe I never should have gone in the first place," he said, surprising her totally. And listening to him worried her. If he lost heart now, he could get hurt. She had heard too many stories like that, of men who lost their girlfriends or their wives, and then got killed in action.

"It's too late to say that now," she scolded him, "you'd better pay attention to what you're doing."

"Look who's talking," he laughed, thinking of what she was facing in barely more than a month. The thought of her tour still worried him sick, as he invited her to take a walk with him, and they walked slowly from her parents' house toward the airport. It just seemed to act like a magnet for them. He told her what England was like for him, and she told him about the tour, and their route across the Pacific.

"It's a damn shame the war won't let you do a proper one. I'd feel better than with those long stretches across the Pacific." But that was where the glory was right now, and they both knew that.

They were at the airport while they talked of it, and almost without thinking, they wandered toward the old Jenny. It was a warm night, and the moon was so bright, they could see easily across the airport.

"Want to go for a ride?" he asked hesitantly. She had a right to tell him to go to hell, but they both knew she didn't want to. She wanted to be alone with him for a while, and forget her other life, and the fact that they had to leave each other again tomorrow. This time maybe forever.

"I'd like that," she said softly. And without another word, she helped him push the plane out, and do their ground check. They sailed into the midnight sky easily, with all the familiar sounds and feelings. But there was something different about doing it at night. They were in their own world up there, a world full of stars and dreams, where no one else could touch or hurt them.

He hesitated only briefly at the old airstrip where they used to meet, and brought the little plane down easily in the moonlight. And then he shut the engine off, and helped Cassie from the plane. They had no idea where they were going, they just knew they needed to be together now, in their own world, away from everyone. And here it was so peaceful. Without thinking, they both wandered toward the place where they used to sit and talk for hours. She felt so much older now, and so much sadder. Her brother was gone, and she had lost all hope of being Nick's now. It was here that he had kissed her for the first time, and told her he loved her. It was the day he had told her he was joining the RAF. And they'd been making bad decisions ever since then.

"Don't you wish you could turn the clock back sometimes?" she asked, looking up at him as he watched her sadly.

"What would you do differently, Cass? Then, I mean?"

"I'd have told you how much I loved you a long time ago. I never thought you'd care because I was just a kid. I thought you'd laugh at me." She looked beautiful as he watched her standing beside him.

"I thought your father would have me arrested." It was strange to realize now that Pat wouldn't have disapproved of him, and they had loved each other for so long. And now she was married to someone else, it was all so crazy.

"My father might have you arrested now," she smiled, "but not then, I guess." But she wasn't even sure he'd object now. He knew how much they loved each other, even though this was exactly what he had told her he didn't want her doing. But he had softened so much over the years. He was her closest friend now. Especially now that Nick was gone. Her father had been surprisingly understanding about everything she'd done. It still surprised her.

They walked over to their old familiar log, and the grass was damp. Nick took the old flight jacket off, and let her sit on it, and then he sat down beside her and took her in his arms and kissed her. They both knew why they had come here. They were grown-ups now. They didn't need permission, or have to tell lies. Not tonight at least. They were here because they loved each other, and needed something to take away with them.

"I don't want to do anything dumb," he said as she nestled close to him, and he worried about her. It was the same worry he had had about her when he left for England. But things were just different enough now to warrant the risk, and in an odd way, this time he almost hoped he'd leave her pregnant. Maybe then she'd have to leave Desmond.

And as she lay down beside him, and felt his powerful arms around her, as he kissed her, she wished the same thing. But within moments, their future paled in comparison to their present.

She felt hot flames shoot through her as they kissed, and within minutes, her silvery flesh shimmered next to his in the moonlight. It was a night that neither of them would ever forget, and they both knew it would have to sustain them for years, maybe forever.

"Cassie . . . I love you so much . . ." he whispered tenderly, holding her, feeling her body next to his in the warm night air. She was more beautiful than he'd ever dreamed as they lay with their clothes scattered in the dew around them. "I was such a fool." He lay on his side, looking at her, carving each moment in memory. In the moonlight, she looked like a goddess.

"I was a fool too," she whispered sleepily, but right now she didn't care, as long as she could lie in his arms and be near him. This was all she wanted. For this one moment in time, this was all that mattered.

"Maybe one of these days, we'll both get smart . . . or lucky," he said, but he doubted it. It was all too complicated now. All they had was this. Tonight. In the silver moonlight.

They lay side by side for a long time, and they made love again just before sunrise. They had both fallen asleep, and awoke in each other's arms, aching for each other in the balmy morning. The sun came up, smiling down at them, and this time he watched her graceful limbs kissed not by silver, but by the golden light of sunrise. And afterward, they held each other close for a long time, wishing they could stay there forever.

When they flew back to her father's airport, the sky was streaked with pink and gold and mauve, and they both looked peaceful as they tied down the Jenny. She turned to him then with a long, slow smile. She didn't regret anything they'd done. This was their destiny.

"I love you, Nick," she said happily.

"I'll always love you," he answered, and then he walked her back to her parents' house. They belonged to each other now. Theirs was a bond that could not be broken.

Her parents' house was quiet as they stood outside. It was still early, and no one was up as Nick held her in his arms, and stroked her hair, trying not to think of the future, or Desmond Williams. They stood there for a long time, not wanting to leave each other as he kissed her again, and she told him again and again how much she loved him.

He left finally when he heard her parents get up and move around. They had no regrets. They needed each other's strength to go back to their lives, with all the terrors and challenges they would be facing.

"I'll see you before I go," she promised him in a whisper, and then she pulled him close to her again, and kissed him on the lips with agonizing softness. He wondered how he would ever leave her again, or watch her go, especially knowing that she was going back to her husband.

"I can't let you go, Cass."

"I know," she said unhappily, "but we have to." They had no choice now, and they knew it.

He left her then and she walked slowly into the room she'd lived in as a child, thinking of him, and wishing things were different.

She showered, and dressed, thinking of Nick, and then she had breakfast with her parents. And as Nick had seen earlier, she noticed that her father was having trouble breathing. But he insisted it was nothing. And as soon as they were finished eating, her father drove her and Billy to the airport. She promised to call her mother frequently before the tour, and maybe even to fly back once more if she could. But she wondered if Desmond would let her. Seeing her father look so pale made her think she ought to.

Nick was in the office when they arrived, and he looked at her long and hard as they said good-bye, and then he walked out to their plane with them, chatting idly with Billy. But every moment, Cassie could sense him close by, she could feel the satin of his flesh on hers, and their exquisite pleasure. The real bond they shared was time and love and caring, but with passion added to it,

Cassie knew now that the flame of her love for him would burn forever.

"Take it away, you two," Nick admonished them, thinking of the tour again. "Watch out that she doesn't fly into a tree somewhere," he warned Billy, and then shook his hand, while Cassie did their ground checks, and he watched her. Nick couldn't keep his eyes from her, and she loved feeling him near her.

She kissed her father then, while Billy settled in, and then there was no escaping it. It was time to say good-bye to Nick. Their eyes met and held, their hands touched, and then he pulled her into his arms and kissed her gently in front of the others. He didn't care anymore. He just wanted to be sure she knew he loved her.

"Take care, Cass," he whispered into her hair after he kissed her. "Don't do anything crazy on that tour of yours." He still wished she wouldn't go but he knew he couldn't stop her.

"I love you," she said softly, with eyes full of tears that told him everything she felt for him and mirrored everything he felt. "Let me know how you are sometime." He nodded, and she stepped up into the cockpit as he squeezed her hand for the last time. It was almost impossible this time to leave each other. Pat was watching them, sorry for both of them. But he said nothing to reproach them.

Her father and Nick were still standing there as they taxied down the runway in the huge Williams Aircraft plane she'd borrowed from Desmond. Once off the ground, she dipped her wings at them, and then they were gone. Nick stood staring at the sky for a long time, long after Pat had walked back into the airport, long after her plane had left the sky. All he could think of now was lying beside her in the moonlight. And in a way, he was relieved that the next morning, he'd be going back to the war. He couldn't stand being here now without her.

She and Billy didn't talk much on the flight back to L.A. Her mother had given them a thermos of coffee, and some fried chicken. But neither of them was hungry. Her eyes told a thousand tales, but he didn't ask her any questions for the first two hours. And then, finally, he couldn't stand the silence any longer.

"How do you feel?" She knew what he was asking her, and she sighed before she answered.

"I don't know. I'm glad I saw him. At least he knows now." She was filled with hope and despair all at once. It was hard to explain it to Billy. At least Nick knew about Desmond now, but in some ways their time together had only made it harder for her to go back to California.

"How did he take it?"

"As well as he could have. He was furious at first. He said a lot of things." She hesitated and then looked at her friend grimly. "He thinks Desmond married me as a publicity stunt to make the tour more appealing to the public."

"Is that what you think?" he asked pointedly, and she thought about it and hesitated. She didn't want to think that. "Sounds like sour grapes to me. Maybe it's hard for Nick to admit to himself that the guy really loves you." But did he? He was so cool to her now, so involved in the tour, and nothing else about her. What if Nick was right, she wondered. It was hard to know, hard to see clearly, especially after the night she'd spent with Nick at the old airstrip. But she knew for certain that she had to put that out of her mind now. She wanted to be fair to Desmond. And she had to think of the tour. She could work the rest out later.

But thinking of the tour reminded her again of everything she owed Desmond. Nick wasn't being fair, and she didn't believe that Desmond had other women. He was completely driven by his work, he was obsessed with it. In a way, that was their biggest problem. That, and Nick Galvin. But she was returning to L.A. determined to play fairly. She wouldn't allow Nick to cast a shadow of doubt on their marriage.

But from the moment she returned, Desmond did everything Nick had predicted. All he did was talk about the press, and the Pacific tour. He didn't even ask about her weekend with her parents. And in spite of herself, she found herself suddenly suspicious of Desmond's coolness, and his constant love affair with photographers and newsreels. She questioned him about some interviews he had scheduled for her, balking at the necessity of it, and the tensions between them were instantly apparent.

"What exactly is it you're complaining about?" he snapped at her nastily at midnight on the day after she got back from her parents. She was exhausted from flying a twelve-hour day, followed by five hours of meetings. And he had ended her day with a bevy of reporters and photographers to take her picture.

"I'm just tired of falling over photographers every time I get out of bed, or climb out of the bathtub. They're everywhere, and I'm tired of it. Get rid of them," she said pointedly, with a look of irritation.

"What is it that you're objecting to?" he said angrily. "The fact that you're the biggest name in the news, or that you've been on the cover of *Life* magazine twice this year? What exactly is your problem?"

"My problem is that I'm exhausted, and I'm tired of being treated like a show dog." Nick's warnings were affecting her. And she realized that she was suspicious of Desmond. But she really was tired of reporters.

And Desmond very clearly didn't like being challenged. He was furious with her. After another hour of arguing pointlessly, he moved into the small guest room off his study. He spent the rest of the week sleeping and working there, claiming he had too much work to do to move back into their bedroom. But she knew he was punishing her for complaining. But in a way it was a relief, and it gave her time to sort out her own confusion. Being with Nick hadn't made things any easier, but she knew that part of that was her own fault.

Eventually, things calmed down again with Desmond. Tensions were high, and their nerves were raw because of the pressures of the tour, but he apologized to her for being "testy." He tried to explain the value of the press to her again, and she decided that

Nick was wrong about him. There was a certain truth to what Desmond was saying. Publicity was an important part of the Pacific tour, and he was right, there was no point accomplishing it in silence.

Desmond was a decent man, she knew. He just had very definite opinions. And he obviously knew what he was doing.

But in spite of their peace treaty over the press, some things didn't improve. For months now, they had had no love life whatsoever. More than once, she had wondered if there was something wrong with him, or with her, but she would never have dared to ask him. All he thought about was the tour. The budding passion of their honeymoon was long since forgotten. She knew that some of that had made her more vulnerable to Nick. But she also knew that her love for Nick was something Desmond had no part in. But her lack of physical relationship with Desmond made it hard for Cassie to feel close to him, and sometimes she wished she had someone to talk to. She thought of saying something to Nancy Firestone, but ever since her marriage to Desmond, Nancy had put a very definite distance between them. It was as though she felt uncomfortable being friendly with Cassie since she was the boss's wife now. But with no friends except Billy, and Desmond so cool, it made Cassie feel lonelier than ever.

In spite of whatever tensions existed, everything moved ahead on schedule. They were within a week of the tour, and they were ready.

Photographers followed her everywhere chronicling her last week before the trip, every action, every meeting, every movement. She felt as though she was spending her entire life smiling and waving. There was no privacy, no quiet time with Desmond. Everything was the Pacific tour, and the endless preparations for it. This was her only life now.

It was also getting very exciting for all of them. Cassie could hardly sleep anymore. And they were down to five days when Glynnis called her late one afternoon, and reached her at the airfield. Cassie was surprised to hear from her, and wondered if anything was wrong.

"Hi, Glynn . . . what's up?"

"It's Dad," she answered quickly. She started to cry before she could say another word, and a vise of steel clutched Cassie's heart as she listened. "He had a heart attack this morning. He's in Mercy Hospital. Mom's with him." Oh God . . . no . . . not her father.

"Is he going to be okay?" Cassie asked her oldest sister quickly.

"They don't know yet," Glynnis said, in tears again.

"I'll come home as soon as I can. Tonight. I'll tell Desmond and start in a little while." Without a moment's hesitation, Cassie knew she had to be there.

"Can you do that?" Glynnis sounded worried, but she knew she had to call her. They had told her at first that her father wasn't going to make it. But in the last hour he had stabilized, and they were cautiously hopeful. "When do you leave on the tour?"

"Not for five more days. I've got time, Glynn. I'm coming . . . I love you . . . tell Dad I love him . . . tell him to wait . . . not to go . . . please . . ." She was sobbing.

"I love you too, baby," Glynnis said, in the strong voice of her older sister, "I'll see you later. Fly safely."

"Tell Mom I love her too." They were both crying as she hung up the phone, and then she went to tell Billy what had happened, and that she was going home to see her father. Without hesitating for an instant, he said he'd go with her. They were inseparable these days, like Siamese twins. They had become like each other's shadows in the six months of training. Sometimes they even seemed to know what the other was thinking.

"I'll meet you back here in half an hour. Do me a favor. Gas up the Phaeton. I'm going to go tell Desmond." But she knew he'd understand, Cassie thought. He knew how much her father meant to her.

But when she got to his office, she was in for a surprise.

"Of course you're not going," he said coldly. "You've got five days of training and briefings left, two press conferences, and we have to plot the final course according to the weather."

"I'll be back in two days," she said quietly. She couldn't believe he was arguing with her about something this important.

"You will not," he said firmly, as Miss Fitzpatrick slipped out of the room discreetly.

"Desmond, my father had a heart attack. He may not survive it." Obviously, he didn't understand, Cassie thought. But he did. Perfectly.

"Let me make myself clear, Cass. You're *not* going. I am *ordering* you to stay here." He sounded like an air marshal in a war. It was ridiculous. He was her husband. What was he talking about? She looked at him in confusion.

"You're *what?*" He repeated himself for her benefit and she stared at him. "My father may die, Desmond. I'm going home to him, whether you like it or not." Something hardened in her eyes as she said it.

"Against my wishes, and not in one of my planes," he said coldly.

"I'll steal one if I have to," she said furiously. "I can't believe you're saying these things. You must be tired, or sick . . . what's wrong with you?" There were tears in her eyes, but he was immovable. The tour meant everything to him. More than her father. Who was this man she had married?

"Do you have any idea how much money is riding on this tour? Do you care?" he spat at her.

"Of course I care, and I wouldn't do anything to jeopardize it, but this is my father we're talking about. Look, I'll be back in two days. I promise." She tried to calm down again, and remind herself that they were both under a lot of pressure.

"You're not going," he repeated coldly. This was ridiculous. What was he trying to do to her? As she looked at him, she started to tremble.

"You have no choice!" she shouted at him, losing control finally. "I'm going! And Billy's coming with me."

"I won't allow it."

"What are you going to do?" She stared at him with new eyes suddenly. She had never seen him so heartless. He had never been cruel to her before. This was a new insight into Desmond. "Fire us both? Isn't it a little close to the trip, or do you think you can replace us?" She was not amused by his behavior.

"Anyone can be replaced. Eventually. And let me explain something to you, Cass, while we're on the subject. If you *don't* come back, I'll divorce you, and sue you for breach of contract. Is that clear? You have a contract with me for this tour, and I intend to hold you to it." She couldn't believe what she was hearing. Who was he? If he meant what he was saying, the man was a monster.

Her mouth opened as she listened to him, but no sound came out. Nick had been right. All that mattered to him was the tour. He didn't care about her or her feelings, or the fact that her father was dying. He would have divorced her for canceling the tour. It was incredible. But so was everything he had just said to her.

She walked slowly to his desk, and looked at him, wondering if she even knew him. "I'll fly the tour for you. Because I want to. But after that, you and I are going to have a serious conversation." He didn't answer her, and she turned around and walked out of his office. She was threatening the only thing in his life he cared about, his precious Pacific tour. But the real shock was that it meant more to him than their marriage.

She said not a word to Billy as she climbed into the plane, and she signed the plane out properly. She suddenly felt like an employee and nothing else. Her face was taut and angry as they took off, and Billy watched her. She had wanted to fly, so he didn't offer to take the controls. It kept her mind occupied while she tried not to worry about her father, but he could see that she did anyway. But she looked angry more than worried, and he wondered what had happened.

"What did he say? . . . about our going, I mean . . ."

"You mean Desmond?" she said icily and he nodded. "He said

he'd divorce me if I didn't do the tour. And he'd sue me for breach of contract." It had to sink in for a minute before Billy reacted.

"He said *what*? He was kidding obviously."

"He was not kidding. He was deadly serious. If we cancel, he's going to sue the pants off us. Me, anyway. Apparently, the tour means a little more to him than I thought. This is the big time, Billy. Big investments, big money, big stakes, big penalties if we blow it. Maybe he'll sue our families if we crack up his plane for him," she said sarcastically, as Billy listened in amazement. She sounded angry and bitterly disappointed.

"But you're his wife, Cass." He was confused by what she was saying.

"Apparently not," she said miserably, "just an employee." He had disappointed her terribly. But then again, families were not his forte. "I told him we'd be back in two days. We're in deep shit, kid, if we aren't." She grinned at him. They were in it now, up to their ears, but at least they were together. She was grateful he had come with her. He was truly her only friend now.

"We'll be back in time. Your dad'll be fine." He tried to reassure her.

But when they got to Mercy Hospital, Pat was anything but fine. Three nuns and a nurse were standing at his bedside, and a priest had just given him the last rites. All of his children and grandchildren were there, and Oona was crying softly.

Cassie cleared the kids out first, she sent them outside with Billy. She knew he could manage them, he was like the pied piper with kids, and one of her brothers-in-law volunteered to go with him. And then she hugged her mother, and talked quietly to her sisters. Pat wasn't rallying, and he hadn't regained consciousness since Glynnis called her. The doctor came to talk to her a few minutes after that, and he said that he was doubtful now that Pat would make it.

Cassie couldn't believe what she was hearing, or what had happened to him. She had seen him only four weeks before, and he hadn't looked great, but she'd had no idea that he was this sick.

Apparently, his heart had been giving him trouble for a while, but he ignored it, despite Oona's pleadings.

Cassie and her mother and all three of her sisters sat with him all night, and by morning there was still no improvement. And it was only late the following day that he regained consciousness, and smiled briefly at Oona. It was the first sign of hope they'd had, and two hours later, he opened his eyes again and squeezed Cassie's hand and told her he loved her. All she could think of then was how much she had loved him as a little girl, how good he had always been to her, and how much she had loved flying with him . . . she thought of a thousand things . . . a hundred special moments.

"Is he going to be okay?" she asked the doctor when he came by that afternoon, and he said it was still too soon to tell. But after another sleepless night for all of them, miraculously, the next morning, as the nuns kept silent vigil with them, saying their rosaries, he stabilized, and the doctor said he was going to make it. It was going to be a long haul, and he predicted two months of solid rest, most of it at home in bed, and after that, with any luck at all, he'd be a new man. But he'd have to take care of himself, not smoke so much, and cut out the whiskey and Oona's home-made ice cream. It was the greatest relief in Cassie's life as she stood crying in the hallway with her sisters. Her mother was still in the room with him, breaking the news to him about the ice cream.

"Who's going to run the airport?" Megan asked as they stood in the hallway. Pat had no assistant these days, and ever since Nick and Cass and Billy had been gone, all the responsibility had fallen on his shoulders. The doctor thought it had probably contributed to the problem. There was no one else around to help him handle the airport.

"Do you know anyone?" she asked Billy in an undertone. He had stood staunchly by them for two days, just as Chris would have. He was almost like their son now. But he didn't know anyone to help out either. A lot of the younger pilots who used to float around had volunteered for the RAF after Nick did.

"I'm stumped," he said, as she looked at him. They were due back in L.A. that night. They were leaving on the Pacific tour in three days. As Billy looked at her, he read her mind, or he thought he did, but he couldn't believe she would do it. "You're not thinking what I think you're thinking . . . are you?"

"I might be." She looked at him seriously. It was a big step. Particularly after what Desmond had said before they left. A very big step. A final one possibly. But the only one, as far as she was concerned. And if he wanted to divorce her for that, let him. This was her father. "You don't have to stay with me though. You can go back so he doesn't get mad at you." Things were going to get rough once she told him.

"I can't go without you," he said calmly.

"Maybe he'll get someone else." She was being naive, and Billy knew it, even if she didn't. After all the publicity she'd had for the past year, and all the careful orchestration, it would never have had the same impact without her, and Desmond knew that.

"What are you going to do?" Billy asked worriedly. He didn't want her to get hurt by her decision, but he also knew what her father meant to her, and what her priorities were. There was no doubt about what she was going to do, just about how she was going to do it.

"I'm going to call him and tell him to postpone it. He doesn't have to cancel it. Just postpone it. All I want is two months, three max, so Dad can get back on his feet, and I can stay here and run the airport."

"I'll stay with you. Possibly permanently," he grinned. "We may both be out of a job in about ten minutes." But it was more than a job to her, he realized. For Cassie it was her marriage. But after Desmond's threats the day before, she wasn't sure if she had a marriage anymore, or if she'd ever had. Maybe Nick had been right about him all along, or maybe Desmond had just let the emotions of the moment get away from him, and by now he was sorry. Interestingly, he had not called Cassie once, at home, or at the hospital, since she'd left. She hadn't heard a thing from him in two days. And when she called him five minutes later from the hospital switchboard, Miss Fitzpatrick answered her with a tone of ice and went to get him.

He came on the line to her almost immediately, and she was sorry about the lack of privacy in the hospital lobby, but it couldn't be helped. She had to tell him as soon as possible, and she didn't want to go all the way to the airport to talk to him from her father's office.

"Where are you?" were his opening words.

"At the hospital in Good Hope. With my father." As though he didn't remember. He did not ask her about his father-in-law, or how she was. For all he knew, her father was dead by then, but he didn't inquire about him. "Desmond, I'm sorry to have to do this."

"Cassie, I'm not going to listen to what you're telling me," he said in a tone of icy fury. "Remember what I said to you when you left, and remember that I meant it." She paused only long enough to catch her breath, and remind herself that this was a man she had married four and a half months before. It was suddenly difficult to believe it. He was everything Nick had said he was, and wasn't.

"I remember everything you said perfectly," she shouted at him across a poor connection. "And I seem to remember marrying you. Apparently, you've forgotten. There's more to life than world tours. I'm not just a machine, or a flyboy in a dress, or one of your employees. I'm a human being with a family and my father almost died two days ago. I'm not leaving him. I want you to postpone the tour for two or three months. I'll go in September or October. You figure out when. Make whatever adjustments you have to for the weather and the course. I'll do whatever you want. But I'm not going three days from now. They need me here. I'm not leaving."

"You bitch," he shouted at her, "you selfish little bitch! Do you know what I've put into this, not only in money, but in time and love and effort? You have no idea what this means to me, or to the country. All you're interested in is your own pathetic little tawdry life with your seamy little family, and your father's embarrassing little airport." He spoke with utter contempt for her, and for them, and she couldn't believe what she was hearing. What a heartless bastard he was to even say things like that to her. It was almost impossible to believe it. And as she listened to him, she felt a physical pain as she realized that she and Desmond Williams had never had a marriage. She had just been a tool to get him what he wanted.

"I don't care what you call me, Desmond," she shouted across the lobby, indifferent to who heard her anymore. "Postpone the trip, or cancel it. It's up to you. But I'm not going now. I'll fly anything you want in the fall, but I'm not going in three days. I'm staying with my father."

"And Billy?" he asked furiously. He wanted to fire both of them, but he knew he couldn't.

"He's staying here with me, with my tawdry little family, at our embarrassing little airport. And I won't fly it for you next time, Desmond, without him. You've got us, if you want us. But later. Let me know what you decide. You know where to reach me."

"I'll never forgive you for this, Cassie."

"So I gather." And then she couldn't help asking. "What exactly is it you're so angry about, Desmond, as long as I've agreed to do it later?"

"The embarrassment, the postponement. Why should we have to put up with this childish garbage from you?"

"Because I could have gotten sick . . . because I'm human. That's it, why don't you just tell the press I'm sick or something." She laughed shallowly, knowing that it was beyond impossible, at the moment. "Tell them I'm pregnant."

"You don't amuse me."

"I'm sorry to hear that. I'm not finding you very amusing either. In fact, I'm finding you very disappointing. Call me, when

315

you decide what you're doing. I'll be at the airport for the next two months. Call me anytime," she said with tears in her eyes, and then hung up on him with a bang. She had wanted to tell him she was sorry for postponing the trip, but he had treated her so abominably that in the end she hadn't. She was sorry to have to postpone it, she knew it was hard on everyone involved, but she just couldn't let her father down now. He had always been there for her, and now she wanted to be there for him. But there were tears of anger and defeat in her eyes when she hung up the phone, and her hands were shaking. And as she put the receiver back in the cradle she happened to glance at the old nun who was running the switchboard. She was smiling at her, and she gave her a sign of victory from her seat at the switchboard.

"You tell 'em," she growled. "America loves you, Cass. They can wait another two or three months. Good for you for staying with your father. God bless you."

Cassie smiled gratefully at her, and went back to report to Billy.

"What did he say?" he asked anxiously.

"I'm not sure yet. I told him to postpone it, and said that we'd fly it for him in September or October. He called me a lot of rude names. I wouldn't exactly say he was pleased. And I told him you were staying here with me, and that I wouldn't fly the next one without you. It's a package deal." Billy whistled at the courage she had shown, and he patted her shoulder. "But listen, if you want to go back, I understand. You can even fly it for yourself if you want to." There was a lot she needed to think about now. About the trip, about her marriage, about everything he had said to her, and the things he hadn't. He had exposed himself to her completely. There were not many illusions left. After four and a half months, their marriage was over. In reality anyway, but not in the papers.

What she hadn't counted on was Desmond arriving in Good Hope the next day, and bringing with him over a hundred reporters and two newsreel crews. He announced right from the steps of Mercy Hospital that due to circumstances beyond their control, the Pacific tour was being postponed until October. He explained that his father-in-law was critically ill, and Cassie couldn't leave him. She would be running her father's airport for him for two months, and then training again for the tour in September. He caught her completely by surprise and he proved once and for all that he was everything Nick had said he was. He was a total fake and a bastard. And through it all, he pretended to care deeply about her father.

But he hadn't even told her he was coming. He had just showed up at the hospital, asked for her, and when she came out to see him, looking surprised, she found him waiting with a lobby full of reporters. He had set up a full press conference on the hospital steps, without even warning her. And she looked haggard and exhausted and unprepared, which was exactly what he wanted. He wanted America to feel sorry for her, so they would forgive her for canceling the tour. But there was no question of it. They would forgive her anything. It was Desmond who wouldn't. She was so overcome, and so tired, and so emotional, and so angry at him, that she ended up crying when the reporters asked her about her father. It was exactly what Desmond wanted.

And when the press had left, he walked her outside and explained to her in no uncertain terms what he expected from her. She had exactly two months "leave," as he put it, from the tour. On September 1, she was to come back to L.A. to train again and attend briefings, and on October 4 they would leave on the same course, with some slight adjustments for weather. Any variation from that plan, or any failure on her part to appear in Los Angeles, as agreed, would result in a lawsuit. And to be sure she understood perfectly, he had brought contracts with him for her and Billy to sign, and he reminded her that he was flying back the plane she had arrived in.

"Anything else? Would you like my underwear or my shoes? I think you paid for them too. I left my engagement ring in L.A., but you're certainly welcome to it, it's yours. You can have my wedding ring too." She slipped it off her shaking hand, and held it out to him with trembling fingers. Everything that had happened in the past few days was a nightmare. And he looked at her now, totally devoid of emotion. He was a man who felt nothing for anyone, not even the girl he had married.

"I suggest you leave it on until after the tour, so as not to cause any gossip. You can dispose of it quietly after that, if you like. That's up to you," he said coldly.

"That's what this was all about then, wasn't it? It was all about a publicity stunt for the tour. America's sweetheart and the big tycoon. Why did you bother? And what happened to you? Why are you so willing to expose yourself now? Just because I postponed it? Is that such a sin? I know it's inconvenient, and expensive to change plans. But what if we'd had a problem with the plane . . . or I got sick . . . what if I did get pregnant?"

"There was never any danger of that, I can't have children." He hadn't told her that either. He had let her think that it was an option, that they would have them one day, when she was ready. She couldn't believe how totally he'd misled her, and how willing he was now to admit it. He had shown his hand to her completely. But he didn't care. All he wanted from her was the tour; he knew that he could sue her, and destroy her publicly if she didn't do it. The stupid thing was that she didn't care what he did to her. All she cared about was that he had lied to her. He had asked her to marry him, told her he loved her, pretended he cared about her. He didn't care about anything except his tour, and the planes he would sell as a result. And the publicity he would derive from organizing it from start to finish.

"What do you want from me?" She looked at him sadly.

"I want you to fly. That's all I ever wanted from you. I want you to fly. And I want everyone to fall in love with you. Whether or not I did was never important."

"It was important to me," she said with tears in her eyes. She had truly believed him.

"You're very young, Cassie," he said quietly. "One day you'll be happy you did this."

"You didn't have to marry me to make me fly the tour. I'd have done it anyway."

"It wouldn't have had the same impact on the public," he said without embarrassment. His marriage to her had been totally calculated. She wondered if he had ever cared for her for a single moment. She felt totally stupid now, gullible and used. It was embarrassing to think of their physical relations. Even their honeymoon had probably been a sham. And everything after that had been business anyway. He hadn't wasted much time on romance.

"You never took the tour seriously. Your postponing it now just proves that. I probably should have picked someone else, but you seemed so perfect." He looked at her as though she had cheated him and she stared at him in amazement.

"I wish you had picked someone else," she said, and meant it.

"It's too late now. For both of us. We have to go through with it. We've all gone too far now."

"We certainly have." She looked at him pointedly. Or at least he had.

He had nothing else to say to her, no apology, no regrets, no words of comfort. He just told her to be in L.A. on schedule on September first, and she and Billy signed their contracts. Desmond drove back to the airport then, and an hour later he was gone. He had gotten what he'd come for, their sworn promise, and a round of publicity using Cassie again. By the following week, the entire country knew about her father's heart attack, they'd seen her cry, they sympathized completely. It only made the tour more exciting.

And at Mercy Hospital, her father was bombarded with flowers and gifts and get-well cards. They had to give them away to other patients, and then start taking the floral arrangements away in trucks, to other hospitals and churches. Cassie had never expected a response like that. But Desmond had. As usual, he had known exactly what he was doing.

He kept feeding them stories regularly, and gave interviews from L.A. about how hard Cassie was working, and what progress they had made on her plane. But interestingly, in August, one of the engineers discovered a potential flaw in one of the engines. They were doing wind tunnel trials at the California Institute of Technology when the engine burst into flame, and it caused untold damage to her airplane. It could be repaired, the press was told, but it had been providential that the tour had been delayed and she'd had to stay home with her father. The first Cassie heard of it was when she read the newspaper to Billy, and he whistled.

"Nice, huh? How would you have liked to be peeing on your number-one engine over the Pacific?" she said with a raised eyebrow.

"Give me enough beer, and I can do great things, Captain." He grinned, and she laughed. But they were both concerned, and they spoke to the engineers several times over it. Everyone assured them that the problem had been taken care of.

It was a tough summer for her. She was still in shock over everything that had happened with Desmond. She thought of Nick a great deal, and she wanted to write to him, but she wasn't sure what to say now. In a funny way, it was hard admitting that Desmond was as bad as Nick thought he was. It made her sound so pathetic. In the end, she just wrote to him about her father, and said that the tour had been postponed, and that she'd always love him. She decided to tell him the rest later, the next time she saw him. She thought of volunteering for the RAF too, but she didn't want to think about that until after the Pacific tour. Maybe afterward, in November, she could fly over to see him. They hadn't heard from him in two months, though that wasn't unusual. The war in Europe was raging on and they could only assume he was safe since they hadn't been notified otherwise. She missed him constantly, and read everything she could about the air war in England.

Most of the fun had gone out of the tour for her. To be doing it under threat was very different from doing it for love, or as a shared project. But she knew it would be interesting anyway, and now all she wanted to do was get it over and done with. She could get on with her life then.

Her father made steady improvements after he went home. He lost some weight, he stopped smoking, and seldom drank, and he looked healthier and stronger day by day. And by the end of August, he came back to the airport. And he seemed better than ever. He was amazed at all that she and Billy had done, and grateful to him for staying with her. But it was his daughter who had won his heart, more than ever. She was a rare and marvelous girl, he said to everyone, she had postponed the Pacific tour just for him, as though they hadn't heard it. And she had told him nothing of her problems with Desmond. Nonetheless he had sensed long since that something was bothering her, and he wondered if it was Nick, or something else. It wasn't until the night before she left that she finally told him.

"Is it Nick that's bothering you, Cass?" He knew she was haunted by the man, and he was worried about how close they had obviously still been the last time she saw him. He was sorry things hadn't worked out for them. But she couldn't have waited for him indefinitely if Nick had told her not to. Pat had tried to tell him it was a mistake, setting her free like that, but young people never listen. Not that Nick was so young anymore. He was old enough to know a thing or two. But like most men, he was foolish when it came to women. "You can't pine for him, Cassie. Not married to another man." She nodded, loath to tell him the truth. She was so ashamed of her own bad judgment. Desmond had taken her in completely.

"There's something you're not telling me, Cassandra Maureen," her father prodded her, and in the end, in spite of herself, she told him. And he was stunned at what she said. It was everything Nick had warned them of and predicted.

"He was right, Dad. Completely."

"What are you going to do now?" He wanted to kill the man. What a rotten trick to pull on a girl like her, to exploit her so totally for his own gain and glory.

"I don't know. Fly the tour, obviously. I really do owe him that. I wouldn't back out on him, though I don't think he knows that. I'll do it. And then"—she took a breath, there weren't many choices—"we'll get divorced, I guess. I'm sure somehow he'll make it look as though I did something terrible. He'll manipulate the press somehow to his advantage. He's much more complicated than I realized. And a whole lot meaner."

"Will he give you anything?" her father wondered. He was a very rich man, and he could have paid her handsomely for her disappointment.

"I doubt it. I'll make my fee for the tour. He was going to reduce it because of the postponement, but he didn't. He considers that a major gift. I don't need more than that. I don't want anything from him. He's been generous enough." And she could live for years on the career he had helped her achieve, that was payment enough. She wanted nothing more from Desmond.

"I'm sorry, Cassie. I'm so very sorry." He was deeply distressed by what he'd heard from her, and they both agreed not to upset her mother.

"Just take care of yourself on the tour. That's all that's important now. You can sort the rest out later."

"Maybe I'll fly bombers to England when I come back, like Jackie Cochran." That June, she had co-piloted a Lockheed Hudson bomber to England, proving once and for all that women could fly heavy airplanes.

"Oh be gone with you," her father rolled his eyes with a groan, "flying bombers to England. You'll give me another heart attack. I swear, you'll make me rue the day I ever took you up in an airplane. Can't you do something ordinary for a while, like answer phones somewhere, or cook, or help your mother clean house?" But he was teasing her, and she knew it. He knew there was no hope of her giving up the skies now. "Fly safely, Cass," he warned her before she left. "Be careful. Watch everything, with all your senses." He knew she was good at that. He had never seen a better pilot.

And the next morning when she left, they all cried at seeing her go, and knowing the danger of the Pacific tour. And Cassie and

Billy cried right along with them. Pat and another pilot flew them
to Chicago, and Billy and Cassie flew back to California commer-
cially from there. It was pleasant actually, for a change. The
Skygirls made a big fuss over her, and she and Billy sat and talked
about their month of training. It had been peaceful for them,
hanging out together at the airport all summer, just like the old
days, only better. They were older now. They had interesting days
ahead. And in spite of Desmond, Cassie was getting excited about
the tour.

"What are you going to do about a place to stay when you get
back to Newport Beach?" Billy asked her quietly as they flew
back.

"I haven't thought of that. I don't know . . . I can't stay at a
hotel, I guess." She suspected Desmond wouldn't like that, because of the scandal. But she couldn't imagine staying in his house
with him after everything that had happened. He hadn't called her
once in the past two months, and the only letters from him were
from his lawyers or his office.

"You can stay with me, if you want. If anyone finds out, we can
say it's for training. What do you think?" Billy offered.

"I think I'd like to," she said honestly. She had nowhere else to
go now.

She went home with him that night, with some clothes she'd
brought from Illinois, and some flight overalls. And she went to
work with him the next day, in his old jalopy. With all the money
he made, Billy still hadn't bought himself a decent car, and he
didn't plan to. He loved his old Model A, even though at least
half the time it never started.

"For a guy who flies the best airplanes in the sky, how can you
drive a car like this?" she asked at three-thirty in the morning.

"Easy," he grinned. "I love it."

They were hard at work by the time the sun came up, and they
didn't finish until late that night. They were also scheduled for a
practice night flight. Cassie didn't even see Desmond until the
second day, and only then because she ran into him in a hangar

near his office. She was surprised to see him there, but he was giving someone a tour, and he dropped by to see her afterward. He wanted to make sure she wasn't going to say anything inappropriate to the press. And he was no nicer to her than he had been the last time she saw him.

"Where exactly is it you're staying?" He had suspected she wouldn't come back to him, and he didn't really care, as long as she kept it quiet. He had packed up all her things and put them in storage in coded boxes in one of the hangars. The only thing he didn't want was for her to create a scandal. But he also knew her well enough to know she wouldn't. She had too much integrity, too much pride. She wanted to do the Pacific tour for him, and do it right. She had no desire to do anything to hurt him.

"I'm staying with Billy," she said with a dignified look, wearing one of her old flight suits.

"Just be discreet about it," he said coldly. But he knew better than anyone that at this point even a tiff reported by the press wouldn't really hurt them.

"Obviously. I don't think anyone even suspects that I'm staying at Billy's." She had thought about calling Nancy Firestone before that, but Cassie had been embarrassed to ask to stay with her and Jane. They weren't close anymore, and Billy had invited her to stay at his place. The one thing she couldn't have done was stay at a hotel. That would have wound up instantly in the papers, unless Desmond was there with her, which of course he wasn't.

Oddly enough, she ran into Nancy Firestone later that day, right after she had run into Desmond. Nancy was leaving work, and Cassie was running out to grab something to eat for herself and Billy, before coming back for a night of meetings.

"It's getting close, isn't it?" Nancy said with a smile. Everyone at Williams Aircraft was counting the days and the minutes. And Cassie looked tired and strained as she smiled and nodded. Seeing Desmond at the end of a long day hadn't done anything to lift Cassie's spirits. He was so unkind to her, so cold, it was impossible to imagine that there had ever been anything more than business between them. But at least Nancy was warmer to her than she'd been in a long time, and it was good to see her.

"It's getting very close," Cassie smiled. "How's Jane? I miss her. I haven't seen her in ages."

"She's fine." The two women stood looking at each other for a long moment, and Cassie suddenly realized that Nancy was looking at her strangely. She looked as though she wanted to say something to her, but she wasn't sure. And for an instant, Cassie wondered if she had ever done anything to offend her, if that was why Nancy had been so cool after Cassie had married Desmond. Or maybe she'd just felt awkward with Cassie's new position. The thought of it almost made Cassie smile. If that was what had bothered her, she could relax now.

"We should get together some time," Cassie said warmly, trying to be friendly in memory of old times. It was Nancy who had made her feel at home when she'd first come to Los Angeles and was so lonely.

But Nancy only looked at her now, as though she couldn't believe what Cassie was saying. "You still don't get it, Cass, do you?"

"Get what?" Cassie felt like a fool, but she had too many other things on her mind to want to play guessing games with Nancy.

"He's not what you ever thought of him. Very few people know him as he is." Cassie stiffened at the oblique mention of Desmond. She wasn't about to get lured into discussing him with Nancy. As far as anyone knew, he was still her husband.

"I don't know what you mean," Cassie said coolly, looking the other woman over. And suddenly she realized that there was a great deal more here than she'd ever seen. There was anger, and jealousy, and envy. Was Nancy in love with him? Had she been jealous of Cassie? Cassie suddenly realized how naive she'd been, about all of them. It seemed as though none of them had been what they'd pretended.

"I don't think we should be talking about Desmond," Cassie said quietly. "Unless you'd like to discuss it with him directly."

"That's a possibility," Nancy said with a supercilious smile. "I knew he wouldn't stay with you for long. It was all for show. Too bad you never figured that out, Cass." But what did she know about all of it? What had Desmond told her?

Cassie blushed as she shrugged a shoulder. "It's a little complicated for me, I guess. Where I come from, people usually get married for other reasons."

"I'm sure he was taken with you. And you might even have hung onto him if you'd played your cards right. But he doesn't like to play with kids. More than anything, Cass, I think you bored him." And then, as Cassie looked at her, she understood what she was saying. She understood all of it, and how vicious they had been to her, how rotten.

"And you don't, Nancy? Is that it?"

"It would appear not. But then again, I'm a little more mature. I play the game better than you do."

"And what game is that?" Cassie wanted to know now.

"It's a game of doing exactly what he wants, when he wants it, and exactly the way he wants it." To Cassie it sounded like a service business and not a marriage.

"Is that your contract with him? Is that how you got your house, and the college education for Janie? I always thought he was so generous. But I guess maybe there's more to it than meets the eye." This was exactly what Nick had meant. Desmond Williams had mistresses, whom he paid handsomely to be on call for him, and do whatever he wanted. For Nancy, it had meant chaperoning Cassie around. And suddenly Cassie realized how much it must have irked her. In a way, if it hadn't been so disgusting, it might almost have been funny.

"Desmond is very generous with me. But I don't have any illusions about him," Nancy said coldly, looking right at Cassie. "He's never going to marry me. He's never going to get involved with me in public. But he knows I'm here for him. And he's good to me. It works out very well for both of us." But suddenly, listening to the cold simplicity of it, the calculated emptiness that allegedly met his needs, Cassie wanted to reach out and slap her.

"Was he with you when he was married to me?" Cassie asked in a strangled voice, terrified by the conversation.

"Obviously. Where do you think he went at night when he wasn't working? And why do you think he wasn't sleeping with you? I told you, Cassie, he doesn't like playing games with children. And he's not as evil as you think. He didn't think there was any point sleeping with you, or misleading you more than he had to. Everything was for the tour. In some ways, Desmond is a purist."

"The bastard." The words escaped Cassie without any thought on her part. But as she looked at Nancy, she suddenly hated her. And him. It had all been a game. For both of them. It was all part of the Pacific tour, and the grander scheme of things, all to sell airplanes.

Marrying her had been just one small part of the plan, for publicity, and all the while he'd been sleeping with Nancy. No wonder Nancy had been so cool to her once they married. And maybe, for a little while, Nancy had even been worried. She was ten years older than Cassie, and not nearly as exciting, or as pretty.

"Weren't you just a little bit afraid he might fall for me?" Cassie eyed her carefully, and was pleased to see the older woman squirm at the question.

"Not really. We talked about it. You're really not his type, Cass."

"Actually, given everything I know, I'd say that's a compliment." Cassie looked at her coolly. And then she decided to deliver a small blow to the opponent. "You're not alone, you know. You're not the only one with an arrangement with Desmond." She said it very confidently, and it was easy to see that she had made Nancy more than a little nervous. Her livelihood and her future depended on her "arrangement" with Desmond.

"What's that supposed to mean?"

327

"There are others like you . . . with houses . . . with contracts . . . with arrangements . . . Desmond's not a man to be satisfied with one woman." Cassie was rewarded with a look of terror.

"That's ridiculous. Who told you that?"

"Someone who knows. He told me that there are quite a number of others. You know, kind of like a little competition."

"I don't believe you." But her words reeked of bravado.

"I didn't believe any of it, Nancy. I do now though. Nice to see you," she smiled. "Say hello to Desmond." And with that, she hurried back into the building. She didn't want anything to eat anymore. Nancy Firestone had ruined her appetite. She felt sick when she went back to find Billy in the hangar.

"Where's my dinner?" They both had to be in a meeting in less than half an hour, and he was starving.

"I ate it on the way back," she quipped, but she was looking deathly pale. He noticed it immediately and was worried.

"You okay, Cass? You look like you've seen a ghost. Did someone call about your dad?"

"No, he's okay. I talked to my mother this morning."

"So what happened?" She hesitated for a long moment, and then sat down in a chair, and told him about Nancy Firestone, and everything she'd told her.

"That sonofabitch," he commented through tightened lips. "He really plays quite a game, doesn't he? Too bad he has to go around ruining other people's lives. It would be nice if he stuck to his own kind."

"I guess he does, at least some of the time." Nancy Firestone had certainly not been the friend she'd thought her. "All I want to do after the tour is leave L.A., and go home for a while. I think I've about done it here. This is a little racy for me." She looked drained as she looked up at him and he nodded. He felt sorry for her, she didn't deserve this.

And for Cassie, it explained why they never made love anymore and why he'd never had any real interest in her after the honeymoon. He had just gone on seeing Nancy, and God only knew who else. Maybe she was lucky he hadn't bothered spending time in bed with her. Maybe she'd have felt worse now if they had. She suspected she would have. What she felt now was betrayed, and more than a little foolish. The worst part was that she had really believed him. The bastard.

"So what do we do now?" Billy asked, worried about her. He kept wondering if, because of Desmond's betrayal of her, she would throw in the towel, with or without a contract. But she didn't do things that way. She had every intention of finishing what she'd started. And Billy admired her for it.

"We finish the race, kid. That's what we came here for. The rest was all icing on the cake anyway." And for Cassie, for a while now, the cake had been poisoned. But nobody had ever called Cassie O'Malley a quitter.

"Good girl." Billy gave her a hug, and took her out for a quick dinner. But she hardly touched it.

There was a press conference every week after that, and Desmond made a point of being friendly to her publicly. There was lots of bantering, some funny little stories about her, and a small show of affection. It was all very touching, if you didn't know what was really happening. And it was surprisingly believable, to anyone who didn't know them.

Cassie seemed more serious than previously, but that was easily explained by the pressures of the upcoming tour. She had an important task set before her. She was training hard, and Desmond reminded the press frequently that she had spent the entire summer taking care of her father.

"How's your dad, Cass?" one of the reporters asked her.

"He's doing great." And then she thanked America for their gifts and cards and letters. "It really helped him. He's flying again, with a co-pilot now," she said proudly. They ate it up. Just the way they ate everything Desmond had fed them. She knew the game now. And Billy marveled at how good at it she was when he watched her.

"You okay?" he asked her in an undertone after one of their press conferences. Desmond had been particularly nice to her, and Billy could see afterward that he had really upset her.

"Yeah. I'm okay," she said, but he knew how hurt she was. And how betrayed she felt. She hated the hypocrisy of it, the pure sham of it. She had nightmares at night. And once from the next room, where he slept, he heard her crying.

She never saw Desmond alone again, until the night before the Pacific tour. There had been a huge press conference that afternoon, and she and Billy had gone out for a quiet dinner at her favorite Mexican restaurant afterward.

When they got back, Desmond was waiting for them. He was sitting in his parked car, and when he got out, he let Billy know he wanted to talk to Cassie.

"I just wanted to wish you luck tomorrow. I'll see you there before you take off, but I wanted you to know that . . . well, I'm sorry things didn't really work out the way we planned." He was trying to be magnanimous, but the way he did it made her very angry.

"What exactly *did* you plan? I was planning to have a life, and a husband and children." He was planning to have a world tour, and a mistress, and a cardboard wife he'd drag out for newsreels.

"Then you should have married someone else, I guess. I was looking for a partnership. And not much more than that. This was business. But isn't that what marriage is, Cassie?" He tried to make it sound as though things just hadn't worked out, and not as though he had lied to her about everything, including being sterile. She could have lived with that, she could have lived with a lot of things, if he'd been honest with her. But they both knew he never had been.

"I don't think you have any idea what marriage is, Desmond."

"Maybe not," he said without embarrassment. "To tell you the truth, it's not something I've ever really wanted."

"So why bother? I would have flown this for you, without all the nonsense, the lies . . . the wedding . . . You didn't have to go that far. You used me," she said, relieved that she had finally had a chance to say it.

"We used each other. You're going to be the biggest star in aviation there ever was two months from now. And I put you there. In one of my planes. It's a wash, Cass. We're even." He seemed pleased with himself. It was all he wanted. She meant nothing to him. She never had. That was the hard part.

"Congratulations. I hope you enjoy it as much as you thought you would."

"I will." He was sure of it. "And so will you. And so will Billy. We all win on this one."

"If everything goes right. You're assuming an awful lot," she said cautiously.

"I have a right to. You're flying a remarkable plane, and you're a great pilot. It doesn't take more than that. Except Lady Luck, and some fine weather." He looked at her long and hard, willing her to do right by him, but offering her nothing in return except glory and money. Love wasn't part of his scheme of things. He didn't have it in him. "Good luck, Cass," he said quietly.

"Thanks," she said, and walked upstairs to Billy's apartment.

"What did he want?" Billy asked suspiciously. He was worried that Desmond might have said something to upset Cassie.

"Just to wish us luck, I guess. In his own way. There's no one in there . . . I finally figured that out . . . the man's completely empty." It was truer than she knew. There was no soul to Desmond Williams. Only greed and calculation, and an unfailing passion for airplanes, never people. She was just a tool, no different from a wrench to tune the engine. She was a vehicle to success, nothing more, a cog in one of his machines, and in fact, a very small one. He was the puppeteer, the designer, the spirit behind it. In his eyes, she was nothing.

331

CHAPTER
18

The *North Star* took off, right on schedule, on the morning of October 4, as planned, with a crowd of hundreds watching. The cardinal of Los Angeles blessed the plane. There was champagne for everyone, and she took off into the horizon on a circuitous route that was designed to break distance records, and accommodate the vagaries of world politics at the moment.

They flew south first to Guatemala City, covering two thousand two hundred miles at one gulp, without refueling. And when they arrived, they checked their maps, the weather, and spent some time investigating the area, and talking to the locals. People were fascinated by the plane, and flocked to the airport to see them. Desmond had done his homework well. People all over the world knew of Cassie's journey.

The press were waiting for them en masse at the Guatemala City airport, along with ambassadors, envoys, diplomats, and politicians. There was a marimba band playing, and Cassie and Billy posed for photographs. No one had gotten as much attention since Charles Lindbergh.

"Not a bad life, huh?" Cassie teased him as they took off for San Cristóbal in the Galápagos the next day, a mere eleven hundred miles, which took them just over three hours in the extraordinary plane Williams Aircraft had built them. Desmond had gotten his first wish this time. They had just set a record for speed and distance.

"Maybe we should just stop somewhere for a vacation," Billy suggested, and she grinned as they were met by Ecuadorian officials, American military personnel, and local natives. There were more photographers, and the governor of the islands invited them to dinner.

The trip was going beautifully, and they spent a day there, checking the plane over carefully, and checking maps and weather again. Things couldn't have looked better.

From the Galápagos, they flew another twenty-four hundred miles to Easter Island in exactly seven hours. But this time they met with unexpected winds, and narrowly missed breaking the record.

"Better luck next time, kid," Billy joked with her as they taxied down the runway at Easter Island. "That husband of yours is liable to burn our homesteads down if we don't get him some more records." They both knew that Desmond had an eye on the Japanese who had been working on a plane for the past year which could fly nonstop from Tokyo to New York, a distance of nearly seven thousand miles, but so far they had encountered nothing but problems, and hadn't even made it as far as Alaska. Their first test flight was scheduled only a year from now. And Desmond had every intention of beating them to it, which was why these long distances across the Pacific interested him so greatly.

They found Easter Island a fascinating place while they re-fueled. It was filled with innocent, beautiful people and intriguing moai statues. There were stories that went back to prehistoric man, and mysteries Cassie would have loved to explore if she'd had the time to stay there.

They stayed on Easter Island for only one night, to rest up for the long leg the following day to Papeete, Tahiti. And this time they managed to just barely shave the record. They traveled two thousand seven hundred miles in seven hours fourteen minutes, without a single problem.

Landing in Tahiti was like arriving in Paradise, and as Billy looked out at the girls lined up along the runway in sarongs, waving at them and carrying leis, he let out a whoop of glee that brought Cassie to gales of laughter.

"My God, they're paying us to do this, Cass? Oh, baby, I don't believe this!"

"Behave yourself, or they're going to put us in jail if you go out there looking like that." He was practically panting and drooling. He was like a big funny kid, and she loved flying with him. More importantly, he was an outstanding navigator and a brilliant me-chanic.

In fact, he had picked up a noise he didn't like just after they took off from Easter Island. And after paying suitable homage to the local girls, he wanted to come back and check it out. When they cabled home that night, they mentioned it, but assured every-one that it was by no means a serious problem. They were giving them daily reports of their progress, and were relieved to be able to announce that they had just broken another record.

In Papeete, almost everyone spoke French, and Billy spoke just enough to get by. There was a dinner given by the French ambas-sador for them, and Cassie apologized that she had nothing to wear but her flight suit. Someone lent her a beautiful sarong in-stead, and she wore a big pink flower in her hair when Billy escorted her to dinner.

"You sure don't look like Lindy to me," he said admiringly,

putting an arm around her as they walked from their hotel to the embassy. But the relationship between them was strictly one of brother and sister. And as they walked along the beach afterward, talking about the trip, Cassie said sadly that she wished Nick could be there. Papeete was a magical place, and the people were wonderful. It was the most beautiful place she'd ever seen, and she resisted any comparison to her honeymoon in Mexico. That was a memory she wanted to forget now.

She and Billy sat on the beach late that night, talking about the people they'd met, the things they'd seen. The dinner at the embassy had been impressively civilized, and even in a sarong she felt somewhat out of place, though less so than she would have in her wrinkled flight suit.

"Sometimes the things we do still stagger me," Cassie said with a smile, fingering the flower she'd worn in her hair that evening. "I mean how did we get so lucky? Look at the plane we're flying all over the world . . . the people we meet . . . the places we go . . . it's like someone else's life . . . how did I get here? Do you ever feel like that, Billy?" She felt so young sometimes, so old at others. At twenty-two, she felt like she'd had a lot of good luck, and not much bad luck, all things considered. But that was the way she saw things.

"I'd say you paid a high price for this trip, Cass . . . higher than I did," he said seriously, thinking of her marriage, "but yeah, I feel like that. I keep waiting for someone to grab me by the scruff of the neck, and say 'hey, what's that kid doing here? He doesn't belong here!' "

"You belong here," she said warmly. "You're the best there is. I wouldn't have done this without you." The only other person she could think of who she would have liked to fly it with was Nick. Maybe some day.

"It's gonna be over too soon, you know that, Cass. I thought of that when we got here. Zip . . . it's over . . . gone . . . you plan and practice and sweat for a whole year, and then whoops . . . ten days . . . it's over." They were almost halfway there already, and Cassie felt sad thinking about it. She didn't want the trip to end so quickly.

They walked slowly back to their hotel after that, and she said something to Billy that surprised him. "I guess I should be grateful to Desmond for all this . . . and I am . . . but in a funny way, it doesn't seem like his trip now. He told all those lies, and did all his scheming, but it's our trip. We're doing it. We're here. He isn't. Somehow, all of a sudden, he doesn't seem all that important." It was a relief for her, and Billy was glad she wasn't tormenting herself about the rotten deal she'd gotten from her erstwhile husband.

"Forget him, Cass. When we go back, all of that will be history. You'll have all the glory."

"I don't think the glory is ever what I wanted," she said honestly. "I just wanted the experience, to know I could do it." But not enough to ruin someone's life for.

"Yeah, me too," he agreed, but he was also realistic about the hullabaloo that would come later. "But the glory won't be bad either." He smiled boyishly and she laughed, and then looked at him seriously.

"I was going to file for divorce before we left, but I decided to wait until after the trip, just in case some nosy reporter got wind of it. I didn't want to screw things up by moving too soon. But all the papers are ready and signed." She sighed as she remembered going to the lawyer's office. It had been a painful experience telling him what had happened.

"What are you going to get him on?" Billy asked with interest. He could think of at least half a dozen things, none of them pleasant, starting with adultery, and ending with breaking Cassie's heart, if that was officially grounds for divorce now.

"I guess fraud, for a start. It sounds terrible, but the lawyer says we have grounds." And then of course there was Nancy. "I think we're going to try to come to some quiet, mutual agreement. Maybe a divorce in Reno, if he'll agree to it. At least then it would be over quickly."

"I'm sure he will," Billy said wisely. And then they left each other for the night, and met again over breakfast on the terrace the next morning.

"What do you say we tell them they can have their plane back, and we just stay here?" He smiled happily at her, eating an omelet and croissants, and a big cup of strong French coffee, all served by a sixteen-year-old native girl with a breathtaking figure in a pareu.

"You don't think you'd get bored?" She smiled as she sat down next to him. She liked it here too, but she was excited about moving on, to Pago Pago, and then Howland Island.

"I'd never get bored," he said, smiling up at the girl and then glancing happily at Cassie. "I think I'd like to end my life on an island. What about you?"

"Maybe." She looked unconvinced, and then she smiled at him over coffee. "I think I'll probably end my life the way I started it, under the belly of an airplane. Maybe they could build me a special wheelchair."

"Sounds great. I'll build you one."

"Maybe you'd better check out the *North Star* first."

"You mean I can't lie on the beach all day?" He pretended to look shocked, but half an hour later, they were both going over the plane with a fine-tooth comb in all seriousness. The jokes were over. And predictably, the photographers, and the visitors, came to watch them.

They were carrying a huge load of fuel on the *North Star*, and very little else except emergency supplies, a radio, life jackets, life raft. They had everything they needed. And the temptation was great at each stop to bring home souvenirs from their travels. But they had no room, and they didn't want to weigh the plane down with a single ounce of anything that was not absolutely essential.

They shared a quiet dinner that night at the hotel, and watched an extravagantly gorgeous sunset, and then they took a walk on the beach and went to bed early. And the next morning, they took off for Pago Pago.

They made it in four and a half hours, and this time broke no records. But it was easy flying, all except for a small noise Billy thought he heard in one of their engines. It was the same thing he'd heard the day before, and it was oddly persistent.

Pago Pago was a fascinating place, though they only spent one night, and they spent most of it at the airport. Billy wanted to find the cause of the noise that had been bothering him, and by midnight he thought he'd located it. It was annoying him, but he was still convinced it wasn't a major problem.

They cabled home again, as they did from every stop, and in the morning they left for Howland Island. They had already covered more than nine thousand miles, and in Cassie's mind they were almost there, though there were still more than three thousand miles between them and Honolulu. But they had already done more than half the trip, and knowing they were approaching Howland, where most people believed Earhart had gone down, made her nostalgic.

"What are you going to do after all this?" she asked Billy as they shared a sandwich two hours out from Pago Pago. The woman at the place they'd stayed had been very nice, and had insisted on giving them a basket of fruit and sandwiches, which turned out to be delicious.

"Me?" Billy thought about it. "I don't know . . . invest my money somewhere, maybe like your father did. I'd like to run a charter service somewhere. Maybe even someplace crazy like Tahiti." He had really loved Papeete. "What about you, Cass?" They had nothing but time on their hands, as they shared the basket of food, and flew over the shimmering Pacific.

"I don't know. I get confused sometimes. Sometimes I think this is it for me . . . planes . . . test flights . . . airports . . . that's all I want . . . other times I wonder if I should do other things, like be married, and have kids." She looked sad for a moment, looking out at the horizon. "I thought I had it worked out with Desmond, but I guess not. I don't know," she shrugged,

"I guess I'll have to refigure it when we go home. I sure didn't win on this one."

"I think you had the right idea, wrong guy. It happens that way sometimes. What about Nick?"

"What about him?" She still didn't have any of the answers. He had been so adamant about not marrying her before, but maybe now, after Desmond, it would be different. She still hadn't told him. And who knew when she'd see him again? Who knew anything now, except what they were doing right now. For the moment, life was very simple.

The stop at Howland was very emotional for her because of Amelia Earhart. She and Billy were carrying a wreath to drop from the plane just before they reached the island.

Billy opened a window for her, just as they came in to land, and she dropped it with a silent prayer for the woman she had never known but admired all her life. She thanked her for being an example to her, and hoped she had had an easy death, and a life that was worthwhile to her. Looking at lives like hers, it was hard to know what people felt, or who they really were. Now that Cassie had been devoured by the press, she knew that most of it meant nothing. But she felt an odd kinship with her idol as she and Billy landed quietly after a twelve-hundred-mile flight. It was so simple for them. It had gone so easily. Why couldn't it have been that way for Amelia Earhart?

Billy patted her knee as the plane came to a stop; it was easy to see all that she was feeling, and he loved her for it.

At Howland, there were photographers waiting for them, courtesy of Desmond Williams. And the expected parallels were drawn between Cassie and Amelia Earhart.

They were only planning to spend one night, before the nearly two-thousand-mile flight to Honolulu. And it was there that Desmond had planned ceremonies and events, awards and honors, press conferences and films, and even a demonstration of the *North Star* to the Army at Hickam Airfield. It sounded exciting to both of them, but it was also a little scary. Everything was so much simpler here. In some ways it would be the last night of peace they had for a long time. And Cassie hated the prospect of seeing Desmond again. Just thinking about it depressed her.

She was quiet when they had dinner alone that night, and with what lay ahead of them, Billy wasn't surprised, that and the fact that she was still feeling emotional about Earhart.

"It's scary going back to all of it again, isn't it?" she said after dinner, sipping a cup of coffee.

"Yeah . . . and exciting." It was less complicated for him, he didn't have the strain of her history with Desmond. "It'll all be over soon, in a great flash of light," he beamed, "like a Fourth of July firework display, now you see it, now you don't, catch the shooting star. We'll be famous for a minute, and then gone," he said prophetically, "until someone else flies farther and faster." But they'd be remembered for a long time. Their fame wouldn't be gone as quickly as he thought. Desmond was right about some things, and what they were doing was important.

"This time tomorrow night, we'll be in Honolulu, Miss O'Malley," he said, toasting her with a small glass of wine. He only had a few sips, knowing that the next day he'd be flying. "Think of the fanfare, the excitement." His eyes danced and she smiled wanly.

"I'd rather not. I go pale thinking of it. Maybe we should just go back, and surprise them by going home the way we came. Now there's a thought." She laughed at the idea and he shook his head, amused by her. They always had a good time together.

"I'm sorry, Mr. Williams, my pilot was confused, well, you know how it is . . . she's just a girl . . . girls can't really fly, everyone knows that . . . actually, she had the map upside down . . ." They were both laughing, amused at their own schemes, but the next day, when they took off, some of what she'd said proved to be prophetic.

They hit an unexpected lightning storm two hundred miles out, and after assessing the situation, and the winds, they agreed to go back to Howland Island. And as they attempted to land, it grew to a tropical storm of surprising proportions, and Cassie couldn't help wondering if this was what had happened to Noonan and Earhart. But she had her hands full bringing the plane down in ferocious winds that almost blew them off the island. In the end, they came down hard and fast in a crosswind, and almost missed the runway. It took everything she had to bring the *North Star* down, and when they stopped, they were within inches of landing in the water.

"May I remind you," Billy said casually to her as she fought to turn the plane around, "that if you drop this airplane in the drink, we're going to be in serious trouble with Mr. Williams."

She couldn't help but laugh at his warning, and she wasn't entirely sorry to spend another night on Howland. It was far from an exciting place, but at least her life was peaceful. Perhaps for the last time. She couldn't imagine what it would be like for them after Honolulu.

By late that night, the storm had calmed down but they discovered early the next morning that it had damaged their direction finder beyond repair. She and Billy both felt it was safe to fly on anyway, but they radioed ahead to Honolulu that they would need a new one upon arrival. The day was sunny and bright as they left early for the eighteen-hundred-mile flight to Honolulu. But three hundred miles out of Howland, they ran into another problem. It seemed to be a problem with one of their engines. Billy was checking for an oil leak, with a quiet frown, and she was watching him, checking their gauges.

"Want to go back?" she asked calmly, keeping her eyes on her instruments.

"I'm not sure yet," he answered, still puzzled.

He played with one of the engines for a while, listening, fixing, adjusting, and after another hundred miles out, he reassured her that everything was in control. She nodded and kept a close eye on the instruments, she wanted to be sure she agreed with him.

Cassie left nothing to chance, which was why she was so good. Billy appeared to be a lot more casual than she was, but he was also extraordinarily careful. And he had an uncanny sixth sense about flying, which was why she loved flying with him. They were a perfect team.

She changed her course slightly after that, to avoid some heavy clouds ahead, and what looked like rough weather. And it was early afternoon when he looked out at the autumn sky, and then at her compass. "Are you sure we're heading right? It feels off to me."

"Trust your compass," she said, sounding like an instructor, as she smiled at him. It was the one instrument she always trusted and the only reliable information they had, since both the sextant and the direction finder had broken in the storm.

"Trust your eyes . . . your nose . . . your guts . . . and then your compass." He was right, as it turned out. With a brisk wind they were slightly off course, but not enough to worry them, and then as she checked the instruments again, she looked up and saw smoke in their number-two engine and thin streams of fuel running back across the number one.

"Shit," she muttered and pointed it out to him as she cut the power to the number-two engine and feathered the prop. They were already a long way from Howland. "We'd better go back." They'd been in the air for two hours, and were already out of radio contact.

"Anything closer than that?" He checked the map, and saw a small island. "What's this?"

"I'm not sure." She looked at it. "It looks like bird shit."

"Very funny. Give me a reading, where are we?" She read the compass off to him, while he looked out at the engine. He wasn't pleased with what he saw, or the knowledge that they were carrying four hundred gallons of fuel near the engine.

They flew on for a few more minutes and decided to try for the island they'd seen on the map. But Cassie was worried about putting the *North Star* down there. If the island was too small, the plane too large, they wouldn't make it. They agreed to land on the beach if they had to. They were out of radio range. Billy checked the engine again, but the news wasn't good. Then he put the headphones on and tried sending distress signals to any ships that might be near them.

But as they looked out the window, they both saw that the engine was burning.

"Happy birthday, Cass. And that's not a cake."

"Shit."

"Precisely. How far are we from Bird Shit Island?"

"Maybe another fifty miles, give or take a few."

"Wonderful. Just what we need, another fifteen minutes with four hundred gallons of fuel in our armpits. Oh goody."

"Go sing to yourself or something," she said calmly.

"You have the worst ideas," he said while flipping some levers, and checking the other engine. "No wonder you can't get a decent job." They were joking, but they were not amused. The *North Star* was in trouble.

Ten minutes later the island came into view, and they checked it out. No flatland. Nothing but trees, and what looked like a small mountain.

"How well can you swim?" he asked conversationally, handing her a life jacket as a matter of routine. He already knew that she was an excellent swimmer. "Looks like we're going to the beach, eh, ducky?"

"Maybe so, cowboy . . . maybe so . . ." She was concentrating on holding the plane. It was starting to pull very badly. And the other engine had begun to smoke too. "What do you suppose is happening?" They were both puzzled by what was going on, but they wouldn't know what till they reached the ground. And that was going to be soon now. At first Billy had thought the fuel lines were clogged, but that wasn't it. Something was defective.

"Too much lighter fluid maybe?"

"Well, don't light up a Lucky now," she warned him, prepared to land. She circled the island twice, made a pass at the beach once, and took off again, with both engines burning. She knew she needed to dump fuel, but there just wasn't time now.

344

"You want to try for New York?" he asked calmly, watching her maneuver the heavy plane over the tiny island.

"I think maybe Tokyo," she answered, never taking her eyes off what she was doing. "Tachikawa is going to pay a fortune for the test flight."

"Great idea. Let's try it. Who needs Desmond Williams?"

"Okay, here we go again," Cassie said, concentrating on every detail. "Christ, that beach is short dammit . . ." And the engines were hot and flaming.

"I hate to say this, my dear," Billy said calmly, putting on his own life jacket, "but if you don't get your ass down there soon, we are going to make a very embarrassing explosion on this island. It might make a very bad impression on the natives."

"I'm working on it," she said through her teeth.

"Want some help?"

"From a kid like you? Hell, no." She came in as low as she could, and used all her strength on the stick; she was almost down, and had just overshot the beach when they hit the water. The plane came to a stop, and sank slowly into three feet of water, as she cut the switches, hoping it wouldn't explode but there was no guarantee now.

"Nice landing, now let's go. Fast." He grabbed her to push her from the plane, before she could take anything. Instinctively, she reached for their emergency kit, while he struggled to get the door open. Both engines were on fire, and you could feel the heat in the cockpit. He had the door open by then, and shouted to her. "Go!" He pushed her out and clear of the plane almost before she knew what had hit her. He had the log and a small knapsack in his hand that she knew held their money, and that was it. They waded through the water as fast as they could and headed for the beach at a dead run. They ran another fifty feet down to the end of it, and just as they reached it, there was an enormous explosion. They turned and watched as the entire plane was outlined in flames, and pieces of it flew into the trees and farther into the water. There was a huge tunnel of fire towering above it, from their fuel, and it burned for hours as they watched it in shocked fascination.

"So long, *North Star*," Billy said, as the last of it disappeared into the water. All that was left was a shell of what had been. All those men and all that work, all those months and hours and calculation, ended in a moment. They had covered eleven thousand miles of their trip. And it was over. They were alive. They had survived it. That was all that mattered. "And here we are," Billy said conversationally, as he handed her a piece of candy from the knapsack, "on Bird Shit Island. Have a great vacation." She looked at him and laughed; she was too tired and too upset to cry, or scream. All she could hope was that someone would figure out that they were gone when they failed to reach Honolulu, and send the troops out looking. She knew all the efforts they'd made to find Earhart four years before. But she also knew how much outcry there had been at the expense. But if nothing else than for the publicity involved, and to recover the plane, she knew that Desmond would stop at nothing to find them. He'd call Roosevelt himself if he had to. He'd play heavily on the fact that she was America's sweetheart and people loved her. They would *have* to find her.

"Well, Miss O'Malley, what do you say we call room service and order a drink?" They had been there for four hours by then, watching their plane disintegrate along with their hope of leaving. Now they had to be rescued. "It wouldn't have been a real record-breaking trip, if this hadn't happened," he said confidently. He was sure that they would be rescued within a day or so, and it would be exciting in the telling.

"Desmond will think I did this as revenge," she grinned. There was a funny side to it too. But barely. If they let themselves, they could have gotten seriously worried. She wondered if it had been like this for Noonan and Earhart, or if it had been more dramatic or quicker. Maybe they had died on impact. Or maybe they were still sitting on an island like this one. It was an intriguing thought, but unlikely. And not very hopeful.

"I kind of figured you did this as revenge too," Billy commented casually. "I can't say I blame you. I wish you'd have done it a little closer to Tahiti. The waitress was great-looking."

"So has been every girl since L.A." She was feeling less cheerful than he, but she was grateful for his sense of humor.

"Not here. Definitely not here." The island was totally deserted.

They went on a reconnaissance mission then, and found a small stream, and a lot of bushes with berries. As desert islands went, it seemed fairly comfortable, with everything they needed. There were some fruits which they didn't recognize, but when they tried them that night they found they were delicious. It was strange being here, but it didn't seem so terrible, as long as they weren't stuck here forever. The prospect of that was more than a little frightening, but Cass wouldn't let herself think of it, as they lay side by side in a cave they found that night.

They were both awake for a long time, and finally, she decided to ask the question. "Billy?"

"Yeah?"

"What if they don't find us?"

"They will."

"What if they don't?"

"They have to."

"Why?" Her eyes were huge in the darkness and he was holding her hand very gently. "Why do they have to find us?"

"Because Desmond will want to sue you for the plane. He's not going to let you get away with this." He grinned in the dark and she laughed.

"Oh shut up."

"See what I mean . . . not to worry." But he rolled over and held her close to him, and he didn't tell her he was scared too. He had never been so frightened in his life, and there was nothing he could do for her but hold her.

CHAPTER
19

Desmond was called in the middle of the night, exactly twenty-two hours after they had left their last destination. The local authorities were absolutely sure by then that the *North Star* had disappeared, and probably gone down in the Pacific Ocean. But there had been no sign, no signal. And no one had any idea what had happened.

"Damn." He called everyone in to help. They had an emergency plan to implement. The Navy was called, the foreign authorities, the Pentagon. The flight of the *North Star* had made world news, and now everyone who had ever heard of her, and some who hadn't, wanted to find her.

There was an aircraft carrier in the vicinity of where she was believed to have gone down, and they dispatched forty-one planes, and called in two destroyers. It was not unlike the search that had gone on four years before, and they were better trained, and better equipped now. They made every conceivable effort, and deployed every man possible. The President called Desmond himself, and then the O'Malleys in Illinois. They were in a state of shock when they heard. They couldn't believe they might lose Cassie. And Oona was particularly afraid for Pat's heart, but he seemed to be taking it fairly calmly. He was desperately afraid for his daughter, but he had a lot of confidence in the armed forces. He only wished that Nick were there to help them.

The search went on for days, in an area that covered hundreds of miles, and all the while Billy and Cass were trying to keep each other's spirits up and eating berries. Cassie had gotten a case of raging dysentery, and Billy had badly scraped his leg swimming over some coral the morning after they crashed. But other than that, they were in pretty good shape. They had whatever fruit they found around them, and enough water. But no sign of anyone coming to rescue them. No plane. No ship. Nothing had even come close. Because Cassie had changed course slightly before they crashed, and because of the winds that had pushed them still further off course before that, the search was being conducted some five hundred miles in the wrong direction. Their radio had gone dead just before they went down and then been destroyed in the explosion, so they had no way of giving anyone their location. And there had been no ship in the vicinity at the time, to hear them. They weren't even sure where they were now. But they had no way to tell anyone even if they had known it.

In L.A. Desmond was doing everything he could to keep the search going. But the press was beginning to question the shocking expense of the search, and began to turn on Desmond. They played up the futility of looking for them, and the likelihood that they'd been killed in the crash or would be dead by now anyway. The search went on at full steam for fourteen days, and then occasional sweeps were made for another week. The search was then called off entirely two days after that, one month to the day of the date they had left Los Angeles. It was over.

"I know she's out there," Desmond insisted to everyone, but no one believed him. "She's too well trained. I don't believe it." But experts assumed that something went wrong with the plane. There could have been some unknown, fatal defect. No one questioned her skill, but there was always the element of fate, or good fortune.

Her parents were devastated once they knew the search was being called off without finding Cassie and Billy. It seemed impossible to believe that they had lost yet another child, and so cruelly. Her mother lay awake night after night, wondering if Cassie was alive somewhere and they just hadn't found her. But her father felt it was unlikely.

Cassie and Billy had been lost for six weeks on Thanksgiving Day, and it was a gloomy holiday for everyone that year. They barely celebrated it at all. They just had a quiet dinner in the kitchen.

"I just can't believe she's gone," her mother sobbed in Megan's arms. It was a terrible time for them.

And for Desmond it was the end of a life's dream. He tormented himself constantly over what must have happened. If only they knew . . . if only they could find something . . . but there was no debris, no evidence, no piece of the plane or of their clothing. It led him to hope they were still alive somewhere. And he hounded the Pentagon constantly, but for them, the search was over. They were convinced that the North Star had gone down without a trace and they were certain there were no survivors.

Cassie's photograph was everywhere, in magazines, and newspapers. Even six weeks after they disappeared, her identity seemed as alive as ever. The press had been devoted to Cass. And appropriately, Desmond portrayed himself as the grieving widower. He had no Thanksgiving that year. And neither did Nick in England. He had heard about Cassie's disappearance about a week after the plane had disappeared. It was such a major event, it had made headlines in England. He couldn't believe it when he heard the news. He had volunteered for the most dangerous missions, until someone had explained the situation to his commander. They had given him a three-day leave and asked him to take some time off. It was obvious to everyone that something was bothering him and he was just taking too many chances. Nick had argued with them, but they didn't want to hear it. He thought about going home for a few days, but he knew he couldn't face Pat yet, knowing what had happened. What a blind fool he had been. What a coward. He knew he'd never forgive himself for not marrying her, and keeping her from Desmond Williams. It never occurred to him that maybe he couldn't have, or that she had wanted to fly the tour more than anything. It was her decision too, and she was very independent.

But he figured Pat would never forgive him either. If he had married her, it might all have been different.

He had seen a photograph of Desmond coming out of a memorial service for Cassie, with a grim face and carrying a homburg. And he hated Desmond for giving Cassie the opportunity to kill herself, and the plane in which to do it. And he knew better than anyone that Williams had probably pushed her into the tour in the first place, all for his own glory. She had deserved better than either of them. He was more convinced of that now than ever.

And on the island with no name, Cassie served Billy berries and a banana and a handful of water for Thanksgiving. They had been living on the same diet for more than a month, and it only rained occasionally, but they were surviving. Billy had gotten an infection in the leg he'd scraped so badly on the coral reef, and he'd been battling with a fever. She'd had a few aspirin in their emergency kit, but they were long gone now. And she'd had some trouble with a spider bite, but other than sunburn, they were in pretty good shape, except for Billy's frequent fevers.

They had managed to keep track of the days since they'd crashed, and they knew it was Thanksgiving. They talked about turkey and pumpkin pie and going to church, and being with their families and friends. Billy was worried about his father being all alone. And Cassie kept thinking about her parents, and her sisters and their husbands and children, and how much she missed them. She talked about Annabelle and Humphrey, the two children from England. They made her think of Nick again. She thought a lot about him. All the time now.

"What do you suppose they all think has happened to us?" she asked as she shared a banana with Billy, and she noticed he was looking flushed again, and his eyes seemed very intense and a little sunken.

"That we're dead probably," he said honestly. Lately, he hadn't been joking as much. All they could do was sit and wait, and think, and eat the same kinds of berries over and over. There was nothing else to eat on the island, and so far they hadn't been able to catch any fish. But they weren't starving.

There was a storm two days after that, and the weather seemed to turn cooler than it had been. She was still wearing her flight suit, but it was torn and not very clean and Billy only had his shorts and a T-shirt. Cassie noticed the morning after the first chill that Billy was shivering even in the sun.

"You okay?" she asked, trying not to look as worried as she felt.

"I'm fine," he said gamely. "I'll go get some bananas." He had to scale up a tree to get them, but he couldn't even get off the ground this time; his leg was hugely swollen and oozing pus, and he was limping when he came back with one banana that had fallen.

She didn't know what to do for him anymore. The leg just kept getting worse, and she could tell that his fever was getting higher. She bathed the leg in salt water, but it didn't help at all. She had nothing else to give him. He dozed a lot that afternoon, and when he woke up, his eyes looked even more glazed than they had been. She laid his head on her lap after that, and stroked his forehead, and as the sun went down he began shaking from the chill again, so she lay next to him, and tried to keep him warm from the heat of her body.

"Thanks, Cass," he whispered in the dark of their cave that night, and she lay holding him, praying that someone would find them. But it seemed almost impossible now. She wondered if they would be there for years, or just die there. It seemed unlikely they'd leave the island. She knew too well that the search had to have been called off by now. They were presumed dead, just as others had been before them.

His teeth chattered constantly during the night, and the next morning, he was delirious as she bathed his head with cool water. There was a storm that day, and she drank too much of the rainwater herself, and wound up with violent dysentery again. Between the berries and the water and the leaves they ate, she had it all the time now. She could tell from the way her flight suit fit that she had lost a lot of weight since they'd reached the island.

Billy never regained consciousness that day, and that night, she lay holding him, crying softly. She had never felt so alone in her entire life, and to make matters worse she felt she had a fever now too. She wondered if she had caught a tropical disease. Billy had an infection from the coral, but they both were very sick.

In the morning, Billy seemed better again, and a lot more lucid. He sat up, and walked around the cave, and then he looked at her and said he was going swimming. It was chilly outside, but he insisted he was hot, and he suddenly became very argumentative, and very powerful. She couldn't stop him. He waded out into the water where the burned hull of their plane was. Even the storms they'd had hadn't washed it away yet, and it lay there like a reproach, and a reminder of all they had had and lost. For Cassie, it was a final reminder of Desmond.

She watched Billy swimming past the plane, and then back again, and when he came out of the water, she saw that he had torn the other leg, but he didn't seem to feel it. He insisted it was nothing, and she watched him scale up the tree, and eat a banana. He seemed to have unusual energy, but an odd kind of dementia.

She could tell that he wasn't himself from the things he said, and the way he looked at her. He was very nervous and very wild-eyed, and by nightfall, he lay shivering in their cave, talking to someone she didn't know about a car, and a candle, and a little boy. She had no idea what he was talking about. And late that night, he looked at her very strangely, and she wondered if he knew her this time.

"Cass?"

"Yes, Billy?" She lay holding him close to her; she could feel his bones, and his whole body shaking.

"I'm tired."

"That's okay. Sleep." They had nothing else to do, and it was very dark there.

"Is it okay?"

"It's okay . . . close your eyes . . ."

"They are," he said, but she could see that they were open.

"It's very dark in here. Close your eyes anyway. You'll feel better tomorrow." Or would they ever feel better, she wondered. She could feel her own fever rising again too, and she was shaking almost as much as he was.

"I love you, Cassie," he said softly after a little while. He sounded like a child, and she found herself thinking of her nieces and nephews, of how sweet they were and how lucky her sisters were to have them.

"I love you too, Billy," she said gently.

He was still curled up in her arms, when she woke up the next morning. Her head ached, and her neck was stiff, and she knew she was slowly getting as sick as he was. Billy was already awake, she thought, he was lying very still and looking at her; and then she gave a small scream as she realized that his eyes were open, and he wasn't breathing. He had died in her arms in the night. She was alone now.

She sat there looking at him for a long time, huddled next to him, not knowing what to do, and not wanting him to leave her. She sat crying, hugging her knees and rocking back and forth. She knew she had to do something with him, to take him away, or bury him, but she couldn't bear for him to leave her.

She pulled him slowly outside that afternoon, and dug a shallow grave with her hands, in the thicker sand near the rocks, and she laid him there. And all she could think of as she did was his telling her not long before that he wanted to end his life on an island. He had. But that all seemed so long ago. It was part of another life, in a place she would never see again. She knew that now. She knew she was going to die like Billy.

She kneeled down next to him, and looked at him, with his eyes closed, and his freckles so big on the thin face, and she touched his cheek for a last time, and stroked his hair.

"I love you, Billy," she said as she had the night before. But this time he didn't answer, and she covered him gently with sand and left him.

She sat alone in the cave that night, hungry and cold and shaking. She hadn't eaten all day. She was too sick to eat, and too sad about Billy. And she hadn't drunk water either. And the next morning, she felt weak and confused and she kept thinking she heard her mother calling her. Whatever she had, it was killing her, just as it had killed Billy. She wondered how long it would take, or if it even mattered. There was nothing left to live for now. Chris was gone. Billy was gone. Nick was lost to her . . . her marriage was over . . . she had crashed Desmond's plane . . . she had let everyone down . . . she had failed them.

She staggered out to the beach and fell down several times, and she was too weak to go up to the rocks and get water. She didn't care anymore. It was too much trouble to stay alive. And there were so many people talking to her now. She saw the sun come out, and she heard them, and as she stood up again, she saw a ship on the horizon. It was a very big ship, and it was coming closer. But it didn't matter, because they would never see her.

The USS *Lexington* was in the area on maneuvers. It passed through these islands regularly, but it hadn't been there in a while, it had been assigned to other positions. But Cassie didn't bother with it, she went back into her cave and lay down. It was too cold outside . . . too cold . . . and there were too many voices . . .

The *Lexington* continued to cruise by, and there were two smaller ships with it. It was the lookout on the smaller one who spotted the burned hull of the *North Star* bobbing in the water half a mile off the island.

"What is that, sir?" he asked an officer next to him, who smiled. "It looks like a scarecrow." It did, from that angle, in the distance. Part of it had gone down, but there was so little left that the skeleton managed to stay afloat, and with another look, the officer gave a series of rapid orders.

"Could it be the plane that O'Malley and Nolan were flying, sir?" the junior officer asked excitedly.

"I don't think so. They went down about five hundred miles from here, give or take a few miles. I don't know what that thing is. Let's take a closer look."

They advanced slowly on it, and several more of the men focused binoculars on it, but when they got there, the skeleton eluded them, and dipped in and out of the water. But it was obvious now that it was part of a plane. Half the cockpit was still there, and one of the wings had been blown off. The other had burned down to the frame and melted.

"What does it say?" one of the men was shouting to the other.

"Get some men in the water now," an officer commanded. "I want that brought aboard." And half an hour later, they had the remains of Cassie's plane spread out on the deck around them. There wasn't much left, but there was one piece that told it all. They had found it. It was painted bright green and yellow. Those had been her colors, they all knew, and the script read *"Star."* They called the captain down to examine what they'd found, and there was no question in his mind. They had found what was left of the *North Star*. It had been burned to a crisp, and it had obviously suffered a severe explosion. But there was no sign of life on

357

it anywhere, or of human remains. They checked carefully. There was no sign of Cassie or Billy.

They radioed their companion ships, and still others in the vicinity, which by late afternoon were scouring the waters for bodies in life vests. They had radioed to shore as well, and there was a news bulletin in L.A., which Desmond heard before anyone called him. Pieces of the plane had been found, but there was no sign of life anywhere. They had been lost for seven weeks now. It was unlikely they were alive, but not impossible. The search for O'Malley and Nolan had been reopened.

Landing parties were organized to search all the surrounding islands. There were three of them, two of them fairly good-sized, and one of them so small as to be unlikely. There wasn't enough vegetation to keep anyone alive for a week, let alone a month, they decided. But the officer in charge told them to search it anyway. There was nothing though. No sign of life, no scraps of clothing, or utensils.

And as Cassie listened, she heard noises again, and then more voices. She wondered if Billy had heard all the same things before he died. She had forgotten to ask him. There were whistles and bells and people calling, and then she realized she was about to die, when a bright light shone in her face. There were voices and people calling again, and that light right in her eyes. She drifted off to sleep again as she looked at it. It was just too much trouble to listen to them anymore. And then she felt them moving her. She was being carried somewhere, just as she had carried Billy . . .

"Sir! Sir!" The whistle shrilled sharply three times signaling for assistance, and four more men came running in the direction of the whistle. There was a small cave, and one of the men was standing there with tears streaming down his face.

"I found her, sir! . . . I found her . . ." She was barely conscious and babbling incoherently, and she kept calling Billy's name over and over. She was rail-thin, and desperately pale, but they all recognized the red hair and the flight suit.

"Oh, my God," one of the officers said. She was filthy and

smelled terrible, and she was obviously deathly ill, but she was alive, although barely. Her pulse was thready, her breathing was shallow, and he wasn't sure she was going to make it. He told the young ensign to signal for help. They put her in the boat quickly, and left three of the men to continue searching the island. They wanted to get her back to the ship as quickly as possible.

They were calling and shouting orders, and she was loaded onto the ship in a sling, and they signaled to the medical personnel on the *Lexington* to assist them. She wore an ID tag around her neck, which identified her correctly as Cassie O'Malley Williams. And within minutes, the Pentagon had the news, she'd been found, barely alive, but there was no sign of Billy Nolan.

But the search party left on the island took less than half an hour to find him. They took him back to the ship, and by then Cassie was already on the *Lexington*, though she was unaware of it. A team of two doctors and three medics were doing what they could to revive her. She was dehydrated and delirious and had an uncontrollable fever.

"How is she?" the captain asked the medical personnel that night.

"Nothing's sure yet," the doctor said quietly, "but nothing's lost yet either."

Her parents had just been called by the Department of the Navy. And Desmond was called shortly after that. It went out over the wire services that night. It was a miracle. The nation's prayers had been answered. Cassie O'Malley had been found, in a cave on an island in the Pacific, in critical condition. It wasn't known yet if she would survive. But it was already known that Billy Nolan hadn't. His father had already been called in San Francisco, and he was crushed to hear the news. Billy was a hero at twenty-six, but he was gone. He had died only a day or two before they found him, they believed, though Miss O'Malley had been unable to tell them anything yet. She was unconscious.

In the O'Malley house everything was still, as Oona and Pat sat staring at each other, unable to believe what they'd been told.

Cassie was alive. And the *Lexington* was steaming toward Hawaii with her at that moment.

"Oh, Pat . . . It's like another chance," Oona said breathlessly, "like a miracle . . ." She smiled through her tears, praying for Cassie silently, her rosary beads in her hand, and her husband patted her hand gently.

"Don't get your hopes up. We already lost her once. She may not make it, Oonie. She's been out there for a long time, and you don't know what kind of shape she was in when they crashed. She may have been pretty banged up then, and that was more than a month ago." She'd been on the ground for seven weeks since they went down. It was a long time to live on rainwater and berries.

They had none of the details yet, and even Desmond had had a hard time prying anything out of them at the Pentagon. They just didn't know enough yet to reassure him.

But the news the next morning from the *Lexington* wasn't very hopeful. She was still unconscious, her fever hadn't gone down, and there were complications.

"What the hell does that mean?" Desmond shouted at them. "What kind of complications?"

"They didn't tell me, sir," the woman on the phone said to him politely.

Cassie's fever didn't respond to any of the medication, and she was dehydrated to the point of death. She was still delirious, and had violent dysentery, and she had started passing blood, which the medics told one of the men was a sure sign it was all over.

"Poor kid," one of the midshipmen said. "She's the same age as my sister, and she can't even drive a car yet."

"Looks like Cassie didn't drive so hot either," one of the men joked, but he had tears in his eyes as he said it. The entire ship was talking about her, and praying for her, and so was the entire country, as well as the world.

In England, Nick had been called into his commander's office at Hornchurch. Word had gotten out eventually that he was extremely close to Cassie O'Malley, though no one knew the details.

And he had been in rough shape since her disappearance in October. They'd sent him back to flying missions eventually, but he'd been hard on all his men, and dangerously willing to take unnatural risks for too long now.

"I wouldn't get my hopes up excessively, Major Galvin, but I thought you ought to know. We've just heard that they found her."

"Found who?" Nick looked confused. He'd been asleep after flying two night missions over Germany back to back, when they'd told him to see the commander.

"I believe the O'Malley woman is a friend of yours, isn't she?" Gossip was everywhere in the Army, all the way to the commander's office.

"Cassie?" Nick looked as though he'd gotten an electric shock as he realized what the commander was telling him. "Cassie's alive? They found her?"

"They found her. She's in critical condition on one of your warships in the Pacific. It sounds as though she might not make it, from what I've seen so far. But we'll keep you informed of any developments, if you like."

"I'd appreciate that, sir," Nick said, looking pale, as the commander watched him.

"You look like you need a break, Major. This might be the right time, depending on what happens."

"I wouldn't know what to do with it, sir," Nick said honestly. He was afraid to go home now. For him, there was nothing to go home to. Cassie would be with Desmond if she survived . . . and oh God, he hoped so . . . he would be willing to sacrifice his own life to make that happen. He would have been willing to do anything, if she just lived . . . even see her with Desmond Williams for the rest of her life. Anything was better than knowing she had died, or fearing it as he had for the past seven weeks. He had given up hope in the last month. It was just impossible that they'd still be alive somewhere in the Pacific. "Any word of her navigator?"

The commander nodded. They were all used to losing friends now, but this was a hard way to do it. "He didn't make it, they found him on the island with her. I'm afraid I don't know the details."

"Thank you, sir." Nick stood up to leave, looking exhausted but hopeful. "Will you let me know if you hear anything else?"

"As soon as we do, Major. We'll call you at once."

"Thank you, sir." They saluted each other, and Nick walked slowly back to his barracks, thinking of Cassie. All he could think of, as he had a thousand times since May, was the night they'd spent at the airstrip in the moonlight. If only he'd held onto her, if only he'd been able to keep her from going . . . if only she'd live . . . for the first time in twenty years, he found himself praying, as tears rolled down his cheeks, and he went back to his barracks.

CHAPTER
20

Three days after they had found Cassie in the cave, the *Lexington* steamed into Pearl Harbor. She had regained consciousness once, but lost it again. She was transferred to the naval hospital by ambulance. And when she got there, Desmond was waiting for her. He had flown over from L.A., leaving Nancy Firestone to control the members of the press who were waiting for her arrival in L.A.

The doctors gave Desmond a report when they first saw her, and Desmond then explained to the reporters what had happened. But they had still heard none of it from Cassie.

"Will she be all right?" they asked with tears in their eyes, and Desmond's tears matched theirs. He was obviously deeply moved by his wife's condition.

"We don't know yet."

A little while later, he went out to see what was left of the plane, which had come in on the *Lexington* too, and Desmond thanked the captain for bringing her home safely, as photographers snapped their picture.

"I only wish we had found her sooner. She's a great gal. We're all rooting for her. You tell her that as soon as she can hear you."

"I will, sir," Desmond said, as they took another picture of him with the captain. Desmond went back to the hospital after that to wait for news and after another hour or two, they finally let him see her. She looked ravaged by everything she'd been through and she had IV tubes in both arms, one giving her medication and the other glucose. But she never stirred. And he never touched her. He simply stood staring at her, and the nurses couldn't tell what he was thinking.

Billy Nolan's body was sent back to San Francisco that day, on a flight Desmond had arranged. And funeral services were set for two days later. And in churches everywhere, people were praying for Cassie.

It was the fourth of December by then, and all over the country, people were talking about Christmas, but all the O'Malleys could think about was Cassie, comatose in Hawaii. They called Honolulu every morning and night for news of Cassie's condition. Pat wanted to fly them there, but his doctor didn't advise it. He was even thinking of calling that miserable husband of hers to lend him a plane, but he had heard he was already in Honolulu. Desmond was milking it for all the publicity he could get out of it. And on December 5, the doctor at the naval hospital called them again. Oona dreaded it now when the phone rang, and at the same time she longed for it. She was desperate for news of Cassie.

"Mrs. O'Malley?"

"Yes." She recognized instantly the scratchy connection of long distance. "There's someone here who'd like to talk to you." She thought it was Desmond, and she didn't want to talk to him, but maybe he had news for them. And then she heard Cassie. Her voice was so weak she could hardly hear her, but it was her. Oona was crying so hard she couldn't even tell Pat what was happening.

"Mama?" Cassie said softly, and her mother nodded, and then forced herself to speak through her tears as Pat understood and began to cry too.

"Cassie? . . . oh, baby . . . oh, sweetheart . . . we love you so much . . . we were so worried about you . . ."

"I'm okay," she said, and ran out of steam almost immediately. The doctor took the phone from her hand, and the nurse explained that Miss O'Malley was very weak, but she was doing much better. And then Cassie insisted on having the phone back again so she could tell her mother she loved her. ". . . and tell Daddy . . ." she whispered and he could hear her anyway, as Oona shared the receiver with Pat and he cried openly as he listened, ". . . I love him too . . ." She wanted to tell them about Billy, but she didn't have the strength, and the nurse took the phone away then. And a little while later they let her see Desmond. The nurse stayed in the room with them, as Cassie needed to be watched constantly. She was so weak that sometimes she even had trouble breathing.

Desmond stood beside her bed, and looked down at her unhappily. He didn't know what to say to her, except that he was glad she had survived. It was an awkward moment for them. Everything he should have felt or said was wrong because of their circumstances, but he was relieved that she was alive. And he couldn't help wondering if she'd been careless about the plane. Or had there been some fatal flaw they hadn't known about before she left? Eventually he would need to ask her, but this wasn't the moment.

". . . I'm sorry . . . about the plane . . ." she said to him with effort, and he nodded.

"You'll do it again one day," he said confidently, but she shook her head. She hadn't even wanted to do it this time in the end. She had done it for him, because she felt she had to. It had always been his idea, his dream, his project. And in the end, she felt she owed it to him. She would never do it again, not for him, not for anyone, and not without Billy. "What happened?" he asked as the nurse looked on disapprovingly. She needed rest desperately, and no one was supposed to upset her, least of all her husband. The nurse had noticed that he hadn't even kissed her. And as he stood there, talking to her, he never touched her or went near her.

But Cassie was trying desperately to answer his question. ". . . first smoke, then fire in the number-two engine . . ." she explained painfully, ". . . then . . . fire . . . in the number . . . one . . . too far from land . . . too much gas . . . brought it down where I could . . . tiny island . . . hit the beach . . . after we got out . . . tremendous explosion . . ."

He nodded, wishing he knew what had caused the fire in the number two. But she couldn't tell him. The nurse told him then that she had exerted herself enough, and had to rest. He could come back later. He was very correct with everyone, and very well bred and polite, but he was as cold as ice, and he had never said a single kind word to Cassie. It was hard to believe he was her husband. Cassie wondered then as she watched him go, if it would have been easier for him if she had died. Now he'd have to face the world when she divorced him.

Cassie sat up in bed the next day, and called her parents again. She was still very weak, but she was feeling a lot better. She had contracted a tropical disease of some kind, but mostly she had suffered from dehydration, malnutrition, and exposure, and it would take time to get back to normal. She was so weak, she couldn't even sit up without assistance. That afternoon Desmond showed up with a few photographers, but the nurse refused to let him bring them in to Cassie. He threatened to report her to her superiors, and she said it made absolutely no difference to her. The doctor had said no visitors except immediate family, and that was all she would allow to see Mrs. Williams.

He was furious and he left almost immediately, and Cassie burst into laughter. "Thank you, Lieutenant Clarke. You stick to your guns."

"I don't think you want to see the press." Cassie still looked very thin and pale and very disheveled. They gave her a bath that afternoon, and she washed her hair, and she almost felt human again by that night. But fortunately, Desmond never came back to see her. He had been very proper with her, but it was obvious that his only interest in her recovery was what he could tell the papers. He had even told them about the lei the crew of the *Lexington* had left for her before setting sail that morning. Her survival had already been announced in newspapers around the world, and in Hornchurch, Nick had cried when his commander told him.

On Saturday, Desmond tried to get the press in to Cassie's room again, and once again, the indomitable Lieutenant Clarke managed to thwart him. It was becoming a game, and Cassie loved it.

"He seems awfully intent on letting the press in to see you," Lieutenant Clarke said cautiously, wondering what Cassie saw in him, but she didn't dare ask her. Other than his good looks and expensive clothes, he seemed to have a heart of stone. The only thing he warmed to was the press, and certainly not Cassie. But that wasn't news to Cassie. She was only amused that her nurse was so good at annoying him. She didn't want to see anyone yet. Except her parents. And they had decided to wait for her to come home, now that she was doing better.

Lieutenant Clarke walked her down the hall for the first time that afternoon, and the doctor said he thought Desmond could fly her home by the end of the week. She needed to build her strength up a little bit, and they wanted to be sure the fever didn't return. But so far it hadn't all day, and she felt a great deal better.

A few men recognized her in the hospital as she walked down the hall awkwardly, she was still so weak, and they shook her hand and congratulated her on her survival. She was a heroine just for being alive, and she wished more than ever that Billy was alive now. She had sent a telegram to his father in San Francisco, expressing her grief to him.

"We were all praying for you, Cassie," people told her in the halls, and she thanked them warmly. Letters and telegrams were pouring in too. President and Mrs. Roosevelt had even called her at the hospital. But it didn't seem fair to Cass that Billy hadn't made it, and she had. She felt terribly guilty and unhappy about it, and she cried whenever anyone mentioned him. She was still emotionally worn out by everything that had happened.

She was pensive as she sat in her room most of the time and the nurses didn't want to disturb her. They could see that she was still troubled, and exhausted by her ordeal. They knew only that her co-pilot had died, but they knew no other details. And Cassie wasn't talking about it to anyone. She did a lot of thinking, and some sleeping. And she found herself thinking of Nick, and wondering where he was. She had never had the opportunity to tell him how right he'd been about Desmond. But maybe it didn't matter anymore. They had their own lives to lead. He wanted his own life, and she needed time just to recover from all that had happened. But when she felt better she wanted to look up Jackie Cochran, and talk to her about the planes she had ferried to England.

Cassie called her parents again that night and she told them she'd be home soon, probably in another week, and she'd be home with them for Christmas. She had no reason to be in L.A. anymore, she didn't want to fly for Desmond, and she was sure he'd agree that she had fulfilled her contract to the best of her ability. It was all over.

Her parents told her on the phone that they had just gotten a telegram from Nick in England, telling them how thrilled he was that she had survived. But he had sent nothing to her, probably because of Desmond.

"Does it say when he's coming home?" she asked casually, and her father laughed.

"You're too sly for your own good, Cassie O'Malley."

"He's probably married by now anyway," she said lightly, but she hoped not.

"No sane woman would have him."

"I hope not." She laughed. She was in much better spirits. And after a brief chat, she went to bed early. She had no idea what Desmond was doing in Honolulu. He never even came to see her. She supposed he was wining and dining the press, lining up interviews for her when she felt better. But he was in for a shock. She was going to do one final press conference for him, to tell them all what they wanted to know. And then she was going home and folding up the road show. It had cost too much. Billy, and almost her own life. She didn't know what she wanted to do now. But whatever it was, it was going to be on a more human scale than what Desmond had pushed her to in the last year. She had made a lot of money, but she had lost a dear friend, and almost her own life. This time the risks had come at too high a price. And she needed time to recover.

Lieutenant Clarke came in at seven o'clock the next morning, and woke her up when she pulled back the curtains and raised the shades. It was a beautiful day, and Cassie was anxious to get up and walk around. She even wanted to shower and dress, but Lieutenant Clarke didn't want her to overdo it.

She had breakfast at seven-fifteen, poached eggs and three strips of bacon. It was a far cry from their island diet of bananas and berries. She never wanted to see either one again, for as long as she lived. And as she finished her breakfast, she glanced over the morning paper.

She saw quickly that Desmond had been at it again. He had granted an interview to the *Honolulu Star Bulletin* and told them all about her condition. He didn't say too much however about what had happened to her on the little island; she suspected that he didn't want to steal any thunder from a major press conference with her. He thought of everything. Except her well-being. It was all business and publicity, airplanes and profit. Nick couldn't have been more accurate in his perceptions and predictions.

She was still reading the paper when she heard the first plane overhead. She thought it was an exercise by the Navy pilots. The hospital was fairly close to the airfield. But then as she listened, she heard an explosion in the distance. And then more of them. Curious, she got up and walked to the window. And then she saw them, wave after wave of bombers. They were being attacked, she realized instantly, with astonishment. It was seven fifty-five on December 7.

The sky was black with planes and they seemed to drone on endlessly, as they flew over the harbor, and systematically bombed every ship they saw beneath them. They strafed the airport simultaneously, and destroyed whatever they found there.

Lieutenant Clarke came running in, and Cassie explained to her quickly what she was seeing. Without thinking, she ran to the closet, and found the clothes that Desmond had brought her. There wasn't much. But there was a skirt and a blouse and a pair of shoes, and she hurriedly took off her robe and nightgown and got dressed for the first time since she'd been there.

In the hospital, people were crowding into the hallways, and dashing around aimlessly. Nurses and orderlies were trying to keep patients calm, and almost instinctively Cassie joined them. They were under attack for an hour, and by then the *Arizona* was in flames, along with a number of smaller ships, and large parts of the harbor. Reports were coming in rapidly, many of them inaccurate. And the radio was explaining that they had been bombed by the Japanese, and it was only moments later when ambulances began bringing in the wounded. There were terrifying burns, and men covered in oil, others with head injuries, some with machine gun wounds, and many with traumatic shock. Nurses were running everywhere, and patients like Cassie were giving up their beds for the men who were being brought in from the harbor.

Cassie worked alongside Lieutenant Clarke tearing bandages, and clean pieces of cloth. She helped to hold wounded men in her arms, lifting them onto beds. She did anything she could to help, but before they could deal with half of the wounded men, the Japanese attacked again. And this time they got the *Nevada*.

Suddenly there were thousands of men, injured and half dead, bleeding from everywhere, streaming into the hospital, or taken to the hospital ship *Solace*.

Rebecca Clarke only looked up at her once with concern and admiration as Cassie worked tirelessly, helping the wounded. She was quite a girl. No wonder the country loved her.

"Are you all right?" the nurse asked her briskly, after Cassie had brought a particularly nasty burn case into a treatment room. The man was screaming and there was flesh hanging everywhere, and even some left on Cassie.

"I'm fine," she said coolly. She remembered her brother and pulling him from the burning plane. She still had a scar on her arm from where the flames on his body had burned her. "Just tell me what to do."

"You're doing just what you need to," Lieutenant Clarke said firmly. "Don't stop unless you feel ill, and if you do, tell me."

"I won't," Cassie said, willing herself not to be sick as she helped the injured men, and a number of women. Civilians began coming into the hospital too. There were casualties everywhere, and after a while there was nowhere to put them. The second bombing lasted till just after ten o'clock, and then they were gone, leaving not only the island in shock, but the entire nation.

Cassie worked feverishly all afternoon, doing what she could, and she felt weak in the knees when she finally sat down at four o'clock. She hadn't stopped, and she hadn't eaten since breakfast. Lieutenant Clarke brought her a cup of tea, and together they checked the lobby for more injured. The last ones had been transferred to the *Solace* just an hour before. The hospital simply couldn't hold another body.

There was nothing left for her to do for the moment, except offer comfort where she could, and as she was doing that, Desmond arrived with a lone photographer beside him. All the others had gone to the harbor to see the damage there, but he had promised the young reporter a picture of Cassie O'Malley if he came with him. He strode across the lobby to her, as Lieutenant Clarke settled a young pregnant woman in a chair. She had come to inquire about her husband, and Lieutenant Clarke had just promised to find him.

"There she is"—Desmond pointed to her dramatically—"darling, are you all right?" he asked, looking at her tenderly, as the photographer snapped a picture of her in her skirt and blouse that were covered with other people's blood, and all she could do was look at Desmond in disgust, and the photographer along with him.

"Oh, for chrissake, Desmond," she railed at him in contempt, "stuff it. Why don't you go do something useful instead of showing off for the press all the time? And you," she wagged a finger at the camera, and the man behind it was too startled to say anything, "why don't you go help someone, instead of standing around taking pictures of me? We've been bombed, you idiot. Get off your lazy ass, and drop your camera." And with that she wheeled out of the lobby with Lieutenant Clarke, and she left the two men with their mouths open behind her. She had won Rebecca Clarke's heart forever that day. She knew that as long as she lived, she would never forget the tireless redhead, helping wounded men, treating burns. She had given up her private room to four of them, and had wheeled the cots in herself and made them with whatever sheets she could find, or steal, from other beds if she had to.

The director of the hospital thanked her himself that afternoon. And they found her a folding cot that she set up in a closet to get some sleep. They had sicker people to take care of now, people who needed them more, and she felt guilty taking any of their attention. She stayed on to help the next day, and they were told, not surprisingly, that the President had declared war on Japan on Monday. There was a cheer in the hospital when it was announced. And on Tuesday, she checked into the Royal Hawaiian Hotel, and called her parents. She had already called them once before to tell them she was all right, but now she wanted to let them know she was going to try and get home as soon as possible.

The hotel promised to try and get a cabin for her on the *Mari-*

posa, which was leaving on Christmas Eve. It was the first ship she could get, and the only thing she wanted to be sure of was that Desmond wasn't on it.

She had no sympathy for him at all, she thought he had behaved abominably. The only thing he was interested in was milking her story one more time. It was disgusting.

He came to see her that afternoon, and told her that the Pentagon had promised him a seat on a military flight to San Francisco in a few days, and he could arrange one for her too, since she was practically a national hero now, but she was adamant that she didn't want to go anywhere with him.

"What difference does it make?" He looked annoyed at how difficult she was being. It would look a lot better to the press if they went home together, although he could still explain it if she didn't. He could even claim that she was suddenly nervous about flying, or blame it on her health. But she was not amenable to any of his excuses.

"I've got real bad news for you, Desmond. The whole world is not watching you, or me, they're thinking about the war we just got ourselves into, though you might not have noticed."

"Think of what you could do now for the war effort," he said hopefully, thinking of the publicity opportunities for him, and for his airplanes. But as far as she was concerned, she had just done it, for three days at the naval hospital, not that he understood that, although Admiral Kimmel had personally thanked her.

"I'll do exactly what I want to do," she said unpleasantly, "and you're not going to advertise, trade, announce, use, or exploit it. You got that? We're finished. I completed my contract."

"You most certainly did not," he said smoothly, and she stared at him in disbelief.

"Are you kidding? I almost killed myself for you."

"You did it for yourself, for your own glory," he corrected.

"I did it because I love flying and I felt I owed it to you. I thought doing the tour for you was the honorable thing to do.

373

Not to mention the fact that you said you'd sue me if I didn't, and I figured my parents didn't need that headache."

"And do they now? What's changed?" Nick was right to the end. Desmond was vicious.

"I flew eleven thousand miles, I did my damnedest, I went down with your goddamn lousy plane, and managed to live forty-five days on an island the size of a dinner plate, while starving to death, I might add. And I watched my best friend die in my arms. Isn't that enough? I'd say it is. And I'll bet a judge would."

"A contract is a contract," he said coolly. "And yours said you would fly fifteen thousand miles across the Pacific in my plane."

"Your plane went up like a matchbook."

"I have others. And your contract said you would do unlimited publicity and endorsements."

"We're at war, Desmond. No one's interested. And whether they are or not, I'm not going to do it. Sue me."

"I might. Maybe you'll give it some thought on the way back."

"I wouldn't waste my time thinking about it. I'll call my lawyer when I get back . . . for a number of reasons," she said pointedly.

"We'll have to discuss that. By the way, you mentioned Billy in rather touching terms a little while ago . . . was that your *best* friend, or your *boy*friend. I'm not sure I understood you."

"You understood me perfectly, you sonofabitch. And if you're talking adultery, why don't you discuss it with Nancy Firestone. She's very clear about calling herself your mistress. I already mentioned that to my attorney."

For once, he blanched, and she was pleased to have gotten him upset for a change.

"I don't know what you're talking about." He was furious with Nancy for talking to Cassie.

"Just ask Nancy. I'm sure she'll explain it to you. She was very direct with me."

His eyes told her he hated her, but she didn't care. She never wanted to see him again after Honolulu.

She spent the next two and a half weeks volunteering to help at the naval hospital again and on the hospital ship *Solace*. It was devastating to see what had happened in the harbor. The *Arizona*, the *Curtiss*, the *West Virginia*, the *Oklahoma*, the *Chew*, the *Oglala* had all been hit by the Japanese, 2,898 had been killed, and another 1,178 had been wounded. It was devastating, and now the country was at war. She wondered what it would mean to Nick, if he would stay in the RAF, or join the American armed forces. Everything was still very confusing.

And when the *Mariposa, Monterey*, and the *Lurline* finally sailed on Christmas Eve, she was touched and surprised when Rebecca Clarke came to see her off, and thanked her for all her help since the bombing. Cassie had done nothing but work with the wounded since the Japanese had bombed Pearl Harbor.

"It was an honor to meet you," Rebecca Clarke said sincerely, "I hope you get home safely."

"So do I," Cassie said honestly. She was anxious to get back to Illinois to see her parents, and to see a lawyer and find out how she could best get out of all her obligations to Desmond.

She was relieved to see that no members of the press had come to see her off. But Desmond had left for San Francisco by military plane the week before, so they hadn't bothered. She was happy not to have flown with him even if this did take longer and was potentially more risky. They were traveling by convoy to ensure greater safety.

Lieutenant Clarke left her on the ship, and they set sail an hour later. Everyone was anxious about the trip, and afraid that the Japanese would come back and sink them. They had complete blackouts every night, and everyone had to wear their life jackets day and night, which was very unnerving. There were a lot of children on the ship, which made it noisy and stressful for the other passengers, but families who had relatives on the mainland were anxious to get away from Hawaii. It was too dangerous there now. Everyone felt sure they would be attacked again at any moment. The *Lurline*, the *Mariposa*, and the *Monterey* sailed quietly with an escort of destroyers, which accompanied them half-way to California, and then left them to complete the trip alone, as the destroyers headed back to Hawaii.

The ships were very quiet as they zigzagged across the Pacific to avoid submarines. There were no parties at night, no one was in the mood. They just wanted to get to San Francisco safely. And Cassie was amazed at how long it took. After flying everywhere all her life, traveling by ship seemed endless and incredibly boring. She hoped she never had to do it again, and the entire ship cheered as they came through the Golden Gate and into the port of San Francisco five days later.

She was even more surprised when she stepped off the gang-plank, carrying her one small bag, and saw her father. She had traveled under the name of Cassandra Williams, and only a hand-ful of people had realized who she was and talked to her. The rest of the time, she kept to herself and minded her own business. She had a lot of thinking to do, and some quiet mourning. But when she saw her father, relief turned to excitement. And her mother was right behind him.

"What are you doing here?" she asked with wide eyes that filled instantly with tears. They were all crying as they hugged each other, her mother more than anyone, but Cassie and her father too. It was the reunion she had thought of a million times on the island. And then as they hugged and talked, out of the corner of her eye, she saw Desmond. He had set up an entire press confer-ence to greet her. There were at least eighty members of the press to welcome her and ask her questions. But as Cassie noticed them, she saw her father's mouth set in a hard line. He was having none of this. Desmond Williams had gone far enough, and he would go no further.

"Welcome home, Cassie!" a flock of reporters shouted at her, as her father grabbed her firmly by the arm, and propelled her through the crowd like a snowplow. Oona was following them closely, and Pat was heading for the car and driver he had hired to meet her. And before the reporters could say anything, she was being pushed into the car, and Desmond had come toward them.

"You're very kind," her father was saying warmly to the members of the press, "but my daughter's not well. She's ill and she's had a traumatic experience in the hospital at the bombing of Pearl Harbor. Thank you . . . thank you very much." He waved his hat at them, shoved his wife into the car after his daughter, and climbed in behind both of them. And then told the driver to pull out as quickly as he could without hitting them. Cassie was laughing at Desmond's expression as they drove off. They had completely foiled him.

"Does that man never stop?" her father said irritably. "Has he no heart at all?"

"None whatsoever," she assured him.

"I don't understand why you married him."

"Neither do I," she sighed, "but he was very convincing then. Until afterward; then he didn't think he had to hide his moves anymore." She told him about his threats to go after her now with his lawyers.

"You owe him nothing!" Pat raged at her, incensed at what Desmond had told her.

"Mind your heart, dear," Oona warned, but he had been fine since the summer. Even during Cassie's ordeal, he had held up surprisingly well. And now he was only angry.

"He'd better mind my fist, not my heart," Pat said bluntly, as they drove back to the Fairmont. Her parents had taken a suite for the three of them, and they spent two days there celebrating her safe return. Before they went home, she went to visit Billy Nolan's father. It was a sad and difficult visit, and she told his father that Billy had died in her arms peacefully, and he hadn't suffered. But even knowing that, it was difficult to console him.

It dawned on Cassie afterward, that with the war now, there would be many young men like Billy dying. It was an awful thought. And she had never been as happy to go home as she was this time.

Her father had brought a co-pilot along, and flown the Vega out for her. Halfway back to Illinois, he turned the controls over to her, and asked her if she'd like to fly it. And much to his surprise, and her own, she hesitated, but he pretended to ignore it.

"It's not as fancy as what you're used to, Cass. But it'll do your heart good to fly again." It was a nice plane to fly, and he was right, she loved the feeling of flying again. She hadn't been in a plane since she'd gone down in the *North Star*, two and a half months before. And it was odd to be flying now, but she still loved it. It was in her blood, just as it was in her father's.

She told him about the crash then on the way home, and she and her father discussed what might have caused the fire in the engines, but it was anyone's guess. Desmond had brought back what was left of the plane, and was hoping they could learn more about what went wrong. But it was unlikely they would find much, the explosion had been so powerful.

"You were damn lucky," her father said, shaking his head, as she flew his plane for him. "You could have been killed on the way down. You could have been blown to bits, or never found an island to light on."

"I know," she said sadly. But it still hadn't helped Billy. She couldn't get over that. She knew she'd never forget him and then as she helped her father put the plane in the hangar that night, he offered her a job at the airport. He said he could use some help with cargo and mail runs, especially now that every able-bodied young boy would be enlisting. Most of his pilots were older than that, but still there was room for her, and he'd love to have her, he said with a shy smile. "Unless you're going to be doing a lot of advertisements for tooth powder and cars." They both laughed at that one.

"I don't think so, Dad. I think I've had enough of all that to last me a lifetime." She wasn't even sure she wanted to do air shows, not after Chris died. She just wanted to fly, nice easy runs, or even long ones.

"Well, I'd love to have you. Think about it, Cass."

"I will, Dad. I'm honored."

He drove them home after that, in his truck, and her sisters and their families were waiting for them at the house. It was New Year's Eve, and they had never looked better to her than at that moment. Everyone cried and hugged, and screamed, and the kids ran around like crazy. They all seemed to have grown, and Annabelle and Humphrey looked cuter than ever. It was a scene she had never thought she'd see again, and she broke down and sobbed as her sisters held her. She only wished that Chris could have been there . . . and Billy . . . and Nick. There were too many people missing now, but she was there. And they thanked God that night for His blessings.

CHAPTER
21

The week after New Year's, Cassie started helping her father at the airport again. But before that, he took her to see an attorney in Chicago. He was an expensive one, with a good reputation, but her father said that she couldn't afford to see anyone less than that if she was going to defend herself against Desmond Williams.

She explained her situation to him, and he advised her that she had nothing to worry about. There wasn't a judge or a jury in the world who would feel that she hadn't fulfilled her contract in good faith, and at great risk and personal expense to herself. "No one's going to take money from you, or put you in jail, or force you to fly for him again. The man sounds like a monster."

"And that brings up another matter," her father said pointedly. The divorce. That was more complicated, but not impossible by any means. It would take time, but it would be easy to say that their marriage had not survived the trauma of her ordeal, and surely no one would contest that. It would be even easier to accuse him of adultery and fraud. And the attorney intended to wave those flags at him. And he was sure he would get Desmond's full cooperation.

He told her to go home, and not to worry about it, and three weeks later some papers arrived for her to sign to set the wheels in motion. And it was shortly after that that Desmond called her.

"How are you feeling, Cass?"

"Why?"

"It's a perfectly reasonable question." He sounded very pleasant but she knew him better than that. He wanted something. She thought maybe he had called to argue about the divorce, but she couldn't imagine why he'd want to. He didn't want to be married to her any more than she wanted to be married to him. And she wasn't asking for money. Much to her surprise, he had sent her the full amount he owed her for the Pacific tour, even though she hadn't completed it, after her lawyer contacted him and pointed out that trying to shortchange her would look very bad to the American public after all she'd been through. Desmond had been furious, but the check for one hundred and fifty thousand was safely put away in her bank account, and her father was well pleased that it was. She had more than earned it.

"I just thought you might like to do a little press conference sometime . . . you know . . . tell the world what happened." She had planned to, at first, just once, but in the meantime, she'd decided against it. Her career as a movie star was over.

"They heard it all from the Department of the Navy, after they rescued me. There's nothing else to say. Do you really think they want to know how Billy died in my arms, or about my dysentery? I don't think so."

"You can leave those parts out."

"No, I can't. And I have nothing to say. I did it. We went down. I was lucky enough to come back, unlike Billy, unlike Noonan, unlike Earhart, unlike a lot of fools like us. I'm here, and I don't want to talk about it anymore. It's over, Desmond. It's history. Find someone else you can mold into a movie star. Maybe Nancy."

"You were good at it," he said nostalgically, "the best."

"I cared about you," she said sadly. "I loved you," she said very softly, but there was no one to love there.

"I'm sorry if you were disappointed," he said pointedly. They were strangers again. They had come full circle. And then he realized that pushing her was pointless. "Let me know if you change your mind. You can have a great career if you ever get serious about it," he said, and she smiled. It had gotten as serious as it gets, and miraculously she'd still survived it.

"Don't count on it." She knew he hated people like her. In his mind, she was a quitter. But she didn't give a damn what he thought now.

"Good-bye, Cassie." End of a career, end of a marriage. End of a nightmare.

They hung up and he never called her again. Her lawyer told her that Mr. Williams had agreed to the divorce, and even offered a small settlement if she would go to Reno. She didn't accept the money, she'd made enough flying for him, but she went to Reno in March for six weeks, and when she came back, she was free again. And predictably, Desmond released a statement to the press afterward that she had been so traumatized by her experience in the Pacific, that continuing their marriage had become impossible for her, and she was living "in seclusion with her parents."

"It makes me sound like a mental case," she complained.

"So what?" her father said. "You're rid of him forever. Good riddance." The press had called a few times after that, and she always refused to talk to them or see them. They had written about her sympathetically, but they didn't pursue her for long. As much as they had loved her before the tour, they had other fish to fry now.

She certainly didn't miss them or Desmond. But she did miss her friends. With Billy gone, the airport was very quiet for her. She was so used to flying with him day after day, that it was odd now to be there without him. And by April, when she got back from Reno, all the young men she knew had either been drafted or enlisted. Even two of her brothers-in-law had gone, although Colleen's husband had flat feet and bad eyes and was 4-F and had stayed. But her two oldest sisters and their children were around the house most of the time now. And that spring, Annabelle and Humphrey's parents were killed in a bombing attack on London. Colleen and her husband had decided to adopt them. And thinking about it, Cassie almost wished that she could have them.

They had news from Nick now and then, but not very often. He was still in England, flying fighter raids now with a vengeance. And killing as many Germans as he could shoot out of the skies, "just like the old days." He was old for those games at forty-one, but with America in the war now, he had full military status in the American Army. He also didn't get leaves back to the States anymore. Not in wartime. Cassie knew that he was still at Hornchurch. He never wrote to her, only to her father. She had never written and told him of Desmond's betrayal and her divorce, and she still wasn't sure what to tell him, or if he'd care. She didn't know if her father had said anything, but she doubted it. Pat wasn't much at writing letters, or at discussing other people's business. Like all men, they discussed world events and politics. But she felt that one of these days, she ought to tell Nick herself what had happened. The question was when and how. She had to assume by now though that if Nick had still been interested in her, he'd have written. She hadn't seen him in almost a year now. And God only knew what he was thinking.

She didn't go out on dates, just with friends, or her sisters. And she worked hard for her father, at the airport. It was almost enough of a life for her, although she had to admit that she missed the thrill of flying Desmond's exotic planes now and then. But you couldn't have everything, and she liked her life just the way it was now. The press had started to forget her, they seldom called now, without Desmond prodding them, and she got an occasional request for endorsements, which she declined. It was a quiet life, and her father worried about her sometimes, and said as much to Oona.

"She's been through a lot, you know," he said. They all had.

"She's a strong girl," her mother said fondly, "she'll be all right." She always was. She was just quiet sometimes, and lonely without the people she'd grown up with. Her brother, Nick, Bobby, even Billy, who had come a little later. But she missed them, and the camaraderie they had all shared in different ways. Now she was just another pilot flying to Chicago and Cleveland, but it felt good to be with her family again. It brought her a great deal of comfort.

In August, she got a phone call that amazed her. Her father took the call, and handed it to her with a blasé look. He didn't even recognize the name, which made her want to shriek at him. Some things never changed. It was Jackie Cochran.

"Are you serious?" She had thought he was kidding at first. She had just come in from a run to Las Vegas. It was hotter than hell. But when she got on the phone, Jackie Cochran said she wanted to meet with her if possible. She said she'd always admired her, and she asked her to come to New York to see her, if she could spare the time. "Sure," Cassie agreed, jotting down the pertinent details. She had agreed to fly there two days later. She had nothing else to do, since it was her day off. And maybe she could even do a little shopping, since she had her money from the tour in the bank, and had never spent a penny. The funny thing was she had wanted to meet Jackie Cochran for ages, but once she got settled at home again, she got lazy and never did anything about it.

She was thinking about inviting her mother to come to New York with her, but then she decided to go alone. She had no idea what Jackie Cochran would want, but she thought it might be something her mother would disapprove of.

And as it turned out, it was something that fascinated Cassie.

She had admitted readily that she was bored at home, and eager for some more exciting flying. Eight months after she had been rescued in the Pacific, she was ready to spread her wings again and do something a little more exciting. And what Jackie Cochran had in mind was right up her alley.

Jackie wanted Cassie to take charge of forming a small group of experienced women pilots under the Army Air Force Flying Training Command, to ferry planes to wherever they were needed in the war, for the moment. The women involved would fly as civilian pilots but have uniforms and honorary rank. Cassie was to start as a captain. There was another women's air corps too, the WAFS, Women's Auxiliary Flying Squadron, if she preferred it, being organized for domestic ferrying by Nancy Harkness Love, another extraordinary female pilot. But Cassie liked the idea of ferrying planes into England right past the Germans. She knew her parents were going to be upset if she left home again, but this was something she believed in. It served a purpose, it wasn't frivolous or self-serving, like her Pacific tour, which just made money for a lot of greedy people. This was something she could do for her country, and if she died . . . she was prepared to accept that. So had Chris . . . so had Billy . . . sadly, so had Bobby Strong by then. He had been killed six weeks after he enlisted. Peggy was a widow again, with four children now. Life was never simple.

The WAFS would begin training in September, for eight weeks in New Jersey, but she could hardly wait. It was time for her to be challenged again and for the first time, she would be flying with other women. She had never had the opportunity to do that.

Jackie Cochran took her to dinner that night at '21' and they talked about their plans. Cassie couldn't remember anything she had wanted to do more, not even the world tour when Desmond had first asked her. This was so different.

It was exactly what she wanted and what she'd been waiting for. For Cassie it was time to move on now. She was still smiling when she flew home the next day, thinking about it.

Her father was at the airport when she got in; he was singing to himself, and filing some papers in his office. She hated to ruin his mood, and she decided to wait and tell him after dinner.

"How was New York?"

"Great," she beamed at him.

"Oh oh. Do I smell romance in the air?" He smelled happiness, but not romance. Airplanes, but not boys. She was right back to where she'd been in the beginning. In love with flying.

"Nope. No romance," she smiled mysteriously. She was twenty-three years old and divorced, and she felt free and independent. And she was about to do exactly what she wanted.

She could hardly contain herself until that night after dinner, and when she told her parents, they stared at her in disbelief.

"Here we go again." Pat looked angry even before she explained it. "You want to do what now?" She had been swimming upstream all her life. It was nothing new for them, or to Cassie.

"I want to join . . . I did join the Army's Flying Training Command," she said happily, and then she explained it to them.

"Wait a minute. You're going to be flying bombers to England? Do you know how heavy and hard to manage those are?"

"I know, Dad." She smiled. She'd flown just about every difficult plane in the sky, when she'd worked for Williams Aircraft. "I'd have a co-pilot." She knew that would make him feel better.

"Probably another woman."

"Sometimes."

"You're crazy," he said tersely, "patriotic, but crazy."

She looked at him hard then. He had to understand. She was grown-up and she had a right to do this. But she had also put them through a lot, especially in the last year and she didn't want to hurt them. She would have preferred to do it with their approval, but her mother was already crying.

"You and your damn flying," Oona said unhappily to her husband, and he patted her hand apologetically.

"Now, Oonie . . . it's always made us a nice living." And it had made Cassie a small fortune, but at what price glory.

She explained the Flying Command to them again, and they

told her they'd think about it. But she had already signed the papers, she reminded them. Pat and Oona looked at each other. There was nothing left to do but support Cassie again. She was always doing this to them. Always putting herself out on a limb, and stretching to the limit.

"When do they want you, Cass?" her father asked, looking somewhat deflated. He hated losing her too. She was such a big help to him at the airport.

"I start in two weeks, on September first. In New Jersey," and then she added gratuitously, "If I were a man, I'd be drafted anyway."

"But you're not, thank God. And you won't be. It's bad enough to have our sons-in-law over there. And Nick," who was like a son to them.

"You'd be there if you could," she pointed out to her father, and he looked at her very strangely. She was right. He would. And Nick had volunteered long before, and he would never have had to go this time.

"Why can't I? Why can't I do something for my country, for a change? Flying is all I know how to do, and I do it well. Why can't I offer that to this country? You would. Why should I be prevented from that because I'm a woman?"

"Oh God," her father rolled his eyes, "it's the Suffragettes again. Where do you get this from? Your mother and your sisters never talk about this nonsense. They stay home where they belong."

"I don't belong there. I'm a flier. Like you. That's the difference." It was hard to argue with her. She was smart, and she was right. And she was gutsy. He loved that about her. She had taught him a lot over the years, and he loved her more for it.

"It's dangerous, Cass. And you'd be flying Lockheed Hudson bombers. They're heavy planes. What if you go down again?"

"What if you go down tomorrow over Cleveland? What's the difference between the two?"

"Maybe nothing. I'll think about it." He knew she was bored

flying mail runs for him, after all the fancy flying she'd done. But at least she was safe here.

He thought about it for days, but in the end, as before, he didn't feel he had the right to stop her. And in September she left for New Jersey. Oona was proud of her too, and her parents flew to New Jersey with her.

"Take it easy, Dad," she said when he left her. She kissed both of them good-bye, and her father stood smiling at her.

"Try not to embarrass yourself," he said mock somberly and she laughed at him.

"Keep your tail up."

"Mind your own!" He saluted her and was gone, and the next time he saw her he almost burst with pride. She was wearing her uniform, with a gleaming pair of silver wings, and she looked older and more mature than she ever had before. She had her long red hair tied into a neat bun, and the uniform looked sensational on her long, lean figure.

Her parents had come to New York because she was shipping out for England that weekend, though they'd only be there briefly. She would be going back and forth with planes, whenever they were needed somewhere else. But her first assignment was to report to Hornchurch with a bomber.

She had dinner with her parents the night before she left, and she took them to a little Italian restaurant she went to whenever she was in New York with the other pilots. She introduced some of them to her parents, and they could see that she had never been happier than she was now. Despite the hardships of the training she'd gone through, to Cassie, more often than not, it seemed like summer camp for female fliers. She liked the women she flew with, and the challenge of ferrying bombers through dangerous airspace suited her completely. She was used to difficult flying, and she liked the fact that she'd have to pay close attention. For this first trip, she had been assigned a male co-pilot, and they were going through Greenland.

"Keep an eye out for Nick," her father had said when he left her at the barracks, and she had promised to write to them from England. She didn't think she'd be there long, but she didn't know yet. She would be doing some flying there, and she would have to wait for a return assignment. She might be there for as little as a week or two, or as long as three months. There was no way of knowing. But one thing she did know and that was that all through her training, she had thought of nothing but Nick Galvin.

She had done a lot of thinking, and she had made some decisions.

All her life she had had to wait for other people to make up their minds about her life, and she wasn't willing to let that happen anymore. She had had to pay her own brother to lie for her and take her up in the plane, so she could learn to fly it. She had had to wait for Nick to notice how badly she wanted to learn, and agree to give her lessons, hidden from her father. She had had to wait for her father to come to his senses years before, and let her fly from his airport.

She had had to wait for Nick to tell her he loved her, and then leave for the RAF. And she had had to wait for Desmond to let her fly his planes, and lie to her, and use her, and then finally tell her the truth of how little he cared for her. All her life she had had to wait for other people's decisions and manipulations. And even now, Nick knew where she was, he knew what she felt for him, but he never wrote her. The only thing he probably didn't know, since it had never been publicized, thanks to Desmond's good relations with the press, was that she had left him.

But she wasn't waiting anymore. It wasn't anyone else's decision this time. It was her turn. And ever since she had found out what a bastard Desmond had been, she had wanted to go to England. She had no idea what would happen when she got there, or what Nick would say. And she didn't care how old he was, or how young she was, or how much money he did or didn't have. All she knew was that she had to be there. She had a right to know what he felt for her. She had a right to a lot of things, she'd decided, and it was time for her to get them. This trip was one of them. It was just exactly what she wanted to be doing at that moment.

They left at five o'clock the next morning, and she found the flying challenging, though dull some of the time. She and her co-pilot chatted for a while, and he was impressed to realize who she was.

"I saw you at an air show once. You cleaned up everything. I think three firsts and a second." It had been her last one. And he remembered correctly.

"I haven't done those in a while."

"They get old."

"I lost my brother at the one the following year, it kind of took the fun out of them for me after that."

"I'll bet." And then he remembered the trick she had pulled, with admiration. "You almost ate it the time I saw you."

"Nah, just looked like it," she said modestly, and he laughed.

"Nervy broads. You guys are all the same. All guts and no brains." He laughed and she grinned at him. To her, it was almost a compliment. She liked the guts part.

"Gee, thanks." She smiled at him, and for an instant he reminded her of Billy.

"No problem."

By the time they arrived over England, they had become friends, and she hoped to fly with him again. He was from Texas, and like all of them, had been flying since he was old enough to climb into the cockpit. He promised to look her up the next time he was in New Jersey.

They'd been lucky that night, there were no German pilots scouting for them. He'd gotten in a couple of dogfights before, and he was happy they hadn't for her first trip. "No big deal though," he reassured her. And much to her delight, he let her land the plane, and she had no problem, despite her father's dire warnings. It was wonderful being treated as an equal.

She took the paperwork to the office they had told her to report to.

They thanked her politely for the paperwork, and handed her a slip of paper with her billeting. And as she walked back outside again, the pilot she'd flown over with invited her for breakfast. But she told him she had other plans. She did, but she wasn't sure where to start looking. She had his address but it meant nothing to her. Not yet, at least. She pulled the piece of paper she'd written it on out of her pocket, and was staring at it, fighting the exhaustion of the flight, when someone jostled her, and she looked up first in irritation, then in amazement.

It was ridiculous. Things didn't happen that way. It was too easy. He was standing there, staring down at her, looking as though he'd seen a ghost. No one had warned him she was coming. And there Cassie stood, in uniform, looking into the startled eyes of Major Nick Galvin.

"What are you doing here?" He said it as though he owned the place, and she laughed at him, her red hair framing her face as the autumn wind blew through it.

"Same thing you are." More or less, except that his job was a lot more dangerous than hers. But they both had their jobs and their missions. And several ferry pilots had already been killed by Germans. "Thanks for all the great letters, by the way. I really enjoyed them." She tried to make light of the pain he had caused her by his silence.

He grinned boyishly at the comment. He could barely make himself listen to her, he was so overwhelmed with just seeing her again. The last time he had seen her was the morning after they had spent the night at their secret airstrip.

"I really enjoyed writing them to you." He quipped back, but all he wanted to do now was reach out and touch her. He couldn't keep his eyes from her, his hands, his arms, his heart, his fingers. Instinctively, he reached out and touched her hair. It still felt like silk and looked like fire. "How are you, Cass?" he said softly, as people in uniform milled around them. Hornchurch was a busy place, but neither of them seemed to notice. They couldn't keep their eyes off each other. Despite the hardships they both had been through, nothing seemed to have changed between them.

"I'm okay," she answered him, as he led her to a quiet spot, where they could sit down on a rock wall for a few minutes, and talk. There was so much to say, so much to catch up on. And he felt guilty suddenly for his silence.

"I was worried sick about you when you went down," he said, and she looked away, thinking of Billy.

"It wasn't much fun," she was honest with him. "It was pretty rough, and . . ." She had trouble saying it, and without thinking, he took her hand and held it in his own. ". . . it was awful when Billy . . ."

"I know." She didn't have to say the words. He understood perfectly. "You can't blame yourself, Cass. I told you that a long time ago. We all do what we have to. We take our chances. Billy knew what he was doing. He wanted to fly the tour with you, for himself, not just for you." She nodded, knowing the wisdom of his words, but it was small comfort.

"I never felt right that I made it back and he didn't." It was the first time she'd said that to anyone, and she couldn't have said it to anyone but Nick. She always told him all her feelings.

"That's life. That's not your decision. It's His." He pointed toward the heavens, and she nodded.

"Why didn't you call when I got back?" she asked sadly. They had gone right to the important things. They always did. He was like that.

"I thought about it a lot . . . I almost did call a couple of times," he smiled, "when I had a pint or two under my belt, as they say here, but I figured your husband wouldn't like it much. Where is he now, by the way?" His question confirmed her suspicion and she smiled at him. It was funny sitting here, talking to Nick, as though he'd been waiting for her to arrive. It was all so simple suddenly. There they were, four thousand miles from home, and chatting on a rock wall in the autumn sunshine.

"He's in Los Angeles." With Nancy Firestone. Or someone like her.

"I'm surprised he let you do this . . . or actually, I'm not," Nick said, looking somewhat bitter. It had torn his heart out when he thought she was lost, and that bastard had risked her life to sell his airplanes. Desmond was the one he'd wanted to call, to tell him what a rotten sonofabitch he was. But he never did it. "I guess he figured this stuff would look good in the newsreels. Patriotic. One of the boys. Was it his idea or yours?" He wanted it to be hers, because he wanted to respect her for it.

"It was mine, Nick. I've wanted to do this for a long time, since the tour. But when I got back, I didn't feel right leaving Dad. It was hard on him even now. There's no one left to help him. He might even have to hire a few women finally, except that most of them are joining the WAFS, the FTC, or the Flying Training Command, like I did."

"What do you mean you didn't feel right leaving him? Did you stay with them when you got back?" The bastard hadn't even had the decency to take care of her, and she must have been pretty sick after seven weeks starving on an atoll.

"Yes, I went back to them," she said quietly, looking at him, remembering their one night of happiness in the moonlight. "I left Desmond, Nick. I left him when Dad had his heart attack." It was over a year before, and Nick was stunned to realize he'd never heard it.

"When I went back to L.A. after the last time I saw you, things were just the way you said they were. He kept pushing me, press conferences, test flights, interviews, newsreels. It was everything you said it would be, but he didn't show his true colors until Dad got sick. He 'ordered' me to do the tour on schedule, and 'forbade' me to go back and see my father."

"But you went anyway, didn't you?" He knew the trip had been postponed, and had seen a newsreel of her at the hospital, so he knew that much.

"Yeah, I went anyway, and Billy came with me. Desmond said

he'd sue us if we didn't do the tour, and he made us sign contracts promising that we'd go in October no matter what."

"Nice guy."

"I know. I never went back to him. He never even called me. All he wanted was for me to keep it from the press till I got back. And you were right about the women too. Nancy Firestone was his mistress. Apparently, the only reason he married me was to publicize the tour, just as you said. He said it wouldn't have had 'the same impact on the public' without it. The marriage was a complete sham. And afterward, when they brought me back, he told me in Hawaii that I still worked for him, and he was going to sue me for not completing my contract. I'd promised him fifteen thousand miles in the *North Star*, and only made eleven before we went down. He figured he'd get some publicity out of me even then, but it was all over. Dad took me to a lawyer in Chicago, and I divorced him."

Nick sat utterly amazed at what she was telling him, although the fact that Williams was a sonofabitch wasn't news to anyone, and certainly not Nick. But he was a lot worse than even Nick had suspected.

"How did you keep all that quiet before you left?"

"He's good at that. That's his business. When I went back to L.A. before the tour, I stayed at Billy's. No one knew anything. We left a few weeks after I got back from Good Hope anyway, and Desmond dressed it all up in clean linen. He's a real snake, Nick. You were right about everything. I always wanted to tell you that, but I wasn't sure what to say, or how to say it. At first, my pride was hurt, and I was ashamed to admit that the whole thing had been a farce. And then, I figured maybe you wouldn't want to know anyway. You were so definite about not wanting me. I don't know . . . I figured maybe it was better to leave it for a while. I kept hoping you'd come home and we'd talk, but I guess after Pearl Harbor, you couldn't."

"We don't get leaves anymore, Cass. And what do you mean I

was 'definite about not wanting you.' Do you remember that night?" He looked hurt that she would say that.

"I remember every minute of it. Sometimes that was the only thing that kept me going on the island . . . thinking of you . . . remembering . . . it was what got me through a lot of things . . . like leaving Desmond. He was so rotten."

"Then why didn't you write and tell me?"

She sighed, thinking about it, and then she looked at him honestly. "I guess I figured you'd just tell me again that you were too old and too poor, and that I should find myself a kid like Billy." He smiled at the truth of it. He might just have been dumb enough to do that. But that was before she had almost died, before he had come to his senses. Just sitting there, looking at her, made him realize what a total fool he'd been when he left her.

"And did you? Find a kid like Billy, I mean?" He looked so worried that for a minute she wished she had the guts to make him jealous.

"I should tell you that I've been out with every man in seven counties."

"I'm not sure I'd believe you." He smiled and lit a cigarette, as he sat back against the wall, and looked at her with pleasure. It was so good to see her again. This was the little girl he'd always loved, all grown-up now.

"Why not? Think I'm too ugly for any man to take out?" she teased him.

"Not ugly. Just difficult. It takes a man of a certain age and sophistication to handle a girl like you, Cass. There aren't too many men in McDonough County who could do it."

"You're so full of it. Does that mean you're the right age these days, or are you still too old for me?" she asked him pointedly, wanting to know just where they were going.

"I used to be. Mostly, I was just too stupid," he said honestly; "they almost had to retire me when you went down, Cass. I thought I'd go crazy, thinking about you. I went nuts for a while there. I should have flown home as soon as I heard. Then at least I could have been in Honolulu when you got there."

"It would have been wonderful," she smiled gently, but she didn't reproach him. Not for anything. She just wanted to know where they stood now.

"I suppose Desmond was there with the reporters," he said with a look of annoyance.

"Naturally. But I had a great nurse who kept throwing them out of my room before they got a foot in the doorway. She absolutely hated Desmond. That was when he was threatening to sue me for not fulfilling my contract. I think he's convinced I blew up his plane on purpose. It was the damnedest thing, Nick," she said solemnly, "both engines caught fire. I don't think they've figured it out yet, and I'm not sure they ever will." She looked far away for a moment as she said it, and he pulled her closer to him.

"Don't think about it, Cass. It's over." So were a lot of things. A whole lifetime had ended for her, and now it was time for a new beginning. He looked down at her with a slow smile, feeling the warmth of her next to him, and remembered a summer night almost two years before that had sustained him ever since then. "So how long are you here for?"

"I get my orders on Thursday," she said quietly, wondering what was in store for them, what he wanted from her, if it was going to be the same game as before, or if he had finally grown up now. "I'll be here anywhere from a week or two to three months. But I'll be back pretty often. I'm in the overseas ferry squadron, that's what we do, taxi service from New Jersey to Hornchurch."

"That's pretty tame for you, Cass. Most of the time at least." He was relieved she hadn't found something more dangerous to do. She'd be just the one to do that. For Desmond, she had tested fighter planes to be adapted for the Army. But that was over.

"It'll do for now. What about you? Where are you now?" she asked him, with a look that searched his soul. There was no escaping her question.

At first he didn't understand what she was asking him, and then he laughed, and looked down at her. He understood perfectly. It was no accident that she had come here. The only coincidence was that he'd run into her so quickly.

"What are you asking me, Cass?"

"How brave are you? How smart have you gotten over here, risking your life against the Germans?"

"I'm smarter than I used to be, if that's what you're asking me. I'm a little older . . . just as poor . . ." He remembered his own words easily, and how foolish he had been when he said them. "How brave are you, little Cassie? How foolish? Is this what you want? After everything you've done and had and been in the last two years, is this what you still want? Just me and the old Jenny? That's all I've got, you know. That, and the Bellanca. It's never going to be fancy." But they both knew she'd had that and it wasn't what she wanted. She wanted him, and everything he meant to her. Nothing more now.

"If I wanted fancy, I'd be in L.A."

"No, you wouldn't," he said quietly, with the stubborn look she knew so well.

"Why not?"

"Because I wouldn't let you. I'll never let you go back to that. I shouldn't have let you go in the first place." They had both learned some expensive lessons. But they were wiser now. They had both come far, and paid dearly for everything they learned and wanted. "I love you, Cass, and always have," he said quietly as he pulled her close to him, and she looked up at him and smiled. It was the face she knew so well, and had always loved since she was a child. The same lines around the eyes from squinting at the sun, the same face she had grown up with. It was a handsome face with character and purpose and kindness, the only one she wanted to look at for an entire lifetime. She had come here to find him again. And she had. With Nick, she had everything she wanted.

"I love you too, Nick," she said peacefully as he held her close to him, feeling the warmth of her, the nearness he had longed for so often. It had been hell being away from her, a hell he'd made for himself, and bitterly regretted, but didn't know how to get out of. It took Cass to come over and find him.

"And if either of us doesn't come back from this?" he asked her honestly. "What then?" He still didn't want to ruin her life, tying her to him, and then dying. That was the price you paid sometimes for loving a flier.

"That's a chance we both take every day. We always have. You taught me that. If this is what we want, we have to have the guts to live with that. And each let the other do what they have to." It was a high price to pay for loving someone, but they had always been willing to do that.

"And afterward?" He still worried about all that, but she had crossed those bridges long since, and she wouldn't have cared anyway if he'd had absolutely nothing.

"Afterward, we go home, my father retires eventually, and he gives us the airport. And if we live in a shack because that's all you've got, so be it. I don't care, and if we do, we'll change it." This time he didn't argue with her. This time he knew it was enough for both of them. They had had more, and less, in their lives, and it didn't matter to them. All they needed was what they had, each other, and a sky to fly in.

He kissed her gently, and afterward she looked into the autumn sky and smiled, remembering the hours they'd spent in his old Jenny. She reminded him of her first loops and spins, and he laughed.

"You used to scare the pants off me."

"The hell I did . . . you told me I was a natural." She pretended to be insulted as they stood up and he walked her slowly toward her barracks. They had resolved a lot that morning.

"I just said that because I was in love with you." He laughed happily, feeling like a kid again. She did that to him. She always had.

"No, you didn't. You weren't in love with me then," she argued with a broad smile, wondering if he had been.

"Yes, I was." He looked happy and at ease and young. And he felt immeasurable pride as he walked along with her.

"Really?"

They laughed and talked and teased like children. Suddenly, life was very simple. She had done what she had come here to do. She had found him, and everything he had always been to her. She was home at last. They both were.